EVERYMAN,
I WILL GO WITH THEE,
AND BE THY GUIDE,
IN THY MOST NEED
TO GO BY THY SIDE

ANTON CHEKHOV

The Steppe and Other Stories

Translated from the Russian by Constance Garnett
with an Introduction by Richard Freeborn

EVERYMAN'S LIBRARY

45

5363
(F)

This book is one of 250 volumes in Everyman's Library
which have been distributed to 4500 state schools
throughout the United Kingdom.
The project has been supported by a grant of £4 million
from the Millennium Commission.

This selection first published in Everyman's Library, 1991
Introduction, Bibliography and Chronology © David Campbell
Publishers Ltd., 1991
Translation © Chatto & Windus
Typography by Peter B. Willberg

ISBN 1-85715-045-7

A CIP catalogue record for this book is available from the
British Library

Published by David Campbell Publishers Ltd.,
Gloucester Mansions, 140A Shaftesbury Avenue,
London WC2H 8HD

Distributed by Random House (UK) Ltd.,
20 Vauxhall Bridge Road, London SW1V 2SA

THE STEPPE AND
OTHER STORIES

———

CONTENTS

Introduction xi

Select Bibliography xxxv

Chronology xxxvi

The Swedish Match (1884) 3

Easter Eve (1886) 35

Mire (1886) 53

On the Road (1886) 81

Verotchka (1887) 107

Volodya (1887) 127

The Kiss (1887) 147

Sleepy (1888) 177

The Steppe (1888) 189

INTRODUCTION

Russian nineteenth-century literature opens with Alexander Pushkin and closes with Anton Chekhov. Between these two figures lie all the greatest achievements of Russian nineteenth-century 'realism' – Gogol's satirical masterpiece *Dead Souls* (1842), Goncharov's *Oblomov* (1859), Turgenev's *Fathers and Children* (1862), the monumental works of Tolstoy, *War and Peace* (1869) and *Anna Karenina* (1878), and Dostoevsky's successive masterpieces from *Crime and Punishment* (1866), *The Idiot* (1868), *The Possessed* (or *The Devils*, 1872), to *The Brothers Karamazov* (1880) – a body of works of unsurpassed scale and power. They established Russian literature as among the greatest in the world and gave the Russian realistic novel pre-eminence in the history of the genre.

As the realistic novel evolved in Russia, it tended to acquire an extra-literary role as a forum for the discussion of topical issues. It aired new ideas and showed how these ideas affected Russian society and the Russian intelligentsia. It epitomized 'tendentiousness' in literature. Frequently this tended to be the principal criterion of excellence by which contemporary criticism judged it. The civic commitment of a writer to the aim of improving society, whether by offering critical depictions of contemporary ills or portraits of positive heroes and heroines, was all that mattered. Literary quality was relegated to second place in the search for a progressive literature.

The evil of demanding such commitment from writers need not be dwelt on here; Soviet literature under the doctrine of Socialist Realism has exemplified it admirably. Needless to say, the commitment was usually more evident to the critic than to the writer. Turgenev, for example, was never strictly speaking 'committed' at all. Tolstoy and Dostoevsky were both committed to a search for the meaning of life in their novels and indeed hoped to provide answers – religious answers, it has to be said – but they were equally fervent in their rejection of commitment in a political sense.

It is a relief, perhaps, certainly a measure of literary sanity, that neither Pushkin nor Chekhov can readily be made to wear the straitjacket of a committed viewpoint. In the ultimate testing of a literature and its values – in a time of revolution and civil war, say – it is the simplest, most direct, truths that emerge most prominently. As Pasternak put it so beautifully through the mouth of his hero, Zhivago, what appealed more than all the rest of Russian literature in the adversity of revolution and civil war was 'the childlike Russian quality of Pushkin and Chekhov, their shy unconcern with such high-sounding matters as the ultimate purpose of mankind or their own salvation'. More than this, given that the two writers stand at opposed ends of the nineteenth century, are the prescient ways in which their 'childlike Russian quality' proved exemplary for the development of Russian literature. Pushkin's genius, by selectively filtering the European literary heritage of the eighteenth century, helped to encourage in Russian nineteenth-century literature a healthy, truthful, unpretentious awareness of its role as a mirror to life. Chekhov's genius seemed similarly to summarize the nineteenth century for the twentieth and to offer a model of literary honesty and unpretentiousness to an age when politicized writing became the norm, as it did in the Soviet Union.

Easy as it may be to pass retrospective judgements, Chekhov's reputation as a story-teller and playwright can withstand innumerable critical generalizations and survive with honour. Both as artist and man he was astonishingly without pretentiousness. His friends have testified to this characteristic in abundance. The most important testimony comes from the only Russian writer approximately of his generation to have rivalled his reputation in his time, Maxim Gorky. It is clear-eyed and fond:

It seems to me, [Gorky wrote in 1904, after Chekhov's death], that everyone in Anton Pavlovich's presence felt in himself a desire to be simpler, more truthful, more himself, and I often observed how people always abandoned the gaudy array of bookish phrases, fashionable words and other cheap trinkets with which Russians, wishing to show how European they are, bedeck themselves like natives arraying themselves in sea-shells and fish-teeth. Anton Pavlovich had no love for fish-teeth or peacock's feathers. Everything gaudy, brash and foreign adopted by people to increase their self-importance was an embarrassment to him, and I noticed that every time he was confronted by someone who decked himself out like this he was seized by a desire to rid the speaker of the oppressive and needless clutter which so distorted his real features and living spirit. All his life A. Chekhov lived off his own spiritual resources, always being himself, inwardly free and never taking into account what some expected of Anton Chekhov and others – cruder people – demanded of him. He disliked talk on 'lofty' subjects – the kind of talk which Russians are so keen on, forgetting that it is comic and not at all clever to discourse about wearing velvet suits in the future when you haven't ever got a decent pair of pants to wear in the present.

As the reminiscence suggests, there was in Chekhov a redemptive sense of humour accompanying the inner resourcefulness and freedom of spirit. It made him assert, in one of the few such pronouncements which he made (and then only in a private letter to his publisher Suvorin), the autonomy of the writer within his own – admittedly limited – ambit. 'An artist,' he wrote (letter of 27 October 1888),

must pass judgement only on what he understands; his sphere is as limited as that of any other specialist, I repeat, and I always insist on this. That his sphere has no questions but contains only answers can only be said by someone who has never written and had no dealings with imagery. An artist observes, chooses, assesses, generalizes – these processes alone presuppose an initial question; if he has not posed himself a question to start with, then he has nothing to assess and there's no point in choosing. To put it briefly, I will end with psychiatry: if you deny in creativity any question and intention, then you have to admit that an artist creates unpremeditatedly, without forethought, under the influence of strong emotion. Therefore, if an author boasted to me that he had written a story without intention or forethought, but only as a result of inspiration, I would call him mad.

In demanding from an artist a conscious attitude to his work, you are right, but you are confusing two ideas: *the answering of a question and the correct formulation of a question.* Only the second is obligatory for an artist. In *Anna Karenina* and in *Onegin* not a single question is answered, but they are fully satisfying because all the questions in them are formulated correctly.

This famous Chekhovian quotation justifies the writer as one who poses questions. He leaves it to the reader to act as jury in deciding the verdict. There is no denying, of course, that a writer's independence is a paramount right, which has to be exercised with due care; and constrained though it may be by commercial or moral considerations, it should never be constrained by *diktat*. Still, Chekhov seems to differ most obviously from his illustrious predecessors through the elusiveness of aim which characterizes his work. He seems to suggest that even the residual certainties of heritage, of the relationship of past to present, of kinship to place, of truth to falsehood, have undergone, or are in process of undergoing, intense tremors of change. That these are not always perceived, or seem hard to identify, reinforces the supposed aimlessness that oppresses so many of the more sensitive individuals portrayed in his world. An absence of certainties naturally involves an uprootedness, so that so many of Chekhov's characters do not 'belong' and, when they do, find themselves disillusioned by the baffling questions posed by their place in life. Faith, therefore, must be sought and rarely found; love and happiness are elusive, not to say illusory; people's lives glide past one another, as if carried on different currents; and his stories have a tendency, as he admitted, to begin very promisingly and look like novels, but the middle appears huddled and timid and the end, as in a short sketch, like fireworks.

Transience and transition are the commonest conditions of Chekhov's world. But for such conditions to have meaning they must presuppose an on-going life. The ultimate up-beat note sounded in Chekhov's work depends precisely on the assumption that changeability contains promise and that hope, however absurd, is the only true human safeguard against extinction.

*

Chekhov lived at a time of rapid change in Russian society and his life (1860–1904) spans almost exactly the period between the Emancipation of the serfs (1861) and the so-called 'first Russian revolution' of 1905. The Emancipation of the serfs paved the way for the movement of peasantry from the land into the cities, aided the construction of a vast railway network, led to the creation of factories and established in Russia a capitalist, market economy. This was subject, of course, to terrible fluctuations and produced great poverty as well as great wealth. It also gave rise to professional and semi-professional classes in practically every area of Russian life. These challenged the previous authority of the landowning nobility, as did the largely urban, mercantile bourgeoisie and the forces for change, however sluggish, which were gradually affecting the masses of the peasantry and the urban working class. The old semi-feudal order was eroded, if not changed beyond recognition so far as the government of the country was concerned. The political culmination of this process was the revolution of 1905, the 'intelligentsia revolution', which brought an end to the Tsarist autocracy and led to the creation of the first elected Russian parliament, the Duma.

Throughout the span of Chekhov's life the most clearly articulate and measurable force for change in Russian life was the intelligentsia. Comprising the most politically conscious and best-educated section of Russian society, its main aim in a political sense was the overthrow of Tsarism. It sought to do this in the name of democracy or, literally, in the name of 'power to the people' (meaning chiefly the peasantry) and in the name of some kind of just, egalitarian society. By the late 1870s intelligentsia activity had begun to take the form of terrorism, culminating in the assassination of Tsar Alexander II in 1881; but so effective was the subsequent repression of such dissidence that the intelligentsia became disillusioned with grandiose, revolutionary plans for social change. It restricted itself for the rest of the century to 'small deeds' in what became known as the 'epoch of small deeds' (*epokha malykh del*). This meant that the intelligentsia limited itself to working largely within the framework of existing institutions to improve the life of the underprivileged. It was a period of intelligentsia disillusionment. Chekhov became its chronicler; he made it 'Chekhovian'.

His birthright and upbringing ensured he was well qualified for the task. Born, in 1860, in the port town of Taganrog on the Sea of Azov, he was the third son of Pavel Chekhov, a small shopkeeper. His father ruined himself by opening a second shop when the harbour trade of Taganrog was already passing to neighbouring Rostov-on-Don. As a boy Chekhov therefore knew from life how precarious and fickle were the ways of capitalism, just as he experienced at first hand the petty tyranny of a father who set himself up as a kind of autocrat in his own household. As a legacy of the oppression associated with serfdom – the Chekhovs (they were originally simply called Chekh) were, in fact, only a generation or so removed from serfdom – this experience gave the young Chekhov a lifelong urge to celebrate the need for human dignity and independence. He was also made inescapably aware of the pettiness and yearnings, the introspective tendencies, the despair and the ineffectual dreaminess that, by common consensus, were ingrained features of Russian provincial life. Chekhov himself defined his heritage by comparison with the equivalent experience of writers from the nobility in the following caustic way (letter to Suvorin, 7 January 1889):

What writers of the nobility take from nature for nothing, the less privileged have to buy at the price of their youth. Just you write a story about a young man, the son of a serf, a former shopkeeper, choirboy, schoolboy and student, raised on respect for rank, kissing priests' hands, worshipping others' ideas, grateful for every scrap of bread, often whipped, going teaching without galoshes, scrapping, teasing animals, enjoying having dinner with rich relatives, playing the hypocrite to God and man just to show how insignificant he was – write how this young man squeezes the slave out of himself drop by drop and how he wakes up one fine morning and feels that the blood of a real man, not of a slave, is flowing in his veins.

Though these elements all become incorporated within the gamut of what may be called the Chekhovian mood, prevailing over it and lightening it was his natural sense of fun. It was clearly on the whole fun to be a member of the Chekhov family in Taganrog. The good spirits expressed themselves most obviously in a love of theatre-going and a talent for amateur theatricals among the Chekhov brothers. For Chekhov, one suspects, this must have taught him something essentially 'Chekhovian' about himself: the art not just of playing a role but of being able to method-act himself into a character. No writer ever subsequently lived himself into so many parts as did Chekhov. The teeming life of the port town of Taganrog supplied many of his role models as did the teeming streets of London for Dickens.

Gorky noted in his reminiscence that 'all his life A. Chekhov lived off his own spiritual resources, always being himself, inwardly free...' but it was an independence and freedom of spirit attained very largely through being left to fend for himself as a teenager. When the rest of the family fled ignominiously to Moscow after the collapse of the father's business, the sixteen-year-old Chekhov had to remain behind in Taganrog to complete his secondary education. He eked out three years there by himself, scraping by with a little tutoring and various handouts. It was a period of loneliness that must have tested his resourcefulness and will-power to the limit. He may have begun writing at this time. Not stories, so far as one knows, but a long play, referred to as *Fatherless* (appropriately enough in the circumstances), which may in fact have been the work we now know as *Platonov*. In short, these were years when he was forced to mature early, but it was a maturity that meant he quickly became the family's mainstay when he rejoined them in Moscow in 1879.

He arrived in Moscow with a scholarship to the university's medical faculty. For five years he was a student who gradually earned a little money on the side by placing short comic pieces with various cheap Moscow magazines such as *The Dragonfly* and *The Alarm Clock*. His writing was done at night, in haste, surrounded by the family, with little thought for the worth of his stories beyond the small sums that could be earned from them. Because he used pseudonyms, it is still not known for sure how many he wrote. Of the forty or so pieces he is known to have published in 1881–2 he himself chose to preserve not a single one. It was only when he met the publisher Leykin in late 1882 and began contributing to his journal *Splinters* (*Oskolki*) that 'Antosha Chekhonte', his most popular pseudonym, began to show in his writing a quality and depth that marked him out as exceptional. Even so, of the hundreds of pieces which he published during his association with *Splinters* he chose to preserve only forty-seven in his *Collected Works* of 1899–1902.

CHEKHOV

Among the stories of this early period which are noteworthy, one may quote *The Death of a Government Clerk*, *The Daughter of Albion* and *A Chameleon* as the most promising. A junior government clerk, for example, chances to sneeze over a senior official during a visit to the theatre and so pesters him with his contrition that when the latter turns on him angrily the junior clerk is so shocked he goes home and dies. Such bald telling does a disservice to the remarkable verbal craftsmanship Chekhov brought to his simple plot. In *The Daughter of Albion* a snooty old maid of an English governess, who speaks not a word of Russian, is ridiculed and finally humiliated by her Russian employer when he strips naked in front of her during a fishing expedition. *A Chameleon* is a dialogue piece in which a policeman chameleon-like changes his tone when he discovers that a dog who has bitten someone on the finger belongs to the brother of a General. Fun at the expense of exaggerated respect for rank, or fun at the expense of an old maid who cannot answer back, couched in idiomatic dialogue and with a minimum of descriptive matter, is an easily comprehensible ingredient of these stories which, like so many others Chekhov wrote at the time, were designed for light reading by railway travellers or a *Punch*-type readership in pubs and clubs. Short, slight, if brilliantly observed, they ran usually to a formula and whetted rather than satisfied a reader's appetite.

Chekhov tired fairly quickly of providing such literary snacks. But it was not until after he had qualified as a doctor in 1884 that he was able to enlarge the scope of his writing. At the same time the newly qualified doctor may have contracted tuberculosis. He overlooked it, it seems, or played it down until it was diagnosed beyond doubt in 1897. His leading English biographer puts it sardonically: 'His sickness, with its intimations of ultimate mortality, declared itself on the threshold of a major change in his evolution. It appeared, in other words, just as the jolly, carefree, joking Antosha Chekhonte was beginning to evolve into the wiser, the more serious, the more mature, the infinitely more talented Anton Chekhov' (R. Hingley, 1976, p. 53). The new stage in his career was marked by a transference from *Splinters* to *The St Petersburg Gazette* as the main outlet for publication in the years 1885–6;

and following that, in 1886, to *New Times* where, under the editorship of Suvorin, whose close friend he was to become, Chekhov began to publish much longer and more mature works.

In social and moral terms, then, Chekhov's is a story of liberation from the servile attitudes of serfdom to something approaching the dignity of a free man which was the political and social dream of the intelligentsia during his lifetime. He entered the professional classes as a doctor and eventually, towards the end of his life, acquired entitlement to nobility status. Upwardly mobile socially, he encompassed in his writing a broad social spectrum from the peasantry at one end to the officer class and aristocracy at the other. Most of his work is concentrated socially within a middle band of the civil service and the professional, merchant and landowning classes, just as, psychologically and temperamentally, his central figures generally exhibit middling characteristics. But he tended always to suggest a detached, uninvolved attitude of medical objectivity towards them even when, as a writer, he was seemingly investing himself with their personalities.

He summed up the balancing act between writer and doctor in his own case by amusingly claiming that medicine was his lawful wife and literature his mistress. More and more time came to be spent with his mistress, though he continued to reside with his wife, as it were, by regularly practising as a doctor. The two activities proved complementary. Something of his diagnostic experience from the practice of medicine was appropriated by his writer's self and made him a remarkable literary diagnostician of the human dilemma. Yet without the social mobility in his own life, the changing quality of the times in which he lived, the transfer from provincial to metropolitan cultures, the awareness, in short, of the inevitable transience that accompanies the act of living, the particular mixture of tragi-comic, elegiac and laconic which adds up to 'Chekhovian' would never have existed.

*

The middle years of the 1880s, when Chekhov was in his mid-twenties, were the most prolific of his entire life. In 1886, for example, he published more than 600 pages of fiction. Anyone attempting to anthologize his work from this period is consequently spoiled for choice. He was to be accused with some justification of not taking his talent seriously. There are undeniably instances in the stories of a certain haste and perfunctoriness, especially in the endings. But the sureness of psychological understanding of character and the sense of irony governing the study of relationships are generally as mature in the mid-1880s as at any time in his later career.

To read Chekhov in Russian is to be confronted by a language with such a hard, sure edge to it, the words seem to be hewn from solid steel. Unless translation can convey this strength and exactitude, the reader will scarcely be aware of Chekhov's power. All good translations convey it to some degree – and there are many excellent translators of Chekhov, notable among them Ronald Hingley (especially as a translator of the stories) and Michael Heim (of the letters) – but none have the abiding sense of first-time freshness, of spontaneous, if rather old-fashioned, turn-of-the century immediacy that one finds in Constance Garnett's translations. Quaint, certainly, in the transliteration of Russian names and references, touched by Edwardian mannerisms that have a flavour of O'Henry, Kipling and Wells, they possess inherent strength and resourcefulness as translations that seem to match similar qualities in Chekhov's own work and bring out with surprising felicity many of the resonances of the original Russian.

When originally published between 1916 and 1926, the seventeen volumes of her translations covered the plays as well as selected letters, but by far the greater part – thirteen volumes in all – was devoted to the stories. Many of these stories (those which pre-date 1888) have not been included in *The Oxford Chekhov*. They have therefore been accessible to an English readership chiefly through Constance Garnett's translations. However, the order in which Constance Garnett published her translations was so haphazard that anyone seeking anything like a chronological pattern to Chekhov's work in her volumes will be disappointed.

This selection of Chekhov's stories in her translation has been designed to illustrate the main features of Chekhov's work in the mid-1880s, shortly, that is, before and after he qualified as a doctor and began to take his talent as a writer more seriously. What might have seemed little more than exercises by a young man in his mid-twenties have the deftness and power of works written by an assured master. The stories culminate with the publication of his first acknowledged masterpiece, *The Steppe*, early in 1888.

*

The Swedish Match is, on the whole, a joke. It is a reminder, if any is needed, that Chekhov always had a sense of fun, a sense of the comic equal to, though often ironically highlighting, the tragic in life. Published originally in the *Dragonfly Almanach for 1884*, this story also reminds us of the fact that Chekhov, heir as he was to the greatest tradition of the novel in European literature, in fact only wrote one novel in his life and then sought to conceal the fact by omitting it from his *Collected Works* and not breathing a word about it later. It is hard to know why. The novel in question, *The Shooting Party*, first published in more or less weekly instalments between August 1884 and April 1885 in the newspaper *Daily News*, has recently been republished in its English translation by A. E. Chamot, with an introduction by Julian Symons (London 1986).

As a novel of detection it is supremely well written, replete with atmospheric nature descriptions and well-observed characters of the sort familiar to us from other, more mature, Chekhov works. It also has a plot which anticipates Agatha Christie's *The Murder of Roger Ackroyd*, as Julian Symons points out. The poking of fun at the conventions of the detective novel which such a plot implies – this Introduction will not let the cat out of the bag – perhaps led Chekhov to regard it as a youthful folly best forgotten. But Chekhov clearly demonstrated his skill as a crime novelist here, even though he never tried his hand at the genre again. It was the basis of a Hollywood film, *Summer Storm*, made towards the end of World War II under the direction of Douglas Sirk, with a cast headed by George Sanders, Linda Darnell and Edward Everett Horton.

The Swedish Match pokes fun at a style of detective yarn very popular in France in the second half of the nineteenth century. A leading exponent was Emile Gaboriau (1835–73) whose detective, Lecoq, employed an indomitable Gallic logic in solving the most complex crimes. Chekhov had a poor opinion of Gaboriau, but in this story, subtitled 'The Story of a Crime', he succeeded in offering a crime which no Gallic logic could possibly solve. It is a murder story in which the victim turns out never to have been murdered! His young detective, Dyukovsky, fabricates what appears to be a watertight case against the suspects, based on the discovery of a Swedish safety match at the scene of the crime. Given to flights of fancy that his grudging superior has to accept, he can exclaim: 'What can sometimes be done by a man who has been expelled from a seminary and studied Gaboriau is beyond all conception!' – a sentiment ever present in the amused reader's mind. The ramifying plot unfolds neatly and entertainingly in a series of dialogue exchanges that have a truer ring to them than the exchanges, say, between Holmes and Watson. There is also a pleasant background irony to the story. Chekhov donated his manuscript to a certain M. M. Dyukovsky in 1886. His heirs deposited the manuscript with the State Literary Museum in Moscow in 1965 and have therefore left us the most telling evidence of the scrupulous way Chekhov recast and refined his work before publication.

Easter Eve, first published in Suvorin's *New Times* in April 1886, could hardly be more different. It depends entirely on a narrator whose eye and ear have an uncannily objective, poetic sensitivity. In responding so perceptively to the nuances of the occasion and the scene, the first-person narrator cannot of course be anyone but Chekhov himself; yet this is more than reportage. His description of crossing the River Goltva by ferry to attend the Easter festival is a framework for the central encounter which enshrines within its depths, almost as if it were iconic, the sacred, devotional and very poignant impact of the monk Ieronim's grief at the loss of his best friend. The movement of the work draws one ever deeper into the centre of the experience, beyond frame to portrait, and from portrayal through dialogue to a spiritual encounter which reveals the very heart and soul of the lay-brother's sweet, unappreciated, saint-like nature.

Chekhov's mastery can be felt instantly in the description of the starry night. The occasion acquires a cosmic frame of reference, as if a mystical quality were being apprehended in the redeemed state of the world through the compact but brilliantly evoked juxtaposition of people and stars at the opening of the second paragraph:

> The weather seemed to me magnificent. It was dark, yet I could see the trees, the water and the people ... The world was lighted by the stars, which were scattered thickly all over the sky. I don't remember ever seeing so many stars. Literally one could not have put a finger in between them. There were some as big as a goose's egg, others tiny as hempseed ... They had come out for the festival procession, every one of them, little and big, washed, renewed and joyful, and every one of them was softly twinkling its beams.

Even to quote is somehow to tear a piece from the solid weft of the description so that the account is left ragged. Yet the prose can stand it. So exact is Chekhov's descriptive power that, even through a translation, one feels in the English the brilliance of the picture of the rocket celebrating the risen Christ:

> All at once, cleaving the darkness, a rocket zigzagged in a golden ribbon up the sky; it described an arc and, as though broken to pieces against the sky, was scattered crackling into sparks. There was a roar from the bank like a far-away hurrah.

The joy, of course, is counterpointed by the monk's rhetorical question about why, even at a time of such popular rejoicing, a man cannot forget his own sorrows. Within his ensuing, obituarial monologue about his dead friend Nikolay there lies a kind of subtext. It is a reminder, however distanced and transmuted by coming from the monk's lips, that Chekhov is telling us here something very important about his own art.

His knowledge of Orthodox church music was deep and had a close relationship to his work. As a boy he acquired the knowledge on his father's orders and on pain of severe beatings, since he was forced to participate regularly in his local church choir. Resented though it was, the experience possibly taught him an appreciation of liturgical rhythms. That they are present in his prose style, especially in descriptive passages, is beyond doubt. They give an often elegiac, psalmic quality to the structure and resonance of his sentences. They frequently have a repeated threefold patterning which makes them seem plaintive and musical. In describing the canticles composed by his friend, Ieronim emphasizes the point by enunciating the rule: 'Everything must be harmonious, brief and complete. There must be in every line softness, graciousness and tenderness; not one word should be harsh or rough or unsuitable.' Such rhythmical and almost chant-like cadences are discernible everywhere in Chekhov, but so carefully incorporated in the very texture of his prose that they rarely ring false or suggest that he is consciously employing a device.

Celebration and sadness commingle in the brief account of the narrator's visit to the monastery church and his attendance at the Easter service. As there is a respect both for the piety of the occasion and the popular bustle and excitement surrounding it, so the contrast between the death and resurrection of the Saviour is matched by the contrast between the monk's grief at his friend's death and the redemptive beauty of deacon Nikolay's gifts as a composer of canticles. More poignant, though, is the clear suggestion that, if Nikolay's gifts lend him a kind of immortality, Ieronim's bereavement is all too mortal, that of a child orphaned by the death of his mother, one widowed by the death of a spouse, one quite simply overlooked and abandoned by the coarse-grained, insensitive peasant monks with whom he will be obliged to live his life in future. The implication is not dwelt on. What emerges finally is the portrait of a friendship so affectionate and gentle it seems to exemplify a perfection of Christian love.

Mire was first published in *New Times* in October 1886. It is hard to imagine a love less Christian than that which Chekhov explores here. Again, implication is what matters. The story of young Lieutenant Sokolsky's visit to the Jewess Susanna in order to persuade her to honour her debt to his cousin undergoes the neatest of ironic twists. The erotic ambience of the house with its pervasive smell of jasmine captivates him as much as its erotic occupant. The consequence is predictable.

Sokolsky, intending marriage, finds himself seduced. His cousin, similarly intent on recovering his IOUs and his money, also falls victim to Susanna's charms.

The story would not succeed were it not for the portrait of the seductive Jewess. Susanna Moiseyevna has a presence within the fiction that breathes intense vivacity. Witty, devious, alluring, violent, she can easily be understood as eating men for breakfast; but the men always come back for more, to be eaten again, to accept again the debasement of their sexuality. The work never for a moment titillates like pornography, but in its allusive, inexplicit treatment of a sexual theme it shows only too remarkably the power of erotic feeling and the moral mire in which men can find themselves as a result.

Naturally it aroused adverse criticism, which in turn elicited one of Chekhov's most interesting letters. A friend of his, a writer of children's stories, Maria Kiselyova reacted hostilely but wittily to the story by complaining that a writer of Chekhov's sort, who was not exactly underendowed by God in terms of talent, should show her in his story nothing more than a 'heap of dung'. 'The world teems with filth,' she wrote in late December 1886, 'with villains and villainesses and the impression produced by them is not a new one, yet with what gratitude one turns to a writer who, while dragging you through all the stink of the dung heap, suddenly pulls a seed-pearl out of it. You are not short-sighted and are splendidly capable of finding such a pearl, so why then nothing but the heap of dung?' Chekhov replied at some length, agreeing that he deplored such 'dung heap' literature as much as anyone, and went on to say:

I haven't, nor have you, nor have critics anywhere in the world any firm grounds for denying this literature. I don't know who's right: Homer, Shakespeare, Lope de Vega and the ancients in general who were not frightened of rooting around in the 'dung heap' but were a lot more stable than we are in a moral sense, or contemporary writers who are prim enough on paper but coldly cynical in their souls and in their lives ... That the world 'teems with villains and villainesses' is true. Human nature is imperfect and it would therefore be odd to find the world populated solely by righteous men. To think that literature is under an obligation to dig up a 'pearl' from a dung heap of villainy is to deny literature itself. Literature is called an art because it depicts life as it is. Its object is unconditional and honest truth. To narrow its function to such a specialism as obtaining 'pearls' would be as fatal as forcing Levitan [I. I. Levitan (1861–1900), famous Russian painter and friend of Chekhov – R.F.] to paint a tree after ordering him not to touch on the dirty bark or the yellowing leaf. I agree a 'pearl' is a fine thing, but a writer is not a pastry-cook, not a cosmetic expert, not an entertainer … He's just like any other simple reporter. What would you say if a reporter out of squeamish-ness or a desire to please his readers made a habit of describing only honest mayors, morally upright women and kindly disposed railway workers?

For chemists nothing on the earth is unclean. A writer must be as objective as a chemist; he must repudiate all day-to-day subjectivity and be certain that dung heaps have a very honourable role to play in any landscape and evil passions are just as essential to life as good ones…

The discovery of 'pearls' in the dung heap of life may not have been Chekhov's conscious aim as a writer, but his chemist's objectivity could help him to discern the uniquely valuable even in what might be regarded as the humanly superfluous or futile. *On the Road* (*New Times*, December, 1886) illustrates this. Its setting is the archetypally transient one of a 'travellers' room' in winter at which a young girl and her father, Liharev, are staying overnight. Into this world, described as meticulously as a stage set, comes Mademoiselle Ilovaisky, so wrapped up against the outer storm that her gradual removal of layers of clothing resembles an emergence from a chrysalis. The child's eye, in the defamiliarizing manner which Chekhov employs here, owes much to Tolstoy. Unkindly, no doubt, the child sees with telling honesty. The brunette Mademoiselle Ilovaisky emerges:

… as slim as a snake, with a long white face and curly hair. Her nose was long and sharp, her chin, too, was long and sharp, her eyelashes were long, the corners of her mouth were sharp, and, thanks to this general sharpness, the expression of her face was biting. Swathed in a closely fitting black dress with a mass of lace at her neck and sleeves, with sharp elbows and long, pink fingers, she recalled the portraits of mediaeval English ladies.

This pearl of a description is not in fact the 'pearl' within the story. It is the little girl's father, Liharev, who personifies the human 'pearl' in life – a figure known to all readers of Russian nineteenth-century literature as the 'superfluous man', the failed intellectual and idealist, a Don Quixote given to expending his energies ineffectually on all manner of good causes. Turgenev's Rudin is no doubt the original portrait of such a type in Russian literature, his Bazarov of *Fathers and Children* the Nihilist development of it; and Liharev, in his autobiographical confession to Mademoiselle Ilovaisky, personifies himself as a paradigm of Russian intelligentsia experience, from Nihilism to Populism, to latter-day Slavophilism, to Tolstoyanism. Chekhov has sucessfully encapsulated the type here and made the portrait both humanly comprehensible and sympathetic. The eloquent testimony to feminine devotion may not please feminists and has, in any case, an over-sentimental, false rhetoric about it, but the sincerity of the man himself is hard to deny. Like so many of Chekhov's characters, he is essentially transient in his relations with others, a condition of things summarized in his impassioned cry to Ilovaisky:

'Oh dear! How glad I am that I have met you! Fate is kind to me, I am always meeting splendid people. Not a day passes but one makes acquaintance with somebody one would give one's soul for. There are ever so many more good people than bad in this world. Here, see, for instance, how openly and from our hearts we have been talking as though we had known each other a hundred years.'

His casual companion is of course touched and appalled when she discovers that this genuinely sensitive, educated and eloquent man is on his way to take up work in the coal mines. Yet what is missing in the very transience of their lives is that elusive, momentary pause, that 'touch or two', as the final paragraph puts it, when they might have stopped long enough to create a relationship. It is a Chekhovian moment, ineffable in its poignant illustration of the transitoriness of life and summarized of course by the couplet from Lermontov which is the story's epigraph.

Precisely the same transitoriness is celebrated in *Verotchka* (*New Times*, February, 1887). Here the transience is enhanced by the prism of reminiscence. Ognev, the viewpoint for the story, brings to it a discernible personality and for that reason seems to endow it with a mood. To describe it as a brief encounter in which the happy, contented mood of Ognev, on finally leaving the Kuznetsov house at the end of summer, is shattered by the discovery that the daughter of the house, Verotchka, has fallen in love with him, is to acknowledge how successful Chekhov can be in his method-acting as a writer. It does not do justice, though, to the resonances and nuances which deepen the emotional effect and turn the experience of a departure into a regret as long as a lifetime. By the end, of course, Ognev has discovered a simple enough truth about himself. Self-pity may induce a sense that he is prematurely old at thirty; his conscience tells him more certainly that 'for the first time in his life it was his lot to learn by experience how little that a man does depends on his own will, and to suffer in his own person the feelings of a decent, kindly man who has against his will caused his neighbour cruel, undeserved anguish'. It is a dilemma Chekhov is to explore again and again.

Volodya (*St Petersburg Gazette*, June 1887) shows the dilemma from a lonely, emotionally insecure adolescent's point of view. The intense, prurient, frustrated feelings of the boy, running the gamut of sexuality from arousal to shame, contrast with the superficial self-indulgences of the Shumihins' world. The hoydenish Nyuta, well observed though she is, victimizes the boy's sensuality. Volodya is simultaneously allured and repelled, until the focus shifts and one realizes he is really the victim of a broken marriage and a mother whom he resents for her failure to satisfy his craving for emotional support and understanding. It is a sombre little story of suicide as a futile act of resentment and vengeance. The image of fatherhood at the end, romantically as remote as Mentone and Biarritz, holiday places, one assumes, where the boy was happy, has about it a bleak, funereal tawdriness. No room is left for supposing that society is to blame, or that religion or morality have an answer; the inadequacy of a Konstantin Treplev, of a seagull's flight interrupted by a bullet, is the final moral. The brevity and power of this study of Volodya's last hours highlight principally a simple failure of human awareness.

Of the hundreds of stories which Chekhov wrote in the 1880s, none seems to capture the essence of the term 'Chekhovian' quite as brilliantly as *The Kiss* (*New Times*, December, 1887). It seems to have been written exceptionally quickly, perhaps over the space of a couple of days while Chekhov was staying in the hotel 'Moscow' in St Petersburg after the production of his first play, *Ivanov*. The very speed of the composition may have helped to fix the story's meaning before it could lose its instantaneous freshness. It emphasizes superbly the eternally Chekhovian message that life's transience acts fatefully on human beings to alter forever their assumptions about themselves.

An artillery officer, Ryabovitch – 'I am the shyest, most modest, and most undistinguished officer in the whole brigade!' – is invited to a party at the house of a local General. He accompanies his brother officers there, takes no part in any of the entertainments, but, losing his way in the darkened rooms, suddenly finds himself embraced by a woman and kissed. He has obviously been mistaken for someone else. The moment, though, permeated by the scents of lilac and roses, and the chilly tingling sensation like peppermint drops remaining on his skin from the kiss, permanently enchants him. He seems to have been caught in the thralls of a vague, inexpressible love that consumes him for the rest of his life.

Though the realities of an artilleryman's bivouac existence are suggested well enough, what is permanent, unchanging for him, his only guarantee against the everyday impermanence surrounding him, is the thought that, as a result of that moment, 'something extraordinary, foolish, but joyful and delightful, had come into his life'. The very vagueness of it can seem unsatisfactory. Chekhov ironically underscores the teasingly vague legacy of Ryabovitch's kiss by describing his ultimate disillusionment. The whole of life became for him, 'an unintelligible, aimless jest' over which he can be said to have had the last laugh. By deliberately ignoring the General's second invitation he snubbed his fate, as it were. The kiss tended to reverse his assumptions about himself, but in doing so it became vampiric.

As a murder story none is more final and inevitable than *Sleepy* (*St Petersburg Gazette*, January, (1888). Chekhov used his pseudonym 'Antosha Chekhonte' for it when it was first published, possibly to distinguish it from the longer, more serious 'Anton Chekhov' work on which he was engaged at the time, *The Steppe*. Both are studies in childhood experience. Yet the nightmare horror of the wretched Varka's struggle to remain awake in *Sleepy* is unforgettable. Through a consciously impressionistic technique Chekhov focuses sharply on the cumulative, uncomprehending awfulness of Varka's predicament, until the desperate final act seems completely devoid of evil intent, let alone of culpability.

*

Chekhov's talent had been recognized by many in the first half of the 1880s, but it was not until he recieved a letter from D. V. Grigorovich in March, 1886, urging him to take his talent more seriously, that he seemed prepared to accept a less modest view of himself than he had entertained previously. Grigorovich (1822–99) had been a close friend of Dostoevsky in the 1840s and the author of such studies of peasant life as *The Village* (1846) and *Anton the Unlucky* (1847). Though famous and influential in their time, these stories had long since lost their appeal. Despite this, Grigorovich himself had survived as a kind of grand old man of Russian letters and his words to Chekhov – 'I am sure that you are called upon to write several truly outstanding works of literature' – had their due effect. Chekhov determined to write a serious work and the determination came to fruition towards the end of 1887.

The Steppe was written over little more than a month, between late December 1887 and early February 1888, and it received the accolade of publication in the prestigious journal *The Northern Herald* shortly after it was completed. By far the longest of Chekhov's stories until that time, it was a reminiscence based on a journey he had made in 1877 from Taganrog when, among other things, he had fallen ill with peritonitis. The autobiographical form of the work is therefore undeniable.

As he wrote it, Chekhov was ever more conscious of its lack

of plot or subject – a characteristic, after all, of so many of his stories – and felt that, as a result, he was not offering a picture, 'in which all the separate parts, like stars in the sky, flowed together into a single whole, but a set of notes, a dry listing of impressions'. Moreover, this was the first work in which he consciously relied on his powers of nature description, consciously made himself, as he admitted, heir to the greatest writing in Russian literature, the work of Lermontov (in 'Taman') or Pushkin (in *The Captain's Daughter*) or Gogol (in *Taras Bulba*), not to mention Turgenev and Tolstoy. The success and power of the work, therefore, had to depend on a unifying presence or narrative eye which could sustain the reader's interest throughout what might, on the face of it, seem little more than a travelogue.

Such unity is, of course, provided by the boy, Yegorushka. As a prose poem, of surpassing beauty in parts, with recurring motifs of music and certain images, such as those relating to the boy's past in his reminiscence of his grandmother, or those relating to the future in his vision of the waving windmill, the work may be thought to have the vague, inconsequent, impressionistic quality of a study in childhood experience. Its freshness and brilliance are in themselves guarantees of its lasting power to work magic. However satisfying it is in this sense, it also has a deeper, subtler meaning that makes it both a watershed in Chekhov's evolution as a writer and an investigation of the very nature of the evolving forces which cause change in life.

The steppe itself exemplifies transition for the impressionable Yegorushka. To travel across it is for him to reach 'a new unknown life that was beginning for him now ... What would that life be like?' The question justifies its formulation, in a Chekhovian sense, throughout the preceding text, throughout the boy's experience of transition. The organic unity of the work is supplied by Yegorushka's experience of the steppe as a kind of rite of passage. Through imagery and episode the boy's journey acquires the character of an initiation into life.

Accompanied by his uncle and a kind of surrogate, or spiritual, father-figure, Father Christopher, the boy Yegorushka sets out one early morning on a journey across the steppe. The object is to receive a good education. The journey itself, though, is an education in life which opens with a departure from the town, passing the prison and cemetery (where 'when the cherries were ripe the white tombstones and crosses were dotted with splashes of red like bloodstains'), and has about it intimations of birth pangs and emergence into light. After such initial tribulations as ferociously barking dogs and the windmill waving like a sorcerer, the boy's fears recede with Father Christopher's extended account of his own education and the stillness which consumes the world during the heat of the day. It is a Joycean epiphany. Meeting for the first time a boy like himself, it is as if time had stood still.

Through successive episodes, merging into each other with passages of such consummate nature description they seem like movements in an ongoing verbal symphony, Yegorushka's experience encompasses the money-orientated world of Moisey Moisevitch at the posting-station, the tender kiss of admiration from the Countess Dranitsky and then seems to burgeon into youthfulness, as do all the natural phenomena of the steppe: 'And then in the churring of insects, in the sinister figures, in the ancient barrows, in the blue sky, in the moonlight, in the flight of the nightbird, in everything you see and hear, triumphant beauty, youth, the fulness of power, and the passionate thirst for life begin to be apparent.' Shortly afterwards, due to his elders' search for the elusive Varlamov, he is consigned to the keeping of peasant waggoners and, as Panteley points out, is no longer 'little Yegor' (i.e. the diminutive form: Yegorushka), but the holy martyr Yegory, the Bearer of Victory, the one who will stand up to his persecutor Dymov and learn, both from the despairing tales of their own lives told by the peasants and Panteley's fictitious tales of bloody murder, the gamut of human emotions, from the horror of violent death to the sweetness of married love.

Varlamov, the man who is described as possessing 'a sense of power and habitual authority over the steppe', is finally found, and the outcome is happy so far as Father Christopher is concerned. But the steppe wields a different power over the boy. Like life itself, he is forced to meet its challenge. It takes the form of an apocalyptic storm − a true *tour de force* of descriptive writing – which, in horrific imagery, projects all the worst fears associated with darkness. It forms the climax to his simulated journey through life in the way it brings Yegorushka close to death. He is only saved through the anointing, with oil and vinegar, which he receives at Father Christopher's hands. The conflict for his soul, as it were, symbolized by so many features of his experience, can be summarized by the contrast between darkness and light, night and day, that has been ever present during his journey and which receives, in the old priest's words, ultimate justification in the simple juxtaposition of learning with light and ignorance with darkness.

Later in the 1880s and during the 1890s Chekhov was to explore other, more sophisticated, themes in stories betraying an even greater mastery. Among these are such powerful and sustained works as *A Dreary Story, The Party, The Duel, Ward No. 6, The Student, The House with the Mezzanine* and *My Life*. But *The Steppe* was the first of his masterpieces as a story-writer and its freshness and vividness have remained untarnished by the century or so which have passed since it was written.

Richard Freeborn

SELECT BIBLIOGRAPHY

This is a select bibliography of works in English relating to Chekhov's life and works and is intended principally as a guide to further reading.

BIOGRAPHIES
The best straightforward biography, based mostly on Chekhov's letters, is R. HINGLEY's *A New Life of Chekhov*, Oxford University Press, 1976. It replaces by and large the earlier biographies by D. MAGARSHACK (1952) and E. J. SIMMONS (1970). Among specialized treatments of aspects of Chekhov's life, especially notable are V. LLEWELLYN SMITH's *Anton Chekhov and the Lady with the Dog*, Oxford University Press, 1973, an erudite examination of his relations with women, and H. PITCHER's *Chekhov's Leading Lady*, John Murray, 1979, about his wife, Olga Knipper. The best selection of his letters is *Letters of Anton Chekhov*, translated by Michael Heim and selected, introduced and with a commentary by SIMON KARLINSKY, Bodley Head, 1973, which comprises a scholarly and stimulating biography in its own right.

CRITICISM
Of the critical studies which relate particularly to the stories in this volume, pride of place must go to D. RAYFIELD, *Chekhov: the evolution of his art*, Elek Books, 1975, a well-written and very perceptive study. Also valuable are T. WINNER, *Chekhov and his Prose*, Henry Holt, New York, 1966 and K. D. KRAMER, *The Chameleon and the Dream*, Mouton, The Hague and Paris, 1970. Rich in insights, if fragmentary in its treatment of Chekhov's works, is S. LAFFITTE's *Chekhov, 1860–1904* (translated by Moura Budberg and Gordon Latta), Angus and Robertson, 1974. Scholarly if uninspired is B. HAHN's *Chekhov. A Study of the Major Stories and Plays*, Cambridge University Press, 1977.

Among specialized critical treatments noteworthy are H. PETER STOWELL's *Literary Impressionism, James and Chekhov*, University of Georgia Press, 1980, and CAROLINA DE MAEGD-SOEP's feminist, but erudite, *Chekhov and Women. Women in the Life and Work of Chekhov*, Slavica, Ohio, 1987.

A very early study is W. GERHARDI's *Anton Chekhov. A Critical Study*, Duffield, New York, 1923, still interesting for its attempt to come to grips with Chekhov's 'elusiveness of aim', and V. S. PRITCHETT's *Chekhov: A Spirit Set Free*, Hodder and Stoughton, 1988, a sensitive and beautifully written general treatment.

CHRONOLOGY

DATE	AUTHOR'S LIFE	LITERARY CONTEXT
1859		Goncharov: *Oblomov*. Ostrovsky: *The Storm*.
1860	Anton Pavlovich Chekhov born in Taganrog on the Sea of Azov in southern Russia (16 January), the third of seven children of a small shopkeeper, and grandson of a serf who had bought his freedom.	Turgenev: *On the Eve*; 'First Love'. Dostoevsky: *The House of the Dead* (to 1862). George Eliot: *The Mill on the Floss*.
1861		Herzen publishes *My Past and Thoughts* (to 1866). Dickens: *Great Expectations*.
1862		Turgenev: *Fathers and Children*. Hugo: *Les Misérables*. Flaubert: *Salammbô*.
1863		Tolstoy: *The Cossacks*. Chernyshevsky: *What is to be Done?* Nekrasov: *Red-Nosed Frost*.
1864		Dostoevsky: *Notes from Underground*. Fet: 'Tormented by life ...'.
1865		Leskov: 'Lady Macbeth of the Mtensk District'. Sleptsov: *Hard Times*. Dickens: *Our Mutual Friend*.
1866		Dostoevsky: *Crime and Punishment*. Daudet: *Lettres de mon moulin*.
1867	Enrolled at parish school attached to Greek Orthodox church. Unable to master modern Greek, he leaves at the end of the school year.	Turgenev: *Smoke*. Dostoevsky: *The Gambler*. Zola: *Thérèse Raquin*. Marx: *Das Kapital*, vol. 1.
1868	Joins preparatory class at the Taganrog *gimnazia*. Following the recent reforms of Dmitry Tolstoy, Minister of Education,	Lavrov: *Historical Letters*. Nekrasov: 'Who Can Be Happy and Free in Russia?'

Alexander II (Tsar since 1855) following a reformist policy, in complete opposition to his predecessor, the reactionary Nicholas I. Port of Vladivostok founded to serve Russia's recent annexations (from China). Huge investment in railway building begins.

Emancipation of the serfs (February), the climax of the Tsar's programme of reform. While his achievement had great moral and symbolic significance, many peasants felt themselves cheated by the terms of the complex emancipation statute. Outbreak of American Civil War. Unification of Italy. Bismarck Prime Minister of Prussia. 1860s and 70s: 'Nihilism' – rationalist philosophy sceptical of all forms of established authority – becomes widespread amongst young radical intelligentsia in Russia.
Polish rebellion. Poland incorporated into Russia. Itinerant movement formed by young artists, led by Ivan Kramskoi and later joined by Ivan Shishkin: drawing inspiration from the Russian countryside and peasant life, they are also concerned to take art to the people.
The first International. Establishment of the Zemstva, organs of self-government and a significant liberal influence in Tsarist Russia. Legal reforms do much towards removing class bias from the administration of justice. Trial by jury instituted and a Russian bar established. Russian colonial expansion in Central Asia (to 1868).
Slavery formally abolished in USA.

Young nobleman Dmitry Karakozov tries to assassinate the Tsar. Radical journals *The Contemporary* and *The Russian Word* suppressed. Austro-Prussian war.

St Petersburg section of Moscow Slavonic Benevolent Committee founded (expansion of Pan-Slav movement). Rimsky-Korsakov's symphonic poem *Sadko*.

DATE	AUTHOR'S LIFE	LITERARY CONTEXT
1868 *cont*	Greek and Latin dominate the curriculum and study of 'subversive' subjects such as Russian literature is severely restricted.	
1869	Embarks on 8-year course which he completes in 10, being twice kept down. Obliged to work in his father's shop in the evenings and holidays.	Tolstoy: *War and Peace*. Goncharov: *The Precipice*. Flaubert: *L'Education sentimentale*. Gaboriau: *Monsieur Lecoq*. Verne: *Vingt mille lieues sous les mers*.
1870		Turgenev: 'King Lear of the Steppes'. Death of Herzen and Dickens.
1871	Death of his infant sister, Evgenia.	Dostoevesky: *The Possessed*. Ostrovsky: *The Forest*. Eliot: *Middlemarch* (to 1872).
1872		Turgenev: 'Spring Torrents'; *A Month in the Country* (1st perf.). Leskov: *Cathedral Folk*. Kushchevsky: *Nikolay Negorev, or The Successful Russian*. Nietzsche: *The Birth of Tragedy*.
1873	Goes to the theatre for the first time (Offenbach's *La Belle Hélène*) and is immediately hooked.	Ostrovsky: *The Snow Maiden*.
1874		
1875	His two elder brothers leave for Moscow, Aleksandr to the University, Nikolai to art college. Anton starts a class magazine, *The Hiccup*.	
1876	Facing bankruptcy, his father flees to Moscow, leaving Anton to negotiate with debtors and creditors (April). His mother and the two youngest children, Maria and Mikhail, follow in July.	Eliot: *Daniel Deronda*. Henry James: *Roderick Hudson*.
1877	When his younger brother Ivan joins the rest of the family, Anton is left alone in Taganrog to complete his education. Finances himself by coaching.	Tolstoy: *Anna Karenina*. Turgenev: *Virgin Soil*. Garshin: 'Four Days'. Zola: *L'Assommoir*. Flaubert: *Trois contes*.

CHRONOLOGY

Chemist D. I. Mendeleyev wins international fame by his periodic table of chemical elements based on atomic weight.

Lenin born. Franco-Prussian war. End of Second Empire in France and establishment of Third Republic. Repin paints *The Volga Boatmen* (to 1873).

Paris Commune set up and suppressed. Fall of Paris ends war. German Empire established.

Three Emperors' League (Germany, Russia and Austria-Hungary) formed in Berlin. During the late 1860s and early 1870s, Narodnik (Populist) 'going to the people' campaign gathers momentum: young intellectuals incite peasantry to rebel against autocracy.

First performance of Rimsky-Korsakov's first opera, *The Maid of Pskov.*

Mussorgsky's *Pictures at an Exhibition*; first performance of *Boris Godunov.*

Bulgarian Atrocities (Bulgarians massacred by Turks). Founding of Land and Freedom, first Russian political party openly to advocate revolution. Death of anarchist Mikhail Bakunin. Official statute for Women's Higher Courses, whereby women able to study at universities of St Petersburg, Moscow, Kiev, Odesssa and Kazan. By 1881 there are 2000 female students. Queen Victoria proclaimed Empress of India.
Russia declares war on Turkey (conflict inspired by Pan-Slav movement). Tchaikovsky: *Swan Lake.*

DATE	AUTHOR'S LIFE	LITERARY CONTEXT
1878	First attempts to write a play.	Saltykov-Shchedrin: *The Sanctuary of Mon Repos.* Garshin: 'An Incident'. James: 'Daisy Miller'.
1879	Matriculates. Leaves Taganrog for Moscow (August) where he joins his parents and younger siblings in lodgings. Enrols as medical student at Moscow University.	Dostoevsky: *The Brothers Karamazov* (to 1880). Saltykov-Shchedrin: *The Golovlev Family.*
1880	First stories published in *The Dragonfly* under a pseudonym.	Maupassant: 'Boule de suif'. Death of Flaubert and George Eliot.
1881	Possibly writing his first surviving play, *Platonov.* Contributing regularly to *The Spectator.* Affair with Natalia Golden (who later marries his brother Aleksandr).	Tolstoy: 'What Men Live By'. Turgenev: 'The Song of Triumphant Love'. Leskov: 'The Lefthanded Craftsman'. Flaubert: *Bouvard et Pécuchet.* Ibsen: *Ghosts.* Death of Dostoevsky.
1882	Writing regularly for *The Alarm Clock.* First contribution to a St Petersburg paper, *Splinters,* after meeting with the editor, Nikolay Leykin.	Kravchinsky: *Underground Russia* (first chronicle of the revolutionary movement). Uspensky: *The Power of the Soil.*
1883	Spends summer at his brother Ivan's house at Voskresensk, a provincial town 40 miles from Moscow. Writes 'The Daughter of Albion', his first piece for *Splinters* to win renown. Friendship with Kiseliov family, neighbouring landowners. Beginning of long relationship with Olga Kundasova.	Turgenev: 'Clara Milich'. Garshin: 'The Red Flower'. Fet: *Evening Lights.* Ostrovsky: *The Handsome Man.* Maupassant: *Une Vie; Clair de Lune.*
1884	Graduates. Summer at Voskresensk, helping at the hospital. Returns to Moscow to practise medicine. First symptoms of TB. Publishes collection of his best stories, *Tales of Melpomene. A Shooting*	Tolstoy: *Confession.* Leskov: 'The Toupée Artist'. Ostrovsky: *Guilty without Guilt.* Ibsen: *The Wild Duck.* Strindberg: *Getting Married* (to 1885). Maupassant: *Miss Harriet.*

CHRONOLOGY

Congress of Berlin ends Russo-Turkish war; other European powers compel Russia to give up many of her territorial gains; partition of Bulgaria between Russia and Turkey. Mass trial of Populist agitators in Russia ('The Trial of the 193'). Shishkin, pioneer of the *plein-air* study in the 1870s, paints *Rye*, classic evocation of Russian countryside.

Birth of Stalin. The People's Will, terrorist offshoot of Land and Freedom, founded. Assassination of Prince Kropotkin, governor of Kharkov.

Tchaikovsky: *Eugene Onegin*. Death of historian S. M. Solovyov, whose history of Russia had been appearing one volume per year since 1851.

Oil drilling begins in Azerbaidzhan; big programme of railway building commences. Borodin: *In Central Asia*. During 1870s and 1880s the Abramtsevo Colony, drawn together by railway tycoon Mamontov, includes Repin, Serov, Vrubel and Chekhov's friend Levitan. Nationalist in outlook, they draw inspiration from Russian folk art and the Russo-Byzantine tradition.

Assassination of Alexander II by Ignatius Grinevitsky, a member of the People's Will, following which the terrorist movement is crushed by the authorities. Revolutionary opposition goes underground until 1900. 'Epoch of small deeds': intelligentsia work for reform through existing institutions. The new Tsar, Alexander III, is much influenced by his former tutor, the extreme conservative Pobedonostsev, who becomes Chief Procurator of the Holy Synod. Resignation of Loris-Melikov, architect of the reforms of Alexander II's reign. Jewish pogroms.

Censorship laws tightened. Student riots in Kazan and St Petersburg. Reactionary regime of Alexander III characterized by stagnation in agriculture, retrogression in education, russification of non-Russian section of the population and narrow bureacratic paternalism.

First Russian Marxist revolutionary organization, the Liberation of Labour, founded in Geneva by Georgi Plekhanov. Increased persecution of religious minorities.

New education minister Delyanov increases powers of inspectors; university appointments made directly by the ministry rather than academic councils; fees increased. *Fatherland Notes*, edited by Saltykov-Shchedrin, suppressed. During 1880s organizations such as the Moscow Law Society and Committee for the Advancement of Literacy become centres for the discussion of political and social ideas amongst the intelligentsia.

DATE	AUTHOR'S LIFE	LITERARY CONTEXT
1884 *cont*	*Party* serialized in *Daily News* (to 1885). First commission for Khudekov's prestigious *Petersburg Gazette*.	
1885	Produces some 100 pieces this year. First of several summers spent in a dacha on the Kiseliov's estate at Babkino (source of *The Cherry Orchard*). Stories written there include 'The Burbot' and 'The Huntsman', his first big success in the *Petersburg Gazette*. Visits St Petersburg for the first time (December) as a guest of Leykin.	Garshin: 'Nadezhda Nikolaevna'. Leskov: 'The Bogey-Man'. Zola: *Germinal*. Maupassant: *Bel-Ami*.
1886	Short, secret engagement to Dunia Efros. Begins working for Aleksey Suvorin's *New Times*, which becomes his principal outlet; writes under his own name for the first time. Receives letter of praise and encouragement from novelist Dmitry Grigorovich. Publishes the collection *Motley Stories*. Two visits to St Petersburg (April and December) where his stories are winning him considerable renown. Individual tales this year include 'Art', 'Easter Eve', 'Difficult People' and 'On the Road'.	Tolstoy: *The Power of Darkness*; *The Death of Ivan Illych*. James: *The Bostonians*; *The Princess Casamassima*. Stevenson: *Dr Jekyll and Mr Hyde*.
1887	Two visits to St Petersburg (March and November). Deepening friendship with Suvorin family. Vacation in Taganrog; trip to the Don Steppe (April). Writes 'Happiness' (summer). Publishes collection *In the Twilight* (September). First play, *Ivanov*, performed in Moscow (November). 'The Kiss' appears in *New Times* (December).	Saltykov-Shchedrin: *Old Days in Poshekhone*. Sluchevsky: *Thirty-three Stories*. Garshin: 'The Signal'. Leskov: 'The Sentry'. Fofanov: *Poems*. Strindberg: *The Father*; *The Dwellers of Hemsö*. Maupassant: *Mont-Oriol*; *Le Horla*.

CHRONOLOGY

Students hold a demonstration to commemorate the 50th anniversary of the birth of Dobrolyubov. Several of them, disgusted by the brutal way in which the demonstration is suppressed, resolve to assassinate the Tsar; the plot is discovered and among those executed is Lenin's brother, Alexander Ulyanov, whose death he swears to avenge.

During the late 1880s Russia begins her industrial revolution.

DATE	AUTHOR'S LIFE	LITERARY CONTEXT
1888	Writes 'The Steppe' (January). The Chekhovs rent a summer dacha at Sumy in the Ukraine; friendship with Lintvariov family. Visits Suvorin in the Crimea; goes to Baku with Suvorin's son. Makes first of several abortive attempts to buy a farm in the Ukraine. Awarded half the Russian Academy's 1888 prize for literature. Stays with Suvorin in St Petersburg (December); meets Tchaikovsky.	Suicide of Vsevolod Garshin. Strindberg: *Miss Julie.* Maupassant: *Pierre et Jean.* James: 'The Aspern Papers'. Hardy: *Wessex Tales.* Kipling: *Plain Tales from the Hills.*
1889	*Ivanov* a success in St Petersburg (January). Death of his brother Nikolai, a talented artist, from tuberculosis (June). Spends the summer in Sumy. Short visit to Odessa where the Moscow Maly Theatre company are on tour; writes 'A Dreary Story' while in the Crimea. *The Wood Demons* produced in Moscow but badly received (November).	Tolstoy: 'The Kreutzer Sonata'. Kravchinksy: *The Career of a Nihilist.* Ertel: *The Gardenins.* Hauptmann: *Before Sunrise.* Maeterlinck: *La Princesse Maleine.*
1890	In April sets off for Sakhalin, a penal colony off the Pacific coast of Siberia, travelling by road and river. Returns via Hong Kong, Singapore and Ceylon, arriving in Moscow in December. Writes 'Gusev'.	Tolstoy: *The Fruits of Enlightenment.* Polonsky: *Evening Bell.* Ibsen: *Hedda Gabler.* Maeterlinck: *Les Aveugles.* Wilde: *The Picture of Dorian Gray.*
1891	To Vienna, Venice, Florence, Rome, Naples, Nice, Monte Carlo and Paris with Suvorin (March–May). Summer spent at Bogimovo, joined by friends including Lika Mizinova (later to provide the inspiration for the character of Nina in *The Seagull*) and the artist Levitan. Writes 'The Duel'. Engaged in fundraising activities for victims of the famine.	Death of Goncharov. Leskov: 'Night Owls'. Ertel: *Change.* Conan Doyle: *The Adventures of Sherlock Holmes.*

HISTORICAL EVENTS

Rimsky-Korsakov: *Scheherazade.*

Land Captains introduced, powerful administrator magnates who increase control of the gentry over the peasants, undermining previous judicial and local government reforms. Shishkin: *Morning in a Pine Forest.*

First performance of Tchaikovsky's opera *The Queen of Spades* and first (posthumous) performance of Borodin's *Prince Igor.* Peasant representation on Zemstva reduced. Bismarck dismissed. During the 1890s growth rate for industrial output averages *c.* 8% per annum. Important development of coal mines in southern European Russia. Industrial expansion sustained by growth of banking and joint stock companies, which begin to attract foreign, later native, investment.

Harvest failure in central Russia causes famine and starvation: up to a million peasants die by the end of the winter. Work commences on Trans-Siberian Railway. 20,000 Jews brutally evicted from Moscow. Rigorously enforced residence restrictions, quotas limiting entry of Jews into high schools and universities, and other anti-Jewish measures drive over a million Russian Jews to emigrate, mainly to North America.

DATE	AUTHOR'S LIFE	LITERARY CONTEXT
1892	Purchases country house and estate at Melikhovo, 50 miles south of Moscow, where he moves with his parents, Maria and Mikhail. During cholera epidemic helps man the local clinic; acts as unpaid 'cholera superintendant' for 25 villages. Writes 'The Grasshopper'. 'Ward No. 6' appears in *Russian Thought*.	Gorky: 'Makar Chudra'. Fofanov: *Shadows and Secrets*. Hauptmann: *The Weavers*. Maeterlinck: *Pelléas et Mélisande*. Ibsen: *The Master Builder*.
1893	Serial publication of *The Island of Sakhalin* (book version published 1895).	Critic Dmitri Merezhkovsky cites Chekhov, Garshin, Fofanov and Minsky as heralds of new era in Russian literature. Zola: *Le Docteur Pascal*.
1894	Writes 'The Student' (spring). Boat trip down the Volga (August). Travels to Europe with Suvorin (autumn).	Bryusov brings out three collections of *The Russian Symbolists* (to 1895). Balmont: *Under Northern Skies*. Rostand: *Les Romanesques*.
1895	Publishes 'Three Years'. Visits Tolstoy at Yasnaya Polyana (August). Works on *The Seagull*. Writes 'The House with the Mezzanine'.	Tolstoy: 'Master and Man'. Gorky: 'The Song of the Falcon'; *Chelkash*. Bryusov: *Chefs d'Oeuvres*. Balmont: *Beyond All Limits*. Fontane: *Effie Briest*. Wilde: *The Importance of Being Earnest*. Rostand: *La Princesse lointaine*.
1896	Writes 'My Life'. Builds school at Melikhovo. *The Seagull* staged in St Petersburg (October). The first night is a disaster, and Chekhov flees to Melikhovo.	Sologub: first collection of Symbolist poetry. Merezhkovsky: *Christ and Antichrist* (to 1905).
1897	Publishes 'Peasants' (February). Collapse in health; TB diagnosed (March). Convalesces in Biarritz and Nice. Sides with Zola in the Dreyfus affair; ceases to write for *New Times* which takes an anti-Semitic line.	Gorky: 'Creatures that Once were Men'. Bunin: *To the Edge of the World*. Bryusov: *Me eum esse*. Kuprin: *Miniatures*. Wells: *The Invisible Man*. Rostand: *Cyrano de Bergerac*.

HISTORICAL EVENTS

Tchaikovsky: *The Nutcracker*. Property qualification for franchise raised, reducing number of voters in St Petersburg from 21,176 to 7,152.

Armenian massacres begin. As part of the russification of the Balkans the German University of Dorpat is reopened as the University of Yuryev, with a majority of Russian students. Death of Tchaikovsky.

Death of Alexander II; accession of Nicholas II. Growth in popularity of Marxist ideas amongst university students encouraged by appearance of Struve's *Critical Notes* and Beltov's *Monistic View*.

A. S. Popov, pioneer of wireless telegraphy, gives demonstration and publishes article on his discoveries, coinciding with Marconi's independent discoveries in this field. Establishment of Marxist newspaper *Samarskii Vestnik*. In May, 2000 people crushed to death on Klondynka field when a stand collapses during the coronation ceremony.
Tsar Nicholas II visits President Faure of France: Russo-French alliance.
Lenin deported for three years to Siberia. Only systematic census carried out in Imperial Russia reports a population of 128,000,000, an increase of three-and-a-half times over the century. The industrial labour force of three million (3%) is small compared with the West but shows a fifteen-fold increase over the century. 13% of the population now urban as opposed to only 4% a century earlier.

DATE	AUTHOR'S LIFE	LITERARY CONTEXT
1898	Returns from Europe (May). Stories include 'Ionych', 'Gooseberries', 'The Man in the Case' and 'About Love'. Death of his father (October). Buys a plot of land for a new house in Yalta, where he is spending the winter for his health. First performance in Moscow of *The Seagull* by the newly founded Moscow Arts Theatre run by Stanislavsky and Nemirovich-Danchenko: a triumph (December). Meets the actress Olga Knipper.	Tolstoy: *What is Art?* Balmont: *Silence.* Zola: *J'Accuse.* Shaw: *Mrs Warren's Profession.* James: 'The Turn of the Screw', 'In the Cage'. Wells: *The War of the Worlds.*
1899	For 75,000 roubles makes over his copyrights to Adolf Marx, who undertakes to republish his Complete Works (1899–1902). Friendship with young writers Gorky and Bunin. Falls in love with Olga Knipper. She visits him at Melikhovo and later at Yalta. Chekhov sells estate at Melikhovo. *Uncle Vanya* (reworking of *The Wood Demons*) opens in Moscow (October). Writes 'The Lady with the Dog' (autumn).	Tolstoy: *Resurrection.* Gorky: *Foma Gordeev*; *Twenty-six Men and a Girl.* Kropotkin: *Memoirs of a Revolutionist.*
1900	'In the Ravine' published in Gorky's Marxist paper, *Life*. Chekhov, his mother and sister installed in new house at Yalta. Elected to the Writers' Section of the Academy. Travels to Caucasus with Gorky. Joins Olga on Moscow Arts Theatre tour at Sevastapol. *Three Sisters* completed in October. Attends rehearsals in Moscow.	Freud: *The Interpretation of Dreams.* Solovyov: *Three Conversations on War, Progress, and the End of Human History.* Balmont: *Buildings on Fire.* Bryusov: *Tertia vigilia.* Conrad: *Lord Jim.*
1901	Spends January in Nice. Successful first night of *Three Sisters* (31 January). Marries Olga Knipper in Moscow (25 May). Honeymoon at sanatorium at Aksionovo. Olga returns to	Blok: 'Verses on the Beautiful Lady' (to 1902). Mann: *Buddenbrooks.* Kipling: *Kim.*

CHRONOLOGY

HISTORICAL EVENTS

Russian Social Democratic Labour Party founded. Between 1898 and 1901 Caucasian oil production is higher than the rest of the world together. Finns begin to lose their rights as a separate nation within the Empire. Sergey Diaghilev and others found the *World of Art* society, prominent members of which are Benois and Bakst; its most notable production is Diaghilev's Ballet Russe. The magazine, to which 'decadent' writers such as Balmont frequently contribute, opposes the 'provincial naturalism' of the Itinerant school, and advocate a philosophy of art for art's sake.

Student riots. All universities in Russia temporarily closed. Moscow Law Society also closed. Reactionary Sipyagin becomes Minister of the Interior. During 1890s the so-called 'Third Element', consisting of doctors, teachers, statisticians, engineers and other professionals employed by the Zemstva, becomes a recognized focus of Liberal opposition to the Tsarist regime. Russian industry enters a period of depression.

Lenin allowed to leave Russia. Founds paper *Iskra* in Germany. Russia ends 19th century with a total of 17,000 students, spread over nine universities: one hundred years before, the Empire had only one university – Moscow. Nevertheless, the proportion of illiterates in the Empire was recorded at this time as 75% of persons aged between 9 and 49.

Murder of Minister of Education Bogolepov by a student marks beginning of wave of political assassinations. For the authorities the principal menace is the Socialist Revolutionary Party, who look for support from the peasantry, rather than the Social Democrats, who hope to rouse the urban proletariat. First performance of Rachmaninov's piano concerto no. 2 with the composer as soloist. Death of Queen Victoria.

DATE	AUTHOR'S LIFE	LITERARY CONTEXT
1901 *cont*	the theatre for the winter season but Chekhov, unable to stand the climate, remains in Yalta. Health deteriorates. Writes 'The Bishop'.	
1902	Olga visits Yalta (February). Back in St Petersburg she miscarries and has to undergo an operation; continues to suffer from peritonitis. Chekhov travels to Perm and the Urals (June). Stays, with Olga, at Stanislavky's country house at Liubimovka (July). Resigns from the Academy when Gorky's election is revoked (September). Visits Olga in Moscow (October–November) and winters in Yalta.	Gorky: *The Lower Depths.* Bely: *Second Symphony.* Andreev: 'The Abyss', 'In the Fog'. Merezhkovsky: *Tolstoy and Dostoevsky.* James: *The Wings of the Dove.* Conrad: *Heart of Darkness.* Gide: *L'Immoraliste.*
1903	Publishes 'The Bride'. Writing *The Cherry Orchard* (March–October). Attends rehearsals in Moscow (December–January).	Balmont: *Let Us Be Like the Sun.* Bryusov: *Urbi et Orbis.* Shaw: *Man and Superman.* Butler: *The Way of All Flesh.* Mann: *Tonio Kröger.*
1904	First night of *The Cherry Orchard* on 17 January, Chekhov's name day. Public tributes. Goes to Yalta (February) where his health continues to deteriorate. Returns to Moscow (May); leaves with Olga for Black Forest spa of Badenweiler (3 June) where he dies on 2 July. Buried at the Novodevichy Cemetry in Moscow.	Tolstoy completes 'Hadji Murad'. Blok: *The City* (to 1908). Bely: *Gold in Azure.* Annensky: *Quiet Songs.* Zinaida Hippius: *Poems.* Shaw: *John Bull's Other Island.* Conrad: *Nostromo.* James: *The Golden Bowl.*
1905		

1

CHRONOLOGY

HISTORICAL EVENTS

Lenin's *What is to be Done?* provides blueprint for future Bolshevik party.
Sipyagin assassinated by Socialist Revolutionaries.

Conflict between Bolsheviks and Mensheviks at second Congress of Russian
Social Democratic Labour Party. Assassination of King Alexander and
Queen Draga of Serbia.

Russo-Japanese war (to 1905), both unpopular and unsuccessful from the
point of view of the Russians. Assassination of V. K. Pleve, Minister of the
Interior, and notorious oppressor of minority peoples within the Empire.

First Russian Revolution.

THE SWEDISH MATCH

THE SWEDISH MATCH

(The Story of a Crime)

I

ON the morning of October 6, 1885, a well-dressed
young man presented himself at the office of the
police superintendent of the 2nd division of the S. district, and announced that his employer, a retired cornet of the guards, called Mark Ivanovitch Klyauzov,
had been murdered. The young man was pale and
extremely agitated as he made this announcement.
His hands trembled and there was a look of horror in
his eyes.

'To whom have I the honour of speaking?' the
superintendent asked him.

'Psyekov, Klyauzov's steward. Agricultural and
engineering expert.'

The police superintendent, on reaching the spot
with Psyekov and the necessary witnesses, found the
position as follows.

Masses of people were crowding about the lodge in
which Klyauzov lived. The news of the event had
flown round the neighbourhood with the rapidity of
lightning, and, thanks to its being a holiday, the
people were flocking to the lodge from all the neigh-

3

bouring villages. There was a regular hubbub of talk.
Pale and tearful faces were to be seen here and there.
The door into Klyauzov's bedroom was found to be
locked. The key was in the lock on the inside.

'Evidently the criminals made their way in by the
window,' Psyekov observed, as they examined the
door.

They went into the garden into which the bedroom
window looked. The window had a gloomy, ominous
air. It was covered by a faded green curtain. One corner of the curtain was slightly turned back, which
made it possible to peep into the bedroom.

'Has anyone of you looked in at the window?'
inquired the superintendent.

'No, your honour,' said Yefrem, the gardener, a little,
grey-haired old man with the face of a veteran non-
commissioned officer. 'No one feels like looking when
they are shaking in every limb!'

'Ech, Mark Ivanitch! Mark Ivanitch!' sighed the
superintendent, as he looked at the window. 'I told
you that you would come to a bad end! I told you,
poor dear – you wouldn't listen! Dissipation leads to
no good!'

'It's thanks to Yefrem,' said Psyekov. 'We should
never have guessed it but for him. It was he who first
thought that something was wrong. He came to me
this morning and said: "Why is it our master hasn't
waked up for so long? He hasn't been out of his bedroom for a whole week!" When he said that to me
I was struck all of a heap ... The thought flashed
through my mind at once. He hasn't made an appearance since Saturday of last week, and to-day's Sunday.
Seven days is no joke!'

'Yes, poor man,' the superintendent sighed again. 'A clever fellow, well-educated, and so good-hearted. There was no one like him, one may say, in company. But a rake; the kingdom of heaven be his! I'm not surprised at anything with him! Stepan,' he said, addressing one of the witnesses, 'ride off this minute to my house and send Andryushka to the police captain's, let him report to him. Say Mark Ivanitch has been murdered! Yes, and run to the inspector – why should he sit in comfort doing nothing? Let him come here. And you go yourself as fast as you can to the examining magistrate, Nikolay Yermolaitch, and tell him to come here. Wait a bit, I will write him a note.'

The police superintendent stationed watchmen round the lodge, and went off to the steward's to have tea. Ten minutes later he was sitting on a stool, carefully nibbling lumps of sugar, and sipping tea as hot as a red-hot coal.

'There it is! . . .' he said to Psyekov, 'there it is! . . . a gentleman, and a well-to-do one, too . . . a favourite of the gods, one may say, to use Pushkin's expression, and what has he made of it? Nothing! He gave himself up to drinking and debauchery, and . . . here now . . . he has been murdered!'

Two hours later the examining magistrate drove up. Nikolay Yermolaitch Tchubikov (that was the magistrate's name), a tall, thick-set old man of sixty, had been hard at work for a quarter of a century. He was known to the whole district as an honest, intelligent, energetic man, devoted to his work. His invariable companion, assistant, and secretary, a tall young man of six and twenty, called Dyukovsky, arrived on the scene of action with him.

'Is it possible, gentlemen?' Tchubikov began, going into Psyekov's room and rapidly shaking hands with everyone. 'Is it possible? Mark Ivanitch? Murdered? No, it's impossible! Im-poss-i-ble!'

'There it is,' sighed the superintendent.

'Merciful heavens! Why I saw him only last Friday. At the fair at Tarabankovo! Saving your presence, I drank a glass of vodka with him!'

'There it is,' the superintendent sighed once more.

They heaved sighs, expressed their horror, drank a glass of tea each, and went to the lodge.

'Make way!' the police inspector shouted to the crowd.

On going into the lodge the examining magistrate first of all set to work to inspect the door into the bedroom. The door turned out to be made of deal, painted yellow, and not to have been tampered with. No special traces that might have served as evidence could be found. They proceeded to break open the door.

'I beg you, gentlemen, who are not concerned, to retire,' said the examining magistrate, when, after long banging and cracking, the door yielded to the axe and the chisel. 'I ask this in the interests of the investigation . . . Inspector, admit no one!'

Tchubikov, his assistant, and the police superintendent opened the door and hesitatingly, one after the other, walked into the room. The following spectacle met their eyes. In the solitary window stood a big wooden bedstead with an immense feather bed on it. On the rumpled feather bed lay a creased and crumpled quilt. A pillow, in a cotton pillow case – also much creased, was on the floor. On a little table beside the bed lay a silver watch, and silver coins to the value of twenty kopecks. Some sulphur matches lay there too. Except the bed, the table, and a solitary chair, there was no furniture in the room. Looking under the bed, the superintendent saw two dozen empty bottles, an old straw hat, and a jar of vodka. Under the table lay one boot, covered with dust. Taking a look round the room, Tchubikov frowned and flushed crimson.

'The blackguards!' he muttered, clenching his fists.

'And where is Mark Ivanitch?' Dyukovsky asked quietly.

'I beg you not to put your spoke in,' Tchubikov answered roughly. 'Kindly examine the floor. This is the second case in my experience, Yergraf Kuzmitch,' he added to the police superintendent, dropping his voice. 'In 1870 I had a similar case. But no doubt you remember it ... The murder of the merchant Portre-tov. It was just the same. The blackguards murdered him, and dragged the dead body out of the window.'

Tchubikov went to the window, drew the curtain aside, and cautiously pushed the window. The window opened.

'It opens, so it was not fastened ... H'm ... there are traces on the window-sill. Do you see? Here is the trace of a knee ... Some one climbed out ... We shall have to inspect the window thoroughly.'

'There is nothing special to be observed on the floor,' said Dyukovsky. 'No stains, nor scratches. The only thing I have found is a used Swedish match. Here it is. As far as I remember, Mark Ivanitch didn't smoke; in a general way he used sulphur ones, never Swedish matches. This match may serve as a clue ...'

'Oh, hold your tongue, please!' cried Tchubikov, with a wave of his hand. 'He keeps on about his match! I can't stand these excitable people! Instead of looking for matches, you had better examine the bed!'

On inspecting the bed, Dyukovsky reported:

'There are no stains of blood or of anything else ... Nor are there any fresh rents. On the pillow there are traces of teeth. A liquid, having the smell of beer and also the taste of it has been spilt on the quilt ... The general appearance of the bed gives grounds for supposing there has been a struggle.'

'I know there was a struggle without your telling me! No one asked you whether there was a struggle. Instead of looking out for a struggle you had better be ...'

'One boot is here, the other one is not on the scene.'

'Well, what of that?'

'Why, they must have strangled him while he was taking off his boots. He hadn't time to take the second boot off when ...'

'He's off again! ... And how do you know that he was strangled?'

'There are marks of teeth on the pillow. The pillow itself is very much crumpled, and has been flung to a distance of six feet from the bed.'

'He argues, the chatterbox! We had better go into the garden. You had better look in the garden instead of rummaging about here ... I can do that without your help.'

When they went out into the garden their first task was the inspection of the grass. The grass had been trampled down under the windows. The clump of burdock against the wall under the window turned out to have been trodden on too. Dyukovsky succeeded in finding on it some broken shoots, and a little bit of wadding. On the topmost burrs, some fine threads of dark blue wool were found.

'What was the colour of his last suit?' Dyukovsky asked Psyekov.

'It was yellow, made of canvas.'

'Capital! Then it was they who were in dark blue . . .'

Some of the burrs were cut off and carefully wrapped up in paper. At that moment Artsybashev-Svistakovsky, the police captain, and Tyutyuev, the doctor, arrived. The police captain greeted the others, and at once proceeded to satisfy his curiosity; the doctor, a tall and extremely lean man with sunken eyes, a long nose, and a sharp chin, greeting no one and asking no questions, sat down on a stump, heaved a sigh, and said:

'The Serbians are in a turmoil again! I can't make out what they want! Ah, Austria, Austria! It's your doing!'

The inspection of the window from outside yielded absolutely no result; the inspection of the grass and surrounding bushes furnished many valuable clues. Dyukovsky succeeded, for instance, in detecting a long, dark streak in the grass, consisting of stains, and stretching from the window for a good many yards into the garden. The streak ended under one of the lilac bushes in a big, brownish stain. Under the same bush was found a boot, which turned out to be the fellow to the one found in the bedroom.

'This is an old stain of blood,' said Dyukovsky, examining the stain.

At the word 'blood,' the doctor got up and lazily took a cursory glance at the stain.

'Yes, it's blood,' he muttered.

'Then he wasn't strangled since there's blood,' said Tchubikov, looking malignantly at Dyukovsky.

'He was strangled in the bedroom, and here, afraid he would come to, they stabbed him with something sharp. The stain under the bush shows that he lay there for a comparatively long time, while they were trying to find some way of carrying him, or something to carry him on out of the garden.'

'Well, and the boot?'

'That boot bears out my contention that he was murdered while he was taking off his boots before going to bed. He had taken off one boot, the other, that is, this boot he had only managed to get half off. While he was being dragged and shaken the boot that was only half on came off of itself . . .'

'What powers of deduction! Just look at him!' Tchubikov jeered. 'He brings it all out so pat! And when will you learn not to put your theories forward? You had better take a little of the grass for analysis instead of arguing!'

After making the inspection and taking a plan of the locality they went off to the steward's to write a report and have lunch. At lunch they talked.

'Watch, money, and everything else . . . are untouched,' Tchubikov began the conversation. 'It is as clear as twice two makes four that the murder was committed not for mercenary motives.'

'It was committed by a man of the educated class,' Dyukovsky put in.

'From what do you draw that conclusion?'

'I base it on the Swedish match which the peasants about here have not learned to use yet. Such matches are only used by landowners and not by all of them. He was murdered, by the way, not by one but by three, at least: two held him while the third strangled him. Klyauzov was strong and the murderers must have known that.'

'What use would his strength be to him, supposing he were asleep?'

'The murderers came upon him as he was taking off his boots. He was taking off his boots, so he was not asleep.'

'It's no good making things up! You had better eat your lunch!'

'To my thinking, your honour,' said Yefrem, the gardener, as he set the samovar on the table, 'this vile deed was the work of no other than Nikolashka.'

'Quite possible,' said Psyekov.

'Who's this Nikolashka?'

'The master's valet, your honour,' answered Yefrem. 'Who else should it be if not he? He's a ruffian, your honour! A drunkard, and such a dissipated fellow! May the Queen of Heaven never bring the like again! He always used to fetch vodka for the master, he always used to put the master to bed ... Who should it be if not he? And what's more, I venture to bring to your notice, your honour, he boasted once in the tavern, the rascal, that he would murder his master. It's all on account of Akulka, on account of a woman ... He had a soldier's wife ... The master took a fancy to her and got intimate with her, and he ... was angered by it, to be sure. He's lolling about in the kitchen now, drunk. He's crying ... making out he is grieving over the master ...'

'And anyone might be angry over Akulka, certainly,' said Psyekov. 'She is a soldier's wife, a peasant woman, but ... Mark Ivanitch might well call her Nana. There is something in her that does suggest Nana ... fascinating ...'

'I have seen her ... I know ...' said the examining magistrate, blowing his nose in a red handkerchief.

Dyukovsky blushed and dropped his eyes. The police superintendent drummed on his saucer with his fingers. The police captain coughed and rummaged in his portfolio for something. On the doctor alone the mention of Akulka and Nana appeared to produce no impression. Tchubikov ordered Nikolashka to be fetched. Nikolashka, a lanky young man with a long pock-marked nose and a hollow chest, wearing a reefer jacket that had been his master's, came into Psyekov's room and bowed down to the ground before Tchubikov. His face looked sleepy and showed traces of tears. He was drunk and could hardly stand up.

'Where is your master?' Tchubikov asked him.

'He's murdered, your honour.'

As he said this Nikolashka blinked and began to cry.

'We know that he is murdered. But where is he now? Where is his body?'

'They say it was dragged out of the window and buried in the garden.'

'H'm ... the results of the investigation are already known in the kitchen then ... That's bad. My good fellow, where were you on the night when your master was killed? On Saturday, that is?'

Nikolashka raised his head, craned his neck, and pondered.

'I can't say, your honour,' he said. 'I was drunk and I don't remember.'

'An alibi!' whispered Dyukovsky, grinning and rubbing his hands.

'Ah! And why is it there's blood under your master's window!'

Nikolashka flung up his head and pondered.

'Think a little quicker,' said the police captain.

'In a minute. That blood's from a trifling matter, your honour. I killed a hen; I cut her throat very simply in the usual way, and she fluttered out of my hands and took and ran off . . . That's what the blood's from.'

Yefrem testified that Nikolashka really did kill a hen every evening and killed it in all sorts of places, and no one had seen the half-killed hen running about the garden, though of course it could not be positively denied that it had done so.

'An alibi,' laughed Dyukovsky, 'and what an idiotic alibi.'

'Have you had relations with Akulka?'

'Yes, I have sinned.'

'And your master carried her off from you?'

'No, not at all. It was this gentleman here, Mr Psyekov, Ivan Mihalitch, who enticed her from me, and the master took her from Ivan Mihalitch. That's how it was.'

Psyekov looked confused and began rubbing his left eye. Dyukovsky fastened his eyes upon him, detected his confusion, and started. He saw on the steward's legs dark blue trousers which he had not previously noticed. The trousers reminded him of the blue threads found on the burdock. Tchubikov in his turn glanced suspiciously at Psyekov.

'You can go!' he said to Nikolashka. 'And now allow me to put one question to you, Mr Psyekov. You were here, of course, on the Saturday of last week?'

'Yes, at ten o'clock I had supper with Mark Ivanitch.'

'And afterwards?'

Psyekov was confused, and got up from the table.

'Afterwards ... afterwards ... I really don't remember,' he muttered. 'I had drunk a good deal on that occasion ... I can't remember where and when I went to bed ... Why do you all look at me like that? As though I had murdered him!'

'Where did you wake up?'

'I woke up in the servants' kitchen on the stove ... They can all confirm that. How I got on to the stove I can't say ...'

'Don't disturb yourself ... Do you know Akulina?'

'Oh well, not particularly.'

'Did she leave you for Klyauzov?'

'Yes ... Yefrem, bring some more mushrooms! Will you have some tea, Yevgraf Kuzmitch?'

There followed an oppressive, painful silence that lasted for some five minutes. Dyukovsky held his tongue, and kept his piercing eyes on Psyekov's face, which gradually turned pale. The silence was broken by Tchubikov.

'We must go to the big house,' he said, 'and speak to the deceased's sister, Marya Ivanovna. She may give us some evidence.'

Tchubikov and his assistant thanked Psyekov for the lunch, then went off to the big house. They found Klyauzov's sister, a maiden lady of five and forty, on her knees before a high family shrine of ikons. When she saw portfolios and caps adorned with cockades in her visitors' hands, she turned pale.

'First of all, I must offer an apology for disturbing your devotions, so to say,' the gallant Tchubikov began with a scrape. 'We have come to you with a request. You have heard, of course, already . . . There is a suspicion that your brother has somehow been murdered. God's will, you know . . . Death no one can escape, neither Tsar nor ploughman. Can you not assist us with some fact, something that will throw light?'

'Oh, do not ask me!' said Marya Ivanovna, turning whiter still, and hiding her face in her hands. 'I can tell you nothing! Nothing! I implore you! I can say nothing . . . What can I do? Oh no, no . . . not a word . . . of my brother! I would rather die than speak!'

Marya Ivanovna burst into tears and went away into another room. The officials looked at each other, shrugged their shoulders, and beat a retreat.

'A devil of a woman!' said Dyukovsky, swearing as they went out of the big house. 'Apparently she knows something and is concealing it. And there is something peculiar in the maid-servant's expression too . . . You wait a bit, you devils! We will get to the bottom of it all!'

In the evening, Tchubikov and his assistant were driving home by the light of a pale-faced moon; they sat in their waggonette, summing up in their minds the incidents of the day. Both were exhausted and sat silent. Tchubikov never liked talking on the road. In spite of his talkativeness, Dyukovsky held his tongue in deference to the old man. Towards the end of the journey, however, the young man could endure the silence no longer, and began:

'That Nikolashka has had a hand in the business,'
he said, '*non dubitandum est*. One can see from his mug
too what sort of a chap he is ... His alibi gives him
away hand and foot. There is no doubt either that he
was not the instigator of the crime. He was only the
stupid hired tool. Do you agree? The discreet Psyekov
plays a not unimportant part in the affair too. His
blue trousers, his embarrassment, his lying on the
stove from fright after the murder, his alibi, and
Akulka.'

'Keep it up, you're in your glory! According to you,
if a man knows Akulka he is the murderer. Ah, you
hot-head! You ought to be sucking your bottle instead
of investigating cases! You used to be running after
Akulka too, does that mean that you had a hand in
this business?'

'Akulka was a cook in your house for a month, too,
but ... I don't say anything. On that Saturday night
I was playing cards with you, I saw you, or I should
be after you too. The woman is not the point, my good
sir. The point is the nasty, disgusting, mean feeling ...
The discreet young man did not like to be cut out, do
you see. Vanity, do you see ... He longed to be
revenged. Then ... His thick lips are a strong indica-
tion of sensuality. Do you remember how he smacked
his lips when he compared Akulka to Nana? That he is
burning with passion, the scoundrel, is beyond doubt!
And so you have wounded vanity and unsatisfied passion. That's enough to lead to murder. Two of them
are in our hands, but who is the third? Nikolashka
and Psyekov held him. Who was it smothered him?
Psyekov is timid, easily embarrassed, altogether a
coward. People like Nikolashka are not equal to

smothering with a pillow, they set to work with an
axe or a mallet ... Some third person must have
smothered him, but who?'

Dyukovsky pulled his cap over his eyes, and
pondered. He was silent till the waggonette had
driven up to the examining magistrate's house.

'Eureka!' he said, as he went into the house, and
took off his overcoat. 'Eureka, Nikolay Yermolaitch!
I can't understand how it is it didn't occur to me
before. Do you know who the third is?'

'Do leave off, please! There's supper ready. Sit down
to supper!'

Tchubikov and Dyukovsky sat down to supper.
Dyukovsky poured himself out a wine-glassful of
vodka, got up, stretched, and with sparkling eyes, said:

'Let me tell you then that the third person who
collaborated with the scoundrel Psyekov and
smothered him was a woman! Yes! I am speaking of
the murdered man's sister, Marya Ivanovna!'

Tchubikov coughed over his vodka and fastened his
eyes on Dyukovsky.

'Are you ... not quite right? Is your head ... not
quite right? Does it ache?'

'I am quite well. Very good, suppose I have gone
out of my mind, but how do you explain her confusion
on our arrival? How do you explain her refusal to give
information? Admitting that that is trivial – very
good! All right! – but think of the terms they were on!
She detested her brother! She is an Old Believer, he
was a profligate, a godless fellow ... that is what has
bred hatred between them! They say he succeeded in
persuading her that he was an angel of Satan! He used
to practise spiritualism in her presence!'

'Well, what then?'

'Don't you understand? She's an Old Believer, she murdered him through fanaticism! She has not merely slain a wicked man, a profligate, she has freed the world from Antichrist – and that she fancies is her merit, her religious achievement! Ah, you don't know these old maids, these Old Believers! You should read Dostoevsky! And what does Lyeskov say . . . and Petchersky! It's she, it's she, I'll stake my life on it. She smothered him! Oh, the fiendish woman! Wasn't she, perhaps, standing before the ikons when we went in to put us off the scent? "I'll stand up and say my prayers," she said to herself, "they will think I am calm and don't expect them." That's the method of all novices in crime. Dear Nikolay Yermolaitch! My dear man! Do hand this case over to me! Let me go through with it to the end! My dear fellow! I have begun it, and I will carry it through to the end.'

Tchubikov shook his head and frowned.

'I am equal to sifting difficult cases myself,' he said. 'And it's your place not to put yourself forward. Write what is dictated to you, that is your business!'

Dyukovsky flushed crimson, walked out, and slammed the door.

'A clever fellow, the rogue,' Tchubikov muttered, looking after him. 'Ve-ery clever! Only inappropriately hasty. I shall have to buy him a cigar-case at the fair for a present.'

Next morning a lad with a big head and a hare lip came from Klyauzovka. He gave his name as the shepherd Danilko, and furnished a very interesting piece of information.

'I had had a drop,' said he. 'I stayed on till midnight

at my crony's. As I was going home, being drunk, I got into the river for a bathe. I was bathing and what do I see! Two men coming along the dam carrying something black. "Tyoo!" I shouted at them. They were scared, and cut along as fast as they could go into the Makarev kitchen-gardens. Strike me dead, if it wasn't the master they were carrying!'

Towards evening of the same day Psyekov and Nikolashka were arrested and taken under guard to the district town. In the town they were put in the prison tower.

II

TWELVE days passed.

It was morning. The examining magistrate, Nikolay Yermolaitch, was sitting at a green table at home, looking through the papers relating to the 'Klyauzov case'; Dyukovsky was pacing up and down the room restlessly, like a wolf in a cage.

'You are convinced of the guilt of Nikolashka and Psyekov,' he said, nervously pulling at his youthful beard. 'Why is it you refuse to be convinced of the guilt of Marya Ivanovna? Haven't you evidence enough?'

'I don't say that I don't believe in it. I am convinced of it, but somehow I can't believe it . . . There is no real evidence. It's all theoretical, as it were . . . Fanaticism and one thing and another . . .'

'And you must have an axe and bloodstained sheets! . . . You lawyers! Well, I will prove it to you then! Do give up your slip-shod attitude to the psychological aspect of the case. Your Marya Ivanovna ought to be in Siberia! I'll prove it. If theoretical proof is not enough for you, I have something material ... It will show you how right my theory is! Only let me go about a little!'

'What are you talking about?'

'The Swedish match! Have you forgotten? I haven't forgotten it! I'll find out who struck it in the murdered man's room! It was not struck by Nikolashka, nor by Psyekov, neither of whom turned out to have matches when searched, but a third person, that is Marya Ivanovna. And I will prove it! ... Only let me drive about the district, make some inquiries ...'

'Oh very well, sit down ... Let us proceed to the examination.'

Dyukovsky sat down to the table, and thrust his long nose into the papers.

'Bring in Nikolay Tetchov!' cried the examining magistrate.

Nikolashka was brought in. He was pale and thin as a chip. He was trembling.

'Tetchov!' began Tchubikov. 'In 1879 you were convicted of theft and condemned to a term of imprisonment. In 1882 you were condemned for theft a second time, and a second time sent to prison ... We know all about it...'

A look of surprise came up into Nikolashka's face. The examining magistrate's omniscience amazed him, but soon wonder was replaced by an expression of extreme distress. He broke into sobs, and asked leave to go to wash, and calm himself. He was led out.

'Bring in Psyekov!' said the examining magistrate.

Psyekov was led in. The young man's face had greatly changed during those twelve days. He was

thin, pale, and wasted. There was a look of apathy in
his eyes.

'Sit down, Psyekov,' said Tchubikov. 'I hope that
to-day you will be sensible and not persist in lying as
on other occasions. All this time you have denied your
participation in the murder of Klyauzov, in spite of
the mass of evidence against you. It is senseless. Confession is some mitigation of guilt. To-day I am talking to you for the last time. If you don't confess to-
day, to-morrow it will be too late. Come, tell us . . .'

'I know nothing, and I don't know your evidence,'
whispered Psyekov.

'That's useless! Well then, allow me to tell you how
it happened. On Saturday evening, you were sitting in
Klyauzov's bedroom drinking vodka and beer with
him.' (Dyukovsky riveted his eyes on Psyekov's face,
and did not remove them during the whole monologue.) 'Nikolay was waiting upon you. Between
twelve and one Mark Ivanitch told you he wanted to
go to bed. He always did go to bed at that time. While
he was taking off his boots and giving you some
instruction regarding the estate, Nikolay and you at a
given signal seized your intoxicated master and flung
him back upon the bed. One of you sat on his feet, the
other on his head. At that moment the lady, you know
who, in a black dress, who had arranged with you
beforehand the part she would take in the crime, came
in from the passage. She picked up the pillow, and
proceeded to smother him with it. During the
struggle, the light went out. The woman took a box of
Swedish matches out of her pocket and lighted the
candle. Isn't that right? I see from your face that what
I say is true. Well, to proceed . . . Having smothered

him, and being convinced that he had ceased to breathe, Nikolay and you dragged him out of the window and put him down near the burdocks. Afraid that he might regain consciousness, you struck him with something sharp. Then you carried him, and laid him for some time under a lilac bush. After resting and considering a little, you carried him ... lifted him over the hurdle ... Then went along the road ... Then comes the dam; near the dam you were frightened by a peasant. But what is the matter with you?'

Psyekov, white as a sheet, got up, staggering.

'I am suffocating!' he said. 'Very well ... So be it ... Only I must go ... Please.'

Psyekov was led out.

'At last he has admitted it!' said Tchubikov, stretching at his ease. 'He has given himself away! How neatly I caught him there.'

'And he didn't deny the woman in black!' said Dyukovsky, laughing. 'I am awfully worried over that Swedish match, though! I can't endure it any longer. Good-bye! I am going!'

Dyukovsky put on his cap and went off. Tchubikov began interrogating Akulka.

Akulka declared that she knew nothing about it ...

'I have lived with you and with nobody else!' she said.

At six o'clock in the evening Dyukovsky returned. He was more excited than ever. His hands trembled so much, that he could not unbutton his overcoat. His cheeks were burning. It was evident that he had not come back without news.

'*Veni, vidi, vici!*' he cried, dashing into Tchubikov's room and sinking into an arm-chair. 'I vow on my

honour, I begin to believe in my own genius. Listen,
damnation take us! Listen and wonder, old friend! It's
comic and it's sad. You have three in your grasp
already ... haven't you? I have found a fourth murderer, or rather murderess, for it is a woman! And what
a woman! I would have given ten years of my life
merely to touch her shoulders. But ... listen. I drove
to Klyauzovka and proceeded to describe a spiral
round it. On the way I visited all the shopkeepers and
innkeepers, asking for Swedish matches. Everywhere
I was told "No." I have been on my round up to now.
Twenty times I lost hope, and as many times regained
it. I have been on the go all day long, and only an hour
ago came upon what I was looking for. A couple of
miles from here they gave me a packet of a dozen
boxes of matches. One box was missing ... I asked at
once: "Who bought that box?" "So-and-so. She took
a fancy to them ... They crackle." My dear fellow!
Nikolay Yermolaitch! What can sometimes be done
by a man who has been expelled from a seminary and
studied Gaboriau is beyond all conception! From to-
day I shall begin to respect myself! ... Ough ... Well,
let us go!'

'Go where?'

'To her, to the fourth ... We must make haste, or
... or I shall explode with impatience! Do you know
who she is? You will never guess! The young wife of
our old police superintendent, Yevgraf Kuzmitch,
Olga Petrovna; that's who it is! She bought that box
of matches!'

'You ... you ... Are you out of your mind?'

'It's very natural! In the first place she smokes, and
in the second she was head over ears in love with

Klyauzov. He rejected her love for the sake of an Akulka. Revenge. I remember now, I once came upon them behind the screen in the kitchen. She was cursing him, while he was smoking her cigarette and puffing the smoke into her face. But do come along; make haste, for it is getting dark already . . . Let us go!'

'I have not gone so completely crazy yet as to disturb a respectable, honourable woman at night for the sake of a wretched boy!'

'Honourable, respectable . . . You are a rag then, not an examining magistrate! I have never ventured to abuse you, but now you force me to it! You rag! you old fogey! Come, dear Nikolay Yermolaitch, I entreat you!'

The examining magistrate waved his hand in refusal and spat in disgust.

'I beg you! I beg you, not for my own sake, but in the interests of justice! I beseech you, indeed! Do me a favour, if only for once in your life!'

Dyukovsky fell on his knees.

'Nikolay Yermolaitch, do be so good! Call me a scoundrel, a worthless wretch if I am in error about that woman! It is such a case, you know! It is a case! More like a novel than a case. The fame of it will be all over Russia. They will make you examining magistrate for particularly important cases! Do understand, you unreasonable old man!'

The examining magistrate frowned and irresolutely put out his hand towards his hat.

'Well, the devil take you!' he said, 'let us go.'

It was already dark when the examining magistrate's waggonette rolled up to the police superintendent's door.

'What brutes we are!' said Tchubikov, as he reached for the bell. 'We are disturbing people.'

'Never mind, never mind, don't be frightened. We will say that one of the springs has broken.'

Tchubikov and Dyukovsky were met in the doorway by a tall, plump woman of three and twenty, with eyebrows as black as pitch and full red lips. It was Olga Petrovna herself.

'Ah, how very nice,' she said, smiling all over her face. 'You are just in time for supper. My Yevgraf Kuzmitch is not at home ... He is staying at the priest's. But we can get on without him. Sit down. Have you come from an inquiry?'

'Yes ... We have broken one of our springs, you know,' began Tchubikov, going into the drawing-room and sitting down in an easy-chair.

'Take her by surprise at once and overwhelm her,' Dyukovsky whispered to him.

'A spring ... er ... yes ... We just drove up ...'

'Overwhelm her, I tell you! She will guess if you go drawing it out.'

'Oh, do as you like, but spare me,' muttered Tchubikov, getting up and walking to the window. 'I can't! You cooked the mess, you eat it!'

'Yes, the spring,' Dyukovsky began, going up to the superintendent's wife and wrinkling his long nose. 'We have not come in to ... er-er-er ... to supper, nor to see Yevgraf Kuzmitch. We have come to ask you, madam, where is Mark Ivanovitch whom you have murdered?'

'What? What Mark Ivanovitch?' faltered the superintendent's wife, and her full face was suddenly in one instant suffused with crimson. 'I ... don't understand.'

'I ask you in the name of the law! Where is Klyau-zov? We know all about it!'

'Through whom?' the superintendent's wife asked slowly, unable to face Dyukovsky's eyes.

'Kindly inform us where he is!'

'But how did you find out? Who told you?'

'We know all about it. I insist in the name of the law.' The examining magistrate, encouraged by the lady's confusion, went up to her:

'Tell us and we will go away. Otherwise we . . .'

'What do you want with him?'

'What is the object of such questions, madam? We ask you for information. You are trembling, confused . . . Yes, he has been murdered, and if you will have it, murdered by you! Your accomplices have betrayed you!'

The police superintendent's wife turned pale.

'Come along,' she said quietly, wringing her hands. 'He is hidden in the bath-house. Only, for God's sake, don't tell my husband! I implore you! It would be too much for him.'

The superintendent's wife took a big key from the wall, and led her visitors through the kitchen and the passage into the yard. It was dark in the yard. There was a drizzle of fine rain. The superintendent's wife went on ahead. Tchubikov and Dyukovsky strode after her through the long grass, breathing in the smell of wild hemp and slops, which made a squelching sound under their feet. It was a big yard. Soon there were no more pools of slops, and their feet felt ploughed land. In the darkness they saw the silhouette of trees, and among the trees a little house with a crooked chimney.

'This is the bath-house,' said the superintendent's wife, 'but, I implore you, do not tell anyone.'

Going up to the bath-house, Tchubikov and Dyukovsky saw a large padlock on the door.

'Get ready your candle-end and matches,' Tchubikov whispered to his assistant.

The superintendent's wife unlocked the padlock and let the visitors into the bath-house. Dyukovsky struck a match and lighted up the entry. In the middle of it stood a table. On the table, beside a podgy little samovar, was a soup tureen with some cold cabbage soup in it, and a dish with traces of some sauce on it.

'Go on!'

They went into the next room, the bath-room. There, too, was a table. On the table there stood a big dish of ham, a bottle of vodka, plates, knives and forks.

'But where is he . . . where's the murdered man?'

'He is on the top shelf,' whispered the superintendent's wife, turning paler than ever and trembling.

Dyukovsky took the candle-end in his hand and climbed up to the upper shelf. There he saw a long, human body, lying motionless on a big feather bed. The body emitted a faint snore . . .

'They have made fools of us, damn it all!' Dyukovsky cried. 'This is not he! It's some living blockhead lying here. Hi! Who are you, damnation take you!'

The body drew in its breath with a whistling sound and moved. Dyukovsky prodded it with his elbow. It lifted up its arms, stretched, and raised its head.

'Who is that poking?' a hoarse, ponderous bass voice inquired. 'What do you want?'

Dyukovsky held the candle-end to the face of the

unknown and uttered a shriek. In the crimson nose, in the ruffled uncombed hair, in the pitch-black moustaches of which one was jauntily twisted and pointed insolently towards the ceiling, he recognised Cornet Klyauzov.

'You ... Mark ... Ivanitch! Impossible!'

The examining magistrate looked up and was dumbfoundered.

'It is I, yes ... And it's you, Dyukovsky! What the devil do you want here? And whose ugly mug is that down there? Holy Saints, it's the examining magistrate! How in the world did you come here?'

Klyauzov hurriedly got down and embraced Tchubikov. Olga Petrovna whisked out of the door.

'However did you come? Let's have a drink! – dash it all! Tra-ta-ti-to-tom ... Let's have a drink! Who brought you here, though? How did you get to know I was here? It doesn't matter, though! Have a drink!'

Klyauzov lighted the lamp and poured out three glasses of vodka.

'The fact is, I don't understand you,' said the examining magistrate, throwing out his hands. 'Is it you, or not you?'

'Stop that ... Do you want to give me a sermon? Don't trouble yourself! Dyukovsky boy, drink up your vodka! Friends, let us pass the ... What are you staring at ...? Drink!'

'All the same, I can't understand,' said the examining magistrate, mechanically drinking his vodka. 'Why are you here?'

'Why shouldn't I be here, if I am comfortable here?'

Klyauzov sipped his vodka and ate some ham.

'I am staying with the superintendent's wife, as you

see. In the wilds among the ruins, like some house goblin. Drink! I felt sorry for her, you know, old man! I took pity on her, and, well, I am living here in the deserted bath-house, like a hermit ... I am well fed. Next week I am thinking of moving on ... I've had enough of it ...'

'Inconceivable!' said Dyukovsky.

'What is there inconceivable in it?'

'Inconceivable! For God's sake, how did your boot get into the garden?'

'What boot?'

'We found one of your boots in the bedroom and the other in the garden.'

'And what do you want to know that for? It is not your business. But do drink, dash it all. Since you have waked me up, you may as well drink! There's an interesting tale about that boot, my boy. I didn't want to come to Olga's. I didn't feel inclined, you know, I'd had a drop too much ... She came under the window and began scolding me ... You know how women ... as a rule ... Being drunk, I up and flung my boot at her ... Ha-ha! ... Don't scold, I said. She clambered in at the window, lighted the lamp, and gave me a good drubbing, as I was drunk. I have plenty to eat here ... Love, vodka, and good things! But where are you off to? Tchubikov, where are you off to?'

The examining magistrate spat on the floor and walked out of the bath-house. Dyukovsky followed him with his head hanging. Both got into the wag-gonette in silence and drove off. Never had the road seemed so long and dreary. Both were silent. Tchubikov was shaking with anger all the way. Dyukovsky hid his face in his collar as though he were afraid the darkness and the drizzling rain might read his shame on his face.

On getting home the examining magistrate found the doctor, Tyutyuev, there. The doctor was sitting at the table and heaving deep sighs as he turned over the pages of the *Neva*.

'The things that are going on in the world,' he said, greeting the examining magistrate with a melancholy smile. 'Austria is at it again ... and Gladstone, too, in a way ...'

Tchubikov flung his hat under the table and began to tremble.

'You devil of a skeleton! Don't bother me! I've told you a thousand times over, don't bother me with your politics! It's not the time for politics! And as for you,' he turned upon Dyukovsky and shook his fist at him, 'as for you ... I'll never forget it, as long as I live!'

'But the Swedish match, you know! How could I tell ...'

'Choke yourself with your match! Go away and don't irritate me, or goodness knows what I shall do to you. Don't let me set eyes on you.'

Dyukovsky heaved a sigh, took his hat, and went out.

'I'll go and get drunk!' he decided as he went out of the gate, and he sauntered dejectedly towards the tavern.

When the superintendent's wife got home from the bath-house she found her husband in the drawing-room.

'What did the examining magistrate come about?' asked her husband.

'He came to say that they had found Klyauzov.

Only fancy, they found him staying with another man's wife.'

'Ah, Mark Ivanitch, Mark Ivanitch!' sighed the police superintendent, turning up his eyes. 'I told you that dissipation would lead to no good! I told you so – you wouldn't heed me!'

EASTER EVE

EASTER EVE

I WAS standing on the bank of the River Goltva, waiting for the ferry-boat from the other side. At ordinary
times the Goltva is a humble stream of moderate size,
silent and pensive, gently glimmering from behind
thick reeds; but now a regular lake lay stretched out
before me. The waters of spring, running riot, had
overflowed both banks and flooded both sides of the
river for a long distance, submerging vegetable gar-
dens, hayfields and marshes, so that it was no unusual
thing to meet poplars and bushes sticking out above
the surface of the water and looking in the darkness
like grim solitary crags.

The weather seemed to me magnificent. It was
dark, yet I could see the trees, the water and the
people ... The world was lighted by the stars, which
were scattered thickly all over the sky. I don't remember ever seeing so many stars. Literally one could not
have put a finger in between them. There were some
as big as a goose's egg, others tiny as hempseed ...
They had come out for the festival procession, every
one of them, little and big, washed, renewed and joyful, and every one of them was softly twinkling its
beams. The sky was reflected in the water; the stars
were bathing in its dark depths and trembling with
the quivering eddies. The air was warm and still ...

Here and there, far away on the further bank in the impenetrable darkness, several bright red lights were gleaming . . .

A couple of paces from me I saw the dark silhouette of a peasant in a high hat, with a thick knotted stick in his hand.

'How long the ferry-boat is in coming!' I said.

'It is time it was here,' the silhouette answered.

'You are waiting for the ferry-boat, too?'

'No, I am not,' yawned the peasant – 'I am waiting for the illumination. I should have gone, but, to tell you the truth, I haven't the five kopecks for the ferry.'

'I'll give you the five kopecks.'

'No; I humbly thank you . . . With that five kopecks put up a candle for me over there in the monastery . . . That will be more interesting, and I will stand here. What can it mean, no ferry-boat, as though it had sunk in the water!'

The peasant went up to the water's edge, took the rope in his hands, and shouted: 'Ieronim! Ieron—im!'

As though in answer to his shout, the slow peal of a great bell floated across from the further bank. The note was deep and low, as from the thickest string of a double bass; it seemed as though the darkness itself had hoarsely uttered it. At once there was the sound of a cannon shot. It rolled away in the darkness and ended somewhere in the far distance behind me. The peasant took off his hat and crossed himself.

'Christ is risen,' he said.

Before the vibrations of the first peal of the bell had time to die away in the air a second sounded, after it at once a third, and the darkness was filled with an unbroken quivering clamour. Near the red lights fresh lights flashed, and all began moving together and twinkling restlessly.

'Ieron—im!' we heard a hollow prolonged shout.

'They are shouting from the other bank,' said the peasant, 'so there is no ferry there either. Our Ieronim has gone to sleep.'

The lights and the velvety chimes of the bell drew one towards them ... I was already beginning to lose patience and grow anxious, but behold at last, staring into the dark distance, I saw the outline of something very much like a gibbet. It was the long-expected ferry. It moved towards us with such deliberation that if it had not been that its lines grew gradually more definite, one might have supposed that it was standing still or moving to the other bank.

'Make haste! Ieronim!' shouted my peasant. 'The gentleman's tired of waiting!'

The ferry crawled to the bank, gave a lurch and stopped with a creak. A tall man in a monk's cassock and a conical cap stood on it, holding the rope.

'Why have you been so long?' I asked, jumping upon the ferry.

'Forgive me, for Christ's sake,' Ieronim answered gently. 'Is there no one else?'

'No one ...'

Ieronim took hold of the rope in both hands, bent himself to the figure of a mark of interrogation, and gasped. The ferry-boat creaked and gave a lurch. The outline of the peasant in the high hat began slowly retreating from me – so the ferry was moving off. Ieronim soon drew himself up and began working with one hand only. We were silent, gazing towards the bank to which we were floating. There the illumination for which the peasant was waiting had begun. At the water's edge barrels of tar were flaring like huge camp fires. Their reflections, crimson as the rising moon, crept to meet us in long broad streaks. The burning barrels lighted up their own smoke and the long shadows of men flitting about the fire; but further to one side and behind them from where the velvety chime floated there was still the same unbroken black gloom. All at once, cleaving the darkness, a rocket zigzagged in a golden ribbon up the sky; it described an arc and, as though broken to pieces against the sky, was scattered crackling into sparks. There was a roar from the bank like a far-away hurrah.

'How beautiful!' I said.

'Beautiful beyond words!' sighed Ieronim. 'Such a night, sir! Another time one would pay no attention to the fireworks, but to-day one rejoices in every vanity. Where do you come from?'

I told him where I came from.

'To be sure ... a joyful day to-day ...' Ieronim went on in a weak sighing tenor like the voice of a convalescent. 'The sky is rejoicing and the earth and what is under the earth. All the creatures are keeping holiday. Only tell me, kind sir, why, even in the time of great rejoicing, a man cannot forget his sorrows?'

I fancied that this unexpected question was to draw me into one of those endless religious conversations which bored and idle monks are so fond of. I was not disposed to talk much, and so I only asked:

'What sorrows have you, father?'

'As a rule only the same as all men, kind sir, but to-day a special sorrow has happened in the monastery:

at mass, during the reading of the Bible, the monk
and deacon Nikolay died.'

'Well, it's God's will!' I said, falling into the mon-
astic tone. 'We must all die. To my mind, you ought
to rejoice indeed . . . They say if anyone dies at Easter
he goes straight to the kingdom of heaven.'

'That's true.'

We sank into silence. The figure of the peasant in
the high hat melted into the lines of the bank. The tar
barrels were flaring up more and more.

'The Holy Scripture points clearly to the vanity of
sorrow, and so does reflection,' said Ieronim, breaking
the silence; 'but why does the heart grieve and refuse
to listen to reason? Why does one want to weep
bitterly?'

Ieronim shrugged his shoulders, turned to me and
said quickly:

'If I died, or anyone else, it would not be worth
notice, perhaps; but, you see, Nikolay is dead! No one
else but Nikolay! Indeed, it's hard to believe that he
is no more! I stand here on my ferry-boat and every
minute I keep fancying that he will lift up his voice
from the bank. He always used to come to the bank
and call to me that I might not be afraid on the ferry.
He used to get up from his bed at night on purpose
for that. He was a kind soul. My God! how kindly and
gracious! Many a mother is not so good to her child as
Nikolay was to me! Lord, save his soul!'

Ieronim took hold of the rope, but turned to me
again at once.

'And such a lofty intelligence, your honour,' he said
in a vibrating voice. 'Such a sweet and harmonious
tongue! Just as they will sing immediately at early

matins: "Oh lovely! oh sweet is Thy Voice!" Besides all other human qualities, he had, too, an extraordinary gift!'

'What gift?' I asked.

The monk scrutinized me, and as though he had convinced himself that he could trust me with a secret, he laughed good-humouredly.

'He had a gift for writing hymns of praise,' he said. 'It was a marvel, sir; you couldn't call it anything else! You will be amazed if I tell you about it. Our Father Archimandrite comes from Moscow, the Father Sub-Prior studied at the Kazan academy, we have wise monks and elders, but, would you believe it, no one could write them; while Nikolay, a simple monk, a deacon, had not studied anywhere, and had not even any outer appearance of it, but he wrote them! A marvel! a real marvel!' Ieronim clasped his hands and, completely forgetting the rope, went on eagerly:

'The Father Sub-Prior has great difficulty in composing sermons; when he wrote the history of the monastery he worried all the brotherhood and drove a dozen times to town, while Nikolay wrote canticles! Hymns of praise! That's a very different thing from a sermon or a history!'

'Is it difficult to write them?' I asked.

'There's great difficulty!' Ieronim wagged his head. 'You can do nothing by wisdom and holiness if God has not given you the gift. The monks who don't understand argue that you only need to know the life of the saint for whom you are writing the hymn, and to make it harmonize with the other hymns of praise. But that's a mistake, sir. Of course, anyone who writes canticles must know the life of the saint to perfection,

to the least trivial detail. To be sure, one must make
them harmonize with the other canticles and know
where to begin and what to write about. To give you
an instance, the first response begins everywhere with
"the chosen" or "the elect." ... The first line must
always begin with the "angel." In the canticle of praise
to Jesus the Most Sweet, if you are interested in the
subject, it begins like this: "Of angels Creator and Lord
of all powers!" In the canticle to the Holy Mother of
God: "Of angels the foremost sent down from on high,"
to Nikolay, the Wonder-worker – "An angel in semblance, though in substance a man," and so on. Everywhere you begin with the angel. Of course, it would be
impossible without making them harmonize, but the
lives of the saints and conformity with the others is
not what matters; what matters is the beauty and
sweetness of it. Everything must be harmonious, brief
and complete. There must be in every line softness,
graciousness and tenderness; not one word should be
harsh or rough or unsuitable. It must be written so
that the worshipper may rejoice at heart and weep,
while his mind is stirred and he is thrown into a tremor.
In the canticle to the Holy Mother are the words:
"Rejoice, O Thou too high for human thought to reach!
Rejoice, O Thou too deep for angels' eyes to fathom!"
In another place in the same canticle: "Rejoice, O tree
that bearest the fair fruit of light that is the food of the
faithful! Rejoice, O tree of gracious spreading shade,
under which there is shelter for multitudes!" '

Ieronim hid his face in his hands, as though
frightened at something or overcome with shame, and
shook his head.

'Tree that bearest the fair fruit of light ... tree of

gracious spreading shade . . .' he muttered. 'To think that a man should find words like those! Such a power is a gift from God! For brevity he packs many thoughts into one phrase, and how smooth and complete it all is! "Light-radiating torch to all that be . . ." comes in the canticle to Jesus the Most Sweet. "Light-radiating!" There is no such word in conversation or in books, but you see he invented it, he found it in his mind! Apart from the smoothness and grandeur of language, sir, every line must be beautified in every way; there must be flowers and lightning and wind and sun and all the objects of the visible world. And every exclamation ought to be put so as to be smooth and easy for the ear. "Rejoice, thou flower of heavenly growth!" comes in the hymn to Nikolay the Wonder-worker. It's not simply "heavenly flower," but "flower of heavenly growth." It's smoother so and sweet to the ear. That was just as Nikolay wrote it! exactly like that! I can't tell you how he used to write!'

'Well, in that case it is a pity he is dead,' I said; 'but let us get on, father, or we shall be late.'

Ieronim started and ran to the rope; they were beginning to peal all the bells. Probably the procession was already going on near the monastery, for all the dark space behind the tar barrels was now dotted with moving lights.

'Did Nikolay print his hymns?' I asked Ieronim.

'How could he print them?' he sighed. 'And, indeed, it would be strange to print them. What would be the object? No one in the monastery takes any interest in them. They don't like them. They knew Nikolay wrote them, but they let it pass unnoticed. No one esteems new writings nowadays, sir!'

'Were they prejudiced against him?'

'Yes, indeed. If Nikolay had been an elder perhaps the brethren would have been interested, but he wasn't forty, you know. There were some who laughed and even thought his writing a sin.'

'What did he write them for?'

'Chiefly for his own comfort. Of all the brotherhood, I was the only one who read his hymns. I used to go to him in secret, that no one else might know of it, and he was glad that I took an interest in them. He would embrace me, stroke my head, speak to me in caressing words as to a little child. He would shut his cell, make me sit down beside him, and begin to read ...'

Ieronim left the rope and came up to me.

'We were dear friends in a way,' he whispered, look-ing at me with shining eyes. 'Where he went I would go. If I were not there he would miss me. And he cared more for me than for anyone, and all because I used to weep over his hymns. It makes me sad to remember. Now I feel just like an orphan or a widow. You know, in our monastery they are all good people, kind and pious, but ... there is no one with softness and refine-ment, they are just like peasants. They all speak loudly, and tramp heavily when they walk; they are noisy, they clear their throats, but Nikolay always talked softly, caressingly, and if he noticed that any-one was asleep or praying he would slip by like a fly or a gnat. His face was tender, compassionate ...'

Ieronim heaved a deep sigh and took hold of the rope again. We were by now approaching the bank. We floated straight out of the darkness and stillness of the river into an enchanted realm, full of stifling smoke, crackling lights and uproar. By now one could distinctly see people moving near the tar barrels. The flickering of the lights gave a strange, almost fantastic, expression to their figures and red faces. From time to time one caught among the heads and faces a glimpse of a horse's head motionless as though cast in copper.

'They'll begin singing the Easter hymn directly ...' said Ieronim, 'and Nikolay is gone; there is no one to appreciate it ... There was nothing written dearer to him than that hymn. He used to take in every word! You'll be there, sir, so notice what is sung; it takes your breath away!'

'Won't you be in church, then?'

'I can't; ... I have to work the ferry ...'

'But won't they relieve you?'

'I don't know ... I ought to have been relieved at eight; but, as you see, they don't come! ... And I must own I should have liked to be in the church ...'

'Are you a monk?'

'Yes ... that is, I am a lay-brother.'

The ferry ran into the bank and stopped. I thrust a five-kopeck piece into Ieronim's hand for taking me across, and jumped on land. Immediately a cart with a boy and a sleeping woman in it drove creaking onto the ferry. Ieronim, with a faint glow from the lights on his figure, pressed on the rope, bent down to it, and started the ferry back ...

I took a few steps through mud, but a little farther walked on a soft freshly trodden path. This path led to the dark monastery gates, that looked like a cavern through a cloud of smoke, through a disorderly crowd of people, unharnessed horses, carts and chaises. All this crowd was rattling, snorting, laughing, and the crimson light and wavering shadows from the smoke flickered over it all ... A perfect chaos! And in this hubbub the people yet found room to load a little cannon and to sell cakes. There was no less commotion on the other side of the wall in the monastery precincts, but there was more regard for decorum and order. Here there was a smell of juniper and incense. They talked loudly, but there was no sound of laughter or snorting. Near the tombstones and crosses people pressed close to one another with Easter cakes and bundles in their arms. Apparently many had come from a long distance for their cakes to be blessed and now were exhausted. Young lay-brothers, making a metallic sound with their boots, ran busily along the iron slabs that paved the way from the monastery gates to the church door. They were busy and shouting on the belfry, too.

'What a restless night!' I thought. 'How nice!'

One was tempted to see the same unrest and sleeplessness in all nature, from the night darkness to the iron slabs, the crosses on the tombs and the trees under which the people were moving to and fro. But nowhere was the excitement and restlessness so marked as in the church. An unceasing struggle was going on in the entrance between the inflowing stream and the outflowing stream. Some were going in, others going out and soon coming back again to stand still for a little and begin moving again. People were scurrying from place to place, lounging about as though they were looking for something. The stream flowed from the entrance all round the church, disturbing even the front rows, where persons of weight and dignity were standing. There could be no thought of concentrated prayer. There were no prayers at all, but a sort of continuous, childishly irresponsible joy, seeking a pretext to break out and vent itself in some movement, even in senseless jostling and shoving.

The same unaccustomed movement is striking in the Easter service itself. The altar gates are flung wide open, thick clouds of incense float in the air near the candelabra; wherever one looks there are lights, the gleam and splutter of candles ... There is no reading; restless and light-hearted singing goes on to the end without ceasing. After each hymn the clergy change their vestments and come out to burn incense, which is repeated every ten minutes.

I had no sooner taken a place, when a wave rushed from in front and forced me back. A tall thick-set deacon walked before me with a long red candle; the grey-headed archimandrite in his golden mitre hurried after him with the censer. When they had vanished from sight the crowd squeezed me back to my former position. But ten minutes had not passed before a new wave burst on me, and again the deacon appeared. This time he was followed by the Father Sub-Prior, the man who, as Ieronim had told me, was writing the history of the monastery.

As I mingled with the crowd and caught the infection of the universal joyful excitement, I felt unbearably sore on Ieronim's account. Why did they not send someone to relieve him? Why could not someone of less feeling and less susceptibility go on the ferry? 'Lift up thine eyes, O Sion, and look around,' they sang in the choir, 'for thy children have come to thee

as to a beacon of divine light from north and south,
and from east and from the sea . . .'

I looked at the faces; they all had a lively expression
of triumph, but not one was listening to what was
being sung and taking it in, and not one was 'holding
his breath.' Why was not Ieronim released? I could
fancy Ieronim standing meekly somewhere by the
wall, bending forward and hungrily drinking in the
beauty of the holy phrase. All this that glided by the
ears of people standing by me he would have eagerly
drunk in with his delicately sensitive soul, and would
have been spell-bound to ecstasy, to holding his
breath, and there would not have been a man happier
than he in all the church. Now he was plying to and
fro over the dark river and grieving for his dead friend
and brother.

The wave surged back. A stout smiling monk, playing with his rosary and looking round behind him,
squeezed sideways by me, making way for a lady in a
hat and velvet cloak. A monastery servant hurried
after the lady, holding a chair over our heads.

I came out of the church. I wanted to have a look
at the dead Nikolay, the unknown canticle writer.
I walked about the monastery wall, where there was a
row of cells, peeped into several windows, and, seeing
nothing, came back again. I do not regret now that
I did not see Nikolay; God knows, perhaps if I had
seen him I should have lost the picture my imagination paints for me now. I imagine that lovable poetical
figure, solitary and not understood, who went out at
nights to call to Ieronim over the water, and filled his
hymns with flowers, stars and sunbeams, as a pale
timid man with soft, mild, melancholy features. His

eyes must have shone, not only with intelligence, but with kindly tenderness and that hardly restrained childlike enthusiasm which I could hear in Ieronim's voice when he quoted to me passages from the hymns.

When we came out of church after mass it was no longer night. The morning was beginning. The stars had gone out and the sky was a morose greyish blue. The iron slabs, the tombstones and the buds on the trees were covered with dew. There was a sharp fresh-ness in the air. Outside the precincts I did not find the same animated scene as I had beheld in the night. Horses and men looked exhausted, drowsy, scarcely moved, while nothing was left of the tar barrels but heaps of black ash. When anyone is exhausted and sleepy he fancies that nature, too, is in the same condi-tion. It seemed to me that the trees and the young grass were asleep. It seemed as though even the bells were not pealing so loudly and gaily as at night. The restlessness was over, and of the excitement nothing was left but a pleasant weariness, a longing for sleep and warmth.

Now I could see both banks of the river; a faint mist hovered over it in shifting masses. There was a harsh cold breath from the water. When I jumped on to the ferry, a chaise and some two dozen men and women were standing on it already. The rope, wet and as I fan-cied drowsy, stretched far away across the broad river and in places disappeared in the white mist.

'Christ is risen! Is there no one else?' asked a soft voice.

I recognized the voice of Ieronim. There was no darkness now to hinder me from seeing the monk. He was a tall narrow-shouldered man of five-and-thirty, with large rounded features, with half-closed listless-looking eyes and an unkempt wedge-shaped beard. He had an extraordinarily sad and exhausted look.

'They have not relieved you yet?' I asked in surprise.

'Me?' he answered, turning to me his chilled and dewy face with a smile. 'There is no one to take my place now till morning. They'll all be going to the Father Archimandrite's to break the fast directly.'

With the help of a little peasant in a hat of reddish fur that looked like the little wooden tubs in which honey is sold, he threw his weight on the rope; they gasped simultaneously, and the ferry started.

We floated across, disturbing on the way the lazily rising mist. Everyone was silent. Ieronim worked mechanically with one hand. He slowly passed his mild lustreless eyes over us; then his glance rested on the rosy face of a young merchant's wife with black eyebrows, who was standing on the ferry beside me silently shrinking from the mist that wrapped her about. He did not take his eyes off her face all the way.

There was little that was masculine in that prolonged gaze. It seemed to me that Ieronim was looking in the woman's face for the soft and tender features of his dead friend.

MIRE

MIRE

I

GRACEFULLY swaying in the saddle, a young man wearing the snow-white tunic of an officer rode into the great yard of the vodka distillery belonging to the heirs of M. E. Rothstein. The sun smiled carelessly on the lieutenant's little stars, on the white trunks of the birch-trees, on the heaps of broken glass scattered here and there in the yard. The radiant, vigorous beauty of a summer day lay over everything, and nothing hindered the sappy young green leaves from dancing gaily and winking at the clear blue sky. Even the dirty and soot-begrimed appearance of the brick-sheds and the stifling fumes of the distillery did not spoil the general good impression. The lieutenant sprang gaily out of the saddle, handed over his horse to a man who ran up, and stroking with his finger his delicate black moustaches, went in at the front door. On the top step of the old but light and softly carpeted staircase he was met by a maidservant with a haughty, not very youthful face. The lieutenant gave her his card without speaking.

As she went through the rooms with the card, the maid could see on it the name 'Alexandr Grigoryevitch Sokolsky.' A minute later she came back and

53

told the lieutenant that her mistress could not see him, as she was not feeling quite well. Sokolsky looked at the ceiling and thrust out his lower lip.

'How vexatious!' he said. 'Listen, my dear,' he said eagerly. 'Go and tell Susanna Moiseyevna that it is very necessary for me to speak to her – very. I will only keep her one minute. Ask her to excuse me.'

The maid shrugged one shoulder and went off languidly to her mistress.

'Very well!' she sighed, returning after a brief interval. 'Please walk in!'

The lieutenant went with her through five or six large, luxuriously furnished rooms and a corridor, and finally found himself in a large and lofty square room, in which from the first step he was impressed by the abundance of flowers and plants and the sweet, almost revoltingly heavy fragrance of jasmine. Flowers were trained to trellis-work along the walls, screening the windows, hung from the ceiling, and were wreathed over the corners, so that the room was more like a greenhouse than a place to live in. Tits, canaries, and goldfinches chirruped among the green leaves and fluttered against the window-panes.

'Forgive me for receiving you here,' the lieutenant heard in a mellow feminine voice with a burr on the letter *r* which was not without charm. 'Yesterday I had a sick headache, and I'm trying to keep still to prevent its coming on again. What do you want?'

Exactly opposite the entrance, he saw sitting in a big low chair, such as old men use, a woman in an expensive Chinese dressing-gown, with her head wrapped up, leaning back on a pillow. Nothing could be seen behind the woollen shawl in which she was muffled but a pale, long, pointed, somewhat aquiline nose, and one large dark eye. Her ample dressing-gown concealed her figure, but judging from her beautiful hand, from her voice, her nose, and her eye, she might be twenty-six or twenty-eight.

'Forgive me for being so persistent ...' began the lieutenant, clinking his spurs. 'Allow me to introduce myself: Sokolsky! I come with a message from my cousin, your neighbour, Alexey Ivanovitch Kryukov, who ...'

'I know!' interposed Susanna Moiseyevna. 'I know Kryukov. Sit down; I don't like anything big standing before me.'

'My cousin charges me to ask you a favour,' the lieutenant went on, clinking his spurs once more and sitting down. 'The fact is, your late father made a purchase of oats from my cousin last winter, and a small sum was left owing. The payment only becomes due next week, but my cousin begs you most particularly to pay him – if possible, to-day.'

As the lieutenant talked, he stole side-glances about him.

'Surely I'm not in her bedroom?' he thought.

In one corner of the room, where the foliage was thickest and tallest, under a pink awning like a funeral canopy, stood a bed not yet made, with the bedclothes still in disorder. Close by on two armchairs lay heaps of crumpled feminine garments. Petticoats and sleeves with rumpled lace and flounces were trailing on the carpet, on which here and there lay bits of white tape, cigarette ends, and the papers of caramels ... Under the bed the toes, pointed and square, of slippers of all kinds peeped out in a long row. And it seemed to the lieutenant that the scent of the jasmine came not from the flowers, but from the bed and the slippers.

'And what is the sum owing?' asked Susanna Moiseyevna.

'Two thousand three hundred.'

'Oho!' said the Jewess, showing another large black eye. 'And you call that – a small sum! However, it's just the same paying it to-day or paying it in a week, but I've had so many payments to make in the last two months since my father's death ... Such a lot of stupid business, it makes my head go round! A nice idea! I want to go abroad, and they keep forcing me to attend to these silly things. Vodka, oats ...' she muttered, half closing her eyes, 'oats, bills, percentages, or, as my head-clerk says, "precentage." ... It's awful. Yesterday I simply turned the excise officer out. He pesters me with his Tralles. I said to him: "Go to the devil with your Tralles! I can't see anyone!" He kissed my hand and went away. I tell you what: can't your cousin wait two or three months?'

'A cruel question!' laughed the lieutenant. 'My cousin can wait a year, but it's I who cannot wait! You see, it's on my own account I'm acting, I ought to tell you. At all costs I must have money, and by ill-luck my cousin hasn't a rouble to spare. I'm forced to ride about and collect debts. I've just been to see a peasant, our tenant; here I'm now calling on you; from here I shall go on to somewhere else, and keep on like that until I get together five thousand roubles. I need money awfully!'

'Nonsense! What does a young man want with money? Whims, mischief. Why, have you been going

in for dissipation? Or losing at cards? Or are you getting married?'

'You've guessed!' laughed the lieutenant, and rising
slightly from his seat, he clinked his spurs. 'I really
am going to be married.'

Susanna Moiseyevna looked intently at her visitor,
made a wry face, and sighed.

'I can't make out what possesses people to get
married!' she said, looking about her for her pocket-
handkerchief. 'Life is so short, one has so little freedom, and they must put chains on themselves!'

'Everyone has his own way of looking at things . . .'

'Yes, yes, of course; everyone has his own way of
looking at things . . . But, I say, are you really going
to marry someone poor? Are you passionately in love?
And why must you have five thousand? Why won't
four do, or three?'

'What a tongue she has!' thought the lieutenant,
and answered: 'The difficulty is that an officer is not
allowed by law to marry till he is twenty-eight; if you
choose to marry, you have to leave the Service or else
pay a deposit of five thousand.'

'Ah, now I understand. Listen. You said just now
that everyone has his own way of looking at things . . .
Perhaps your fiancée is someone special and remarkable, but . . . but I am utterly unable to understand
how any decent man can live with a woman. I can't
for the life of me understand it. I have lived, thank
the Lord, twenty-seven years, and I have never yet
seen an endurable woman. They're all affected minxes,
immoral, liars . . . The only ones I can put up with are
cooks and housemaids, but so-called ladies I won't let
come within shooting distance of me. But, thank God,

they hate me and don't force themselves on me! If one of them wants money she sends her husband, but nothing will induce her to come herself, not from pride – no, but from cowardice; she's afraid of my making a scene. Oh, I understand their hatred very well! Rather! I openly display what they do their very utmost to conceal from God and man. How can they help hating me? No doubt you've heard bushels of scandal about me already ...'

'I've only arrived here so lately ...'

'Tut, tut, tut! ... I see from your eyes! But your brother's wife, surely she primed you for this expedition? Think of letting a young man come to see such an awful woman without warning him – how could she? Ha, ha! ... But tell me, how is your brother? He's a fine fellow, such a handsome man! ... I've seen him several times at mass. Why do you look at me like that? I very often go to church! We all have the same God. To an educated person externals matter less than the idea ... That's so, isn't it?'

'Yes, of course ...' smiled the lieutenant.

'Yes, the idea ... But you are not a bit like your brother. You are handsome, too, but your brother is a great deal better-looking. There's wonderfully little likeness!'

'That's quite natural; he's not my brother, but my cousin.'

'Ah, to be sure! So you must have the money to-day? Why to-day?'

'My furlough is over in a few days.'

'Well, what's to be done with you!' sighed Susanna Moiseyevna. 'So be it. I'll give you the money, though I know you'll abuse me for it afterwards. You'll quarrel with your wife after you are married, and say: "If that mangy Jewess hadn't given me the money, I should perhaps have been as free as a bird to-day!" Is your fiancée pretty?'

'Oh yes ...'

'H'm! ... Anyway, better something, if it's only beauty, than nothing. Though however beautiful a woman is, it can never make up to her husband for her silliness.'

'That's original!' laughed the lieutenant. 'You are a woman yourself, and such a woman-hater!'

'A woman ...' smiled Susanna. 'It's not my fault that God has cast me into this mould, is it? I'm no more to blame for it than you are for having moustaches. The violin is not responsible for the choice of its case. I am very fond of myself, but when anyone reminds me that I am a woman, I begin to hate myself. Well, you can go away, and I'll dress. Wait for me in the drawing-room.'

The lieutenant went out, and the first thing he did was to draw a deep breath, to get rid of the heavy scent of jasmine, which had begun to irritate his throat and to make him feel giddy.

'What a strange woman!' he thought, looking about him. 'She talks fluently, but ... far too much, and too freely. She must be neurotic.'

The drawing-room, in which he was standing now, was richly furnished, and had pretensions to luxury and style. There were dark bronze dishes with patterns in relief, views of Nice and the Rhine on the tables, old-fashioned sconces, Japanese statuettes, but all this striving after luxury and style only emphasized the lack of taste which was glaringly apparent in the gilt cornices, the gaudy wall-paper, the bright velvet table-cloths, the common oleographs in heavy frames. The bad taste of the general effect was the more complete from the lack of finish and the over-crowding of the room, which gave one a feeling that something was lacking, and that a great deal should have been thrown away. It was evident that the furniture had not been bought all at once, but had been picked up at auctions and other favourable opportunities.

Heaven knows what taste the lieutenant could boast of, but even he noticed one characteristic peculiarity about the whole place, which no luxury or style could efface – a complete absence of all trace of womanly, careful hands, which, as we all know, give a warmth, poetry, and snugness to the furnishing of a room. There was a chilliness about it such as one finds in waiting-rooms at stations, in clubs, and foyers at the theatres.

There was scarcely anything in the room definitely Jewish, except, perhaps, a big picture of the meeting of Jacob and Esau. The lieutenant looked round about him, and, shrugging his shoulders, thought of his strange, new acquaintance, of her free-and-easy manners, and her way of talking. But then the door opened, and in the doorway appeared the lady herself, in a long black dress, so slim and tightly laced that her figure looked as though it had been turned in a lathe. Now the lieutenant saw not only the nose and eyes, but also a thin white face, a head black and as curly as lamb's-wool. She did not attract him, though she did not strike him as ugly. He had a prejudice against un-Russian faces in general, and he considered, too,

that the lady's white face, the whiteness of which for
some reason suggested the cloying scent of jasmine,
did not go well with her little black curls and thick
eyebrows; that her nose and ears were astoundingly
white, as though they belonged to a corpse, or had
been moulded out of transparent wax. When she
smiled she showed pale gums as well as her teeth, and
he did not like that either.

'Anæmic debility . . .' he thought; 'she's probably as
nervous as a turkey.'

'Here I am! Come along!' she said, going on rapidly
ahead of him and pulling off the yellow leaves from
the plants as she passed.

'I'll give you the money directly, and if you like I'll
give you some lunch. Two thousand three hundred
roubles! After such a good stroke of business you'll
have an appetite for your lunch. Do you like my
rooms? The ladies about here declare that my rooms
always smell of garlic. With that culinary gibe their
stock of wit is exhausted. I hasten to assure you that
I've no garlic, even in the cellar. And one day when a
doctor came to see me who smelt of garlic, I asked
him to take his hat and go and spread his fragrance
elsewhere. There is no smell of garlic here, but the
place does smell of drugs. My father lay paralyzed for
a year and a half, and the whole house smelt of medicine. A year and a half! I was sorry to lose him, but
I'm glad he's dead: he suffered so!'

She led the officer through two rooms similar to
the drawing-room, through a large reception hall, and
came to a stop in her study, where there was a lady's
writing-table covered with little knick-knacks. On the
carpet near it several books lay strewn about, opened

and folded back. Through a small door leading from the study he saw a table laid for lunch.

Still chatting, Susanna took out of her pocket a bunch of little keys and unlocked an ingeniously made cupboard with a curved, sloping lid. When the lid was raised the cupboard emitted a plaintive note which made the lieutenant think of an Æolian harp. Susanna picked out another key and clicked another lock.

'I have underground passages here and secret doors,' she said, taking out a small morocco portfolio. 'It's a funny cupboard, isn't it? And in this portfolio I have a quarter of my fortune. Look how podgy it is! You won't strangle me, will you?'

Susanna raised her eyes to the lieutenant and laughed good-naturedly. The lieutenant laughed too.

'She's rather jolly,' he thought, watching the keys flashing between her fingers.

'Here it is,' she said, picking out the key of the portfolio. 'Now, Mr Creditor, trot out the IOU. What a silly thing money is really! How paltry it is, and yet how women love it! I am a Jewess, you know, to the marrow of my bones. I am passionately fond of Shmuls and Yankels, but how I loathe that passion for gain in our Semitic blood. They hoard and they don't know what they are hoarding for. One ought to live and enjoy oneself, but they're afraid of spending an extra farthing. In that way I am more like a hussar than a Shmul. I don't like money to be kept long in one place. And altogether I fancy I'm not much like a Jewess. Does my accent give me away much, eh?'

'What shall I say?' mumbled the lieutenant. 'You speak good Russian, but you do roll your *r*s.'

Susanna laughed and put the little key in the lock

of the portfolio. The lieutenant took out of his pocket a little roll of IOUs and laid them with a notebook on the table.

'Nothing betrays a Jew as much as his accent,' Susanna went on, looking gaily at the lieutenant. 'However much he twists himself into a Russian or a Frenchman, ask him to say "feather" and he will say "fedder" ... but I pronounce it correctly: "Feather! feather! feather!"'

Both laughed.

'By Jove, she's very jolly!' thought Sokolsky.

Susanna put the portfolio on a chair, took a step towards the lieutenant, and bringing her face close to his, went on gaily:

'Next to the Jews I love no people so much as the Russian and the French. I did not do much at school and I know no history, but it seems to me that the fate of the world lies in the hands of those two nations. I lived a long time abroad ... I spent six months in Madrid ... I've gazed my fill at the public, and the conclusion I've come to is that there are no decent peoples except the Russian and the French. Take the languages, for instance ... The German language is like the neighing of horses; as for the English ... you can't imagine anything stupider. Fight – feet – foot! Italian is only pleasant when they speak it slowly. If you listen to Italians gabbling you get the effect of the Jewish jargon. And the Poles? Mercy on us! There's no language so disgusting! "Nie pieprz, Pietrze, pieprzem wieprza, bo możesz przepieprzyé wieprza pieprzem." That means: "Don't pepper a sucking pig with pepper, Pyotr, or perhaps you'll over-pepper the sucking pig with pepper." Ha, ha, ha!'

Susanna Moiseyevna rolled her eyes and broke into
such a pleasant, infectious laugh that the lieutenant,
looking at her, went off into a loud and merry peal
of laughter. She took the visitor by the button, and
went on:

'You don't like Jews, of course ... they've many
faults, like all nations. I don't dispute that. But are
the Jews to blame for it? No, it's not the Jews who are
to blame, but the Jewish women! They are narrow-
minded, greedy; there's no sort of poetry about them,
they're dull ... You have never lived with a Jewess, so
you don't know how charming it is!' Susanna Moiseyevna pronounced the last words with deliberate
emphasis and with no eagerness or laughter. She
paused as though frightened at her own openness, and
her face was suddenly distorted in a strange, unaccountable way. Her eyes stared at the lieutenant
without blinking, her lips parted and showed clenched
teeth. Her whole face, her throat, and even her bosom,
seemed quivering with a spiteful, catlike expression.
Still keeping her eyes fixed on her visitor, she rapidly
bent to one side, and swiftly, like a cat, snatched something from the table. All this was the work of a few
seconds. Watching her movements, the lieutenant saw
five fingers crumple up his IOUs and caught a glimpse
of the white rustling paper as it disappeared in her
clenched fist. Such an extraordinary transition from
good-natured laughter to crime so appalled him that
he turned pale and stepped back ...

And she, still keeping her frightened, searching eyes
upon him, felt along her hip with her clenched fist
for her pocket. Her fist struggled convulsively for the
pocket, like a fish in the net, and could not find the

opening. In another moment the IOUs would have vanished in the recesses of her feminine garments, but at that point the lieutenant uttered a faint cry, and, moved more by instinct than reflection, seized the Jewess by her arm above the clenched fist. Showing her teeth more than ever, she struggled with all her might and pulled her hand away. Then Sokolsky put his right arm firmly round her waist, and the other round her chest, and a struggle followed. Afraid of outraging her sex or hurting her, he tried only to prevent her moving, and to get hold of the fist with the IOUs; but she wriggled like an eel in his arms with her supple, flexible body, struck him in the chest with her elbows, and scratched him, so that he could not help touching her all over, and was forced to hurt her and disregard her modesty.

'How unusual this is! How strange!' he thought, utterly amazed, hardly able to believe his senses, and feeling rather sick from the scent of jasmine.

In silence, breathing heavily, stumbling against the furniture, they moved about the room. Susanna was carried away by the struggle. She flushed, closed her eyes, and forgetting herself, once even pressed her face against the face of the lieutenant, so that there was a sweetish taste left on his lips. At last he caught hold of her clenched hand . . . Forcing it open, and not finding the papers in it, he let go the Jewess. With flushed faces and dishevelled hair, they looked at one another, breathing hard. The spiteful, catlike expression on the Jewess's face was gradually replaced by a good-natured smile. She burst out laughing, and turning on one foot, went towards the room where lunch was ready. The lieutenant moved slowly after her. She sat down to the table, and, still flushed and breathing hard, tossed off half a glass of port.

'Listen' – the lieutenant broke the silence – 'I hope you are joking?'

'Not a bit of it,' she answered, thrusting a piece of bread into her mouth.

'H'm! .... How do you wish me to take all this?'

'As you choose. Sit down and have lunch!'

'But ... it's dishonest!'

'Perhaps. But don't trouble to give me a sermon; I have my own way of looking at things.'

'Won't you give them back?'

'Of course not! If you were a poor unfortunate man, with nothing to eat, then it would be a different matter. But – he wants to get married!'

'It's not my money, you know; it's my cousin's!'

'And what does your cousin want with money? To get fashionable clothes for his wife? But I really don't care whether your *belle-sœur* has dresses or not.'

The lieutenant had ceased to remember that he was in a strange house with an unknown lady, and did not trouble himself with decorum. He strode up and down the room, scowled and nervously fingered his waistcoat. The fact that the Jewess had lowered herself in his eyes by her dishonest action made him feel bolder and more free-and-easy.

'The devil knows what to make of it!' he muttered. 'Listen. I shan't go away from here until I get the IOUs!'

'Ah, so much the better,' laughed Susanna. 'If you stay here for good, it will make it livelier for me.'

Excited by the struggle, the lieutenant looked at Susanna's laughing, insolent face, at her munching mouth, at her heaving bosom, and grew bolder and more audacious. Instead of thinking about the IOUs he began for some reason recalling with a sort of relish his cousin's stories of the Jewess's romantic adventures, of her free way of life, and these reminiscences only provoked him to greater audacity. Impulsively he sat down beside the Jewess and thinking no more of the IOUs began to eat . . .

'Will you have vodka or wine?' Susanna asked with a laugh. 'So you will stay till you get the IOUs? Poor fellow! How many days and nights you will have to spend with me, waiting for those IOUs! Won't your fiancée have something to say about it?'

II

FIVE hours had passed. The lieutenant's cousin, Alexey Ivanovitch Kryukov, was walking about the rooms of his country-house in his dressing-gown and slippers, and looking impatiently out of the window. He was a tall, sturdy man, with a large black beard and a manly face; and as the Jewess had truly said, he was handsome, though he had reached the age when men are apt to grow too stout, puffy, and bald. By mind and temperament he was one of those natures in which the Russian intellectual classes are so rich: warm-hearted, good-natured, well-bred, having some knowledge of the arts and sciences, some faith, and the most chivalrous notions about honour, but indolent and lacking in depth. He was fond of good eating and drinking, was an ideal whist-player, was a connoisseur in women and horses, but in other things he was apathetic and sluggish as a seal, and to rouse him from his lethargy something extraordinary and quite revolting was needed, and then he would forget everything in the world and display intense activity; he would fume and talk of a duel, write a petition of seven pages to a Minister, gallop at breakneck speed about the district, call someone publicly 'a scoundrel,' would go to law, and so on.

'How is it our Sasha's not back yet?' he kept asking his wife, glancing out of the window. 'Why, it's dinner-time!'

After waiting for the lieutenant till six o'clock, they sat down to dinner. When supper-time came, however, Alexey Ivanovitch was listening to every footstep, to every sound of the door, and kept shrugging his shoulders.

'Strange!' he said. 'The rascally dandy must have stayed on at the tenant's.'

As he went to bed after supper, Kryukov made up his mind that the lieutenant was being entertained at the tenant's, where after a festive evening he was staying the night.

Alexandr Grigoryevitch only returned next morning. He looked extremely crumpled and confused.

'I want to speak to you alone . . .' he said mysteriously to his cousin.

They went into the study. The lieutenant shut the door, and he paced for a long time up and down before he began to speak.

'Something's happened, my dear fellow,' he began, 'that I don't know how to tell you about. You wouldn't believe it . . .'

And blushing, faltering, not looking at his cousin, he told what had happened with the IOUs. Kryukov,

standing with his feet wide apart and his head bent,
listened and frowned.

'Are you joking?' he asked.

'How the devil could I be joking? It's no joking
matter!'

'I don't understand!' muttered Kryukov, turning
crimson and flinging up his hands. 'It's positively ...
immoral on your part. Before your very eyes a hussy
is up to the devil knows what, a serious crime, plays a
nasty trick, and you go and kiss her!'

'But I can't understand myself how it happened!'
whispered the lieutenant, blinking guiltily. 'Upon my
honour, I don't understand it! It's the first time in my
life I've come across such a monster! It's not her
beauty that does for you, not her mind, but that ...
you understand ... insolence, cynicism ...'

'Insolence, cynicism ... it's unclean! If you've such
a longing for insolence and cynicism, you might have
picked a sow out of the mire and have devoured her
alive. It would have been cheaper, anyway! Instead of
two thousand three hundred!'

'You do express yourself elegantly!' said the lieutenant, frowning. 'I'll pay you back the two thousand
three hundred!'

'I know you'll pay it back, but it's not a question of
money! Damn the money! What revolts me is your
being such a limp rag ... such filthy feebleness! And
engaged! With a fiancée!'

'Don't speak of it ...' said the lieutenant, blushing.
'I loathe myself as it is. I should like to sink into the
earth. It's sickening and vexatious that I shall have
to bother my aunt for that five thousand ...'

Kryukov continued for some time longer expressing his indignation and grumbling, then, as he grew calmer, he sat down on the sofa and began to jeer at his cousin.

'You young officers!' he said with contemptuous irony. 'Nice bridegrooms.'

Suddenly he leapt up as though he had been stung, stamped his foot, and ran about the study.

'No, I'm not going to leave it like that!' he said, shaking his fist. 'I will have those IOUs, I will! I'll give it her! One doesn't beat women, but I'll break every bone in her body . . . I'll pound her to a jelly! I'm not a lieutenant! You won't touch me with insolence or cynicism! No-o-o, damn her! Mishka!' he shouted, 'run and tell them to get the racing droshky out for me!'

Kryukov dressed rapidly, and, without heeding the agitated lieutenant, got into the droshky, and with a wave of his hand resolutely raced off to Susanna Moiseyevna. For a long time the lieutenant gazed out of the window at the clouds of dust that rolled after his cousin's droshky, stretched, yawned, and went to his own room. A quarter of an hour later he was sound asleep.

At six o'clock he was waked up and summoned to dinner.

'How nice this is of Alexey!' his cousin's wife greeted him in the dining-room. 'He keeps us waiting for dinner.'

'Do you mean to say he's not come back yet?' yawned the lieutenant. 'H'm! . . . he's probably gone round to see the tenant.'

But Alexey Ivanovitch was not back by supper either. His wife and Sokolsky decided that he was playing cards at the tenant's and would most likely stay the night there. What had happened was not what they had supposed, however.

Kryukov returned next morning, and without greeting anyone, without a word, dashed into his study.

'Well?' whispered the lieutenant, gazing at him round-eyed.

Kryukov waved his hand and gave a snort.

'Why, what's the matter? What are you laughing at?'

Kryukov flopped on the sofa, thrust his head in the pillow, and shook with suppressed laughter. A minute later he got up, and looking at the surprised lieutenant, with his eyes full of tears from laughing, said:

'Close the door. Well ... she *is* a fe-e-male, I beg to inform you!'

'Did you get the IOUs?'

Kryukov waved his hand and went off into a peal of laughter again.

'Well! she is a female!' he went on. '*Merci* for the acquaintance, my boy! She's a devil in petticoats. I arrived; I walked in like such an avenging Jove, you know, that I felt almost afraid of myself ... I frowned, I scowled, even clenched my fists to be more awe-inspiring ... "Jokes don't pay with me, madam!" said I, and more in that style. And I threatened her with the law and with the Governor. To begin with she burst into tears, said she'd been joking with you, and even took me to the cupboard to give me the money. Then she began arguing that the future of Europe lies in the hands of the French and the Russians, swore at women ... Like you, I listened, fascinated, ass that I was ... She kept singing the praises of my beauty, patted me on the arm near the shoulder, to see how strong I was, and ... and as you see, I've only just got away from her! Ha, ha! She's enthusiastic about you!'

'You're a nice fellow!' laughed the lieutenant. 'A married man! highly respected ... Well, aren't you ashamed? Disgusted? Joking apart, though, old man, you've got your Queen Tamara in your own neighbourhood ...'

'In my own neighbourhood! Why, you wouldn't find another such chameleon in the whole of Russia! I've never seen anything like it in my life, though I know a good bit about women, too. I have known regular devils in my time, but I never met anything like this. It is, as you say, by insolence and cynicism she gets over you. What is so attractive in her is the diabolical suddenness, the quick transitions, the swift shifting hues ... Brrr! And the IOU – phew! Write it off for lost. We are both great sinners, we'll go halves in our sin. I shall put down to you not two thousand three hundred, but half of it. Mind, tell my wife I was at the tenant's.'

Kryukov and the lieutenant buried their heads in the pillows, and broke into laughter; they raised their heads, glanced at one another, and again subsided into their pillows.

'Engaged! A lieutenant!' Kryukov jeered.

'Married!' retorted Sokolsky. 'Highly respected! Father of a family!'

At dinner they talked in veiled allusions, winked at one another, and, to the surprise of the others, were continually gushing with laughter into their dinnernapkins. After dinner, still in the best of spirits, they dressed up as Turks, and, running after one another with guns, played at soldiers with the children. In the evening they had a long argument. The lieutenant maintained that it was mean and contemptible to accept a dowry with your wife, even when there was passionate love on both sides. Kryukov thumped the table with his fists and declared that this was absurd, and that a husband who did not like his wife to have property of her own was an egoist and a despot. Both shouted, boiled over, did not understand each other, drank a good deal, and in the end, picking up the skirts of their dressing-gowns, went to their bedrooms. They soon fell asleep and slept soundly.

Life went on as before, even, sluggish and free from sorrow. The shadows lay on the earth, thunder pealed from the clouds, from time to time the wind moaned plaintively, as though to prove that nature, too, could lament, but nothing troubled the habitual tranquillity of these people. Of Susanna Moiseyevna and the IOUs they said nothing. Both of them felt, somehow, ashamed to speak of the incident aloud. Yet they remembered it and thought of it with pleasure, as of a curious farce, which life had unexpectedly and casually played upon them, and which it would be pleasant to recall in old age.

On the sixth or seventh day after his visit to the Jewess, Kryukov was sitting in his study in the morning writing a congratulatory letter to his aunt. Alexandr Grigoryevitch was walking to and fro near the table in silence. The lieutenant had slept badly that night; he woke up depressed, and now he felt bored. He paced up and down, thinking of the end of his furlough, of his fiancée, who was expecting him, of how people could live all their lives in the country without feeling bored. Standing at the window, for a long time he

stared at the trees, smoked three cigarettes one after
another, and suddenly turned to his cousin.

'I have a favour to ask you, Alyosha,' he said. 'Let
me have a saddle-horse for the day ...'

Kryukov looked searchingly at him and continued
his writing with a frown.

'You will, then?' asked the lieutenant.

Kryukov looked at him again, then deliberately
drew out a drawer in the table, and taking out a thick
roll of notes, gave it to his cousin.

'Here's five thousand ...' he said. 'Though it's not
my money, yet, God bless you, it's all the same.
I advise you to send for post-horses at once and go
away. Yes, really!'

The lieutenant in his turn looked searchingly at
Kryukov and laughed.

'You've guessed right, Alyosha,' he said, reddening.
'It was to her I meant to ride. Yesterday evening when
the washerwoman gave me that damned tunic, the one
I was wearing then, and it smelt of jasmine, why ...
I felt I must go!'

'You must go away.'

'Yes, certainly. And my furlough's just over. I really
will go to-day! Yes, by Jove! However long one stays,
one has to go in the end ... I'm going!'

The post-horses were brought after dinner the same
day; the lieutenant said good-bye to the Kryukovs
and set off, followed by their good wishes.

Another week passed. It was a dull but hot and
heavy day. From early morning Kryukov walked aim-
lessly about the house, looking out of window, or turning over the leaves of albums, though he was sick of
the sight of them already. When he came across his

wife or children, he began grumbling crossly. It seemed to him, for some reason that day, that his children's manners were revolting, that his wife did not know how to look after the servants, that their expenditure was quite disproportionate to their income. All this meant that 'the master' was out of humour.

After dinner, Kryukov, feeling dissatisfied with the soup and the roast meat he had eaten, ordered out his racing droshky. He drove slowly out of the courtyard, drove at a walking pace for a quarter of a mile, and stopped.

'Shall I . . . drive to her . . . that devil?' he thought, looking at the leaden sky.

And Kryukov positively laughed, as though it were the first time that day he had asked himself that question. At once the load of boredom was lifted from his heart, and there rose a gleam of pleasure in his lazy eyes. He lashed the horse . . .

All the way his imagination was picturing how surprised the Jewess would be to see him, how he would laugh and chat, and come home feeling refreshed . . .

'Once a month one needs something to brighten one up . . . something out of the common round,' he thought, 'something that would give the stagnant organism a good shaking up, a reaction . . . whether it's a drinking bout, or . . . Susanna. One can't get on without it.'

It was getting dark when he drove into the yard of the vodka distillery. From the open windows of the owner's house came sounds of laughter and singing:

' "Brighter than lightning, more burning than flame . . ." '

sang a powerful, mellow bass voice.

'Aha! she has visitors,' thought Kryukov.

And he was annoyed that she had visitors.

'Shall I go back?' he thought with his hand on the bell, but he rang all the same, and went up the familiar staircase. From the entry he glanced into the reception hall. There were about five men there – all landowners and officials of his acquaintance; one, a tall, thin gentleman, was sitting at the piano, singing, and striking the keys with his long, thin fingers. The others were listening and grinning with enjoyment. Kryukov looked himself up and down in the looking-glass, and was about to go into the hall, when Susanna Moiseyevna herself darted into the entry, in high spirits and wearing the same black dress ... Seeing Kryukov, she was petrified for an instant, then she uttered a little scream and beamed with delight.

'Is it you?' she said, clutching his hand. 'What a surprise!'

'Here she is!' smiled Kryukov, putting his arm round her waist. 'Well! Does the destiny of Europe still lie in the hands of the French and the Russians?'

'I'm so glad,' laughed the Jewess, cautiously removing his arm. 'Come, go into the hall; they're all friends there ... I'll go and tell them to bring you some tea. Your name's Alexey, isn't it? Well, go in, I'll come directly ...'

She blew him a kiss and ran out of the entry, leaving behind her the same sickly smell of jasmine. Kryukov raised his head and walked into the hall. He was on terms of friendly intimacy with all the men in the room, but scarcely nodded to them; they, too, scarcely responded, as though the place in which they met were not quite decent, and as though they were in tacit agreement with one another that it was more suitable for them not to recognize one another.

From the hall Kryukov walked into the drawing-room, and from it into a second drawing-room. On the way he met three or four other guests, also men whom he knew, though they barely recognized him. Their faces were flushed with drink and merriment. Alexey Ivanovitch glanced furtively at them and marvelled that these men, respectable heads of families, who had known sorrow and privation, could demean them-selves to such pitiful, cheap gaiety! He shrugged his shoulders, smiled, and walked on.

'There are places,' he reflected, 'where a sober man feels sick, and a drunken man rejoices. I remember I never could go to the operetta or the gipsies when I was sober: wine makes a man more good-natured and reconciles him with vice . . .'

Suddenly he stood still, petrified, and caught hold of the door-post with both hands. At the writing-table in Susanna's study was sitting Lieutenant Alexandr Grigoryevitch. He was discussing something in an undertone with a fat, flabby-looking Jew, and seeing his cousin, flushed crimson and looked down at an album.

The sense of decency was stirred in Kryukov and the blood rushed to his head. Overwhelmed with amazement, shame, and anger, he walked up to the table without a word. Sokolsky's head sank lower than ever. His face worked with an expression of agon-izing shame.

'Ah, it's you, Alyosha!' he articulated, making a desperate effort to raise his eyes and to smile. 'I called here to say good-bye, and, as you see ... But to-morrow I am certainly going.'

'What can I say to him? What?' thought Alexey Ivanovitch. 'How can I judge him since I'm here myself?'

And clearing his throat without uttering a word, he went out slowly.

' "Call her not heavenly, and leave her on earth ..." '

The bass was singing in the hall. A little while after, Kryukov's racing droshky was bumping along the dusty road.

ON THE ROAD

ON THE ROAD

'Upon the breast of a gigantic crag,
A golden cloudlet rested for one night.'

LERMONTOV.

IN the room which the tavern keeper, the Cossack
Semyon Tchistopluy, called the 'travellers' room,'
that is kept exclusively for travellers, a tall, broad-
shouldered man of forty was sitting at the big
unpainted table. He was asleep with his elbows on the
table and his head leaning on his fist. An end of tallow
candle, stuck into an old pomatum pot, lighted up his
light brown beard, his thick, broad nose, his sunburnt
cheeks, and the thick, black eyebrows overhanging his
closed eyes ... The nose and the cheeks and the eyebrows, all the features, each taken separately, were
coarse and heavy, like the furniture and the stove in
the 'travellers' room,' but taken all together they gave
the effect of something harmonious and even beautiful. Such is the lucky star, as it is called, of the Russian
face: the coarser and harsher its features the softer
and more good-natured it looks. The man was dressed
in a gentleman's reefer jacket, shabby, but bound with
wide new braid, a plush waistcoat, and full black
trousers thrust into big high boots.

On one of the benches, which stood in a continuous

row along the wall, a girl of eight, in a brown dress and long black stockings, lay asleep on a coat lined with fox. Her face was pale, her hair was flaxen, her shoulders were narrow, her whole body was thin and frail, but her nose stood out as thick and ugly a lump as the man's. She was sound asleep, and unconscious that her semi-circular comb had fallen off her head and was cutting her cheek.

The 'travellers' room' had a festive appearance. The air was full of the smell of freshly scrubbed floors, there were no rags hanging as usual on the line that ran diagonally across the room, and a little lamp was burning in the corner over the table, casting a patch of red light on the ikon of St George the Victorious. From the ikon stretched on each side of the corner a row of cheap oleographs, which maintained a strict and careful gradation in the transition from the sacred to the profane. In the dim light of the candle end and the red ikon lamp the pictures looked like one continuous stripe, covered with blurs of black. When the tiled stove, trying to sing in unison with the weather, drew in the air with a howl, while the logs, as though waking up, burst into bright flame and hissed angrily, red patches began dancing on the log walls, and over the head of the sleeping man could be seen first the Elder Seraphim, then the Shah Nasir-ed-Din, then a fat, brown baby with goggle eyes, whispering in the ear of a young girl with an extraordinarily blank, and indifferent face ...

Outside a storm was raging. Something frantic and wrathful, but profoundly unhappy, seemed to be flinging itself about the tavern with the ferocity of a wild beast and trying to break in. Banging at the

doors, knocking at the windows and on the roof,
scratching at the walls, it alternately threatened and
besought, then subsided for a brief interval, and then
with a gleeful, treacherous howl burst into the chimney, but the wood flared up, and the fire, like a chained
dog, flew wrathfully to meet its foe, a battle began,
and after it – sobs, shrieks, howls of wrath. In all of
this there was the sound of angry misery and unsatisfied hate, and the mortified impatience of something
accustomed to triumph.

Bewitched by this wild, inhuman music the 'travellers' room' seemed spellbound for ever, but all at once
the door creaked and the potboy, in a new print shirt,
came in. Limping on one leg, and blinking his sleepy
eyes, he snuffed the candle with his fingers, put some
more wood on the fire and went out. At once from
the church, which was three hundred paces from the
tavern, the clock struck midnight. The wind played
with the chimes as with the snowflakes; chasing the
sounds of the clock it whirled them round and round
over a vast space, so that some strokes were cut short
or drawn out in long, vibrating notes, while others
were completely lost in the general uproar. One stroke
sounded as distinctly in the room as though it had
chimed just under the window. The child, sleeping on
the fox-skin, started and raised her head. For a minute
she stared blankly at the dark window, at Nasir-ed-
Din, over whom a crimson glow from the fire flickered
at that moment, then she turned her eyes upon the
sleeping man.

'Daddy,' she said.

But the man did not move. The little girl knitted
her brow angrily, lay down, and curled up her legs.

Someone in the tavern gave a loud, prolonged yawn. Soon afterwards there was the squeak of the swing door and the sound of indistinct voices. Someone came in, shaking the snow off, and stamping in felt boots which made a muffled thud.

'What is it?' a woman's voice asked languidly.

'Mademoiselle Ilovaisky has come ...' answered a bass voice.

Again there was the squeak of the swing door. Then came the roar of the wind rushing in. Someone, probably the lame boy, ran to the door leading to the 'travellers' room,' coughed deferentially, and lifted the latch.

'This way, lady, please,' said a woman's voice in dulcet tones. 'It's clean in here, my beauty ...'

The door was opened wide and a peasant with a beard appeared in the doorway, in the long coat of a coachman, plastered all over with snow from head to foot, and carrying a big trunk on his shoulder. He was followed into the room by a feminine figure, scarcely half his height, with no face and no arms, muffled and wrapped up like a bundle and also covered with snow. A damp chill, as from a cellar, seemed to come to the child from the coachman and the bundle, and the fire and the candles flickered.

'What nonsense!' said the bundle angrily. 'We could go perfectly well. We have only nine more miles to go, mostly by the forest, and we should not get lost ...'

'As for getting lost, we shouldn't, but the horses can't go on, lady!' answered the coachman. 'And it is Thy Will, O Lord! As though I had done it on purpose!'

'God knows where you have brought me ... Well,

be quiet . . . There are people asleep here, it seems. You can go . . .'

The coachman put the portmanteau on the floor, and as he did so, a great lump of snow fell off his shoulders. He gave a sniff and went out.

Then the little girl saw two little hands come out from the middle of the bundle, stretch upwards and begin angrily disentangling the network of shawls, kerchiefs, and scarves. First a big shawl fell on the ground, then a hood, then a white knitted kerchief. After freeing her head, the traveller took off her pelisse and at once shrank to half the size. Now she was in a long, grey coat with big buttons and bulging pockets. From one pocket she pulled out a paper parcel, from the other a bunch of big, heavy keys, which she put down so carelessly that the sleeping man started and opened his eyes. For some time he looked blankly round him as though he didn't know where he was, then he shook his head, went to the corner and sat down . . . The newcomer took off her great coat, which made her shrink to half her size again, she took off her big felt boots, and sat down too.

By now she no longer resembled a bundle: she was a thin little brunette of twenty, as slim as a snake, with a long white face and curly hair. Her nose was long and sharp, her chin, too, was long and sharp, her eyelashes were long, the corners of her mouth were sharp, and, thanks to this general sharpness, the expression of her face was biting. Swathed in a closely fitting black dress with a mass of lace at her neck and sleeves, with sharp elbows and long pink fingers, she recalled the portraits of medieval English ladies. The grave concentration of her face increased this likeness.

The lady looked round at the room, glanced sideways at the man and the little girl, shrugged her shoulders, and moved to the window. The dark windows were shaking from the damp west wind. Big flakes of snow, glistening in their whiteness, lay on the window frame, but at once disappeared, borne away by the wind. The savage music grew louder and louder ...

After a long silence the little girl suddenly turned over, and said angrily, emphasizing each word:

'Oh, goodness, goodness, how unhappy I am! Unhappier than anyone!'

The man got up and moved with little steps to the child with a guilty air, which was utterly out of keeping with his huge figure and big beard.

'You are not asleep, dearie?' he said, in an apologetic voice. 'What do you want?'

'I don't want anything, my shoulder aches! You are a wicked man, Daddy, and God will punish you! You'll see He will punish you.'

'My darling, I know your shoulder aches, but what can I do, dearie?' said the man, in the tone in which men who have been drinking excuse themselves to their stern spouses. 'It's the journey has made your shoulder ache, Sasha. To-morrow we shall get there and rest, and the pain will go away ...'

'To-morrow, to-morrow ... Every day you say to-morrow. We shall be going on another twenty days.'

'But we shall arrive to-morrow, dearie, on your father's word of honour. I never tell a lie, but if we are detained by the snowstorm it is not my fault.'

'I can't bear any more, I can't, I can't!'

Sasha jerked her leg abruptly and filled the room

with an unpleasant wailing. Her father made a despairing gesture, and looked hopelessly towards the
young lady. The latter shrugged her shoulders, and
hesitatingly went up to Sasha.

'Listen, my dear,' she said, 'it's no use crying. It's
really naughty; if your shoulder aches it can't be
helped.'

'You see, Madam,' said the man quickly, as though
defending himself, 'we have not slept for two nights,
and have been travelling in a revolting conveyance.
Well, of course, it is natural she should be ill and miserable ... and then, you know, we had a drunken
driver, our portmanteau has been stolen ... the snowstorm all the time, but what's the use of crying,
Madam? I am exhausted, though, by sleeping in a sitting position, and I feel as though I were drunk. Oh,
dear! Sasha, I feel sick as it is, and then you cry!'

The man shook his head, and with a gesture of despair sat down.

'Of course you mustn't cry,' said the young lady.
'It's only little babies cry. If you are ill, dear, you must
undress and go to sleep ... Let us take off your
things!'

When the child had been undressed and pacified a
silence reigned again. The young lady seated herself
at the window, and looked round wonderingly at the
room of the inn, at the ikon, at the stove ... Apparently the room and the little girl with the thick nose,
in her short boy's nightgown, and the child's father,
all seemed strange to her. This strange man was sitting
in a corner; he kept looking about him helplessly, as
though he were drunk, and rubbing his face with the
palm of his hand. He sat silent, blinking, and judging

from his guilty-looking figure it was difficult to imagine that he would soon begin to speak. Yet he was
the first to begin. Stroking his knees, he gave a cough,
laughed, and said:

'It's a comedy, it really is ... I look and I cannot
believe my eyes: for what devilry has destiny driven
us to this accursed inn? What did she want to show
by it? Life sometimes performs such "*salto mortale*,"
one can only stare and blink in amazement. Have you
come from far, Madam?'

'No, not from far,' answered the young lady. 'I am
going from our estate, fifteen miles from here, to our
farm, to my father and brother. My name is Ilovaisky,
and the farm is called Ilovaiskoe. It's nine miles away.
What unpleasant weather!'

'It couldn't be worse.'

The lame boy came in and stuck a new candle in the
pomatum pot.

'You might bring us the samovar, boy,' said the
man, addressing him.

'Who drinks tea now?' laughed the boy. 'It is a sin
to drink tea before mass ...'

'Never mind, boy, you won't burn in hell if we do ...'

Over the tea the new acquaintances got into
conversation.

Mlle Ilovaisky learned that her companion was
called Grigory Petrovitch Liharev, that he was the
brother of the Liharev who was Marshal of Nobility in
one of the neighbouring districts, and he himself had
once been a landowner, but had 'run through everything in his time.' Liharev learned that her name was
Marya Mihailovna, that her father had a huge estate,
but that she was the only one to look after it as her

father and brother looked at life through their fingers, were irresponsible, and were too fond of harriers.

'My father and brother are all alone at the farm,' she told him, brandishing her fingers (she had the habit of moving her fingers before her pointed face as she talked, and after every sentence moistened her lips with her sharp little tongue). 'They, I mean men, are an irresponsible lot, and don't stir a finger for themselves. I can fancy there will be no one to give them a meal after the fast! We have no mother, and we have such servants that they can't lay the tablecloth properly when I am away. You can imagine their condition now! They will be left with nothing to break their fast, while I have to stay here all night. How strange it all is.'

She shrugged her shoulders, took a sip from her cup, and said:

'There are festivals that have a special fragrance: at Easter, Trinity and Christmas there is a peculiar scent in the air. Even unbelievers are fond of those festivals. My brother, for instance, argues that there is no God, but he is the first to hurry to Matins at Easter.'

Liharev raised his eyes to Mlle Ilovaisky and laughed.

'They argue that there is no God,' she went on, laughing too, 'but why is it, tell me, all the celebrated writers, the learned men, clever people generally, in fact, believe towards the end of their life?'

'If a man does not know how to believe when he is young, Madam, he won't believe in his old age if he is ever so much of a writer.'

Judging from Liharev's cough he had a bass voice, but, probably from being afraid to speak aloud or

from exaggerated shyness, he spoke in a tenor. After a
brief pause he heaved a sigh and said:

'The way I look at it is that faith is a faculty of the
spirit. It is just the same as a talent, one must be born
with it. So far as I can judge by myself, by the people
I have seen in my time, and by all that is done around
us, this faculty is present in Russians in its highest
degree. Russian life presents us with an uninterrupted
succession of convictions and aspirations, and, if you
care to know, it has not yet the faintest notion of lack
of faith or scepticism. If a Russian does not believe in
God, it means he believes in something else.'

Liharev took a cup of tea from Mlle Ilovaisky, drank
off half at one gulp, and went on:

'I will tell you about myself. Nature has implanted
in my breast an extraordinary faculty for belief. Whisper it not to the night, but half my life I was in the
ranks of the Atheists and Nihilists, but there was not
one hour in my life in which I ceased to believe. All
talents, as a rule, show themselves in early childhood,
and so my faculty showed itself when I could still walk
upright under the table. My mother liked her children
to eat a great deal, and when she gave me food she
used to say: "Eat! Soup is the great thing in life!"
I believed, and ate the soup ten times a day, ate like a
shark, ate till I was disgusted and stupefied. My nurse
used to tell me fairy tales, and I believed in house-
spirits, in wood-elves, and in goblins of all kinds.
I used sometimes to steal corrosive sublimate from
my father, sprinkle it on cakes, and carry them up to
the attic that the house-spirits, you see, might eat
them and be killed. And when I was taught to read
and understand what I read, then there was a fine to-

do. I ran away to America and went off to join the brigands, and wanted to go into a monastery, and hired boys to torture me for being a Christian. And note that my faith was always active, never dead. If I was running away to America I was not alone, but seduced someone else, as great a fool as I was, to go with me, and was delighted when I was nearly frozen outside the town gates and when I was thrashed; if I went to join the brigands I always came back with my face battered. A most restless childhood, I assure you! And when they sent me to the high school and pelted me with all sorts of truths – that is, that the earth goes round the sun, or that white light is not white, but is made up of seven colours – my poor little head began to go round! Everything was thrown into a whirl in me: Navin who made the sun stand still, and my mother who in the name of the Prophet Elijah disapproved of lightning conductors, and my father who was indifferent to the truths I had learned. My enlightenment inspired me. I wandered about the house and stables like one possessed, preaching my truths, was horrified by ignorance, glowed with hatred for anyone who saw in white light nothing but white light ... But all that's nonsense and childishness. Serious, so to speak, manly enthusiasms began only at the university. You have, no doubt, Madam, taken your degree somewhere?'

'I studied at Novotcherkask at the Don Institute.'

'Then you have not been to a university? So you don't know what science means. All the sciences in the world have the same passport, without which they regard themselves as meaningless ... the striving towards truth! Every one of them, even pharmacology, has for its aim not utility, not the alleviation of life, but truth. It's remarkable! When you set to work to study any science, what strikes you first of all is its beginning. I assure you there is nothing more attractive and grander, nothing is so staggering, nothing takes a man's breath away like the beginning of any science. From the first five or six lectures you are soaring on wings of the brightest hopes, you already seem to yourself to be welcoming truth with open arms. And I gave myself up to science, heart and soul, passionately, as to the woman one loves. I was its slave; I found it the sun of my existence, and asked for no other. I studied day and night without rest, ruined myself over books, wept when before my eyes men exploited science for their own personal ends. But my enthusiasm did not last long. The trouble is that every science has a beginning but not an end, like a recurring decimal. Zoology has discovered 35,000 kinds of insects, chemistry reckons 60 elements. If in time tens of noughts can be written after these figures, zoology and chemistry will be just as far from their end as now, and all contemporary scientific work consists in increasing these numbers. I saw through this trick when I discovered the 35,001-st and felt no satisfaction. Well, I had no time to suffer from disillusionment, as I was soon possessed by a new faith. I plunged into Nihilism with its manifestoes, its "black divisions," and all the rest of it. I "went to the people," worked in factories, worked as an oiler, as a barge hauler. Afterwards, when wandering over Russia, I had a taste of Russian life, I turned into a fervent devotee of that life. I loved the Russian people with poignant intensity; I loved their God and believed in Him, and in their language, their creative genius ... And so on, and so on ... I have been a Slavophile in my time, I used to pester Aksakov with letters, and I was a Ukrainophile, and an archeologist, and a collector of specimens of peasant art ... I was enthusiastic over ideas, people, events, places ... my enthusiasm was endless! Five years ago I was working for the abolition of private property; my last creed was non-resistance to evil.'

Sasha gave an abrupt sigh and began moving. Liharev got up and went to her.

'Won't you have some tea, dearie?' he asked tenderly.

'Drink it yourself,' the child answered rudely.

Liharev was disconcerted, and went back to the table with a guilty step.

'Then you have had a lively time,' said Mlle Ilovai-sky; 'you have something to remember.'

'Well, yes, it's all very lively when one sits over tea and chatters to a kind listener, but you should ask what that liveliness has cost me! What price have I paid for the variety of my life? You see, Madam, I have not held my convictions like a German doctor of philosophy, *zierlich männerlich*, I have not lived in solitude, but every conviction I have had has bound my back to the yoke, has torn my body to pieces. Judge for yourself. I was wealthy like my brothers, but now I am a beggar. In the delirium of my enthusiasm I smashed up my own fortune and my wife's – a heap of other people's money. Now I am forty-two, old age is close upon me, and I am homeless, like a dog that has dropped behind its waggon at night. All my life I have not known what peace meant, my soul has been

in continual agitation, distressed even by its hopes ...
I have been wearied out with heavy, irregular work,
have endured privation, have five times been in
prison, have dragged myself across the provinces of
Archangel and of Tobolsk ... it's painful to think of
it! I have lived, but in my fever I have not even been
conscious of the process of life itself. Would you
believe it, I don't remember a single spring, I never
noticed how my wife loved me, how my children were
born. What more can I tell you? I have been a misfortune to all who have loved me ... My mother has worn
mourning for me these fifteen years, while my proud
brothers, who have had to wince, to blush, to bow
their heads, to waste their money on my account, have
come in the end to hate me like poison.'

Liharev got up and sat down again.

'If I were simply unhappy I should thank God,' he
went on without looking at his listener. 'My personal
unhappiness sinks into the background when
I remember how often in my enthusiasms I have been
absurd, far from the truth, unjust, cruel, dangerous!
How often I have hated and despised those whom
I ought to have loved, and *vice versa*, I have changed
a thousand times. One day I believe, fall down and
worship, and the next I flee like a coward from the
gods and friends of yesterday, and swallow in silence
the "scoundrel!" they hurl after me. God alone has
seen how often I have wept and bitten my pillow in
shame for my enthusiasms. Never once in my life have
I intentionally lied or done evil, but my conscience is
not clear! I cannot even boast, Madam, that I have no
one's life upon my conscience, for my wife died before
my eyes, worn out by my reckless activity. Yes, my

wife! I tell you they have two ways of treating women nowadays. Some measure women's skulls to prove woman is inferior to man, pick out her defects to mock at her, to look original in her eyes, and to justify their sensuality. Others do their utmost to raise women to their level, that is, force them to learn by heart the 35,000 species, to speak and write the same foolish things as they speak and write themselves.'

Liharev's face darkened.

'I tell you that woman has been and always will be the slave of man,' he said in a bass voice, striking his fist on the table. 'She is the soft, tender wax which a man always moulds into anything he likes . . . My God! for the sake of some trumpery masculine enthusiasm she will cut off her hair, abandon her family, die among strangers! . . . among the ideas for which she has sacrificed herself there is not a single feminine one . . . An unquestioning, devoted slave! I have not measured skulls, but I say this from hard, bitter experience: the proudest, most independent women, if I have succeeded in communicating to them my enthusiasm, have followed me without criticism, without question, and done anything I chose; I have turned a nun into a Nihilist who, as I heard afterwards, shot a gendarme; my wife never left me for a minute in my wanderings, and like a weathercock changed her faith in step with my changing enthusiasms.'

Liharev jumped up and walked up and down the room.

'A noble, sublime slavery!' he said, clasping his hands. 'It is just in it that the highest meaning of woman's life lies! Of all the fearful medley of thoughts and impressions accumulated in my brain from my association with women my memory, like a filter, has retained no ideas, no clever saying, no philosophy, nothing but that extraordinary resignation to fate, that wonderful mercifulness, forgiveness of everything.'

Liharev clenched his fists, stared at a fixed point, and with a sort of passionate intensity, as though he were savouring each word as he uttered it, hissed through his clenched teeth:

'That ... that great-hearted fortitude, faithfulness unto death, poetry of the heart ... The meaning of life lies in just that unrepining martyrdom, in the tears which would soften a stone, in the boundless, all-forgiving love which brings light and warmth into the chaos of life ...'

Mlle Ilovaisky got up slowly, took a step towards Liharev, and fixed her eyes upon his face. From the tears that glittered on his eyelashes, from his quivering, passionate voice, from the flush on his cheeks, it was clear to her that women were not a chance, not a simple subject of conversation. They were the object of his new enthusiasm, or, as he said himself, his new faith! For the first time in her life she saw a man carried away, fervently believing. With his gesticulations, with his flashing eyes he seemed to her mad, frantic, but there was a feeling of such beauty in the fire of his eyes, in his words, in all the movements of his huge body, that without noticing what she was doing she stood facing him as though rooted to the spot, and gazed into his face with delight.

'Take my mother,' he said, stretching out his hand to her with an imploring expression on his face, 'I poisoned her existence, according to her ideas disgraced the name of Liharev, did her as much harm as the most malignant enemy, and what do you think? My brothers give her little sums for holy bread and church services, and, outraging her religious feelings, she saves that money and sends it in secret to her erring Grigory. This trifle alone elevates and ennobles the soul far more than all the theories, all the clever sayings and the 35,000 species. I can give you thousands of instances. Take you, even, for instance! With tempest and darkness outside you are going to your father and your brother to cheer them with your affection in the holiday, though very likely they have forgotten and are not thinking of you. And, wait a bit, and you will love a man and follow him to the North Pole. You would, wouldn't you?'

'Yes, if I loved him.'

'There, you see,' cried Liharev delighted, and he even stamped with his foot. 'Oh dear! How glad I am that I have met you! Fate is kind to me, I am always meeting splendid people. Not a day passes but one makes acquaintance with somebody one would give one's soul for. There are ever so many more good people than bad in this world. Here, see, for instance, how openly and from our hearts we have been talking as though we had known each other a hundred years. Sometimes, I assure you, one restrains oneself for ten years and holds one's tongue, is reserved with one's friends and one's wife, and meets some cadet in a train and babbles one's whole soul out to him. It is the first time I have the honour of seeing you, and yet I have confessed to you as I have never confessed in my life. Why is it?'

Rubbing his hands and smiling good-humouredly

Liharev walked up and down the room, and fell to talking about women again. Meanwhile they began ringing for matins.

'Goodness,' wailed Sasha. 'He won't let me sleep with his talking!'

'Oh, yes!' said Liharev, startled. 'I am sorry, darling, sleep, sleep ... I have two boys besides her,' he whispered. 'They are living with their uncle, Madam, but this one can't exist a day without her father. She's wretched, she complains, but she sticks to me like a fly to honey. I have been chattering too much, Madam, and it would do you no harm to sleep. Wouldn't you like me to make up a bed for you?'

Without waiting for permission he shook the wet pelisse, stretched it on a bench, fur side upwards, collected various shawls and scarves, put the overcoat folded up into a roll for a pillow, and all this he did in silence with a look of devout reverence, as though he were not handling a woman's rags, but the fragments of holy vessels. There was something apologetic, embarrassed about his whole figure, as though in the presence of a weak creature he felt ashamed of his height and strength ...

When Mlle Ilovaisky had lain down, he put out the candle and sat down on a stool by the stove.

'So, Madam,' he whispered, lighting a fat cigarette and puffing the smoke into the stove, 'Nature has put into the Russian an extraordinary faculty for belief, a searching intelligence, and the gift of speculation, but all that is reduced to ashes by irresponsibility, laziness, and dreamy frivolity ... Yes ...'

She gazed wonderingly into the darkness, and saw only a spot of red on the ikon and the flicker of the light of the stove on Liharev's face. The darkness, the chime of the bells, the roar of the storm, the lame boy, Sasha with her fretfulness, unhappy Liharev and his sayings – all this was mingled together, and seemed to grow into one huge impression, and God's world seemed to her fantastic, full of marvels and magical forces. All that she had just heard was ringing in her ears, and human life presented itself to her as a beautiful poetic fairy-tale without an end.

The immense impression grew and grew, clouded consciousness, and turned into a sweet dream. She was asleep, though she saw the little ikon lamp, and a big nose with the light playing on it.

She heard the sound of weeping.

'Daddy, darling,' a child's voice was tenderly entreating, 'let's go back to uncle! There is a Christmas-tree there! Styopa and Kolya are there!'

'My darling, what can I do?' a man's bass persuaded softly. 'Understand me! Come, understand!'

And the man's weeping blended with the child's. This voice of human sorrow, in the midst of the howling of the storm, touched the girl's ear with such sweet human music that she could not bear the delight of it, and wept too. She was conscious afterwards of a big, black shadow coming softly up to her, picking up a shawl that had dropped on to the floor and carefully wrapping it round her feet.

Mlle Ilovaisky was awakened by a strange uproar. She jumped up and looked about her in astonishment. The deep blue dawn was looking in at the window half-covered with snow. In the room there was a grey twilight, through which the stove and the sleeping child and Nasir-ed-Din stood out distinctly. The stove and the lamp were both out. Through the wide-open door she could see the big tavern room with a counter and chairs. A man, with a stupid, gipsy face and astonished eyes, was standing in the middle of the room in a puddle of melting snow, holding a big red star on a stick. He was surrounded by a group of boys, motionless as statues, and plastered over with snow. The light shone through the red paper of the star, throwing a glow of red on their wet faces. The crowd was shouting in disorder, and from its uproar Mlle Ilovaisky could make out only one couplet:

'Hi, you Little Russian lad,
Bring your sharp knife,
We will kill the Jew, we will kill him,
The son of tribulation . . .'

Liharev was standing near the counter, looking feel-ingly at the singers and tapping his feet in time. See-ing Mlle Ilovaisky, he smiled all over his face and came up to her. She smiled too.

'A happy Christmas!' he said. 'I saw you slept well.'

She looked at him, said nothing, and went on smiling.

After the conversation in the night he seemed to her not tall and broad shouldered, but little, just as the biggest steamer seems to us a little thing when we hear that it has crossed the ocean.

'Well, it is time for me to set off,' she said. 'I must put on my things. Tell me where you are going now?'

'I? To the station of Klinushki, from there to Sergi-evo, and from Sergievo, with horses, thirty miles to the coal mines that belong to a horrid man, a general called Shashkovsky. My brothers have got me the post of superintendent there … I am going to be a coal miner.'

'Stay, I know those mines. Shashkovsky is my uncle, you know. But … what are you going there for?' asked Mlle Ilovaisky, looking at Liharev in surprise.

'As superintendent. To superintend the coal mines.'

'I don't understand!' she shrugged her shoulders. 'You are going to the mines. But, you know, it's the bare steppe, a desert, so dreary that you couldn't exist a day there! It's horrible coal, no one will buy it, and my uncle's a maniac, a despot, a bankrupt … You won't get your salary!'

'No matter,' said Liharev, unconcernedly, 'I am thankful even for coal mines.'

She shrugged her shoulders, and walked about the room in agitation.

'I don't understand, I don't understand,' she said, moving her fingers before her face. 'It's impossible, and … and irrational! You must understand that it's … it's worse than exile. It is a living tomb! O Heavens!' she said hotly, going up to Liharev and moving her fingers before his smiling face; her upper lip was quivering, and her sharp face turned pale, 'Come, picture it, the bare steppe, solitude. There is no one to say a word to there, and you … are enthusiastic over women! Coal mines … and women!'

Mlle Ilovaisky was suddenly ashamed of her heat and, turning away from Liharev, walked to the window.

'No, no, you can't go there,' she said, moving her fingers rapidly over the pane.

Not only in her heart, but even in her spine she felt

that behind her stood an infinitely unhappy man, lost and outcast, while he, as though he were unaware of his unhappiness, as though he had not shed tears in the night, was looking at her with a kindly smile. Better he should go on weeping! She walked up and down the room several times in agitation, then stopped short in a corner and sank into thought. Liharev was saying something, but she did not hear him. Turning her back on him she took out of her purse a money note, stood for a long time crumpling it in her hand, and looking round at Liharev, blushed and put it in her pocket.

The coachman's voice was heard through the door. With a stern, concentrated face she began putting on her things in silence. Liharev wrapped her up, chatting gaily, but every word he said lay on her heart like a weight. It is not cheering to hear the unhappy or the dying jest.

When the transformation of a live person into a shapeless bundle had been completed, Mlle Ilovaisky looked for the last time round the 'travellers' room,' stood a moment in silence, and slowly walked out. Liharev went to see her off . . .

Outside, God alone knows why, the winter was raging still. Whole clouds of big soft snowflakes were whirling restlessly over the earth, unable to find a resting-place. The horses, the sledge, the trees, a bull tied to a post, all were white and seemed soft and fluffy.

'Well, God help you,' muttered Liharev, tucking her into the sledge. 'Don't remember evil against me . . .'

She was silent. When the sledge started, and had to go round a huge snowdrift, she looked back at Liharev with an expression as though she wanted to say something to him. He ran up to her, but she did not say a word to him, she only looked at him through her long eyelashes with little specks of snow on them.

Whether his finely intuitive soul were really able to read that look, or whether his imagination deceived him, it suddenly began to seem to him that with another touch or two that girl would have forgiven him his failures, his age, his desolate position, and would have followed him without question or reasonings. He stood a long while as though rooted to the spot, gazing at the tracks left by the sledge runners. The snowflakes greedily settled on his hair, his beard, his shoulders ... Soon the track of the runners had vanished, and he himself, covered with snow, began to look like a white rock, but still his eyes kept seeking something in the clouds of snow.

VEROTCHKA

VEROTCHKA

IVAN ALEXEYITCH OGNEV remembers how on that August evening he opened the glass door with a rattle and went out on to the verandah. He was wearing a light Inverness cape and a wide-brimmed straw hat, the very one that was lying with his top-boots in the dust under his bed. In one hand he had a big bundle of books and notebooks, in the other a thick knotted stick.

Behind the door, holding the lamp to show the way, stood the master of the house, Kuznetsov, a bald old man with a long grey beard, in a snow-white piqué jacket. The old man was smiling cordially and nodding his head.

'Good-bye, old fellow!' said Ognev.

Kuznetsov put the lamp on a little table and went out on to the verandah. Two long narrow shadows moved down the steps towards the flower-beds, swayed to and fro, and leaned their heads on the trunks of the lime-trees.

'Good-bye and once more thank you, my dear fellow!' said Ivan Alexeyitch. 'Thank you for your welcome, for your kindness, for your affection ... I shall never forget your hospitality as long as I live. You are so good, and your daughter is so good, and everyone here is so kind, so good-humoured and friendly ...

Such a splendid set of people that I don't know how to say what I feel!'

From excess of feeling and under the influence of the home-made wine he had just drunk, Ognev talked in a singing voice like a divinity student, and was so touched that he expressed his feelings not so much by words as by the blinking of his eyes and the twitching of his shoulders. Kuznetsov, who had also drunk a good deal and was touched, craned forward to the young man and kissed him.

'I've grown as fond of you as if I were your dog,' Ognev went on. 'I've been turning up here almost every day; I've stayed the night a dozen times. It's dreadful to think of all the home-made wine I've drunk. And thank you most of all for your co-operation and help. Without you I should have been busy here over my statistics till October. I shall put in my preface: "I think it my duty to express my gratitude to the President of the District Zemstvo of N——, Kuznetsov, for his kind co-operation." There is a brilliant future before statistics! My humble respects to Vera Gavrilovna, and tell the doctors, both the lawyers and your secretary, that I shall never forget their help! And now, old fellow, let us embrace one another and kiss for the last time!'

Ognev, limp with emotion, kissed the old man once more and began going down the steps. On the last step he looked round and asked: 'Shall we meet again some day?'

'God knows!' said the old man. 'Most likely not!'

'Yes, that's true! Nothing will tempt you to Petersburg and I am never likely to turn up in this district again. Well, good-bye!'

'You had better leave the books behind!' Kuznetsov called after him. 'You don't want to drag such a weight with you. I would send them by a servant to-morrow!'

But Ognev was rapidly walking away from the house and was not listening. His heart, warmed by the wine, was brimming over with good-humour, friendliness, and sadness. He walked along thinking how frequently one met with good people, and what a pity it was that nothing was left of those meetings but memories. At times one catches a glimpse of cranes on the horizon, and a faint gust of wind brings their plaintive, ecstatic cry, and a minute later, however greedily one scans the blue distance, one cannot see a speck nor catch a sound; and, like that, people with their faces and their words flit through our lives and are drowned in the past, leaving nothing except faint traces in the memory. Having been in the N—— District from the early spring, and having been almost every day at the friendly Kuznetsovs', Ivan Alexeyitch had become as much at home with the old man, his daughter, and the servants as though they were his own people; he had grown familiar with the whole house to the smallest detail, with the cosy verandah, the windings of the avenues, the silhouettes of the trees over the kitchen and the bath-house; but as soon as he was out of the gate all this would be changed to memory and would lose its meaning as reality for ever, and in a year or two all these dear images would grow as dim in his consciousness as stories he had read or things he had imagined.

'Nothing in life is so precious as people!' Ognev thought in his emotion, as he strode along the avenue to the gate. 'Nothing!'

It was warm and still in the garden. There was a scent of the mignonette, of the tobacco-plants, and of the heliotrope, which were not yet over in the flower-beds. The spaces between the bushes and the tree-trunks were filled with a fine soft mist soaked through and through with moonlight, and, as Ognev long remembered, coils of mist that looked like phantoms slowly but perceptibly followed one another across the avenue. The moon stood high above the garden, and below it transparent patches of mist were floating eastward. The whole world seemed to consist of nothing but black silhouettes and wandering white shadows. Ognev, seeing the mist on a moonlight August evening almost for the first time in his life, imagined he was seeing, not nature, but a stage effect in which unskilful workmen, trying to light up the garden with white Bengal fire, hid behind the bushes and let off clouds of white smoke together with the light.

When Ognev reached the garden gate a dark shadow moved away from the low fence and came towards him.

'Vera Gavrilovna!' he said, delighted. 'You here? And I have been looking everywhere for you; wanted to say good-bye ... Good-bye; I am going away!'

'So early? Why, it's only eleven o'clock.'

'Yes, it's time I was off. I have a four-mile walk and then my packing. I must be up early to-morrow.'

Before Ognev stood Kuznetsov's daughter Vera, a girl of one-and-twenty, as usual melancholy, carelessly dressed, and attractive. Girls who are dreamy and spend whole days lying down, lazily reading whatever they come across, who are bored and melancholy, are usually careless in their dress. To those of them who have been endowed by nature with taste and an instinct of beauty, the slight carelessness adds a special charm. When Ognev later on remembered her, he could not picture pretty Verotchka except in a full blouse which was crumpled in deep folds at the belt and yet did not touch her waist; without her hair done up high and a curl that had come loose from it on her forehead; without the knitted red shawl with ball fringe at the edge which hung disconsolately on Vera's shoulders in the evenings, like a flag on a windless day, and in the daytime lay about, crushed up, in the hall near the men's hats or on a box in the dining-room, where the old cat did not hesitate to sleep on it. This shawl and the folds of her blouse suggested a feeling of freedom and laziness, of good-nature and sitting at home. Perhaps because Vera attracted Ognev he saw in every frill and button something warm, naive, cosy, something nice and poetical, just what is lacking in cold, insincere women that have no instinct for beauty.

Verotchka had a good figure, a regular profile, and beautiful curly hair. Ognev, who had seen few women in his life, thought her a beauty.

'I am going away,' he said as he took leave of her at the gate. 'Don't remember evil against me! Thank you for everything!'

In the same singing divinity student's voice in which he had talked to her father, with the same blinking and twitching of his shoulders, he began thanking Vera for her hospitality, kindness, and friendliness.

'I've written about you in every letter to my mother,' he said. 'If everyone were like you and your dad, what a jolly place the world would be! You are such a splendid set of people! All such genuine, friendly people with no nonsense about you.'

'Where are you going to now?' asked Vera.

'I am going now to my mother's at Oryol; I shall be a fortnight with her, and then back to Petersburg and work.'

'And then?'

'And then? I shall work all the winter and in the spring go somewhere into the provinces again to collect material. Well, be happy, live a hundred years . . . don't remember evil against me. We shall not see each other again.'

Ognev stooped down and kissed Vera's hand. Then, in silent emotion, he straightened his cape, shifted his bundle of books to a more comfortable position, paused, and said:

'What a lot of mist!'

'Yes. Have you left anything behind?'

'No, I don't think so . . .'

For some seconds Ognev stood in silence, then he moved clumsily towards the gate and went out of the garden.

'Stay; I'll see you as far as our wood,' said Vera, following him out.

They walked along the road. Now the trees did not obscure the view, and one could see the sky and the distance. As though covered with a veil, all nature was hidden in a transparent, colourless haze through which her beauty peeped gaily; where the mist was thicker and whiter it lay heaped unevenly about the stones, stalks, and bushes or drifted in coils over the road, clung close to the earth and seemed trying not to conceal the view. Through the haze they could see all the road as far as the wood, with dark ditches at the sides and tiny bushes which grew in the ditches and caught the straying wisps of mist. Half a mile from the gate they saw the dark patch of Kuznetsov's wood.

'Why has she come with me? I shall have to see her back,' thought Ognev, but looking at her profile he gave a friendly smile and said: 'One doesn't want to go away in such lovely weather. It's quite a romantic evening, with the moon, the stillness, and all the etceteras. Do you know, Vera Gavrilovna, here I have lived twenty-nine years in the world and never had a romance. No romantic episode in my whole life, so that I only know by hearsay of rendezvous, "avenues of sighs," and kisses. It's not normal! In town, when one sits in one's lodgings, one does not notice the blank, but here in the fresh air one feels it ... One resents it!'

'Why is it?'

'I don't know. I suppose I've never had time, or perhaps it was I have never met women who ... In fact, I have very few acquaintances and never go anywhere.'

For some three hundred paces the young people walked on in silence. Ognev kept glancing at Verotchka's bare head and shawl, and days of spring and summer rose to his mind one after another. It had been a period when far from his grey Petersburg lodgings, enjoying the friendly warmth of kind people, nature, and the work he loved, he had not had time to notice how the sunsets followed the glow of dawn, and how, one after another, foretelling the end of summer, first the nightingale ceased singing, then the quail, then a little later the landrail. The days slipped by unnoticed, so that life must have been happy and easy. He began recalling aloud how reluctantly he, poor and unaccustomed to change of scene and society, had come at the end of April to the N—— District, where he had expected dreariness, loneliness, and indifference to statistics, which he considered was now the foremost among the sciences. When he arrived on an April morning at the little town of N—— he had put up at the inn kept by Ryabuhin, the Old Believer, where for twenty kopecks a day they had given him a light, clean room on condition that he should not smoke indoors. After resting and finding out who was the president of the District Zemstvo, he had set off at once on foot to Kuznetsov. He had to walk three miles through lush meadows and young copses. Larks were hovering in the clouds, filling the air with silvery notes, and rooks flapping their wings with sedate dignity floated over the green cornland.

'Good heavens!' Ognev had thought in wonder; 'can it be that there's always air like this to breathe here, or is this scent only to-day, in honour of my coming?'

Expecting a cold business-like reception, he went in to Kuznetsov's diffidently, looking up from under his eyebrows and shyly pulling his beard. At first Kuznetsov wrinkled up his brows and could not understand what use the Zemstvo could be to the young man and his statistics; but when the latter explained at length what was material for statistics and how such material was collected, Kuznetsov brightened, smiled, and with childish curiosity began looking at his note-

books. On the evening of the same day Ivan Alexeyitch was already sitting at supper with the
Kuznetsovs, was rapidly becoming exhilarated by
their strong home-made wine, and, looking at the
calm faces and lazy movements of his new acquaintances, felt all over that sweet, drowsy indolence which
makes one want to sleep and stretch and smile; while
his new acquaintances looked at him good-naturedly
and asked him whether his father and mother were
living, how much he earned a month, how often he
went to the theatre ...

Ognev recalled his expeditions about the neighbourhood, the picnics, the fishing parties, the visit of
the whole party to the convent to see the Mother
Superior Marfa, who had given each of the visitors
a bead purse; he recalled the hot, endless, typically
Russian arguments in which the opponents, spluttering and banging the table with their fists, misun-
derstand and interrupt one another, unconsciously
contradict themselves at every phrase, continually
change the subject, and after arguing for two or three
hours, laugh and say:

'Goodness knows what we have been arguing about!
Beginning with one thing and going on to another!'

'And do you remember how the doctor and you and
I rode to Shestovo?' said Ivan Alexeyitch to Vera as
they reached the copse. 'It was there that the crazy
saint met us: I gave him a five-kopeck piece, and he
crossed himself three times and flung it into the rye.
Good heavens! I am carrying away such a mass of
memories that if I could gather them together into a
whole it would make a good nugget of gold! I don't
understand why clever, perceptive people crowd into

Petersburg and Moscow and don't come here. Is there more truth and freedom in the Nevsky and in the big damp houses than here? Really, the idea of artists, scientific men, and journalists all living crowded together in furnished rooms has always seemed to me a mistake.'

Twenty paces from the copse the road was crossed by a small narrow bridge with posts at the corners, which had always served as a resting-place for the Kuznetsovs and their guests on their evening walks. From there those who liked could mimic the forest echo, and one could see the road vanish in the dark woodland track.

'Well, here is the bridge!' said Ognev. 'Here you must turn back.'

Vera stopped and drew a breath.

'Let us sit down,' she said, sitting down on one of the posts. 'People generally sit down when they say good-bye before starting on a journey.'

Ognev settled himself beside her on his bundle of books and went on talking. She was breathless from the walk, and was looking, not at Ivan Alexeyitch, but away into the distance so that he could not see her face.

'And what if we meet in ten years' time?' he said. 'What shall we be like then? You will be by then the respectable mother of a family, and I shall be the author of some weighty statistical work of no use to anyone, as thick as forty thousand such works. We shall meet and think of old days ... Now we are conscious of the present; it absorbs and excites us, but when we meet we shall not remember the day, nor the month, nor even the year in which we saw each other for the last time on this bridge. You will be changed, perhaps ... Tell me, will you be different?'

Vera started and turned her face towards him.

'What?' she asked.

'I asked you just now ...'

'Excuse me, I did not hear what you were saying.'

Only then Ognev noticed a change in Vera. She was pale, breathing fast, and the tremor in her breathing affected her hands and lips and head, and not one curl as usual, but two, came loose and fell on her forehead ... Evidently she avoided looking him in the face, and, trying to mask her emotion, at one moment fingered her collar, which seemed to be rasping her neck, at another pulled her red shawl from one shoulder to the other.

'I am afraid you are cold,' said Ognev. 'It's not at all wise to sit in the mist. Let me see you back *nach-haus*.'

Vera sat mute.

'What is the matter?' asked Ognev, with a smile. 'You sit silent and don't answer my questions. Are you cross, or don't you feel well? Eh?'

Vera pressed the palm of her hand to the cheek nearest to Ognev, and then abruptly jerked it away.

'An awful position!' she murmured, with a look of pain on her face. 'Awful!'

'How is it awful?' asked Ognev, shrugging his shoulders and not concealing his surprise. 'What's the matter?'

Still breathing hard and twitching her shoulders, Vera turned her back to him, looked at the sky for half a minute, and said:

'There is something I must say to you, Ivan Alexe-yitch ...'

'I am listening.'

'It may seem strange to you ... You will be surprised, but I don't care ...'

Ognev shrugged his shoulders once more and prepared himself to listen.

'You see ...' Verotchka began, bowing her head and fingering a ball on the fringe of her shawl. 'You see ... this is what I wanted to tell you ... You'll think it strange ... and silly, but I ... can't bear it any longer.'

Vera's words died away in an indistinct mutter and were suddenly cut short by tears. The girl hid her face in her handkerchief, bent lower than ever, and wept bitterly. Ivan Alexeyitch cleared his throat in confusion and looked about him hopelessly, at his wits' end, not knowing what to say or do. Being unused to the sight of tears, he felt his own eyes, too, beginning to smart.

'Well, what next!' he muttered helplessly. 'Vera Gavrilovna, what's this for, I should like to know? My dear girl, are you ... are you ill? Or has someone been nasty to you? Tell me, perhaps I could, so to say ... help you ...'

When, trying to console her, he ventured cautiously to remove her hands from her face, she smiled at him through her tears and said:

'I ... love you!'

These words, so simple and ordinary, were uttered in ordinary human language, but Ognev, in acute embarrassment, turned away from Vera, and got up, while his confusion was followed by terror.

The sad, warm, sentimental mood induced by leave-taking and the home-made wine suddenly vanished, and gave place to an acute and unpleasant feeling of awkwardness. He felt an inward revulsion; he looked askance at Vera, and now that by declaring her love for him she had cast off the aloofness which so adds to a woman's charm, she seemed to him, as it were, shorter, plainer, more ordinary.

'What's the meaning of it?' he thought with horror. 'But I ... do I love her or not? That's the question!'

And she breathed easily and freely now that the worst and most difficult thing was said. She, too, got up, and looking Ivan Alexeyitch straight in the face, began talking rapidly, warmly, irrepressibly.

As a man suddenly panic-stricken cannot afterwards remember the succession of sounds accompanying the catastrophe that overwhelmed him, so Ognev cannot remember Vera's words and phrases. He can only recall the meaning of what she said, and the sensation her words evoked in him. He remembers her voice, which seemed stifled and husky with emotion, and the extraordinary music and passion of her intonation. Laughing, crying, with tears glistening on her eyelashes, she told him that from the first day of their acquaintance he had struck her by his originality, his intelligence, his kind intelligent eyes, by his work and objects in life; that she loved him passionately, deeply, madly; that when coming into the house from the garden in the summer she saw his cape in the hall or heard his voice in the distance, she felt a cold shudder at her heart, a foreboding of happiness; even his slightest jokes had made her laugh; in every figure in his notebooks she saw something extraordinarily wise and grand; his knotted stick seemed to her more beautiful than the trees.

The copse and the wisps of mist and the black

ditches at the side of the road seemed hushed listening to her, whilst something strange and unpleasant was passing in Ognev's heart ... Telling him of her love, Vera was enchantingly beautiful; she spoke eloquently and passionately, but he felt neither pleasure nor gladness, as he would have liked to; he felt nothing but compassion for Vera, pity and regret that a good girl should be distressed on his account. Whether he was affected by generalizations from reading or by the insuperable habit of looking at things objectively, which so often hinders people from living, but Vera's ecstasies and suffering struck him as affected, not to be taken seriously, and at the same time rebellious feeling whispered to him that all he was hearing and seeing now, from the point of view of nature and personal happiness, was more important than any statistics and books and truths ... And he raged and blamed himself, though he did not understand exactly where he was in fault.

To complete his embarrassment, he was absolutely at a loss what to say, and yet something he must say. To say bluntly, 'I don't love you,' was beyond him, and he could not bring himself to say 'Yes,' because however much he rummaged in his heart he could not find one spark of feeling in it ...

He was silent, and she meanwhile was saying that for her there was no greater happiness than to see him, to follow him wherever he liked this very moment, to be his wife and helper, and that if he went away from her she would die of misery.

'I cannot stay here!' she said, wringing her hands. 'I am sick of the house and this wood and the air. I cannot bear the everlasting peace and aimless

life, I can't endure our colourless, pale people, who are
all as like one another as two drops of water! They
are all good-natured and warm-hearted because they
are all well-fed and know nothing of struggle or suffering ... I want to be in those big damp houses where
people suffer, embittered by work and need ...'

And this, too, seemed to Ognev affected and not to
be taken seriously. When Vera had finished he still did
not know what to say, but it was impossible to be
silent, and he muttered:

'Vera Gavrilovna, I am very grateful to you, though
I feel I've done nothing to deserve such ... feeling ...
on your part. Besides, as an honest man I ought to tell
you that ... happiness depends on equality – that is,
when both parties are ... equally in love ...'

But he was immediately ashamed of his muttering
and ceased. He felt that his face at that moment
looked stupid, guilty, blank, that it was strained and
affected ... Vera must have been able to read the
truth on his countenance, for she suddenly became
grave, turned pale, and bent her head.

'You must forgive me,' Ognev muttered, not able to
endure the silence. 'I respect you so much that ... it
pains me ...'

Vera turned sharply and walked rapidly home-
wards. Ognev followed her.

'No, don't!' said Vera, with a wave of her hand.
'Don't come; I can go alone.'

'Oh, yes ... I must see you home, anyway.'

Whatever Ognev said, it all to the last word struck
him as loathsome and flat. The feeling of guilt grew
greater at every step. He raged inwardly, clenched his
fists, and cursed his coldness and his stupidity with

women. Trying to stir his feelings, he looked at Verotchka's beautiful figure, at her hair and the traces of her little feet on the dusty road; he remembered her words and her tears, but all that only touched his heart and did not quicken his pulse.

'Ach! one can't force oneself to love,' he assured himself, and at the same time he thought, 'But shall I ever fall in love without? I am nearly thirty! I have never met anyone better than Vera and I never shall ... Oh, this premature old age! Old age at thirty!'

Vera walked on in front more and more rapidly, without looking back at him or raising her head. It seemed to him that sorrow had made her thinner and narrower in the shoulders.

'I can imagine what's going on in her heart now!' he thought, looking at her back. 'She must be ready to die with shame and mortification! My God, there's so much life, poetry, and meaning in it that it would move a stone, and I ... I am stupid and absurd!'

At the gate Vera stole a glance at him, and, shrugging and wrapping her shawl round her, walked rapidly away down the avenue.

Ivan Alexeyitch was left alone. Going back to the copse, he walked slowly, continually standing still and looking round at the gate with an expression in his whole figure that suggested that he could not believe his own memory. He looked for Vera's footprints on the road, and could not believe that the girl who had so attracted him had just declared her love, and that he had so clumsily and bluntly 'refused' her. For the first time in his life it was his lot to learn by experience how little that a man does depends on his own will, and to suffer in his own person the feelings of a decent,

kindly man who has against his will caused his neighbour cruel, undeserved anguish.

His conscience tormented him, and when Vera disappeared he felt as though he had lost something very
precious, something very near and dear, which he
could never find again. He felt that with Vera a part
of his youth had slipped away from him, and that the
moments which he had passed through so fruitlessly
would never be repeated.

When he reached the bridge he stopped and sank
into thought. He wanted to discover the reason of his
strange coldness. That it was due to something within
him and not outside himself was clear to him. He
frankly acknowledged to himself that it was not the
intellectual coldness of which clever people so often
boast, not the coldness of a conceited fool, but simply
impotence of soul, incapacity for being moved by
beauty, premature old age brought on by education,
his casual existence, struggling for a livelihood, his
homeless life in lodgings. From the bridge he walked
slowly, as it were reluctantly, into the wood. Here,
where in the dense black darkness glaring patches of
moonlight gleamed here and there, where he felt nothing except his thoughts, he longed passionately to
regain what he had lost.

And Ivan Alexeyitch remembers that he went back
again. Urging himself on with his memories, forcing
himself to picture Vera, he strode rapidly towards the
garden. There was no mist by then along the road or
in the garden, and the bright moon looked down from
the sky as though it had just been washed; only the
eastern sky was dark and misty ... Ognev remembers
his cautious steps, the dark windows, the heavy scent

of heliotrope and mignonette. His old friend Karo, wagging his tail amicably, came up to him and sniffed his hand. This was the one living creature who saw him walk two or three times round the house, stand near Vera's dark window, and with a deep sigh and a wave of his hand walk out of the garden.

An hour later he was in the town, and, worn out and exhausted, leaned his body and hot face against the gatepost of the inn as he knocked at the gate. Somewhere in the town a dog barked sleepily, and as though in response to his knock, someone clanged the hour on an iron plate near the church.

'You prowl about at night,' grumbled his host, the Old Believer, opening the door to him in a long nightgown like a woman's. 'You had better be saying your prayers instead of prowling about.'

When Ivan Alexeyitch reached his room he sank on the bed and gazed a long, long time at the light. Then he tossed his head and began packing.

VOLODYA

VOLODYA

AT five o'clock one Sunday afternoon in summer, Volodya, a plain, shy, sickly-looking lad of seventeen, was sitting in the arbour of the Shumihins' country villa, feeling dreary. His despondent thoughts flowed in three directions. In the first place, he had next day, Monday, an examination in mathematics; he knew that if he did not get through the written examination on the morrow, he would be expelled, for he had already been two years in the sixth form and had two and three-quarter marks for algebra in his annual report. In the second place, his presence at the villa of the Shumihins, a wealthy family with aristocratic pretensions, was a continual source of mortification to his amour-propre. It seemed to him that Madame Shumihin looked upon him and his *maman* as poor relations and dependents, that they laughed at his *maman* and did not respect her. He had on one occasion accidentally overheard Madame Shumihin, in the verandah, telling her cousin Anna Fyodorovna that his *maman* still tried to look young and got herself up, that she never paid her losses at cards, and had a partiality for other people's shoes and tobacco. Every day Volodya besought his *maman* not to go to the Shumihins', and drew a picture of the humiliating part she played with these gentlefolk. He tried to

127

persuade her, said rude things, but she – a frivolous, pampered woman, who had run through two fortunes, her own and her husband's, in her time, and always gravitated towards acquaintances of high rank – did not understand him, and twice a week Volodya had to accompany her to the villa he hated.

In the third place, the youth could not for one instant get rid of a strange, unpleasant feeling which was absolutely new to him ... It seemed to him that he was in love with Anna Fyodorovna, the Shumihins' cousin, who was staying with them. She was a vivacious, loud-voiced, laughter-loving, healthy, and vigorous lady of thirty, with rosy cheeks, plump shoulders, a plump round chin and a continual smile on her thin lips. She was neither young nor beautiful – Volodya knew that perfectly well; but for some reason he could not help thinking of her, looking at her while she shrugged her plump shoulders and moved her flat back as she played croquet, or after prolonged laughter and running up and down stairs, sank into a low chair, and, half closing her eyes and gasping for breath, pretended that she was stifling and could not breathe. She was married. Her husband, a staid and dignified architect, came once a week to the villa, slept soundly, and returned to town. Volodya's strange feeling had begun with his conceiving an unaccountable hatred for the architect, and feeling relieved every time he went back to town.

Now, sitting in the arbour, thinking of his examination next day, and of his *maman*, at whom they laughed, he felt an intense desire to see Nyuta (that was what the Shumihins called Anna Fyodorovna), to hear her laughter and the rustle of her dress ... This

desire was not like the pure, poetic love of which he
read in novels and about which he dreamed every
night when he went to bed; it was strange, incomprehensible; he was ashamed of it, and afraid of it as of
something very wrong and impure, something which
it was disagreeable to confess even to himself.

'It's not love,' he said to himself. 'One can't fall in
love with women of thirty who are married. It is only
a little intrigue ... Yes, an intrigue ...'

Pondering on the 'intrigue,' he thought of his
uncontrollable shyness, his lack of moustache, his
freckles, his narrow eyes, and put himself in his
imagination side by side with Nyuta, and the juxtaposition seemed to him impossible; then he made
haste to imagine himself bold, handsome, witty,
dressed in the latest fashion.

When his dreams were at their height, as he sat
huddled together and looking at the ground in a dark
corner of the arbour, he heard the sound of light footsteps. Someone was coming slowly along the avenue.
Soon the steps stopped and something white gleamed
in the entrance.

'Is there anyone here?' asked a woman's voice.

Volodya recognized the voice, and raised his head
in a fright.

'Who is here?' asked Nyuta, going into the arbour.
'Ah, it is you, Volodya? What are you doing here?
Thinking? And how can you go on thinking, thinking,
thinking? ... That's the way to go out of your mind!'

Volodya got up and looked in a dazed way at
Nyuta. She had only just come back from bathing.
Over her shoulder there was hanging a sheet and a
rough towel, and from under the white silk kerchief

on her head he could see the wet hair sticking to her forehead. There was the cool damp smell of the bath-house and of almond soap still hanging about her. She was out of breath from running quickly. The top but-ton of her blouse was undone, so that the boy saw her throat and bosom.

'Why don't you say something?' said Nyuta, look-ing Volodya up and down. 'It's not polite to be silent when a lady talks to you. What a clumsy seal you are though, Volodya! You always sit, saying nothing, thinking like some philosopher. There's not a spark of life or fire in you! You are really horrid! ... At your age you ought to be living, skipping, and jumping, chattering, flirting, falling in love.'

Volodya looked at the sheet that was held by a plump white hand, and thought ...

'He's mute,' said Nyuta, with wonder; 'it is strange, really ... Listen! Be a man! Come, you might smile at least! Phew, the horrid philosopher!' she laughed. 'But do you know, Volodya, why you are such a clumsy seal? Because you don't devote yourself to the ladies. Why don't you? It's true there are no girls here, but there is nothing to prevent your flirting with the mar-ried ladies! Why don't you flirt with me, for instance?'

Volodya listened and scratched his forehead in acute and painful irresolution.

'It's only very proud people who are silent and love solitude,' Nyuta went on, pulling his hand away from his forehead. 'You are proud, Volodya. Why do you look at me like that from under your brows? Look me straight in the face, if you please! Yes, now then, clumsy seal!'

Volodya made up his mind to speak. Wanting to

smile, he twitched his lower lip, blinked, and again put his hand to his forehead.

'I . . . I love you,' he said.

Nyuta raised her eyebrows in surprise, and laughed.

'What do I hear?' she sang, as prima-donnas sing at the opera when they hear something awful. 'What? What did you say? Say it again, say it again . . .'

'I . . . I love you!' repeated Volodya.

And without his will's having any part in his action, without reflection or understanding, he took half a step towards Nyuta and clutched her by the arm. Everything was dark before his eyes, and tears came into them. The whole world was turned into one big, rough towel which smelt of the bath-house.

'Bravo, bravo!' he heard a merry laugh. 'Why don't you speak? I want you to speak! Well?'

Seeing that he was not prevented from holding her arm, Volodya glanced at Nyuta's laughing face, and clumsily, awkwardly, put both arms round her waist, his hands meeting behind her back. He held her round the waist with both arms, while, putting her hands up to her head, showing the dimples in her elbows, she set her hair straight under the kerchief and said in a calm voice:

'You must be tactful, polite, charming, and you can only become that under feminine influence. But what a wicked, angry face you have! You must talk, laugh . . . Yes, Volodya, don't be surly; you are young and will have plenty of time for philosophizing. Come, let go of me; I am going. Let go.'

Without effort she released her waist, and, humming something, walked out of the arbour. Volodya was left alone. He smoothed his hair, smiled, and walked three times to and fro across the arbour, then he sat down on the bench and smiled again. He felt insufferably ashamed, so much so that he wondered that human shame could reach such a pitch of acuteness and intensity. Shame made him smile, gesticulate, and whisper some disconnected words.

He was ashamed that he had been treated like a small boy, ashamed of his shyness, and, most of all, that he had had the audacity to put his arms round the waist of a respectable married woman, though, as it seemed to him, he had neither through age nor by external quality, nor by social position any right to do so.

He jumped up, went out of the arbour, and, without looking round, walked into the recesses of the garden furthest from the house.

'Ah! only to get away from here as soon as possible,' he thought, clutching his head. 'My God! as soon as possible.'

The train by which Volodya was to go back with his *maman* was at eight-forty. There were three hours before the train started, but he would with pleasure have gone to the station at once without waiting for his *maman*.

At eight o'clock he went to the house. His whole figure was expressive of determination: what would be, would be! He made up his mind to go in boldly, to look them straight in the face, to speak in a loud voice, regardless of everything.

He crossed the terrace, the big hall and the drawing-room, and there stopped to take breath. He could hear them in the dining-room, drinking tea. Madame Shumihin, *maman*, and Nyuta were talking and laughing about something.

Volodya listened.

'I assure you!' said Nyuta. 'I could not believe my eyes! When he began declaring his passion and – just imagine! – put his arms round my waist, I should not have recognized him. And you know he has a way with him! When he told me he was in love with me, there was something brutal in his face, like a Circassian.'

'Really!' gasped *maman*, going off into a peal of laughter. 'Really! How he does remind me of his father!'

Volodya ran back and dashed out into the open air.

'How could they talk of it aloud!' he wondered in agony, clasping his hands and looking up to the sky in horror. 'They talk aloud in cold blood . . . and *maman* laughed! . . . *Maman!* My God, why didst Thou give me such a mother? Why?'

But he had to go to the house, come what might. He walked three times up and down the avenue, grew a little calmer, and went into the house.

'Why didn't you come in in time for tea?' Madame Shumihin asked sternly.

'I am sorry, it's . . . it's time for me to go,' he muttered, not raising his eyes. '*Maman*, it's eight o'clock!'

'You go alone, my dear,' said his *maman* languidly. 'I am staying the night with Lili. Good-bye, my dear . . . Let me make the sign of the cross over you.'

She made the sign of the cross over her son, and said in French, turning to Nyuta:

'He's rather like Lermontov . . . isn't he?'

Saying good-bye after a fashion, without looking anyone in the face, Volodya went out of the dining-room. Ten minutes later he was walking along the road to the station, and was glad of it. Now he felt neither frightened nor ashamed; he breathed freely and easily.

About half a mile from the station, he sat down on a stone by the side of the road, and gazed at the sun, which was half hidden behind a barrow. There were lights already here and there at the station, and one green light glimmered dimly, but the train was not yet in sight. It was pleasant to Volodya to sit still without moving, and to watch the evening coming little by little. The darkness of the arbour, the footsteps, the smell of the bath-house, the laughter, and the waist – all these rose with amazing vividness before his imagination, and all this was no longer so terrible and important as before.

'It's of no consequence . . . She did not pull her hand away, and laughed when I held her by the waist,' he thought. 'So she must have liked it. If she had disliked it she would have been angry . . .'

And now Volodya felt sorry that he had not had more boldness there in the arbour. He felt sorry that he was so stupidly going away, and he was by now persuaded that if the same thing happened again he would be bolder and look at it more simply.

And it would not be difficult for the opportunity to occur again. They used to stroll about for a long time after supper at the Shumihins'. If Volodya went for a walk with Nyuta in the dark garden, there would be an opportunity!

'I will go back,' he thought, 'and will go by the morning train to-morrow . . . I will say I have missed the train.'

And he turned back . . . Madame Shumihin, *maman*, Nyuta, and one of the nieces were sitting on the verandah, playing *vint*. When Volodya told them the lie that he had missed the train, they were uneasy that he might be late for the examination next day and advised him to get up early. All the while they were playing he sat on one side, greedily watching Nyuta and waiting ... He already had a plan prepared in his mind: he would go up to Nyuta in the dark, would take her by the hand, then would embrace her; there would be no need to say anything, as both of them would understand without words.

But after supper the ladies did not go for a walk in the garden, but went on playing cards. They played till one o'clock at night, and then broke up to go to bed.

'How stupid it all is!' Volodya thought with vexation as he got into bed. 'But never mind; I'll wait till to-morrow ... to-morrow in the arbour. It doesn't matter ...'

He did not attempt to go to sleep, but sat in bed, hugging his knees and thinking. All thought of the examination was hateful to him. He had already made up his mind that they would expel him, and that there was nothing terrible about his being expelled. On the contrary, it was a good thing – a very good thing, in fact. Next day he would be as free as a bird; he would put on ordinary clothes instead of his school uniform, would smoke openly, come out here, and make love to Nyuta when he liked; and he would not be a schoolboy but 'a young man.' And as for the rest of it, what is called a career, a future, that was clear; Volodya would go into the army or the telegraph service, or he would go into a chemist's shop and work his way up till he was a dispenser ... There were lots of callings. An hour or two passed, and he was still sitting and thinking ...

Towards three o'clock, when it was beginning to get
light, the door creaked cautiously and his *maman*
came into the room.

'Aren't you asleep?' she asked, yawning. 'Go to
sleep; I have only come in for a minute ... I am only
fetching the drops ...'

'What for?'

'Poor Lili has got spasms again. Go to sleep, my
child, your examination's to-morrow ...'

She took a bottle of something out of the cupboard,
went to the window, read the label, and went away.

'Marya Leontyevna, those are not the drops!' Volodya heard a woman's voice, a minute later. 'That's con-
vallaria, and Lili wants morphine. Is your son asleep?
Ask him to look for it ...'

It was Nyuta's voice. Volodya turned cold. He hurriedly put on his trousers, flung his coat over his
shoulders, and went to the door.

'Do you understand? Morphine,' Nyuta explained
in a whisper. 'There must be a label in Latin. Wake
Volodya; he will find it.'

Maman opened the door and Volodya caught sight
of Nyuta. She was wearing the same loose wrapper in
which she had gone to bathe. Her hair hung loose and
disordered on her shoulders, her face looked sleepy
and dark in the half-light ...

'Why, Volodya is not asleep,' she said. 'Volodya, look
in the cupboard for the morphine, there's a dear! What
a nuisance Lili is! She has always something the matter.'

Maman muttered something, yawned, and went
away.

'Look for it,' said Nyuta. 'Why are you standing
still?'

Volodya went to the cupboard, knelt down, and began looking through the bottles and boxes of medicine. His hands were trembling, and he had a feeling in his chest and stomach as though cold waves were running all over his inside. He felt suffocated and giddy from the smell of ether, carbolic acid, and various drugs, which he quite unnecessarily snatched up with his trembling fingers and spilled in so doing.

'I believe *maman* has gone,' he thought. 'That's a good thing ... a good thing ...'

'Will you be quick?' said Nyuta, drawling.

'In a minute ... Here, I believe this is morphine,' said Volodya, reading on one of the labels the word 'morph ...' 'Here it is!'

Nyuta was standing in the doorway in such a way that one foot was in his room and one was in the passage. She was tidying her hair, which was difficult to put in order because it was so thick and long, and looked absent-mindedly at Volodya. In her loose wrap, with her sleepy face and her hair down, in the dim light that came into the white sky not yet lit by the sun, she seemed to Volodya captivating, magnificent ... Fascinated, trembling all over, and remembering with relish how he had held that exquisite body in his arms in the arbour, he handed her the bottle and said:

'How wonderful you are!'

'What?'

She came into the room.

'What?' she asked, smiling.

He was silent and looked at her, then, just as in the arbour, he took her hand, and she looked at him with a smile and waited for what would happen next.

'I love you,' he whispered.

She left off smiling, thought a minute, and said:

'Wait a little; I think somebody is coming. Oh, these schoolboys!' she said in an undertone, going to the door and peeping out into the passage. 'No, there is no one to be seen ...'

She came back.

Then it seemed to Volodya that the room, Nyuta, the sunrise and himself – all melted together in one sensation of acute, extraordinary, incredible bliss, for which one might give up one's whole life and face eternal torments ... But half a minute passed and all that vanished. Volodya saw only a fat, plain face, distorted by an expression of repulsion, and he himself suddenly felt a loathing for what had happened.

'I must go away, though,' said Nyuta, looking at Volodya with disgust. 'What a wretched, ugly ... fie, ugly duckling!'

How unseemly her long hair, her loose wrap, her steps, her voice seemed to Volodya now! ...

' "Ugly duckling" ...' he thought after she had gone away. 'I really am ugly ... everything is ugly.'

The sun was rising, the birds were singing loudly; he could hear the gardener walking in the garden and the creaking of his wheelbarrow ... and soon afterwards he heard the lowing of the cows and the sounds of the shepherd's pipe. The sunlight and the sounds told him that somewhere in this world there is a pure, refined, poetical life. But where was it? Volodya had never heard a word of it from his *maman* or any of the people round about him.

When the footman came to wake him for the morning train, he pretended to be asleep ...

'Bother it! Damn it all!' he thought.

He got up between ten and eleven.

Combing his hair before the looking-glass, and looking at his ugly face, pale from his sleepless night, he thought:

'It's perfectly true . . . an ugly duckling!'

When *maman* saw him and was horrified that he was not at his examination, Volodya said:

'I overslept myself, *maman* . . . But don't worry, I will get a medical certificate.'

Madame Shumihin and Nyuta waked up at one o'clock. Volodya heard Madame Shumihin open her window with a bang, heard Nyuta go off into a peal of laughter in reply to her coarse voice. He saw the door open and a string of nieces and other toadies (among the latter was his *maman*) file in to lunch, caught a glimpse of Nyuta's freshly washed laughing face, and, beside her, the black brows and beard of her husband the architect, who had just arrived.

Nyuta was wearing a Little Russian dress which did not suit her at all, and made her look clumsy; the architect was making dull and vulgar jokes. The rissoles served at lunch had too much onion in them – so it seemed to Volodya. It also seemed to him that Nyuta laughed loudly on purpose, and kept glancing in his direction to give him to understand that the memory of the night did not trouble her in the least, and that she was not aware of the presence at table of the 'ugly duckling.'

At four o'clock Volodya drove to the station with his *maman*. Foul memories, the sleepless night, the prospect of expulsion from school, the stings of conscience – all roused in him now an oppressive, gloomy anger. He looked at *maman's* sharp profile, at her little nose, and at the raincoat which was a present from Nyuta, and muttered:

'Why do you powder? It's not becoming at your age! You make yourself up, don't pay your debts at cards, smoke other people's tobacco ... It's hateful! I don't love you ... I don't love you!'

He was insulting her, and she moved her little eyes about in alarm, flung up her hands, and whispered in horror:

'What are you saying, my dear! Good gracious! the coachman will hear! Be quiet or the coachman will hear! He can overhear everything.'

'I don't love you ... I don't love you!' he went on breathlessly. 'You've no soul and no morals ... Don't dare to wear that raincoat! Do you hear? Or else I will tear it into rags ...'

'Control yourself, my child,' *maman* wept; 'the coachman can hear!'

'And where is my father's fortune? Where is your money? You have wasted it all. I am not ashamed of being poor, but I am ashamed of having such a mother ... When my schoolfellows ask questions about you, I always blush.'

In the train they had to pass two stations before they reached the town. Volodya spent all the time on the little platform between two carriages and shivered all over. He did not want to go into the compartment because there the mother he hated was sitting. He hated himself, hated the ticket collectors, the smoke from the engine, the cold to which he attributed his shivering. And the heavier the weight on his heart, the more strongly he felt that somewhere in the world, among some people, there was a pure, honourable, warm, refined life, full of love, affection, gaiety, and serenity ... He felt this and was so intensely miserable that one of the passengers, after looking in his face attentively, actually asked:

'You have the toothache, I suppose?'

In the town *maman* and Volodya lived with Marya Petrovna, a lady of noble rank, who had a large flat and let rooms to boarders. *Maman* had two rooms, one with windows and two pictures in gold frames hanging on the walls, in which her bed stood and in which she lived, and a little dark room opening out of it in which Volodya lived. Here there was a sofa on which he slept, and, except that sofa, there was no other furniture; the rest of the room was entirely filled up with wicker baskets full of clothes, cardboard hat-boxes, and all sorts of rubbish, which *maman* preserved for some reason or other. Volodya prepared his lessons either in his mother's room or in the 'general room,' as the large room in which the boarders assembled at dinner-time and in the evening was called.

On reaching home he lay down on his sofa and put the quilt over him to stop his shivering. The cardboard hat-boxes, the wicker baskets, and the other rubbish, reminded him that he had not a room of his own, that he had no refuge in which he could get away from his mother, from her visitors, and from the voices that were floating up from the 'general room.' The satchel and the books lying about in the corners reminded him of the examination he had missed ... For some reason there came into his mind, quite inappropriately, Mentone, where he had lived with his father when he was seven years old; he thought of

Biarritz and two little English girls with whom he ran about on the sand ... He tried to recall to his memory the colour of the sky, the sea, the height of the waves, and his mood at the time, but he could not succeed. The English girls flitted before his imagination as though they were living; all the rest was a medley of images that floated away in confusion ...

'No; it's cold here,' thought Volodya. He got up, put on his overcoat, and went into the 'general room.'

There they were drinking tea. There were three people at the samovar: *maman*; an old lady with tortoiseshell pince-nez, who gave music lessons; and Avgustin Mihalitch, an elderly and very stout Frenchman, who was employed at a perfumery factory.

'I have had no dinner to-day,' said *maman*. 'I ought to send the maid to buy some bread.'

'Dunyasha!' shouted the Frenchman.

It appeared that the maid had been sent out somewhere by the lady of the house.

'Oh, that's of no consequence,' said the Frenchman, with a broad smile. 'I will go for some bread myself at once. Oh, it's nothing.'

He laid his strong, pungent cigar in a conspicuous place, put on his hat and went out. After he had gone away *maman* began telling the music teacher how she had been staying at the Shumihins', and how warmly they welcomed her.

'Lili Shumihin is a relation of mine, you know,' she said. 'Her late husband, General Shumihin, was a cousin of my husband. And she was a Baroness Kolb by birth ...'

'*Maman*, that's false!' said Volodya irritably. 'Why tell lies?'

He knew perfectly well that what his mother said was true; in what she was saying about General Shumihin and about Baroness Kolb there was not a word of lying, but nevertheless he felt that she was lying. There was a suggestion of falsehood in her manner of speaking, in the expression of her face, in her eyes, in everything.

'You are lying,' repeated Volodya; and he brought his fist down on the table with such force that all the crockery shook and *maman*'s tea was spilt over. 'Why do you talk about generals and baronesses? It's all lies!'

The music teacher was disconcerted, and coughed into her handkerchief, affecting to sneeze, and *maman* began to cry.

'Where can I go?' thought Volodya.

He had been in the street already; he was ashamed to go to his schoolfellows. Again, quite incongruously, he remembered the two little English girls ... He paced up and down the 'general room,' and went into Avgustin Mihalitch's room. Here there was a strong smell of ethereal oils and glycerine soap. On the table, in the window, and even on the chairs, there were a number of bottles, glasses, and wineglasses containing fluids of various colours. Volodya took up from the table a newspaper, opened it and read the title *Figaro* ... There was a strong and pleasant scent about the paper. Then he took a revolver from the table ...

'There, there! Don't take any notice of it.' The music teacher was comforting *maman* in the next room. 'He is young! Young people of his age never restrain themselves. One must resign oneself to that.'

'No, Yevgenya Andreyevna; he's too spoilt,' said

maman in a singsong voice. 'He has no one in authority over him, and I am weak and can do nothing. Oh, I am unhappy!'

Volodya put the muzzle of the revolver to his mouth, felt something like a trigger or spring, and pressed it with his finger ... Then felt something else projecting, and once more pressed it. Taking the muzzle out of his mouth, he wiped it with the lapel of his coat, looked at the lock. He had never in his life taken a weapon in his hand before ...

'I believe one ought to raise this ...' he reflected. 'Yes, it seems so.'

Avgustin Mihalitch went into the 'general room' and with a laugh began telling them about something. Volodya put the muzzle in his mouth again, pressed it with his teeth, and pressed something with his fingers. There was a sound of a shot ... Something hit Volodya in the back of his head with terrible violence, and he fell on the table with his face downwards among the bottles and glasses. Then he saw his father, as in Mentone, in a top-hat with a wide black band on it, wearing mourning for some lady, suddenly seize him by both hands, and they fell headlong into a very deep, dark pit.

Then everything was blurred and vanished.

THE KISS

THE KISS

AT eight o'clock on the evening of the twentieth of May all the six batteries of the N—— Reserve Artillery Brigade halted for the night in the village of Myestetchki on their way to camp. When the general commotion was at its height, while some officers were busily occupied around the guns, while others, gathered together in the square near the church enclosure, were listening to the quartermasters, a man in civilian dress, riding a strange horse, came into sight round the church. The little dun-coloured horse with a good neck and a short tail came, moving not straight forward, but as it were sideways, with a sort of dance step, as though it were being lashed about the legs. When he reached the officers the man on the horse took off his hat and said:

'His Excellency Lieutenant-General von Rabbek invites the gentlemen to drink tea with him this minute . . .'

The horse turned, danced, and retired sideways; the messenger raised his hat once more, and in an instant disappeared with his strange horse behind the church.

'What the devil does it mean?' grumbled some of the officers, dispersing to their quarters. 'One is sleepy, and here this Von Rabbek with his tea! We know what tea means.'

The officers of all the six batteries remembered vividly an incident of the previous year, when during manoeuvres they, together with the officers of a Cossack regiment, were in the same way invited to tea by a count who had an estate in the neighbourhood and was a retired army officer: the hospitable and genial count made much of them, fed them, and gave them drink, refused to let them go to their quarters in the village and made them stay the night. All that, of course, was very nice – nothing better could be desired, but the worst of it was, the old army officer was so carried away by the pleasure of the young men's company that till sunrise he was telling the officers anecdotes of his glorious past, taking them over the house, showing them expensive pictures, old engravings, rare guns, reading them autograph letters from great people, while the weary and exhausted officers looked and listened, longing for their beds and yawning in their sleeves; when at last their host let them go, it was too late for sleep.

Might not this Von Rabbek be just such another? Whether he were or not, there was no help for it. The officers changed their uniforms, brushed themselves, and went all together in search of the gentleman's house. In the square by the church they were told they could get to His Excellency's by the lower path – going down behind the church to the river, going along the bank to the garden, and there an avenue would take them to the house; or by the upper way – straight from the church by the road which, half a mile from the village, led right up to His Excellency's granaries. The officers decided to go by the upper way.

'What Von Rabbek is it?' they wondered on the

way. 'Surely not the one who was in command of the N—— cavalry division at Plevna?'

'No, that was not Von Rabbek, but simply Rabbe and no "von." '

'What lovely weather!'

At the first of the granaries the road divided in two: one branch went straight on and vanished in the evening darkness, the other led to the owner's house on the right. The officers turned to the right and began to speak more softly ... On both sides of the road stretched stone granaries with red roofs, heavy and sullen-looking, very much like barracks of a district town. Ahead of them gleamed the windows of the manor-house.

'A good omen, gentlemen,' said one of the officers. 'Our setter is the foremost of all; no doubt he scents game ahead of us! ...'

Lieutenant Lobytko, who was walking in front, a tall and stalwart fellow, though entirely without moustache (he was over five-and-twenty, yet for some reason there was no sign of hair on his round, well-fed face), renowned in the brigade for his peculiar faculty for divining the presence of women at a distance, turned round and said:

'Yes, there must be women here; I feel that by instinct.'

On the threshold the officers were met by Von Rabbek himself, a comely-looking man of sixty in civilian dress. Shaking hands with his guests, he said that he was very glad and happy to see them, but begged them earnestly for God's sake to excuse him for not asking them to stay the night; two sisters with their children, some brothers, and some neighbours, had

come on a visit to him, so that he had not one spare
room left.

The General shook hands with everyone, made his
apologies, and smiled, but it was evident by his face
that he was by no means so delighted as their last
year's count, and that he had invited the officers
simply because, in his opinion, it was a social obligation to do so. And the officers themselves, as they
walked up the softly carpeted stairs, as they listened
to him, felt that they had been invited to this house
simply because it would have been awkward not to
invite them; and at the sight of the footmen, who
hastened to light the lamps in the entrance below and
in the anteroom above, they began to feel as though
they had brought uneasiness and discomfort into the
house with them. In a house in which two sisters and
their children, brothers, and neighbours were gathered
together, probably on account of some family festiv-
ity, or event, how could the presence of nineteen
unknown officers possibly be welcome?

At the entrance to the drawing-room the officers
were met by a tall, graceful old lady with black eyebrows and a long face, very much like the Empress
Eugénie. Smiling graciously and majestically, she said
she was glad and happy to see her guests, and apologized that her husband and she were on this occasion
unable to invite *messieurs les officiers* to stay the
night. From her beautiful majestic smile which instantly vanished from her face every time she turned
away from her guests, it was evident that she had seen
numbers of officers in her day, that she was in no
humour for them now, and if she invited them to her
house and apologized for not doing more, it was only

because her breeding and position in society required it of her.

When the officers went into the big dining-room, there were about a dozen people, men and ladies, young and old, sitting at tea at the end of a long table. A group of men was dimly visible behind their chairs, wrapped in a haze of cigar smoke; and in the midst of them stood a lanky young man with red whiskers, talking loudly, with a lisp, in English. Through a door beyond the group could be seen a light room with pale blue furniture.

'Gentlemen, there are so many of you that it is impossible to introduce you all!' said the General in a loud voice, trying to sound very cheerful. 'Make each other's acquaintance, gentlemen, without any ceremony!'

The officers – some with very serious and even stern faces, others with forced smiles, and all feeling extremely awkward – somehow made their bows and sat down to tea.

The most ill at ease of them all was Ryabovitch – a little officer in spectacles, with sloping shoulders, and whiskers like a lynx's. While some of his comrades assumed a serious expression, while others wore forced smiles, his face, his lynx-like whiskers, and spectacles seemed to say: 'I am the shyest, most modest, and most undistinguished officer in the whole brigade!' At first, on going into the room and sitting down to the table, he could not fix his attention on any one face or object. The faces, the dresses, the cut-glass decanters of brandy, the steam from the glasses, the moulded cornices – all blended in one general impression that inspired in Ryabovitch alarm and a desire to hide his head. Like a lecturer making his first appearance before the public, he saw everything that was before his eyes, but apparently only had a dim understanding of it (among physiologists this condition, when the subject sees but does not understand, is called psychical blindness). After a little while, growing accustomed to his surroundings, Ryabovitch saw clearly and began to observe. As a shy man, unused to society, what struck him first was that in which he had always been deficient – namely, the extraordinary boldness of his new acquaintances. Von Rabbek, his wife, two elderly ladies, a young lady in a lilac dress, and the young man with the red whiskers, who was, it appeared, a younger son of Von Rabbek, very cleverly, as though they had rehearsed it beforehand, took seats between the officers, and at once got up a heated discussion in which the visitors could not help taking part. The lilac young lady hotly asserted that the artillery had a much better time than the cavalry and the infantry, while Von Rabbek and the elderly ladies maintained the opposite. A brisk interchange of talk followed. Ryabovitch watched the lilac young lady who argued so hotly about what was unfamiliar and utterly uninteresting to her, and watched artificial smiles come and go on her face.

Von Rabbek and his family skilfully drew the officers into the discussion, and meanwhile kept a sharp lookout over their glasses and mouths, to see whether all of them were drinking, whether all had enough sugar, why someone was not eating cakes or not drinking brandy. And the longer Ryabovitch watched and listened, the more he was attracted by this insincere but splendidly disciplined family.

After tea the officers went into the drawing-room. Lieutenant Lobytko's instinct had not deceived him. There were a great number of girls and young married ladies. The 'setter' lieutenant was soon standing by a very young, fair girl in a black dress, and, bending down to her jauntily, as though leaning on an unseen sword, smiled and shrugged his shoulders coquettishly. He probably talked very interesting nonsense, for the fair girl looked at his well-fed face condescendingly and asked indifferently, 'Really?' And from that uninterested 'Really?' the setter, had he been intelligent, might have concluded that she would never call him to heel.

The piano struck up; the melancholy strains of a valse floated out of the wide open windows, and everyone, for some reason, remembered that it was spring, a May evening. Everyone was conscious of the fragrance of roses, of lilac, and of the young leaves of the poplar. Ryabovitch, in whom the brandy he had drunk made itself felt, under the influence of the music stole a glance towards the window, smiled, and began watching the movements of the women, and it seemed to him that the smell of roses, of poplars, and lilac came not from the garden, but from the ladies' faces and dresses.

Von Rabbek's son invited a scraggy-looking young lady to dance, and waltzed round the room twice with her. Lobytko, gliding over the parquet floor, flew up to the lilac young lady and whirled her away. Dancing began ... Ryabovitch stood near the door among those who were not dancing and looked on. He had never once danced in his whole life, and he had never once in his life put his arm round the waist of a respectable woman. He was highly delighted that a man should in the sight of all take a girl he did not know round the waist and offer her his shoulder to put her hand on, but he could not imagine himself in the position of such a man. There were times when he envied the boldness and swagger of his companions and was inwardly wretched; the consciousness that he was timid, that he was round-shouldered and uninteresting, that he had a long waist and lynx-like whiskers, had deeply mortified him, but with years he had grown used to this feeling, and now, looking at his comrades dancing or loudly talking, he no longer envied them, but only felt touched and mournful.

When the quadrille began, young Von Rabbek came up to those who were not dancing and invited two officers to have a game at billiards. The officers accepted and went with him out of the drawing-room. Ryabovitch, having nothing to do and wishing to take part in the general movement, slouched after them. From the big drawing-room they went into the little drawing-room, then into a narrow corridor with a glass roof, and thence into a room in which on their entrance three sleepy-looking footmen jumped up quickly from the sofa. At last, after passing through a long succession of rooms, young Von Rabbek and the officers came into a small room where there was a billiard-table. They began to play.

Ryabovitch, who had never played any game but cards, stood near the billiard-table and looked indifferently at the players, while they in unbuttoned coats, with cues in their hands, stepped about, made puns, and kept shouting out unintelligible words. The players took no notice of him, and only now and then one of them, shoving him with his elbow or accidentally touching him with the end of his cue, would turn round and say 'Pardon!' Before the first game was over he was weary of it, and began to feel he was not wanted and in the way ... He felt disposed to return to the drawing-room, and he went out.

On his way back he met with a little adventure. When he had gone half-way he noticed he had taken a wrong turning. He distinctly remembered that he ought to meet three sleepy footmen on his way, but he had passed five or six rooms, and those sleepy figures seemed to have vanished into the earth. Noticing his mistake, he walked back a little way and turned to the right; he found himself in a little dark room which he had not seen on his way to the billiard-room. After standing there a little while, he resolutely opened the first door that met his eyes and walked into an absolutely dark room. Straight in front could be seen the crack in the doorway through which there was a gleam of vivid light; from the other side of the door came the muffled sound of a melancholy mazurka. Here, too, as in the drawing-room, the windows were wide open and there was a smell of poplars, lilac and roses ...

Ryabovitch stood still in hesitation ... At that moment, to his surprise, he heard hurried footsteps and the rustling of a dress, a breathless feminine voice whispered 'At last!' And two soft, fragrant, unmistakably feminine arms were clasped about his neck; a warm cheek was pressed to his cheek, and simultaneously there was the sound of a kiss. But at once the bestower of the kiss uttered a faint shriek and skipped back from him, as it seemed to Ryabovitch, with aversion. He, too, almost shrieked and rushed towards the gleam of light at the door ...

When he went back into the drawing-room his heart was beating and his hands were trembling so noticeably that he made haste to hide them behind his back. At first he was tormented by shame and dread that the whole drawing-room knew that he had just been kissed and embraced by a woman. He shrank into himself and looked uneasily about him, but as he became convinced that people were dancing and talking as calmly as ever, he gave himself up entirely to the new sensation which he had never experienced before in his life. Something strange was happening to him ... His neck, round which soft, fragrant arms had so lately been clasped, seemed to him to be anointed with oil; on his left cheek near his moustache where the unknown had kissed him there was a faint chilly tingling sensation as from peppermint drops, and the more he rubbed the place the more distinct was the chilly sensation; all over, from head to foot, he was full of a strange new feeling which grew stronger and stronger ... He wanted to dance, to talk, to run into the garden, to laugh aloud ... He quite forgot that he was round-shouldered and uninteresting, that he had lynx-like whiskers and an 'undistinguished appearance' (that was how his appearance had been described by some ladies whose conversation he had accidentally overheard). When Von Rabbek's wife happened to pass by him, he gave her such a broad and friendly smile that she stood still and looked at him inquiringly.

'I like your house immensely!' he said, setting his spectacles straight.

The General's wife smiled and said that the house had belonged to her father; then she asked whether his parents were living, whether he had long been in the army, why he was so thin, and so on ... After receiving answers to her questions, she went on, and after his conversation with her his smiles were more friendly than ever, and he thought he was surrounded by splendid people ...

At supper Ryabovitch ate mechanically everything offered him, drank, and without listening to anything, tried to understand what had just happened to him ... The adventure was of a mysterious and romantic character, but it was not difficult to explain it. No doubt some girl or young married lady had arranged a tryst with someone in the dark room; had waited a long time, and being nervous and excited had taken Ryabovitch for her hero; this was the more probable as Ryabovitch had stood still hesitating in the dark room, so that he, too, had seemed like a person expecting something ... This was how Ryabovitch explained to himself the kiss he had received.

'And who is she?' he wondered, looking round at the women's faces. 'She must be young, for elderly ladies don't give rendezvous. That she was a lady, one could tell by the rustle of her dress, her perfume, her voice ...'

His eyes rested on the lilac young lady, and he thought her very attractive; she had beautiful shoulders and arms, a clever face, and a delightful voice. Ryabovitch, looking at her, hoped that she and no one else was his unknown ... But she laughed somehow artificially and wrinkled up her long nose, which seemed to him to make her look old. Then he turned his eyes upon the fair girl in a black dress. She was younger, simpler, and more genuine, had a charming brow, and drank very daintily out of her wineglass. Ryabovitch now hoped that it was she. But soon he began to think her face flat and fixed his eyes upon the one next to her.

'It's difficult to guess,' he thought, musing. 'If one takes the shoulders and arms of the lilac one only, adds the brow of the fair one and the eyes of the one on the left of Lobytko, then ...'

He made a combination of these things in his mind and so formed the image of the girl who had kissed him, the image that he wanted her to have, but could not find at the table ...

After supper, replete and exhilarated, the officers began to take leave and say thank you. Von Rabbek and his wife began again apologizing that they could not ask them to stay the night.

'Very, very glad to have met you, gentlemen,' said Von Rabbek, and this time sincerely (probably because people are far more sincere and good-humoured at speeding their parting guests than on meeting them). 'Delighted. I hope you will come on your way back! Don't stand on ceremony! Where are you going? Do you want to go by the upper way? No, go across the garden; it's nearer here by the lower way.'

The officers went out into the garden. After the bright light and the noise the garden seemed very dark and quiet. They walked in silence all the way to the gate. They were a little drunk, pleased, and in good spirits, but the darkness and silence made them thoughtful for a minute. Probably the same idea occurred to each one of them as to Ryabovitch: would

there ever come a time for them when, like Von Rabbek, they would have a large house, a family, a garden
– when they, too, would be able to welcome people,
even though insincerely, feed them, make them drunk
and contented?

Going out of the garden gate, they all began talking at once and laughing loudly about nothing. They
were walking now along the little path that led down
to the river, and then ran along the water's edge,
winding round the bushes on the bank, the pools,
and the willows that overhung the water. The bank
and the path were scarcely visible, and the other
bank was entirely plunged in darkness. Stars were
reflected here and there on the dark water; they
quivered and were broken up on the surface – and
from that alone it could be seen that the river was
flowing rapidly. It was still. Drowsy curlews cried
plaintively on the further bank, and in one of the
bushes on the nearest side a nightingale was trilling
loudly, taking no notice of the crowd of officers. The
officers stood round the bush, touched it, but the
nightingale went on singing.

'What a fellow!' they exclaimed approvingly. 'We
stand beside him and he takes not a bit of notice!
What a rascal!'

At the end of the way the path went uphill, and,
skirting the church enclosure, turned into the road.
Here the officers, tired with walking uphill, sat down
and lighted their cigarettes. On the other side of the
river a murky red fire came into sight, and having
nothing better to do, they spent a long time in discussing whether it was a camp fire or a light in a window, or something else ... Ryabovitch, too, looked at

the light, and he fancied that the light looked and winked at him, as though it knew about the kiss.

On reaching his quarters, Ryabovitch undressed as quickly as possible and got into bed. Lobytko and Lieutenant Merzlyakov – a peaceable, silent fellow, who was considered in his own circle a highly educated officer, and was always, whenever it was possible, reading the 'Vyestnik Evropi,' which he carried about with him everywhere – were quartered in the same hut with Ryabovitch. Lobytko undressed, walked up and down the room for a long while with the air of a man who has not been satisfied, and sent his orderly for beer. Merzlyakov got into bed, put a candle by his pillow, and plunged into reading the 'Vyestnik Evropi.'

'Who was she?' Ryabovitch wondered, looking at the smoky ceiling.

His neck still felt as though he had been anointed with oil, and there was still the chilly sensation near his mouth as though from peppermint drops. The shoulders and arms of the young lady in lilac, the brow and the truthful eyes of the fair girl in black, waists, dresses, and brooches, floated through his imagination. He tried to fix his attention on these images, but they danced about, broke up and flickered. When these images vanished altogether from the broad dark background which every man sees when he closes his eyes, he began to hear hurried footsteps, the rustle of skirts, the sound of a kiss and – an intense groundless joy took possession of him ... Abandoning himself to this joy, he heard the orderly return and announce that there was no beer. Lobytko was terribly indignant, and began pacing up and down again.

'Well, isn't he an idiot?' he kept saying, stopping first before Ryabovitch and then before Merzlyakov. 'What a fool and a dummy a man must be not to get hold of any beer! Eh? Isn't he a scoundrel?'

'Of course you can't get beer here,' said Merzlyakov, not removing his eyes from the 'Vyestnik Evropi.'

'Oh! Is that your opinion?' Lobytko persisted. 'Lord have mercy upon us, if you dropped me on the moon I'd find you beer and women directly! I'll go and find some at once ... You may call me an impostor if I don't!'

He spent a long time in dressing and pulling on his high boots, then finished smoking his cigarette in silence and went out.

'Rabbek, Grabbek, Labbek,' he muttered, stopping in the outer room. 'I don't care to go alone, damn it all! Ryabovitch, wouldn't you like to go for a walk? Eh?'

Receiving no answer, he returned, slowly undressed, and got into bed. Merzlyakov sighed, put the 'Vyestnik Evropi' away, and put out the light.

'H'm! ...' muttered Lobytko, lighting a cigarette in the dark.

Ryabovitch pulled the bed-clothes over his head, curled himself up in bed, and tried to gather together the floating images in his mind and to combine them into one whole. But nothing came of it. He soon fell asleep, and his last thought was that someone had caressed him and made him happy – that something extraordinary, foolish, but joyful and delightful, had come into his life. The thought did not leave him even in his sleep.

When he woke up the sensations of oil on his neck

and the chill of peppermint about his lips had gone, but joy flooded his heart just as the day before. He looked enthusiastically at the window-frames, gilded by the light of the rising sun, and listened to the movement of the passers-by in the street. People were talking loudly close to the window. Lebedetsky, the commander of Ryabovitch's battery, who had only just overtaken the brigade, was talking to his sergeant at the top of his voice, being always accustomed to shout.

'What else?' shouted the commander.

'When they were shoeing yesterday, your high nobility, they drove a nail into Pigeon's hoof. The vet. put on clay and vinegar; they are leading him apart now. And also, your honour, Artemyev got drunk yesterday, and the lieutenant ordered him to be put in the limber of a spare gun-carriage.'

The sergeant reported that Karpov had forgotten the new cords for the trumpets and the rings for the tents, and that their honours, the officers, had spent the previous evening visiting General Von Rabbek. In the middle of this conversation the red-bearded face of Lebedetsky appeared in the window. He screwed up his short-sighted eyes, looking at the sleepy faces of the officers, and said good-morning to them.

'Is everything all right?' he asked.

'One of the horses has a sore neck from the new collar,' answered Lobytko, yawning.

The commander sighed, thought a moment, and said in a loud voice:

'I am thinking of going to see Alexandra Yev-grafovna. I must call on her. Well, good-bye. I shall catch you up in the evening.'

A quarter of an hour later the brigade set off on its way. When it was moving along the road by the granaries, Ryabovitch looked at the house on the right. The blinds were down in all the windows. Evidently the household was still asleep. The one who had kissed Ryabovitch the day before was asleep, too. He tried to imagine her asleep. The wide-open windows of the bedroom, the green branches peeping in, the morning freshness, the scent of the poplars, lilac, and roses, the bed, a chair, and on it the skirts that had rustled the day before, the little slippers, the little watch on the table – all this he pictured to himself clearly and distinctly, but the features of the face, the sweet sleepy smile, just what was characteristic and important, slipped through his imagination like quicksilver through the fingers. When he had ridden on half a mile, he looked back: the yellow church, the house, and the river, were all bathed in light; the river with its bright green banks, with the blue sky reflected in it and glints of silver in the sunshine here and there, was very beautiful. Ryabovitch gazed for the last time at Myestetchki, and he felt as sad as though he were parting with something very near and dear to him.

And before him on the road lay nothing but long familiar, uninteresting pictures . . . To right and to left, fields of young rye and buckwheat with rooks hopping about in them. If one looked ahead, one saw dust and the backs of men's heads; if one looked back, one saw the same dust and faces . . . Foremost of all marched four men with sabres – this was the vanguard. Next, behind, the crowd of singers, and behind them the trumpeters on horseback. The vanguard and the

chorus of singers, like torch-bearers in a funeral procession, often forgot to keep the regulation distance
and pushed a long way ahead . . . Ryabovitch was with
the first cannon of the fifth battery. He could see all
the four batteries moving in front of him. For anyone
not a military man this long tedious procession of a
moving brigade seems an intricate and unintelligible
muddle; one cannot understand why there are so
many people round one cannon, and why it is drawn
by so many horses in such a strange network of har-
ness, as though it really were so terrible and heavy. To
Ryabovitch it was all perfectly comprehensible and
therefore uninteresting. He had known for ever so long
why at the head of each battery there rode a stalwart
bombardier, and why he was called a bombardier;
immediately behind this bombardier could be seen
the horsemen of the first and then of the middle units.
Ryabovitch knew that the horses on which they rode,
those on the left, were called one name, while those
of the right were called another – it was extremely
uninteresting. Behind the horsemen came two shaft-
horses. On one of them sat a rider with the dust of yesterday on his back and a clumsy and funny-looking
piece of wood on his leg. Ryabovitch knew the object
of this piece of wood, and did not think it funny. All
the riders waved their whips mechanically and
shouted from time to time. The cannon itself was ugly.
On the fore part lay sacks of oats covered with canvas,
and the cannon itself was hung all over with kettles,
soldiers' knapsacks, bags, and looked like some small
harmless animal surrounded for some unknown
reason by men and horses. To the leeward of it
marched six men, the gunners, swinging their arms.

After the cannon there came again more bombardiers, riders, shaft-horses, and behind them another cannon, as ugly and unimpressive as the first. After the second followed a third, a fourth; near the fourth an officer, and so on. There were six batteries in all in the brigade, and four cannon in each battery. The procession covered half a mile; it ended in a string of waggons near which an extremely attractive creature – the ass, Magar, brought by a battery commander from Turkey – paced pensively with his long-eared head drooping.

Ryabovitch looked indifferently before and behind, at the backs of heads and at faces; at any other time he would have been half asleep, but now he was entirely absorbed in his new agreeable thoughts. At first when the brigade was setting off on the march he tried to persuade himself that the incident of the kiss could only be interesting as a mysterious little adventure, that it was in reality trivial, and to think of it seriously, to say the least of it, was stupid; but now he bade farewell to logic and gave himself up to dreams . . . At one moment he imagined himself in Von Rabbek's drawing-room beside a girl who was like the young lady in lilac and the fair girl in black; then he would close his eyes and see himself with another, entirely unknown girl, whose features were very vague. In his imagination he talked, caressed her, leaned on her shoulder, pictured war, separation, then meeting again, supper with his wife, children . . .

'Brakes on!' the word of command rang out every time they went downhill.

He, too, shouted 'Brakes on!' and was afraid this shout would disturb his reverie and bring him back to reality . . .

As they passed by some landowner's estate Ryabovitch looked over the fence into the garden. A long avenue, straight as a ruler, strewn with yellow sand and bordered with young birch-trees, met his eyes ... With the eagerness of a man given up to dreaming, he pictured to himself little feminine feet tripping along yellow sand, and quite unexpectedly had a clear vision in his imagination of the girl who had kissed him and whom he had succeeded in picturing to himself the evening before at supper. This image remained in his brain and did not desert him again.

At midday there was a shout in the rear near the string of waggons:

'Easy! Eyes to the left! Officers!'

The General of the brigade drove by in a carriage with a pair of white horses. He stopped near the second battery, and shouted something which no one understood. Several officers, among them Ryabovitch, galloped up to him.

'Well?' asked the General, blinking his red eyes. 'Are there any sick?'

Receiving an answer, the General, a little skinny man, chewed, thought for a moment and said, addressing one of the officers:

'One of your drivers of the third cannon has taken off his leg-guard and hung it on the fore part of the cannon, the rascal. Reprimand him.'

He raised his eyes to Ryabovitch and went on:

'It seems to me your front strap is too long.'

Making a few other tedious remarks, the General looked at Lobytko and grinned.

'You look very melancholy to-day, Lieutenant Lobytko,' he said. 'Are you pining for Madame Lopuhov? Eh? Gentlemen, he is pining for Madame Lopuhov.'

The lady in question was a very stout and tall person who had long passed her fortieth year. The General, who had a predilection for solid ladies, whatever their ages, suspected a similar taste in his officers. The officers smiled respectfully. The General, delighted at having said something very amusing and biting, laughed loudly, touched his coachman's back, and saluted. The carriage rolled on ...

'All I am dreaming about now which seems to me so impossible and unearthly is really quite an ordinary thing,' thought Ryabovitch, looking at the clouds of dust racing after the General's carriage. 'It's all very ordinary, and everyone goes through it ... That General, for instance, has once been in love; now he is married and has children. Captain Vahter, too, is married and beloved, though the nape of his neck is very red and ugly and he has no waist ... Salmanov is coarse and very Tatar, but he has had a love affair that has ended in marriage ... I am the same as everyone else, and I, too, shall have the same experience as everyone else, sooner or later ...'

And the thought that he was an ordinary person, and that his life was ordinary, delighted him and gave him courage. He pictured *her* and his happiness as he pleased, and put no rein on his imagination ...

When the brigade reached their halting-place in the evening, and the officers were resting in their tents, Ryabovitch, Merzlyakov, and Lobytko were sitting round a box having supper. Merzlyakov ate without haste, and, as he munched deliberately, read the 'Vyestnik Evropi,' which he held on his knees.

Lobytko talked incessantly and kept filling up his glass with beer, and Ryabovitch, whose head was confused from dreaming all day long, drank and said nothing. After three glasses he got a little drunk, felt weak, and had an irresistible desire to impart his new sensations to his comrades.

'A strange thing happened to me at those Von Rabbeks',' he began, trying to put an indifferent and ironical tone into his voice. 'You know I went into the billiard-room . . .'

He began describing very minutely the incident of the kiss, and a moment later relapsed into silence . . . In the course of that moment he had told everything, and it surprised him dreadfully to find how short a time it took him to tell it. He had imagined that he could have been telling the story of the kiss till next morning. Listening to him, Lobytko, who was a great liar and consequently believed no one, looked at him sceptically and laughed. Merzlyakov twitched his eyebrows and, without removing his eyes from the 'Vyestnik Evropi,' said:

'That's an odd thing! How strange! . . . throws herself on a man's neck, without addressing him by name . . . She must be some sort of hysterical neurotic.'

'Yes, she must,' Ryabovitch agreed.

'A similar thing once happened to me,' said Lobytko, assuming a scared expression. 'I was going last year to Kovno . . . I took a second-class ticket. The train was crammed, and it was impossible to sleep. I gave the guard half a rouble; he took my luggage and led me to another compartment . . . I lay down and covered myself with a rug . . . It was dark, you understand. Suddenly I felt someone touch me on

the shoulder and breathe in my face. I made a movement with my hand and felt somebody's elbow ...
I opened my eyes and only imagine – a woman. Black
eyes, lips red as a prime salmon, nostrils breathing
passionately – a bosom like a buffer ...'

'Excuse me,' Merzlyakov interrupted calmly,
'I understand about the bosom, but how could you
see the lips if it was dark?'

Lobytko began trying to put himself right and
laughing at Merzlyakov's unimaginativeness. It made
Ryabovitch wince. He walked away from the box, got
into bed, and vowed never to confide again.

Camp life began ... The days flowed by, one very
much like another. All those days Ryabovitch felt,
thought, and behaved as though he were in love.
Every morning when his orderly handed him water to
wash with, and he sluiced his head with cold water, he
thought there was something warm and delightful in
his life.

In the evenings when his comrades began talking
of love and women, he would listen, and draw up
closer; and he wore the expression of a soldier when
he hears the description of a battle in which he has
taken part. And on the evenings when the officers,
out on the spree with the setter – Lobytko – at their
head, made Don Juan excursions to the 'suburb,' and
Ryabovitch took part in such excursions, he always
was sad, felt profoundly guilty, and inwardly begged
her forgiveness ... In hours of leisure or on sleepless
nights, when he felt moved to recall his childhood,
his father and mother – everything near and dear,
in fact, he invariably thought of Myestetchki, the
strange horse, Von Rabbek, his wife who was like the

Empress Eugénie, the dark room, the crack of light at the door ...

On the thirty-first of August he went back from the camp, not with the whole brigade, but with only two batteries of it. He was dreaming and excited all the way, as though he were going back to his native place. He had an intense longing to see again the strange horse, the church, the insincere family of the Von Rabbeks, the dark room. The 'inner voice,' which so often deceives lovers, whispered to him for some reason that he would be sure to see her ... and he was tortured by the questions, How he should meet her? What he would talk to her about? Whether she had forgotten the kiss? If the worst came to the worst, he thought, even if he did not meet her, it would be a pleasure to him merely to go through the dark room and recall the past ...

Towards evening there appeared on the horizon the familiar church and white granaries. Ryabovitch's heart beat ... He did not hear the officer who was riding beside him and saying something to him, he forgot everything, and looked eagerly at the river shining in the distance, at the roof of the house, at the dovecote round which the pigeons were circling in the light of the setting sun.

When they reached the church and were listening to the billeting orders, he expected every second that a man on horseback would come round the church enclosure and invite the officers to tea, but ... the billeting orders were read, the officers were in haste to go on to the village, and the man on horseback did not appear.

'Von Rabbek will hear at once from the peasants

that we have come and will send for us,' thought Ryabovitch, as he went into the hut, unable to understand
why a comrade was lighting a candle and why the
orderlies were hurriedly setting samovars ...

A painful uneasiness took possession of him. He lay
down, then got up and looked out of the window to
see whether the messenger were coming. But there
was no sign of him.

He lay down again, but half an hour later he got up,
and, unable to restrain his uneasiness, went into the
street and strode towards the church. It was dark and
deserted in the square near the church ... Three soldiers were standing silent in a row where the road
began to go downhill. Seeing Ryabovitch, they roused
themselves and saluted. He returned the salute and
began to go down the familiar path.

On the further side of the river the whole sky was
flooded with crimson: the moon was rising; two peasant women, talking loudly, were picking cabbage in
the kitchen garden; behind the kitchen garden there
were some dark huts ... And everything on the near
side of the river was just as it had been in May: the
path, the bushes, the willows overhanging the water
... but there was no sound of the brave nightingale,
and no scent of poplar and fresh grass.

Reaching the garden, Ryabovitch looked in at the
gate. The garden was dark and still ... He could see
nothing but the white stems of the nearest birch-trees
and a little bit of the avenue; all the rest melted
together into a dark blur. Ryabovitch looked and
listened eagerly, but after waiting for a quarter of an
hour without hearing a sound or catching a glimpse of
a light, he trudged back ...

He went down to the river. The General's bath-house and the bath-sheets on the rail of the little bridge showed white before him ... He went on to the bridge, stood a little, and, quite unnecessarily, touched the sheets. They felt rough and cold. He looked down at the water ... The river ran rapidly and with a faintly audible gurgle round the piles of the bath-house. The red moon was reflected near the left bank; little ripples ran over the reflection, stretching it out, breaking it into bits, and seemed trying to carry it away ...

'How stupid, how stupid!' thought Ryabovitch, looking at the running water. 'How unintelligent it all is!'

Now that he expected nothing, the incident of the kiss, his impatience, his vague hopes and disappointment, presented themselves in a clear light. It no longer seemed to him strange that he had not seen the General's messenger, and that he would never see the girl who had accidentally kissed him instead of someone else; on the contrary, it would have been strange if he had seen her ...

The water was running, he knew not where or why, just as it did in May. In May it had flowed into the great river, from the great river into the sea; then it had risen in vapour, turned into rain, and perhaps the very same water was running now before Ryabovitch's eyes again ... What for? Why?

And the whole world, the whole of life, seemed to Ryabovitch an unintelligible, aimless jest ... And turning his eyes from the water and looking at the sky, he remembered again how fate in the person of an unknown woman had by chance caressed him, he remembered his summer dreams and fancies, and his life struck him as extraordinarily meagre, poverty-stricken, and colourless ...

When he went back to his hut he did not find one of his comrades. The orderly informed him that they had all gone to 'General von Rabbek's, who had sent a messenger on horseback to invite them ...'

For an instant there was a flash of joy in Ryabovitch's heart, but he quenched it at once, got into bed, and in his wrath with his fate, as though to spite it, did not go to the General's.

SLEEPY

SLEEPY

NIGHT. Varka, the little nurse, a girl of thirteen, is rocking the cradle in which the baby is lying, and humming hardly audibly:

> 'Hush-a-bye, my baby wee,
> While I sing a song for thee.'

A little green lamp is burning before the ikon; there is a string stretched from one end of the room to the other, on which baby-clothes and a pair of big black trousers are hanging. There is a big patch of green on the ceiling from the ikon lamp, and the baby-clothes and the trousers throw long shadows on the stove, on the cradle, and on Varka ... When the lamp begins to flicker, the green patch and the shadows come to life, and are set in motion, as though by the wind. It is stuffy. There is a smell of cabbage soup, and of the inside of a boot-shop.

The baby is crying. For a long while he has been hoarse and exhausted with crying; but he still goes on screaming, and there is no knowing when he will stop. And Varka is sleepy. Her eyes are glued together, her head droops, her neck aches. She cannot move her eyelids or her lips, and she feels as though her face is dried and wooden, as though her head has become as small as the head of a pin.

'Hush-a-bye, my baby wee,' she hums, 'while I cook the groats for thee . . .'

A cricket is churring in the stove. Through the door in the next room the master and the apprentice Afanasy are snoring ... The cradle creaks plaintively, Varka murmurs – and it all blends into that soothing music of the night to which it is so sweet to listen, when one is lying in bed. Now that music is merely irritating and oppressive, because it goads her to sleep, and she must not sleep; if Varka – God forbid! – should fall asleep, her master and mistress would beat her.

The lamp flickers. The patch of green and the shadows are set in motion, forcing themselves on Varka's fixed, half-open eyes, and in her half slumbering brain are fashioned into misty visions. She sees dark clouds chasing one another over the sky, and screaming like the baby. But then the wind blows, the clouds are gone, and Varka sees a broad high road covered with liquid mud; along the high road stretch files of wagons, while people with wallets on their backs are trudging along and shadows flit backwards and forwards; on both sides she can see forests through the cold harsh mist. All at once the people with their wallets and their shadows fall on the ground in the liquid mud. 'What is that for?' Varka asks. 'To sleep, to sleep!' they answer her. And they fall sound asleep, and sleep sweetly, while crows and magpies sit on the telegraph wires, scream like the baby, and try to wake them.

'Hush-a-bye, my baby wee, and I will sing a song to thee,' murmurs Varka, and now she sees herself in a dark stuffy hut.

Her dead father, Yefim Stepanov, is tossing from side to side on the floor. She does not see him, but she hears him moaning and rolling on the floor from pain. 'His guts have burst,' as he says; the pain is so violent that he cannot utter a single word, and can only draw in his breath and clack his teeth like the rattling of a drum:

'Boo—boo—boo—boo . . .'

Her mother, Pelageya, has run to the master's house to say that Yefim is dying. She has been gone a long time, and ought to be back. Varka lies awake on the stove, and hears her father's 'boo—boo—boo.' And then she hears someone has driven up to the hut. It is a young doctor from the town, who has been sent from the big house where he is staying on a visit. The doctor comes into the hut; he cannot be seen in the darkness, but he can be heard coughing and rattling the door.

'Light a candle,' he says.

'Boo—boo—boo,' answers Yefim.

Pelageya rushes to the stove and begins looking for the broken pot with the matches. A minute passes in silence. The doctor, feeling in his pocket, lights a match.

'In a minute, sir, in a minute,' says Pelageya. She rushes out of the hut, and soon afterwards comes back with a bit of candle.

Yefim's cheeks are rosy and his eyes are shining, and there is a peculiar keenness in his glance, as though he were seeing right through the hut and the doctor.

'Come, what is it? What are you thinking about?' says the doctor, bending down to him. 'Aha! have you had this long?'

'What? Dying, your honour, my hour has come ...
I am not to stay among the living ...'

'Don't talk nonsense! We will cure you!'

'That's as you please, your honour, we humbly
thank you, only we understand ... Since death has
come, there it is.'

The doctor spends a quarter of an hour over Yefim,
then he gets up and says:

'I can do nothing. You must go into the hospital,
there they will operate on you. Go at once ... You
must go! It's rather late, they will all be asleep in the
hospital, but that doesn't matter, I will give you a
note. Do you hear?'

'Kind sir, but what can he go in?' says Pelageya.
'We have no horse.'

'Never mind. I'll ask your master, he'll let you have
a horse.'

The doctor goes away, the candle goes out, and
again there is the sound of 'boo—boo—boo.' Half an
hour later someone drives up to the hut. A cart has
been sent to take Yefim to the hospital. He gets ready
and goes ...

But now it is a clear bright morning. Pelageya is
not at home; she has gone to the hospital to find what
is being done to Yefim. Somewhere there is a baby
crying, and Varka hears someone singing with her own
voice:

'Hush-a-bye, my baby wee, I will sing a song to
thee.'

Pelageya comes back; she crosses herself ' and
whispers:

'They put him to rights in the night, but towards
morning he gave up his soul to God ... The Kingdom

of Heaven be his and peace everlasting ... They say
he was taken too late ... He ought to have gone
sooner ...'

Varka goes out into the road and cries there, but all
at once someone hits her on the back of her head so
hard that her forehead knocks against a birch tree.
She raises her eyes, and sees facing her, her master, the
shoemaker.

'What are you about, you scabby slut?' he says.
'The child is crying, and you are asleep!'

He gives her a sharp slap behind the ear, and she
shakes her head, rocks the cradle, and murmurs her
song. The green patch and the shadows from the
trousers and the baby-clothes move up and down, nod
to her, and soon take possession of her brain again.
Again she sees the high road covered with liquid mud.
The people with wallets on their backs and the
shadows have lain down and are fast asleep. Looking
at them, Varka has a passionate longing for sleep; she
would lie down with enjoyment, but her mother Pelageya is walking beside her, hurrying her on. They are
hastening together to the town to find situations.

'Give alms, for Christ's sake!' her mother begs of the
people they meet. 'Show us the Divine Mercy, kind-
hearted gentlefolk!'

'Give the baby here!' a familiar voice answers. 'Give
the baby here!' the same voice repeats, this time
harshly and angrily. 'Are you asleep, you wretched
girl?'

Varka jumps up, and looking round grasps what
is the matter: there is no high road, no Pelageya,
no people meeting them, there is only her mistress,
who has come to feed the baby, and is standing in

the middle of the room. While the stout, broad-shouldered woman nurses the child and soothes it, Varka stands looking at her and waiting till she has done. And outside the windows the air is already turning blue, the shadows and the green patch on the ceiling are visibly growing pale, it will soon be morning.

'Take him,' says her mistress, buttoning up her chemise over her bosom; 'he is crying. He must be bewitched.'

Varka takes the baby, puts him in the cradle, and begins rocking it again. The green patch and the shadows gradually disappear, and now there is nothing to force itself on her eyes and cloud her brain. But she is as sleepy as before, fearfully sleepy! Varka lays her head on the edge of the cradle, and rocks her whole body to overcome her sleepiness, but yet her eyes are glued together, and her head is heavy.

'Varka, heat the stove!' she hears the master's voice through the door.

So it is time to get up and set to work. Varka leaves the cradle, and runs to the shed for firewood. She is glad. When one moves and runs about, one is not so sleepy as when one is sitting down. She brings the wood, heats the stove, and feels that her wooden face is getting supple again, and that her thoughts are growing clearer.

'Varka, set the samovar!' shouts her mistress.

Varka splits a piece of wood, but has scarcely time to light the splinters and put them in the samovar, when she hears a fresh order:

'Varka, clean the master's goloshes!'

She sits down on the floor, cleans the goloshes, and thinks how nice it would be to put her head into a big deep golosh, and have a little nap in it ... And all at once the golosh grows, swells, fills up the whole room. Varka drops the brush, but at once shakes her head, opens her eyes wide, and tries to look at things so that they may not grow big and move before her eyes.

'Varka, wash the steps outside; I am ashamed for the customers to see them!'

Varka washes the steps, sweeps and dusts the rooms, then heats another stove and runs to the shop. There is a great deal of work: she hasn't one minute free.

But nothing is so hard as standing in the same place at the kitchen table peeling potatoes. Her head droops over the table, the potatoes dance before her eyes, the knife tumbles out of her hand while her fat, angry mistress is moving about near her with her sleeves tucked up, talking so loud that it makes a ringing in Varka's ears. It is agonising, too, to wait at dinner, to wash, to sew, there are minutes when she longs to flop on to the floor regardless of everything, and to sleep.

The day passes. Seeing the windows getting dark, Varka presses her temples that feel as though they were made of wood, and smiles, though she does not know why. The dusk of evening caresses her eyes that will hardly keep open, and promises her sound sleep soon. In the evening visitors come.

'Varka, set the samovar!' shouts her mistress.

The samovar is a little one, and before the visitors have drunk all the tea they want, she has to heat it five times. After tea Varka stands for a whole hour on the same spot, looking at the visitors, and waiting for orders.

'Varka, run and buy three bottles of beer!'

She starts off, and tries to run as quickly as she can, to drive away sleep.

'Varka, fetch some vodka! Varka, where's the cork-screw? Varka, clean a herring!'

But now, at last, the visitors have gone; the lights are put out, the master and mistress go to bed.

'Varka, rock the baby!' she hears the last order.

The cricket churrs in the stove; the green patch on the ceiling and the shadows from the trousers and the baby-clothes force themselves on Varka's half-opened eyes again, wink at her and cloud her mind.

'Hush-a-bye, my baby wee,' she murmurs, 'and I will sing a song to thee.'

And the baby screams, and is worn out with scream-ing. Again Varka sees the muddy high road, the people with wallets, her mother Pelageya, her father Yefim. She understands everything, she recognises everyone, but through her half sleep she cannot understand the force which binds her, hand and foot, weighs upon her, and prevents her from living. She looks round, searches for that force that she may escape from it, but she cannot find it. At last, tired to death, she does her very utmost, strains her eyes, looks up at the flickering green patch, and listening, to the screaming, finds the foe who will not let her live.

That foe is the baby.

She laughs. It seems strange to her that she has failed to grasp such a simple thing before. The green patch, the shadows, and the cricket seem to laugh and wonder too.

The hallucination takes possession of Varka. She gets up from her stool, and with a broad smile on her face and wide unblinking eyes, she walks up and down the room. She feels pleased and tickled at the thought that she will be rid directly of the baby that binds her hand and foot ... Kill the baby and then sleep, sleep, sleep ...

Laughing and winking and shaking her fingers at the green patch, Varka steals up to the cradle and bends over the baby. When she has strangled him, she quickly lies down on the floor, laughs with delight that she can sleep, and in a minute is sleeping as sound as the dead.

THE STEPPE

THE STEPPE

THE STORY OF A JOURNEY

I

EARLY one morning in July a shabby covered chaise, one of those antediluvian chaises without springs in which no one travels in Russia nowadays, except merchants' clerks, dealers and the less well-to-do among priests, drove out of N., the principal town of the province of Z., and rumbled noisily along the posting-track. It rattled and creaked at every movement; the pail, hanging on behind, chimed in gruffly, and from these sounds alone and from the wretched rags of leather hanging loose about its peeling body one could judge of its decrepit age and readiness to drop to pieces.

Two of the inhabitants of N. were sitting in the chaise; they were a merchant of N. called Ivan Ivanitch Kuzmitchov, a man with a shaven face, wearing glasses and a straw hat, more like a government clerk than a merchant, and Father Christopher Sireysky, the priest of the Church of St Nikolay at N., a little old man with long hair, in a grey canvas cassock, a wide-brimmed top-hat and a coloured embroidered girdle. The former was absorbed in thought, and kept tossing his head to shake off drowsiness; in his countenance an habitual business-like reserve was struggling with the genial expression of a man who has just said good-bye to his relatives and has had a good drink at parting. The latter gazed with moist eyes wonderingly at God's world, and his smile was so broad that it seemed to embrace even the brim of his hat; his face was red and looked frozen. Both of them, Father Christopher as well as Kuzmitchov, were going to sell wool. At parting with their families they had just eaten heartily of pastry puffs and cream, and although it was so early in the morning had had a glass or two ... Both were in the best of humours.

Apart from the two persons described above and the coachman Deniska, who lashed the pair of frisky bay horses, there was another figure in the chaise – a boy of nine with a sunburnt face, wet with tears. This was Yegorushka, Kuzmitchov's nephew. With the sanction of his uncle and the blessing of Father Christopher, he was now on his way to go to school. His mother, Olga Ivanovna, the widow of a collegiate secretary, and Kuzmitchov's sister, who was fond of educated people and refined society, had entreated her brother to take Yegorushka with him when he went to sell wool and to put him to school; and now the boy was sitting on the box beside the coachman Deniska, holding on to his elbow to keep from falling off, and dancing up and down like a kettle on the hob, with no notion where he was going or what he was going for. The rapid motion through the air blew out his red shirt like a balloon on his back and made his new hat with a peacock's feather in it, like a coachman's, keep slipping on to the back of his head. He felt himself an intensely unfortunate person, and had an inclination to cry.

When the chaise drove past the prison, Yegorushka glanced at the sentinels pacing slowly by the high white walls, at the little barred windows, at the cross shining on the roof, and remembered how the week before, on the day of the Holy Mother of Kazan, he had been with his mother to the prison church for the Dedication Feast, and how before that, at Easter, he had gone to the prison with Deniska and Ludmila the cook, and had taken the prisoners Easter bread, eggs, cakes and roast beef. The prisoners had thanked them and made the sign of the cross, and one of them had given Yegorushka a pewter buckle of his own making.

The boy gazed at the familiar places, while the hateful chaise flew by and left them all behind. After the prison he caught glimpses of black grimy foundries, followed by the snug green cemetery surrounded by a wall of cobblestones; white crosses and tombstones, nestling among green cherry-trees and looking in the distance like patches of white, peeped out gaily from behind the wall. Yegorushka remembered that when the cherries were in blossom those white patches melted with the flowers into a sea of white; and that when the cherries were ripe the white tombstones and crosses were dotted with splashes of red like bloodstains. Under the cherry-trees in the cemetery Yegorushka's father and granny, Zinaida Danilovna, lay sleeping day and night. When Granny had died she had been put in a long narrow coffin and two pennies had been put upon her eyes, which would not keep shut. Up to the time of her death she had been brisk, and used to bring soft rolls covered with poppy seeds from the market. Now she did nothing but sleep and sleep . . .

Beyond the cemetery came the smoking brickyards. From under the long roofs of reeds that looked as though pressed flat to the ground, a thick black smoke rose in great clouds and floated lazily upwards. The sky was murky above the brickyards and the cemetery, and great shadows from the clouds of smoke crept over the fields and across the roads. Men and horses covered with red dust were moving about in the smoke near the roofs ...

The town ended with the brickyards and the open country began. Yegorushka looked at the town for the last time, pressed his face against Deniska's elbow, and wept bitterly ...

'Come, not done howling yet, cry-baby!' cried Kuzmitchov. 'You are blubbering again, little milksop! If you don't want to go, stay behind; no one is taking you by force!'

'Never mind, never mind, Yegor boy, never mind,' Father Christopher muttered rapidly – 'never mind, my boy ... Call upon God ... You are not going for your harm, but for your good. Learning is light, as the saying is, and ignorance is darkness ... That is so, truly.'

'Do you want to go back?' asked Kuzmitchov.

'Yes ... yes ...' answered Yegorushka, sobbing.

'Well, you'd better go back then. Anyway, you are going for nothing; it's a day's journey for a spoonful of porridge.'

'Never mind, never mind, my boy,' Father Christopher went on. 'Call upon God ... Lomonosov set off with the fishermen in the same way, and he became a man famous all over Europe. Learning in conjunction with faith brings forth fruit pleasing to God. What are the words of the prayer? For the glory of our Maker, for the comfort of our parents, for the benefit of our Church and our country . . . Yes, indeed!'

'The benefit is not the same in all cases,' said Kuzmitchov, lighting a cheap cigar; 'some will study twenty years and get no sense from it.'

'That does happen.'

'Learning is a benefit to some, but others only muddle their brains. My sister is a woman who does not understand; she is set upon refinement, and wants to turn Yegorka into a learned man, and she does not understand that with my business I could settle Yegorka happily for the rest of his life. I tell you this, that if everyone were to go in for being learned and refined there would be no one to sow the corn and do the trading; they would all die of hunger.'

'And if all go in for trading and sowing corn there will be no one to acquire learning.'

And considering that each of them had said something weighty and convincing, Kuzmitchov and Father Christopher both looked serious and cleared their throats simultaneously.

Deniska, who had been listening to their conversation without understanding a word of it, shook his head and, rising in his seat, lashed at both the bays. A silence followed.

Meanwhile a wide boundless plain encircled by a chain of low hills lay stretched before the travellers' eyes. Huddling together and peeping out from behind one another, these hills melted together into rising ground, which stretched right to the very horizon and disappeared into the lilac distance; one drives on and on and cannot discern where it begins or where it ends

... The sun had already peeped out from beyond the town behind them, and quietly, without fuss, set to its accustomed task. At first in the distance before them a broad, bright, yellow streak of light crept over the ground where the earth met the sky, near the little barrows and the windmills, which in the distance looked like tiny men waving their arms. A minute later a similar streak gleamed a little nearer, crept to the right and embraced the hills. Something warm touched Yegorushka's spine; the streak of light, stealing up from behind, darted between the chaise and the horses, moved to meet the other streak, and soon the whole wide steppe flung off the twilight of early morning, and was smiling and sparkling with dew.

The cut rye, the coarse steppe grass, the milkwort, the wild hemp, all withered from the sultry heat, turned brown and half dead, now washed by the dew and caressed by the sun, revived, to fade again. Arctic petrels flew across the road with joyful cries; marmots called to one another in the grass. Somewhere, far away to the left, lapwings uttered their plaintive notes. A covey of partridges, scared by the chaise, fluttered up and with their soft 'trrrr!' flew off to the hills. In the grass crickets, locusts and grasshoppers kept up their churring, monotonous music.

But a little time passed, the dew evaporated, the air grew stagnant, and the disillusioned steppe began to wear its jaded July aspect. The grass drooped, everything living was hushed. The sun-baked hills, brownish-green and lilac in the distance, with their quiet shadowy tones, the plain with the misty distance and, arched above them, the sky, which seems terribly deep and transparent in the steppes, where there are no woods or high hills, seemed now endless, petrified with dreariness . . .

How stifling and oppressive it was! The chaise raced along, while Yegorushka saw always the same – the sky, the plain, the low hills . . . The music in the grass was hushed, the petrels had flown away, the partridges were out of sight, rooks hovered idly over the withered grass; they were all alike and made the steppe even more monotonous.

A hawk flew just above the ground, with an even sweep of its wings, suddenly halted in the air as though pondering on the dreariness of life, then fluttered its wings and flew like an arrow over the steppe, and there was no telling why it flew off and what it wanted. In the distance a windmill waved its sails . . .

Now and then a glimpse of a white potsherd or a heap of stones broke the monotony; a grey stone stood out for an instant or a parched willow with a blue crow on its top branch; a marmot would run across the road and – again there flitted before the eyes only the high grass, the low hills, the rooks . . .

But at last, thank God, a waggon loaded with sheaves came to meet them; a peasant wench was lying on the very top. Sleepy, exhausted by the heat, she lifted her head and looked at the travellers. Deniska gaped, looking at her; the horses stretched out their noses towards the sheaves; the chaise, squeaking, kissed the waggon, and the pointed ears passed over Father Christopher's hat like a brush.

'You are driving over folks, fatty!' cried Deniska. 'What a swollen lump of a face, as though a bumble-bee had stung it!'

The girl smiled drowsily, and moving her lips lay down again; then a solitary poplar came into sight on the low hill. Someone had planted it, and God only knows why it was there. It was hard to tear the eyes away from its graceful figure and green drapery. Was that lovely creature happy? Sultry heat in summer, in winter frost and snowstorms, terrible nights in autumn when nothing is to be seen but darkness and nothing is to be heard but the senseless angry howling wind, and, worst of all, alone, alone for the whole of life ... Beyond the poplar stretches of wheat extended like a bright yellow carpet from the road to the top of the hills. On the hills the corn was already cut and laid up in sheaves, while at the bottom they were still cutting ... Six mowers were standing in a row swinging their scythes, and the scythes gleamed gaily and uttered in unison together 'Vzhee, vzhee!' From the movements of the peasant women binding the sheaves, from the faces of the mowers, from the glitter of the scythes, it could be seen that the sultry heat was baking and stifling. A black dog with its tongue hanging out ran from the mowers to meet the chaise, probably with the intention of barking, but stopped halfway and stared indifferently at Deniska, who shook his whip at him; it was too hot to bark! One peasant woman got up and, putting both hands to her aching back, followed Yegorushka's red shirt with her eyes. Whether it was that the colour pleased her or that he reminded her of her children, she stood a long time motionless staring after him ...

But now the wheat, too, had flashed by; again the

parched plain, the sunburnt hills, the sultry sky stretched before them; again a hawk hovered over the earth. In the distance, as before, a windmill whirled its sails, and still it looked like a little man waving his arms. It was wearisome to watch, and it seemed as though one would never reach it, as though it were running away from the chaise.

Father Christopher and Kuzmitchov were silent. Deniska lashed the horses and kept shouting to them, while Yegorushka had left off crying, and gazed about him listlessly. The heat and the tedium of the steppes overpowered him. He felt as though he had been travelling and jolting up and down for a very long time, that the sun had been baking his back a long time. Before they had gone eight miles he began to feel 'It must be time to rest.' The geniality gradually faded out of his uncle's face, and nothing else was left but the air of business reserve; and to a gaunt shaven face, especially when it is adorned with spectacles and the nose and temples are covered with dust, this reserve gives a relentless, inquisitorial appearance. Father Christopher never left off gazing with wonder at God's world, and smiling. Without speaking, he brooded over something pleasant and nice, and a kindly, genial smile remained imprinted on his face. It seemed as though some nice and pleasant thought were imprinted on his brain by the heat . . .

'Well, Deniska, shall we overtake the waggons to-day?' asked Kuzmitchov.

Deniska looked at the sky, rose in his seat, lashed at his horses and then answered:

'By nightfall, please God, we shall overtake them.'

There was a sound of dogs barking. Half a dozen

steppe sheep-dogs, suddenly leaping out as though from ambush, with ferocious howling barks, flew to meet the chaise. All of them, extraordinarily furious, surrounded the chaise, with their shaggy spider-like muzzles and their eyes red with anger, and jostling against one another in their anger, raised a hoarse howl. They were filled with passionate hatred of the horses, of the chaise, and of the human beings, and seemed ready to tear them into pieces. Deniska, who was fond of teasing and beating, was delighted at the chance of it, and with a malignant expression bent over and lashed at the sheep-dogs with his whip. The brutes growled more than ever, the horses flew on; and Yegorushka, who had difficulty in keeping his seat on the box, realized, looking at the dogs' eyes and teeth, that if he fell down they would instantly tear him to bits; but he felt no fear and looked at them as malignantly as Deniska, and regretted that he had no whip in his hand.

The chaise came upon a flock of sheep.

'Stop!' cried Kuzmitchov. 'Pull up! Woa!'

Deniska threw his whole body backwards and pulled up the horses.

'Come here!' Kuzmitchov shouted to the shepherd. 'Call off the dogs, curse them!'

The old shepherd, tattered and barefoot, wearing a fur cap, with a dirty sack round his loins and a long crook in his hand – a regular figure from the Old Testament – called off the dogs, and taking off his cap, went up to the chaise. Another similar Old Testament figure was standing motionless at the other end of the flock, staring without interest at the travellers.

'Whose sheep are these?' asked Kuzmitchov.

'Varlamov's,' the old man answered in a loud voice.

'Varlamov's,' repeated the shepherd standing at the other end of the flock.

'Did Varlamov come this way yesterday or not?'

'He did not; his clerk came ...'

'Drive on!'

The chaise rolled on and the shepherds, with their angry dogs, were left behind. Yegorushka gazed listlessly at the lilac distance in front, and it began to seem as though the windmill, waving its sails, were getting nearer. It became bigger and bigger, grew quite large, and now he could distinguish clearly its two sails. One sail was old and patched, the other had only lately been made of new wood and glistened in the sun. The chaise drove straight on, while the windmill, for some reason, began retreating to the left. They drove on and on, and the windmill kept moving away to the left, and still did not disappear.

'A fine windmill Boltva has put up for his son,' observed Deniska.

'And how is it we don't see his farm?'

'It is that way, beyond the creek.'

Boltva's farm, too, soon came into sight, but yet the windmill did not retreat, did not drop behind; it still watched Yegorushka with its shining sail and waved. What a sorcerer!

II

TOWARDS midday the chaise turned off the road to the right; it went on a little way at walking pace and then stopped. Yegorushka heard a soft, very caressing gurgle, and felt a different air breathe on his face with a cool velvety touch. Through a little pipe of hemlock stuck there by some unknown benefactor, water was running in a thin trickle from a low hill, put together by nature of huge monstrous stones. It fell to the ground, and limpid, sparkling gaily in the sun, and softly murmuring as though fancying itself a great tempestuous torrent, flowed swiftly away to the left. Not far from its source the little stream spread itself out into a pool; the burning sunbeams and the parched soil greedily drank it up and sucked away its strength; but a little further on it must have mingled with another rivulet, for a hundred paces away thick reeds showed green and luxuriant along its course, and three snipe flew up from them with a loud cry as the chaise drove by.

The travellers got out to rest by the stream and feed the horses. Kuzmitchov, Father Christopher and Yegorushka sat down on a mat in the narrow strip of shade cast by the chaise and the unharnessed horses. The nice pleasant thought that the heat had imprinted in Father Christopher's brain craved expression after he had had a drink of water and eaten a hard-boiled egg. He bent a friendly look upon Yegorushka, munched, and began:

'I studied too, my boy; from the earliest age God instilled into me good sense and understanding, so that while I was just such a lad as you I was beyond others, a comfort to my parents and preceptors by my good sense. Before I was fifteen I could speak and make verses in Latin, just as in Russian. I was the crosier-bearer to his Holiness Bishop Christopher. After mass one day, as I remember it was the patron saint's day of His Majesty Tsar Alexandr Pavlovitch of blessed memory, he unrobed at the altar, looked kindly at me and asked, "Puer bone, quam appelaris?" And I answered, "Christopherus sum;" and he said, "Ergo connominati sumus" – that is, that we were namesakes ... Then he asked in Latin, "Whose son are you?" To which I answered, also in Latin, that I was the son of deacon Sireysky of the village of Lebedinskoe. Seeing my readiness and the clearness of my answers, his Holiness blessed me and said, "Write to your father that I will not forget him, and that I will keep you in view." The holy priests and fathers who were standing round the altar, hearing our discussion in Latin, were not a little surprised, and everyone expressed his pleasure in praise of me. Before I had moustaches, my boy, I could read Latin, Greek, and French; I knew philosophy, mathematics, secular history, and all the sciences. The Lord gave me a marvellous memory. Sometimes, if I read a thing once or twice, I knew it by heart. My preceptors and patrons were amazed, and so they expected I should make a learned man, a luminary of the Church. I did think of going to Kiev to continue my studies, but my parents did not approve. "You'll be studying all your life," said my father; "when shall we see you finished?" Hearing such words, I gave up study and took a post ... Of course, I did not become a learned man, but then I did not disobey my parents; I was a comfort to them in their old age and gave them a creditable funeral. Obedience is more than fasting and prayer.'

'I suppose you have forgotten all your learning?' observed Kuzmitchov.

'I should think so! Thank God, I have reached my

eightieth year! Something of philosophy and rhetoric I do remember, but languages and mathematics I have quite forgotten.'

Father Christopher screwed up his eyes, thought a minute and said in an undertone:

'What is a substance? A creature is a self-existing object, not requiring anything else for its completion.'

He shook his head and laughed with feeling.

'Spiritual nourishment!' he said. 'Of a truth matter nourishes the flesh and spiritual nourishment the soul.'

'Learning is all very well,' sighed Kuzmitchov, 'but if we don't overtake Varlamov, learning won't do much for us.'

'A man isn't a needle – we shall find him. He must be going his rounds in these parts.'

Among the sedge were flying the three snipe they had seen before, and in their plaintive cries there was a note of alarm and vexation at having been driven away from the stream. The horses were steadily munching and snorting. Deniska walked about by them and, trying to appear indifferent to the cucumbers, pies, and eggs that the gentry were eating, he concentrated himself on the gadflies and horseflies that were fastening upon the horses' backs and bellies; he squashed his victims apathetically, emitting a peculiar, fiendishly triumphant, guttural sound, and when he missed them cleared his throat with an air of vexation and looked after every lucky one that escaped death.

'Deniska, where are you? Come and eat,' said Kuzmitchov, heaving a deep sigh, a sign that he had had enough.

Deniska diffidently approached the mat and picked out five thick and yellow cucumbers (he did not venture to take the smaller and fresher ones), took two hard-boiled eggs that looked dark and were cracked, then irresolutely, as though afraid he might get a blow on his outstretched hand, touched a pie with his finger.

'Take them, take them,' Kuzmitchov urged him on.

Deniska took the pies resolutely, and, moving some distance away, sat down on the grass with his back to the chaise. At once there was such a sound of loud munching that even the horses turned round to look suspiciously at Deniska.

After his meal Kuzmitchov took a sack containing something out of the chaise and said to Yegorushka:

'I am going to sleep, and you mind that no one takes the sack from under my head.'

Father Christopher took off his cassock, his girdle, and his full coat, and Yegorushka, looking at him, was dumb with astonishment. He had never imagined that priests wore trousers, and Father Christopher had on real canvas trousers thrust into high boots, and a short striped jacket. Looking at him, Yegorushka thought that in this costume, so unsuitable to his dignified position, he looked with his long hair and beard very much like Robinson Crusoe. After taking off their outer garments Kuzmitchov and Father Christopher lay down in the shade under the chaise, facing one another, and closed their eyes. Deniska, who had finished munching, stretched himself out on his back and also closed his eyes.

'You look out that no one takes away the horses!' he said to Yegorushka, and at once fell asleep.

Stillness reigned. There was no sound except the munching and snorting of the horses and the snoring of the sleepers; somewhere far away a lapwing wailed, and from time to time there sounded the shrill cries of the three snipe who had flown up to see whether their uninvited visitors had gone away; the rivulet babbled, lisping softly, but all these sounds did not break the stillness, did not stir the stagnation, but, on the contrary, lulled all nature to slumber.

Yegorushka, gasping with the heat, which was particularly oppressive after a meal, ran to the sedge and from there surveyed the country. He saw exactly the same as he had in the morning: the plain, the low hills, the sky, the lilac distance; only the hills stood nearer; and he could not see the windmill, which had been left far behind. From behind the rocky hill from which the stream flowed rose another, smoother and broader; a little hamlet of five or six homesteads clung to it. No people, no trees, no shade were to be seen about the huts; it looked as though the hamlet had expired in the burning air and was dried up. To while away the time Yegorushka caught a grasshopper in the grass, held it in his closed hand to his ear, and spent a long time listening to the creature playing on its instrument. When he was weary of its music he ran after a flock of yellow butterflies who were flying towards the sedge on the watercourse, and found himself again beside the chaise, without noticing how he came there. His uncle and Father Christopher were sound asleep; their sleep would be sure to last two or three hours till the horses had rested ... How was he to get through that long time, and where was he to get away from the heat? A hard problem ... Mechanically Yegorushka put his lips to the trickle that ran from the waterpipe; there was a chilliness in his mouth and there was the smell of hemlock. He drank at first eagerly, then went on with effort till the sharp cold had run from his mouth all over his body and the water was spilt on his shirt. Then he went up to the chaise and began looking at the sleeping figures. His uncle's face wore, as before, an expression of businesslike reserve. Fanatically devoted to his work, Kuzmitchov always, even in his sleep and at church when they were singing, 'Like the cherubim,' thought about his business and could never forget it for a moment; and now he was probably dreaming about bales of wool, waggons, prices, Varlamov ... Father Christopher, now, a soft, frivolous and absurd person, had never all his life been conscious of anything which could, like a boa-constrictor, coil about his soul and hold it tight. In all the numerous enterprises he had undertaken in his day what attracted him was not so much the business itself, but the bustle and the contact with other people involved in every undertaking. Thus, in the present expedition, he was not so much interested in wool, in Varlamov, and in prices, as in the long journey, the conversations on the way, the sleeping under a chaise, and the meals at odd times ... And now, judging from his face, he must have been dreaming of Bishop Christopher, of the Latin discussion, of his wife, of puffs and cream and all sorts of things that Kuzmitchov could not possibly dream of.

While Yegorushka was watching their sleeping faces he suddenly heard a soft singing; somewhere at a distance a woman was singing, and it was difficult to tell where and in what direction. The song was subdued, dreary and melancholy, like a dirge, and hardly audible, and seemed to come first from the right, then from the left, then from above, and then from underground, as though an unseen spirit were hovering over the steppe and singing. Yegorushka looked about him, and could not make out where the strange song came from. Then as he listened he began to fancy that the grass was singing; in its song, withered and half-dead, it was without words, but plaintively and passionately, urging that it was not to blame, that the sun was burning it for no fault of its own; it urged that it ardently longed to live, that it was young and might have been beautiful but for the heat and the drought; it was guiltless, but yet it prayed forgiveness and protested that it was in anguish, sad and sorry for itself . . .

Yegorushka listened for a little, and it began to seem as though this dreary, mournful song made the air hotter, more suffocating and more stagnant . . . To drown the singing he ran to the sedge, humming to himself and trying to make a noise with his feet. From there he looked about in all directions and found out who was singing. Near the furthest hut in the hamlet stood a peasant woman in a short petticoat, with long thin legs like a heron. She was sowing something. A white dust floated languidly from her sieve down the hillock. Now it was evident that she was singing. A couple of yards from her a little bare-headed boy in nothing but a smock was standing motionless. As though fascinated by the song, he stood stock-still, staring away into the distance, probably at Yegorushka's crimson shirt.

The song ceased. Yegorushka sauntered back to the

chaise, and to while away the time went again to the trickle of water.

And again there was the sound of the dreary song. It was the same long-legged peasant woman in the hamlet over the hill. Yegorushka's boredom came back again. He left the pipe and looked upwards. What he saw was so unexpected that he was a little frightened. Just above his head on one of the big clumsy stones stood a chubby little boy, wearing nothing but a shirt, with a prominent stomach and thin legs, the same boy who had been standing before by the peasant woman. He was gazing with open mouth and unblinking eyes at Yegorushka's crimson shirt and at the chaise, with a look of blank astonishment and even fear, as though he saw before him creatures of another world. The red colour of the shirt charmed and allured him. But the chaise and the men sleeping under it excited his curiosity; perhaps he had not noticed how the agreeable red colour and curiosity had attracted him down from the hamlet, and now probably he was surprised at his own boldness. For a long while Yegorushka stared at him, and he at Yegorushka. Both were silent and conscious of some awkwardness. After a long silence Yegorushka asked:

'What's your name?'

The stranger's cheeks puffed out more than ever; he pressed his back against the rock, opened his eyes wide, moved his lips, and answered in a husky bass: 'Tit!'

The boys said not another word to each other; after a brief silence, still keeping his eyes fixed on Yegorushka, the mysterious Tit kicked up one leg, felt with his heel for a niche and clambered up the rock; from that point he ascended to the next rock, staggering backwards and looking intently at Yegorushka, as though afraid he might hit him from behind, and so made his way upwards till he disappeared altogether behind the crest of the hill.

After watching him out of sight, Yegorushka put his arms round his knees and leaned his head on them ... The burning sun scorched the back of his head, his neck, and his spine. The melancholy song died away, then floated again on the stagnant stifling air. The rivulet gurgled monotonously, the horses munched, and time dragged on endlessly, as though it, too, were stagnant and had come to a standstill. It seemed as though a hundred years had passed since the morning. Could it be that God's world, the chaise and the horses would come to a standstill in that air, and, like the hills, turn to stone and remain for ever in one spot? Yegorushka raised his head, and with smarting eyes looked before him; the lilac distance, which till then had been motionless, began heaving, and with the sky floated away into the distance ... It drew after it the brown grass, the sedge, and with extraordinary swiftness Yegorushka floated after the flying distance. Some force noiselessly drew him onwards, and the heat and the wearisome song flew after in pursuit. Yegorushka bent his head and shut his eyes ...

Deniska was the first to wake up. Something must have bitten him, for he jumped up, quickly scratched his shoulder and said:

'Plague take you, cursed idolater!'

Then he went to the brook, had a drink and slowly washed. His splashing and puffing roused Yegorushka

from his lethargy. The boy looked at his wet face with
drops of water and big freckles which made it look like
marble, and asked:

'Shall we soon be going?'

Deniska looked at the height of the sun and
answered:

'I expect so.'

He dried himself with the tail of his shirt and, making a very serious face, hopped on one leg.

'I say, which of us will get to the sedge first?' he
said.

Yegorushka was exhausted by the heat and drowsiness, but he raced off after him all the same. Deniska
was in his twentieth year, was a coachman and going
to be married, but he had not left off being a boy. He
was very fond of flying kites, chasing pigeons, playing
knuckle-bones, running races, and always took part in
children's games and disputes. No sooner had his master turned his back or gone to sleep than Deniska
would begin doing something such as hopping on one
leg or throwing stones. It was hard for any grown-up
person, seeing the genuine enthusiasm with which he
frolicked about in the society of children, to resist saying, 'What a baby!' Children, on the other hand, saw
nothing strange in the invasion of their domain by the
big coachman. 'Let him play,' they thought, 'as long
as he doesn't fight!' In the same way little dogs see
nothing strange in it when a simple-hearted big dog
joins their company uninvited and begins playing
with them.

Deniska outstripped Yegorushka, and was evidently very much pleased at having done so. He
winked at him, and to show that he could hop on

one leg any distance, suggested to Yegorushka that he should hop with him along the road and from there, without resting, back to the chaise. Yegorushka declined this suggestion, for he was very much out of breath and exhausted.

All at once Deniska looked very grave, as he did not look even when Kuzmitchov gave him a scolding or threatened him with a stick; listening intently, he dropped quietly on one knee and an expression of sternness and alarm came into his face, such as one sees in people who hear heretical talk. He fixed his eyes on one spot, raised his hand curved into a hollow, and suddenly fell on his stomach on the ground and slapped the hollow of his hand down upon the grass.

'Caught!' he wheezed triumphantly, and, getting up, lifted a big grasshopper to Yegorushka's eyes.

The two boys stroked the grasshopper's broad green back with their fingers and touched his antennae, supposing that this would please the creature. Then Deniska caught a fat fly that had been sucking blood and offered it to the grasshopper. The latter moved his huge jaws, that were like the visor of a helmet, with the utmost unconcern, as though he had been long acquainted with Deniska, and bit off the fly's stomach. They let him go. With a flash of the pink lining of his wings, he flew down into the grass and at once began his churring notes again. They let the fly go, too. It preened its wings, and without its stomach flew off to the horses.

A loud sigh was heard from under the chaise. It was Kuzmitchov waking up. He quickly raised his head, looked uneasily into the distance, and from that look, which passed by Yegorushka and Deniska without sympathy or interest, it could be seen that his thought on awaking was of the wool and of Varlamov.

'Father Christopher, get up; it is time to start,' he said anxiously. 'Wake up; we've slept too long as it is! Deniska, put the horses in.'

Father Christopher woke up with the same smile with which he had fallen asleep; his face looked creased and wrinkled from sleep, and seemed only half the size. After washing and dressing, he proceeded without haste to take out of his pocket a little greasy psalter; and standing with his face towards the east, began in a whisper repeating the psalms of the day and crossing himself.

'Father Christopher,' said Kuzmitchov reproachfully, 'it's time to start; the horses are ready, and here are you . . . upon my word.'

'In a minute, in a minute,' muttered Father Christopher. 'I must read the psalms . . . I haven't read them to-day.'

'The psalms can wait.'

'Ivan Ivanitch, that is my rule every day . . . I can't . . .'

'God will overlook it.'

For a full quarter of an hour Father Christopher stood facing the east and moving his lips, while Kuzmitchov looked at him almost with hatred and impatiently shrugged his shoulders. He was particularly irritated when, after every 'Hallelujah,' Father Christopher drew a long breath, rapidly crossed himself and repeated three times, intentionally raising his voice so that the others might cross themselves, 'Hallelujah, hallelujah, hallelujah! Glory be to Thee, O Lord!' At last he smiled, looked upwards at the sky, and, putting the psalter in his pocket, said:

'*Finis!*'

A minute later the chaise had started on the road. As though it were going backwards and not forwards, the travellers saw the same scene as they had before midday.

The low hills were still plunged in the lilac distance, and no end could be seen to them. There were glimpses of high grass and heaps of stones; strips of stubble land passed by them and still the same rooks, the same hawk, moving its wings with slow dignity, moved over the steppe. The air was more sultry than ever; from the sultry heat and the stillness submissive nature was spellbound into silence ... No wind, no fresh cheering sound, no cloud.

But at last, when the sun was beginning to sink into the west, the steppe, the hills and the air could bear the oppression no longer, and, driven out of all patience, exhausted, tried to fling off the yoke. A fleecy ashen-grey cloud unexpectedly appeared behind the hills. It exchanged glances with the steppe, as though to say, 'Here I am,' and frowned. Suddenly something burst in the stagnant air; there was a violent squall of wind which whirled round and round, roaring and whistling over the steppe. At once a murmur rose from the grass and last year's dry herbage, the dust curled in spiral eddies over the road, raced over the steppe, and carrying with it straws, dragon flies and feathers, rose up in a whirling black column towards the sky and darkened the sun. Prickly uprooted plants ran stumbling and leaping in all directions over the steppe, and one of them got caught in the whirlwind, turned round and round like a bird, flew towards the sky, and turning into a little black speck, vanished from sight. After it flew another, and then a third, and Yegorushka saw two of them meet in the blue height and clutch at one another as though they were wrestling.

A bustard flew up by the very road. Fluttering his wings and his tail, he looked, bathed in the sunshine, like an angler's glittering tin fish or a waterfly flashing so swiftly over the water that its wings cannot be told from its antennae, which seem to be growing before, behind and on all sides ... Quivering in the air like an insect with a shimmer of bright colours, the bustard flew high up in a straight line, then, probably frightened by a cloud of dust, swerved to one side, and for a long time the gleam of his wings could be seen ...

Then a corncrake flew up from the grass, alarmed by the hurricane and not knowing what was the matter. It flew with the wind and not against it, like all the other birds, so that all its feathers were ruffled up and it was puffed out to the size of a hen and looked very angry and impressive. Only the rooks who had grown old on the steppe and were accustomed to its vagaries hovered calmly over the grass, or taking no notice of anything, went on unconcernedly pecking with their stout beaks at the hard earth.

There was a dull roll of thunder beyond the hills; there came a whiff of fresh air. Deniska gave a cheerful whistle and lashed his horses. Father Christopher and Kuzmitchov held their hats and looked intently towards the hills ... How pleasant a shower of rain would have been!

One effort, one struggle more, and it seemed the

steppe would have got the upper hand. But the unseen oppressive force gradually riveted its fetters on the wind and the air, laid the dust, and the stillness came back again as though nothing had happened, the cloud hid, the sun-baked hills frowned submissively, the air grew calm, and only somewhere the troubled lapwings wailed and lamented their destiny . . .

Soon after that the evening came on.

III

IN the dusk of evening a big house of one storey, with a rusty iron roof and with dark windows, came into sight. This house was called a posting inn, though it had nothing like a stableyard, and it stood in the middle of the steppe, with no kind of enclosure round it. A little to one side of it a wretched little cherry orchard shut in by a hurdle fence made a dark patch, and under the windows stood sleepy sunflowers drooping their heavy heads. From the orchard came the clatter of a little toy windmill, set there to frighten away hares by the rattle. Nothing more could be seen near the house, and nothing could be heard but the steppe. The chaise had scarcely stopped at the porch with an awning over it, when from the house there came the sound of cheerful voices, one a man's, another a woman's; there was the creak of a swing-door, and in a flash a tall gaunt figure, swinging its arms and fluttering its coat, was standing by the chaise. This was the innkeeper, Moisey Moisevitch, a man no longer young, with a very pale face and a handsome beard as black as charcoal. He was wearing a threadbare black coat, which hung flapping on his

narrow shoulders as though on a hatstand, and fluttered its skirts like wings every time Moisey Moisevitch flung up his hands in delight or horror. Besides
his coat the innkeeper was wearing full white trousers,
not stuck into his boots, and a velvet waistcoat with
brown flowers on it that looked like gigantic bugs.

Moisey Moisevitch was at first dumb with excess of
feeling on recognizing the travellers, then he clasped
his hands and uttered a moan. His coat swung its
skirts, his back bent into a bow, and his pale face
twisted into a smile that suggested that to see the
chaise was not merely a pleasure to him, but actually
a joy so sweet as to be painful.

'Oh dear! oh dear!' he began in a thin sing-song
voice, breathless, fussing about and preventing the
travellers from getting out of the chaise by his antics.
'What a happy day for me! Oh, what am I to do now?
Ivan Ivanitch! Father Christopher! What a pretty
little gentleman sitting on the box, God strike me
dead! Oh, my goodness! why am I standing here
instead of asking the visitors indoors? Please walk in,
I humbly beg you ... You are kindly welcome! Give
me all your things ... Oh, my goodness me!'

Moisey Moisevitch, who was rummaging in the
chaise and assisting the travellers to alight, suddenly
turned back and shouted in a voice as frantic and
choking as though he were drowning and calling for
help:

'Solomon! Solomon!'

'Solomon! Solomon!' a woman's voice repeated
indoors.

The swing-door creaked, and in the doorway
appeared a rather short young Jew with a big beak-

like nose, with a bald patch surrounded by rough red curly hair; he was dressed in a short and very shabby reefer jacket, with rounded lappets and short sleeves, and in short serge trousers, so that he looked skimpy and short-tailed like an unfledged bird. This was Solomon, the brother of Moisey Moisevitch. He went up to the chaise, smiling rather queerly, and did not speak or greet the travellers.

'Ivan Ivanitch and Father Christopher have come,' said Moisey Moisevitch in a tone as though he were afraid his brother would not believe him. 'Dear, dear! What a surprise! Such honoured guests to have come to us so suddenly! Come, take their things, Solomon. Walk in, honoured guests.'

A little later Kuzmitchov, Father Christopher, and Yegorushka were sitting in a big gloomy empty room at an old oak table. The table was almost in solitude, for, except a wide sofa covered with torn American leather and three chairs, there was no other furniture in the room. And, indeed, not everybody would have given the chairs that name. They were a pitiful semblance of furniture, covered with American leather that had seen its best days, and with backs bent backwards at an unnaturally acute angle, so that they looked like children's sledges. It was hard to imagine what had been the unknown carpenter's object in bending the chair-backs so mercilessly, and one was tempted to imagine that it was not the carpenter's fault, but that some athletic visitor had bent the chairs like this as a feat, then had tried to bend them back again and had made them worse. The room looked gloomy, the walls were grey, the ceilings and the cornices were grimy; on the floor were chinks and

yawning holes that were hard to account for (one
might have fancied they were made by the heel of the
same athlete), and it seemed as though the room
would still have been dark if a dozen lamps had hung
in it. There was nothing approaching an ornament on
the walls or the windows. On one wall, however, there
hung a list of regulations of some sort under a two-
headed eagle in a grey wooden frame, and on another
wall in the same sort of frame an engraving with the
inscription, 'The Indifference of Man.' What it was to
which men were indifferent it was impossible to make
out, as the engraving was very dingy with age and was
extensively flyblown. There was a smell of something
decayed and sour in the room.

As he led the visitors into the room, Moisey Moisevitch went on wriggling, gesticulating, shrugging and
uttering joyful exclamations; he considered these
antics necessary in order to seem polite and agreeable.

'When did our waggons go by?' Kuzmitchov asked.

'One party went by early this morning, and the
other, Ivan Ivanitch, put up here for dinner and went
on towards evening.'

'Ah! ... Has Varlamov been by or not?'

'No, Ivan Ivanitch. His clerk, Grigory Yegoritch,
went by yesterday morning and said that he had to be
to-day at the Molokans' farm.'

'Good! so we will go after the waggons directly and
then on to the Molokans'.'

'Mercy on us, Ivan Ivanitch!' Moisey Moisevitch
cried in horror, flinging up his hands. 'Where are you
going for the night? You will have a nice little supper
and stay the night, and to-morrow morning, please
God, you can go on and overtake anyone you like.'

'There is no time for that ... Excuse me, Moisey Moisevitch, another time; but now I must make haste. We'll stay a quarter of an hour and then go on; we can stay the night at the Molokans'.'

'A quarter of an hour!' squealed Moisey Moisevitch. 'Have you no fear of God, Ivan Ivanitch? You will compel me to hide your caps and lock the door! You must have a cup of tea and a snack of something, anyway.'

'We have no time for tea,' said Kuzmitchov.

Moisey Moisevitch bent his head on one side, crooked his knees, and put his open hands before him as though warding off a blow, while with a smile of agonized sweetness he began imploring:

'Ivan Ivanitch! Father Christopher! Do be so good as to take a cup of tea with me. Surely I am not such a bad man that you can't even drink tea in my house? Ivan Ivanitch!'

'Well, we may just as well have a cup of tea,' said Father Christopher, with a sympathetic smile; 'that won't keep us long.'

'Very well,' Kuzmitchov assented.

Moisey Moisevitch, in a fluster, uttered an exclamation of joy, and shrugging as though he had just stepped out of cold water into warm, ran to the door and cried in the same frantic voice in which he had called Solomon:

'Rosa! Rosa! Bring the samovar!'

A minute later the door opened, and Solomon came into the room carrying a large tray in his hands. Setting the tray on the table, he looked away sarcastically with the same queer smile as before. Now, by the light of the lamp, it was possible to see his smile distinctly; it was very complex, and expressed a variety of emotions, but the predominant element in it was undisguised contempt. He seemed to be thinking of something ludicrous and silly, to be feeling contempt and dislike, to be pleased at something and waiting for the favourable moment to turn something into ridicule and to burst into laughter. His long nose, his thick lips, and his sly prominent eyes seemed tense with the desire to laugh. Looking at his face, Kuzmitchov smiled ironically and asked:

'Solomon, why did you not come to our fair at N. this summer, and act some Jewish scenes?'

Two years before, as Yegorushka remembered very well, at one of the booths at the fair at N., Solomon had performed some scenes of Jewish life, and his acting had been a great success. The allusion to this made no impression whatever upon Solomon. Making no answer, he went out and returned a little later with the samovar.

When he had done what he had to do at the table he moved a little aside, and, folding his arms over his chest and thrusting out one leg, fixed his sarcastic eyes on Father Christopher. There was something defiant, haughty, and contemptuous in his attitude, and at the same time it was comic and pitiful in the extreme, because the more impressive his attitude the more vividly it showed up his short trousers, his bobtail coat, his caricature of a nose, and his bird-like plucked-looking little figure.

Moisey Moisevitch brought a footstool from the other room and sat down a little way from the table.

'I wish you a good appetite! Tea and sugar!' he

began, trying to entertain his visitors. 'I hope you will enjoy it. Such rare guests, such rare ones; it is years since I last saw Father Christopher. And will no one tell me who is this nice little gentleman?' he asked, looking tenderly at Yegorushka.

'He is the son of my sister, Olga Ivanovna,' answered Kuzmitchov.

'And where is he going?'

'To school. We are taking him to a high school.'

In his politeness, Moisey Moisevitch put on a look of wonder and wagged his head expressively.

'Ah, that is a fine thing,' he said, shaking his finger at the samovar. 'That's a fine thing. You will come back from the high school such a gentleman that we shall all take off our hats to you. You will be wealthy and wise and so grand that your mamma will be delighted. Oh, that's a fine thing!'

He paused a little, stroked his knees, and began again in a jocose and deferential tone.

'You must excuse me, Father Christopher, but I am thinking of writing to the bishop to tell him you are robbing the merchants of their living. I shall take a sheet of stamped paper and write that I suppose Father Christopher is short of pence, as he has taken up with trade and begun selling wool.'

'H'm, yes ... it's a queer notion in my old age,' said Father Christopher, and he laughed. 'I have turned from priest to merchant, brother. I ought to be at home now saying my prayers, instead of galloping about the country like a Pharaoh in his chariot ... Vanity!'

'But it will mean a lot of pence!'

'Oh, I dare say! More kicks than halfpence, and

serve me right. The wool's not mine, but my son-in-law Mihail's!'

'Why doesn't he go himself?'

'Why, because ... His mother's milk is scarcely dry upon his lips. He can buy wool all right, but when it comes to selling, he has no sense; he is young yet. He has wasted all his money; he wanted to grow rich and cut a dash, but he tried here and there, and no one would give him his price. And so the lad went on like that for a year, and then he came to me and said "Daddy, you sell the wool for me; be kind and do it! I am no good at the business!" And that is true enough. As soon as there is anything wrong then it's "Daddy," but till then they could get on without their dad. When he was buying he did not consult me, but now when he is in difficulties it's Daddy's turn. And what does his dad know about it? If it were not for Ivan Ivanitch, his dad could do nothing. I have a lot of worry with them.'

'Yes; one has a lot of worry with one's children, I can tell you that,' sighed Moisey Moisevitch. 'I have six of my own. One needs schooling, another needs doctoring, and a third needs nursing, and when they grow up they are more trouble still. It is not only nowadays, it was the same in Holy Scripture. When Jacob had little children he wept, and when they grew up he wept still more bitterly.'

'H'm, yes ...' Father Christopher assented pensively, looking at his glass. 'I have no cause myself to rail against the Lord. I have lived to the end of my days as any man might be thankful to live ... I have married my daughters to good men, my sons I have set up in life, and now I am free; I have done my work and can go where I like. I live in peace with my wife. I eat and drink and sleep and rejoice in my grandchildren, and say my prayers and want nothing more. I live on the fat of the land, and don't need to curry favour with anyone. I have never had any trouble from childhood, and now suppose the Tsar were to ask me, "What do you need? What would you like?" why, I don't need anything. I have everything I want and everything to be thankful for. In the whole town there is no happier man than I am. My only trouble is I have so many sins, but there – only God is without sin. That's right, isn't it?'

'No doubt it is.'

'I have no teeth, of course; my poor old back aches; there is one thing and another . . . asthma and that sort of thing . . . I ache . . . The flesh is weak, but then think of my age! I am in the eighties! One can't go on for ever; one mustn't outstay one's welcome.'

Father Christopher suddenly thought of something, spluttered into his glass and choked with laughter. Moisey Moisevitch laughed, too, from politeness, and he, too, cleared his throat.

'So funny!' said Father Christopher, and he waved his hand. 'My eldest son Gavrila came to pay me a visit. He is in the medical line, and is a district doctor in the province of Tchernigov . . . "Very well . . ." I said to him, "here I have asthma and one thing and another . . . You are a doctor; cure your father!" He undressed me on the spot, tapped me, listened, and all sorts of tricks . . . kneaded my stomach, and then he said, "Dad, you ought to be treated with compressed air." Father Christopher laughed convulsively, till the tears came into his eyes, and got up.

'And I said to him, "God bless your compressed

air!"' he brought out through his laughter, waving both hands. 'God bless your compressed air!'

Moisey Moisevitch got up, too, and with his hands on his stomach, went off into shrill laughter like the yap of a lap-dog.

'God bless the compressed air!' repeated Father Christopher, laughing.

Moisey Moisevitch laughed two notes higher and so violently that he could hardly stand on his feet.

'Oh dear!' he moaned through his laughter. 'Let me get my breath ... You'll be the death of me.'

He laughed and talked, though at the same time he was casting timorous and suspicious looks at Solomon. The latter was standing in the same attitude and still smiling. To judge from his eyes and his smile, his contempt and hatred were genuine, but that was so out of keeping with his plucked-looking figure that it seemed to Yegorushka as though he were putting on his defiant attitude and biting sarcastic smile to play the fool for the entertainment of their honoured guests.

After drinking six glasses of tea in silence, Kuzmitchov cleared a space before him on the table, took his bag, the one which he kept under his head when he slept under the chaise, untied the string and shook it. Rolls of paper notes were scattered out of the bag on the table.

'While we have the time, Father Christopher, let us reckon up,' said Kuzmitchov.

Moisey Moisevitch was embarrassed at the sight of the money. He got up, and, as a man of delicate feeling unwilling to pry into other people's secrets, he went out of the room on tiptoe, swaying his arms. Solomon remained where he was.

'How many are there in the rolls of roubles?' Father Christopher began.

'The rouble notes are done up in fifties ... the three-rouble notes in nineties, the twenty-five and hundred roubles in thousands. You count out seven thousand eight hundred for Varlamov, and I will count out for Gusevitch. And mind you don't make a mistake ...'

Yegorushka had never in his life seen so much money as was lying on the table before him. There must have been a great deal of money, for the roll of seven thousand eight hundred, which Father Christopher put aside for Varlamov, seemed very small compared with the whole heap. At any other time such a mass of money would have impressed Yegorushka, and would have moved him to reflect how many cracknels, buns and poppy-cakes could be bought for that money. Now he looked at it listlessly, only conscious of the disgusting smell of kerosene and rotten apples that came from the heap of notes. He was exhausted by the jolting ride in the chaise, tired out and sleepy. His head was heavy, his eyes would hardly keep open and his thoughts were tangled like threads. If it had been possible he would have been relieved to lay his head on the table, so as not to see the lamp and the fingers moving over the heaps of notes, and to have let his tired sleepy thoughts go still more at random. When he tried to keep awake, the light of the lamp, the cups and the fingers grew double, the samovar heaved and the smell of rotten apples seemed even more acrid and disgusting.

'Ah, money, money!' sighed Father Christopher, smiling. 'You bring trouble! Now I expect my Mihailo is asleep and dreaming that I am going to bring him a heap of money like this.'

'Your Mihailo Timofevitch is a man who doesn't
understand business,' said Kuzmitchov in an undertone; 'he undertakes what isn't his work, but you
understand and can judge. You had better hand over
your wool to me, as I have said already, and I would
give you half a rouble above my own price – yes,
I would, simply out of regard for you . . .'

'No, Ivan Ivanitch,' Father Christopher sighed.
'I thank you for your kindness . . . Of course, if it were
for me to decide, I shouldn't think twice about it; but
as it is, the wool is not mine, as you know . . .'

Moisey Moisevitch came in on tiptoe. Trying from
delicacy not to look at the heaps of money, he stole up
to Yegorushka and pulled at his shirt from behind.

'Come along, little gentleman,' he said in an undertone, 'come and see the little bear I can show you!
Such a queer cross little bear. Oo-oo!'

The sleepy boy got up and listlessly dragged himself
after Moisey Moisevitch to see the bear. He went into a
little room, where, before he saw anything, he felt he
could not breathe from the smell of something sour and
decaying, which was much stronger here than in the
big room and probably spread from this room all over
the house. One part of the room was occupied by a big
bed, covered with a greasy quilt, and another by a
chest of drawers and heaps of rags of all kinds from a
woman's stiff petticoat to children's little breeches and
braces. A tallow candle stood on the chest of drawers.

Instead of the promised bear, Yegorushka saw a big
fat Jewess with her hair hanging loose, in a red flannel
skirt with black sprigs on it; she turned with difficulty
in the narrow space between the bed and the chest of
drawers and uttered drawn-out moaning as though

she had toothache. On seeing Yegorushka, she made a doleful, woebegone face, heaved a long-drawn-out sigh, and before he had time to look round, put to his lips a slice of bread smeared with honey.

'Eat it, dearie, eat it!' she said. 'You are here without your mamma, and no one to look after you. Eat it up.'

Yegorushka did eat it, though after the goodies and poppy-cakes he had every day at home, he did not think very much of the honey, which was mixed with wax and bees' wings. He ate while Moisey Moisevitch and the Jewess looked at him and sighed.

'Where are you going, dearie?' asked the Jewess.

'To school,' answered Yegorushka.

'And how many brothers and sisters have you got?'

'I am the only one; there are no others.'

'O-oh!' sighed the Jewess, and turned her eyes upward. 'Poor mamma, poor mamma! How she will weep and miss you! We are going to send our Nahum to school in a year. O-oh!'

'Ah, Nahum, Nahum!' sighed Moisey Moisevitch, and the skin of his pale face twitched nervously. 'And he is so delicate.'

The greasy quilt quivered, and from beneath it appeared a child's curly head on a very thin neck; two black eyes gleamed and stared with curiosity at Yegorushka. Still sighing, Moisey Moisevitch and the Jewess went to the chest of drawers and began talking in Yiddish. Moisey Moisevitch spoke in a low bass undertone, and altogether his talk in Yiddish was like a continual 'ghaal-ghaal-ghaal-ghaal . . .' while his wife answered him in a shrill voice like a turkeycock's, and the whole effect of her talk was something like 'Too-

too-too-too!' While they were consulting, another
little curly head on a thin neck peeped out of the
greasy quilt, then a third, then a fourth ... If Yegorushka had had a fertile imagination he might have
imagined that the hundred-headed hydra was hiding
under the quilt.

'Ghaal-ghaal-ghaal-ghaal!' said Moisey Moisevitch.

'Too-too-too-too!' answered the Jewess.

The consultation ended in the Jewess's diving with
a deep sigh into the chest of drawers, and, unwrapping
some sort of green rag there, she took out a big rye
cake made in the shape of a heart.

'Take it, dearie,' she said, giving Yegorushka the
cake; 'you have no mamma now – no one to give you
nice things.'

Yegorushka stuck the cake in his pocket and stag-
gered to the door, as he could not go on breathing the
foul, sour air in which the innkeeper and his wife lived.
Going back to the big room, he settled himself more
comfortably on the sofa and gave up trying to check
his straying thoughts.

As soon as Kuzmitchov had finished counting out
the notes he put them back into the bag. He did not
treat them very respectfully and stuffed them into
the dirty sack without ceremony, as indifferently as
though they had not been money but waste paper.

Father Christopher was talking to Solomon.

'Well, Solomon the Wise!' he said, yawning and
making the sign of the cross over his mouth. 'How is
business?'

'What sort of business are you talking about?'
asked Solomon, and he looked as fiendish, as though
it were a hint of some crime on his part.

'Oh, things in general. What are you doing?'

'What am I doing?' Solomon repeated, and he shrugged his shoulders. 'The same as everyone else . . . You see, I am a menial, I am my brother's servant; my brother's the servant of the visitors; the visitors are Varlamov's servants; and if I had ten millions, Varlamov would be my servant.'

'Why would he be your servant?'

'Why, because there isn't a gentleman or millionaire who isn't ready to lick the hand of a scabby Jew for the sake of making a kopeck. Now, I am a scabby Jew and a beggar. Everybody looks at me as though I were a dog, but if I had money Varlamov would play the fool before me just as Moisey does before you.'

Father Christopher and Kuzmitchov looked at each other. Neither of them understood Solomon. Kuzmitchov looked at him sternly and dryly, and asked:

'How can you compare yourself with Varlamov, you blockhead?'

'I am not such a fool as to put myself on a level with Varlamov,' answered Solomon, looking sarcastically at the speaker. 'Though Varlamov is a Russian, he is at heart a scabby Jew; money and gain are all he lives for, but I threw my money in the stove! I don't want money, or land, or sheep, and there is no need for people to be afraid of me and to take off their hats when I pass. So I am wiser than your Varlamov and more like a man!'

A little later Yegorushka, half asleep, heard Solomon in a hoarse hollow voice choked with hatred, in hurried stuttering phrases, talking about the Jews. At first he talked correctly in Russian, then he fell into the tone of a Jewish recitation, and began speaking as he had done at the fair with an exaggerated Jewish accent.

'Stop! ...' Father Christopher said to him. 'If you don't like your religion you had better change it, but to laugh at it is a sin; it is only the lowest of the low who will make fun of his religion.'

'You don't understand,' Solomon cut him short rudely. 'I am talking of one thing and you are talking of something else ...'

'One can see you are a foolish fellow,' sighed Father Christopher. 'I admonish you to the best of my ability, and you are angry. I speak to you like an old man quietly, and you answer like a turkeycock: "Bla— bla—bla!" You really are a queer fellow ...'

Moisey Moisevitch came in. He looked anxiously at Solomon and at his visitors, and again the skin on his face quivered nervously. Yegorushka shook his head and looked about him; he caught a passing glimpse of Solomon's face at the very moment when it was turned three-quarters towards him and when the shadow of his long nose divided his left cheek in half; the contemptuous smile mingled with that shadow; the gleaming sarcastic eyes, the haughty expression, and the whole plucked-looking little figure, dancing and doubling itself before Yegorushka's eyes, made him now not like a buffoon, but like something one sometimes dreams of, like an evil spirit.

'What a ferocious fellow you've got here, Moisey Moisevitch! God bless him!' said Father Christopher with a smile. 'You ought to find him a place or a wife or something ... There's no knowing what to make of him ...'

Kuzmitchov frowned angrily. Moisey Moisevitch

looked uneasily and inquiringly at his brother and the visitors again.

'Solomon, go away!' he said shortly. 'Go away!' and he added something in Yiddish. Solomon gave an abrupt laugh and went out.

'What was it?' Moisey Moisevitch asked Father Christopher anxiously.

'He forgets himself,' answered Kuzmitchov. 'He's rude and thinks too much of himself.'

'I knew it!' Moisey Moisevitch cried in horror, clasping his hands. 'Oh dear, oh dear!' he muttered in a low voice. 'Be so kind as to excuse it, and don't be angry. He is such a queer fellow, such a queer fellow! Oh dear, oh dear! He is my own brother, but I have never had anything but trouble from him. You know he's ...'

Moisey Moisevitch crooked his finger by his forehead and went on:

'He is not in his right mind; ... he's hopeless. And I don't know what I am to do with him! He cares for nobody, he respects nobody, and is afraid of nobody ... You know he laughs at everybody, he says silly things, speaks familiarly to anyone. You wouldn't believe it, Varlamov came here one day and Solomon said such things to him that he gave us both a taste of his whip ... But why whip me? Was it my fault? God has robbed him of his wits, so it is God's will, and how am I to blame?'

Ten minutes passed and Moisey Moisevitch was still muttering in an undertone and sighing:

'He does not sleep at night, and is always thinking and thinking and thinking, and what he is thinking about God only knows. If you go to him at night he is angry and laughs. He doesn't like me either ... And there is nothing he wants! When our father died he left us each six thousand roubles. I bought myself an inn, married, and now I have children; and he burnt all his money in the stove. Such a pity, such a pity! Why burn it? If he didn't want it he could give it to me, but why burn it?'

Suddenly the swing-door creaked and the floor shook under footsteps. Yegorushka felt a draught of cold air, and it seemed to him as though some big black bird had passed by him and had fluttered its wings close in his face. He opened his eyes ... His uncle was standing by the sofa with his sack in his hands ready for departure; Father Christopher, holding his broad-brimmed top-hat, was bowing to someone and smiling – not his usual soft kindly smile, but a respectful forced smile which did not suit his face at all – while Moisey Moisevitch looked as though his body had been broken into three parts, and he were balancing and doing his utmost not to drop to pieces. Only Solomon stood in the corner with his arms folded, as though nothing had happened, and smiled contemptuously as before.

'Your Excellency must excuse us for not being tidy,' moaned Moisey Moisevitch with the agonizingly sweet smile, taking no more notice of Kuzmitchov or Father Christopher, but swaying his whole person so as to avoid dropping to pieces. 'We are plain folks, your Excellency.'

Yegorushka rubbed his eyes. In the middle of the room there really was standing an Excellency, in the form of a young plump and very beautiful woman in a black dress and a straw hat. Before Yegorushka had time to examine her features the image of the solitary graceful poplar he had seen that day on the hill for some reason came into his mind.

'Has Varlamov been here to-day?' a woman's voice inquired.

'No, your Excellency,' said Moisey Moisevitch.

'If you see him to-morrow, ask him to come and see me for a minute.'

All at once, quite unexpectedly, Yegorushka saw half an inch from his eyes velvety black eyebrows, big brown eyes, delicate feminine cheeks with dimples, from which smiles seemed radiating all over the face like sunbeams. There was a glorious scent.

'What a pretty boy!' said the lady. 'Whose boy is it? Kazimir Mihalovitch, look what a charming fellow! Good heavens, he is asleep!'

And the lady kissed Yegorushka warmly on both cheeks, and he smiled and, thinking he was asleep, shut his eyes. The swing-door squeaked, and there was the sound of hurried footsteps, coming in and going out.

'Yegorushka, Yegorushka!' he heard two bass voices whisper. 'Get up; it is time to start.'

Somebody, it seemed to be Deniska, set him on his feet and led him by the arm. On the way he half-opened his eyes and once more saw the beautiful lady in the black dress who had kissed him. She was standing in the middle of the room and watched him go out, smiling at him and nodding her head in a friendly way. As he got near the door he saw a handsome, stoutly built, dark man in a bowler hat and in leather gaiters. This must have been the lady's escort.

'Woa!' he heard from the yard.

At the front door Yegorushka saw a splendid new

carriage and a pair of black horses. On the box sat a groom in livery, with a long whip in his hands. No one but Solomon came to see the travellers off. His face was tense with a desire to laugh; he looked as though he were waiting impatiently for the visitors to be gone, so that he might laugh at them without restraint.

'The Countess Dranitsky,' whispered Father Christopher, clambering into the chaise.

'Yes, Countess Dranitsky,' repeated Kuzmitchov, also in a whisper.

The impression made by the arrival of the countess was probably very great, for even Deniska spoke in a whisper, and only ventured to lash his bays and shout when the chaise had driven a quarter of a mile away and nothing could be seen of the inn but a dim light.

IV

WHO was this elusive, mysterious Varlamov of whom people talked so much, whom Solomon despised, and whom even the beautiful countess needed? Sitting on the box beside Deniska, Yegorushka, half asleep, thought about this person. He had never seen him. But he had often heard of him and pictured him in his imagination. He knew that Varlamov possessed several tens of thousands of acres of land, about a hundred thousand sheep, and a great deal of money. Of his manner of life and occupation Yegorushka knew nothing, except that he was always 'going his rounds in these parts,' and he was always being looked for.

At home Yegorushka had heard a great deal of the

Countess Dranitsky, too. She, too, had some tens of thousands of acres, a great many sheep, a stud farm and a great deal of money, but she did not 'go rounds,' but lived at home in a splendid house and grounds, about which Ivan Ivanitch, who had been more than once at the countess's on business, and other acquaintances told many marvellous tales; thus, for instance, they said that in the countess's drawing-room, where the portraits of all the kings of Poland hung on the walls, there was a big table-clock in the form of a rock, on the rock a gold horse with diamond eyes, rearing, and on the horse the figure of a rider also of gold, who brandished his sword to right and to left whenever the clock struck. They said, too, that twice a year the countess used to give a ball, to which the gentry and officials of the whole province were invited, and to which even Varlamov used to come; all the visitors drank tea from silver samovars, ate all sorts of extraordinary things (they had straw-berries and raspberries, for instance, in winter at Christmas), and danced to a band which played day and night …

'And how beautiful she is,' thought Yegorushka, remembering her face and smile.

Kuzmitchov, too, was probably thinking about the countess. For when the chaise had driven a mile and a half he said:

'But doesn't that Kazimir Mihalovitch plunder her right and left! The year before last when, do you remember, I bought some wool from her, he made over three thousand from my purchase alone.'

'That is just what you would expect from a Pole,' said Father Christopher.

'And little does it trouble her. Young and foolish, as they say, her head is full of nonsense.'

Yegorushka, for some reason, longed to think of nothing but Varlamov and the countess, particularly the latter. His drowsy brain utterly refused ordinary thoughts, was in a cloud and retained only fantastic fairy-tale images, which have the advantage of springing into the brain of themselves without any effort on the part of the thinker, and completely vanishing of themselves at a mere shake of the head; and, indeed, nothing that was around him disposed to ordinary thoughts. On the right there were the dark hills which seemed to be screening something unseen and terrible; on the left the whole sky about the horizon was covered with a crimson glow, and it was hard to tell whether there was a fire somewhere, or whether it was the moon about to rise. As by day the distance could be seen, but its tender lilac tint had gone, quenched by the evening darkness, in which the whole steppe was hidden like Moisey Moisevitch's children under the quilt.

Corncrakes and quails do not call in the July nights, the nightingale does not sing in the woodland marsh, and there is no scent of flowers, but still the steppe is lovely and full of life. As soon as the sun goes down and the darkness enfolds the earth, the day's weariness is forgotten, everything is forgiven, and the steppe breathes a light sigh from its broad bosom. As though because the grass cannot see in the dark that it has grown old, a gay youthful twitter rises up from it, such as is not heard by day; chirruping, twittering, whistling, scratching, the basses, tenors and sopranos of the steppe all mingle in an incessant, monotonous

roar of sound in which it is sweet to brood on memories and sorrows. The monotonous twitter soothes to
sleep like a lullaby; you drive and feel you are falling
asleep, but suddenly there comes the abrupt agitated
cry of a wakeful bird, or a vague sound like a voice
crying out in wonder 'A-ah, a-ah!' and slumber closes
one's eyelids again. Or you drive by a little creek
where there are bushes and hear the bird, called by
the steppe dwellers 'the sleeper,' call 'Asleep, asleep,
asleep!' while another laughs or breaks into trills of
hysterical weeping – that is the owl. For whom do
they call and who hears them on that plain, God only
knows, but there is deep sadness and lamentation in
their cry ... There is a scent of hay and dry grass
and belated flowers, but the scent is heavy, sweetly
mawkish and soft.

Everything can be seen through the mist, but it is
hard to make out the colours and the outlines of
objects. Everything looks different from what it is.
You drive on and suddenly see standing before you
right in the roadway a dark figure like a monk; it
stands motionless, waiting, holding something in its
hands ... Can it be a robber? The figure comes closer,
grows bigger; now it is on a level with the chaise, and
you see it is not a man, but a solitary bush or a great
stone. Such motionless expectant figures stand on the
low hills, hide behind the old barrows, peep out from
the high grass, and they all look like human beings
and arouse suspicion.

And when the moon rises the night becomes pale
and dim. The mist seems to have passed away. The air
is transparent, fresh and warm; one can see well in all
directions and even distinguish the separate stalks of

grass by the wayside. Stones and bits of pots can be seen at a long distance. The suspicious figures like monks look blacker against the light background of the night, and seem more sinister. More and more often in the midst of the monotonous chirruping there comes the sound of the 'A-ah, a-ah!' of astonishment troubling the motionless air, and the cry of a sleepless or delirious bird. Broad shadows move across the plain like clouds across the sky, and in the inconceivable distance, if you look long and intently at it, misty monstrous shapes rise up and huddle one against another ... It is rather uncanny. One glances at the pale green, star-spangled sky on which there is no cloudlet, no spot, and understands why the warm air is motionless, why nature is on her guard, afraid to stir: she is afraid and reluctant to lose one instant of life. Of the unfathomable depth and infinity of the sky one can only form a conception at sea and on the steppe by night when the moon is shining. It is terribly lonely and caressing; it looks down languid and alluring, and its caressing sweetness makes one giddy.

You drive on for one hour, for a second ... You meet upon the way a silent old barrow or a stone figure put up God knows when and by whom; a nightbird floats noiselessly over the earth, and little by little those legends of the steppes, the tales of men you have met, the stories of some old nurse from the steppe, and all the things you have managed to see and treasure in your soul, come back to your mind. And then in the churring of insects, in the sinister figures, in the ancient barrows, in the blue sky, in the moonlight, in the flight of the nightbird, in everything you see and hear, triumphant beauty, youth, the fulness of power, and the passionate thirst for life begin to be apparent; the soul responds to the call of her lovely austere fatherland, and longs to fly over the steppes with the nightbird. And in the triumph of beauty, in the exuberance of happiness you are conscious of yearning and grief, as though the steppe knew she was solitary, knew that her wealth and her inspiration were wasted for the world, not glorified in song, not wanted by anyone; and through the joyful clamour one hears her mournful, hopeless call for singers, singers!

'Woa! Good-evening, Panteley! Is everything all right?'

'First-rate, Ivan Ivanitch!'

'Haven't you seen Varlamov, lads?'

'No, we haven't.'

Yegorushka woke up and opened his eyes. The chaise had stopped. On the right the train of waggons stretched for a long way ahead on the road, and men were moving to and fro near them. All the waggons being loaded up with great bales of wool looked very high and fat, while the horses looked short-legged and little.

'Well, then, we shall go on to the Molokans'!' Kuzmitchov said aloud. 'The Jew told us that Varlamov was putting up for the night at the Molokans'. So good-bye lads! Good luck to you!'

'Good-bye, Ivan Ivanitch,' several voices replied.

'I say, lads,' Kuzmitchov cried briskly, 'you take my little lad along with you! Why should he go jolting off with us for nothing? You put him on the bales, Panteley, and let him come on slowly, and we shall overtake you. Get down, Yegor! Go on; it's all right ...'

Yegorushka got down from the box-seat. Several

hands caught him, lifted him high into the air, and he found himself on something big, soft, and rather wet with dew. It seemed to him now as though the sky were quite close and the earth far away.

'Hey, take his little coat!' Deniska shouted from somewhere far below.

His coat and bundle flung up from far below fell close to Yegorushka. Anxious not to think of anything, he quickly put his bundle under his head and covered himself with his coat, and stretching his legs out and shrinking a little from the dew, he laughed with content.

'Sleep, sleep, sleep . . .' he thought.

'Don't be unkind to him, you devils!' he heard Deniska's voice below.

'Good-bye lads; good luck to you,' shouted Kuzmitchov. 'I rely upon you!'

'Don't you be uneasy, Ivan Ivanitch!'

Deniska shouted to the horses, the chaise creaked and started, not along the road, but somewhere off to the side. For two minutes there was silence, as though the waggons were asleep and there was no sound except the clanking of the pails tied on at the back of the chaise as it slowly died away in the distance. Then someone at the head of the waggons shouted:

'Kiruha! Sta-art!'

The foremost of the waggons creaked, then the second, then the third . . . Yegorushka felt the waggon he was on sway and creak also. The waggons were moving. Yegorushka took a tighter hold of the cord with which the bales were tied on, laughed again with content, shifted the cake in his pocket, and fell asleep just as he did in his bed at home . . .

When he woke up the sun had risen, it was screened by an ancient barrow, and, trying to shed its light upon the earth, it scattered its beams in all directions and flooded the horizon with gold. It seemed to Yegorushka that it was not in its proper place, as the day before it had risen behind his back, and now it was much more to his left ... And the whole landscape was different. There were no hills now, but on all sides, wherever one looked, there stretched the brown cheerless plain; here and there upon it small barrows rose up and rooks flew as they had done the day before. The belfries and huts of some village showed white in the distance ahead; as it was Sunday the Little Russians were at home baking and cooking – that could be seen by the smoke which rose from every chimney and hung, a dark blue transparent veil, over the village. In between the huts and beyond the church there were blue glimpses of a river, and beyond the river a misty distance. But nothing was so different from yesterday as the road. Something extraordinarily broad, spread out and titanic, stretched over the steppe by way of a road. It was a grey streak well trodden down and covered with dust, like all roads. Its width puzzled Yegorushka and brought thoughts of fairy tales to his mind. Who travelled along that road? Who needed so much space? It was strange and unintelligible. It might have been supposed that giants with immense strides, such as Ilya Muromets and Solovy the Brigand, were still surviving in Russia, and that their gigantic steeds were still alive. Yegorushka, looking at the road, imagined some half a dozen high chariots racing along side by side, like some he used to see in pictures in his Scripture his-

tory; these chariots were each drawn by six wild furious horses, and their great wheels raised a cloud of
dust to the sky, while the horses were driven by men
such as one may see in one's dreams or in imagination
brooding over fairy tales. And if those figures had
existed, how perfectly in keeping with the steppe and
the road they would have been!

Telegraph-poles with two wires on them stretched
along the right side of the road to its furthermost
limit. Growing smaller and smaller, they disappeared
near the village behind the huts and green trees, and
then again came into sight in the lilac distance in the
form of very small thin sticks that looked like pencils
stuck into the ground. Hawks, falcons, and crows sat
on the wires and looked indifferently at the moving
waggons.

Yegorushka was lying in the last of the waggons,
and so could see the whole string. There were about
twenty waggons, and there was a driver to every three
waggons. By the last waggon, the one in which Yegorushka was, there walked an old man with a grey
beard, as short and lean as Father Christopher, but
with a sunburnt, stern and brooding face. It is very
possible that the old man was not stern and not
brooding, but his red eyelids and his sharp long nose
gave his face a stern frigid expression such as is common with people in the habit of continually thinking
of serious things in solitude. Like Father Christopher
he was wearing a wide-brimmed top-hat, not like a
gentleman's, but made of brown felt, and in shape
more like a cone with the top cut off than a real top-
hat. Probably from a habit acquired in cold winters,
when he must more than once have been nearly frozen

as he trudged beside the waggons, he kept slapping his thighs and stamping with his feet as he walked. Noticing that Yegorushka was awake, he looked at him and said, shrugging his shoulders as though from the cold:

'Ah, you are awake, youngster! So you are the son of Ivan Ivanitch?'

'No; his nephew ...'

'Nephew of Ivan Ivanitch? Here I have taken off my boots and am hopping along barefoot. My feet are bad; they are swollen, and it's easier without my boots ... easier, youngster ... without boots, I mean ... So you are his nephew? He is a good man; no harm in him ... God give him health ... No harm in him ... I mean Ivan Ivanitch ... He has gone to the Molokans' ... O Lord, have mercy upon us!'

The old man talked, too, as though it were very cold, pausing and not opening his mouth properly; and he mispronounced the labial consonants, stuttering over them as though his lips were frozen. As he talked to Yegorushka he did not once smile, and he seemed stern.

Two waggons ahead of them there walked a man wearing a long reddish-brown coat, a cap and high boots with sagging bootlegs, and carrying a whip in his hand. This was not an old man, only about forty. When he looked round Yegorushka saw a long red face with a scanty goat beard and a spongy-looking swelling under his right eye. Apart from this very ugly swelling, there was another peculiar thing about him which caught the eye at once: in his left hand he carried a whip, while he waved the right as though he were conducting an unseen choir; from time to time he put the whip under his arm, and then he conducted with both hands and hummed something to himself.

The next driver was a long rectilinear figure with extremely sloping shoulders and a back as flat as a board. He held himself as stiffly erect as though he were marching or had swallowed a yard measure. His hands did not swing as he walked, but hung down as if they were straight sticks, and he strode along in a wooden way, after the manner of toy soldiers, almost without bending his knees, and trying to take as long steps as possible. While the old man or the owner of the spongy swelling were taking two steps he succeeded in taking only one, and so it seemed as though he were walking more slowly than any of them, and would drop behind. His face was tied up in a rag, and on his head something stuck up that looked like a monk's peaked cap; he was dressed in a short Little Russian coat, with full dark blue trousers and bark shoes.

Yegorushka did not even distinguish those that were farther on. He lay on his stomach, picked a little hole in the bale, and, having nothing better to do, began twisting the wool into a thread. The old man trudging along below him turned out not to be so stern as one might have supposed from his face. Having begun a conversation, he did not let it drop.

'Where are you going?' he asked, stamping with his feet.

'To school,' answered Yegorushka.

'To school? Aha! . . . Well, may the Queen of Heaven help you. Yes. One brain is good, but two are better. To one man God gives one brain, to another two brains, and to another three . . . To another three, that is true ... One brain you are born with, one you get from learning, and a third with a good life. So you see, my lad, it is a good thing if a man has three brains. Living is easier for him, and, what's more, dying is, too. Dying is, too ... And we shall all die for sure.'

The old man scratched his forehead, glanced upwards at Yegorushka with his red eyes, and went on:

'Maxim Nikolaitch, the gentleman from Slavyano-serbsk, brought a little lad to school, too, last year. I don't know how he is getting on there in studying the sciences, but he was a nice good little lad ... God give them help, they are nice gentlemen. Yes, he, too, brought his boy to school ... In Slavyanoserbsk there is no establishment, I suppose, for study. No ... But it is a nice town ... There's an ordinary school for simple folks, but for the higher studies there is nothing. No, that's true. What's your name? ...'

'Yegorushka.'

'Yegory, then ... The holy martyr Yegory, the Bearer of Victory, whose day is the twenty-third of April. And my christian name is Panteley ... Panteley Zaharov Holodov ... We are Holodovs ... I am a native of – maybe you've heard of it – Tim in the province of Kursk. My brothers are artisans and work at trades in the town, but I am a peasant ... I have remained a peasant. Seven years ago I went there – home, I mean. I went to the village and to the town ... To Tim, I mean. Then, thank God, they were all alive and well; ... but now I don't know ... Maybe some of them are dead ... And it's time they did die, for some of them are older than I am. Death is all right; it is good so long, of course, as one does not die without repentance. There is no worse evil than an impenitent death; an impenitent death is a joy to the devil. And if you want to die penitent so that you may not be forbidden to enter the mansions of the Lord, pray to the holy martyr Varvara. She is the intercessor. She is, that's the truth ... For God has given her such a place in the heavens that everyone has the right to pray to her for penitence.'

Panteley went on muttering, and apparently did not trouble whether Yegorushka heard him or not. He talked listlessly, mumbling to himself, without raising or dropping his voice, but succeeded in telling him a great deal in a short time. All he said was made up of fragments that had very little connection with one another, and quite uninteresting for Yegorushka. Possibly he talked only in order to reckon over his thoughts aloud after the night spent in silence, in order to see if they were all there. After talking of repentance, he spoke about a certain Maxim Nikolaitch from Slavyanoserbsk.

'Yes, he took his little lad; ... he took him, that's true ...'

One of the waggoners walking in front darted from his place, ran to one side and began lashing on the ground with his whip. He was a stalwart, broad-shouldered man of thirty, with curly flaxen hair and a look of great health and vigour. Judging from the movements of his shoulders and the whip, and the eagerness expressed in his attitude, he was beating something alive. Another waggoner, a short stubby little man with a bushy black beard, wearing a waistcoat and a shirt outside his trousers, ran up to him. The latter broke into a deep guffaw of laughter and coughing and said: 'I say, lads, Dymov has killed a snake!'

There are people whose intelligence can be gauged at once by their voice and laughter. The man with the black beard belonged to that class of fortunate individuals; impenetrable stupidity could be felt in his voice and laugh. The flaxen-headed Dymov had finished, and lifting from the ground with his whip something like a cord, flung it with a laugh into the cart.

'That's not a viper; it's a grass snake!' shouted someone.

The man with the wooden gait and the bandage round his face strode up quickly to the dead snake, glanced at it and flung up his stick-like arms.

'You jail-bird!' he cried in a hollow wailing voice. 'What have you killed a grass snake for? What had he done to you, you damned brute? Look, he has killed a grass snake; how would you like to be treated so?'

'Grass snakes ought not to be killed, that's true,' Panteley muttered placidly, 'they ought not ... They are not vipers; though it looks like a snake, it is a gentle, innocent creature ... It's friendly to man, the grass snake is.'

Dymov and the man with the black beard were probably ashamed, for they laughed loudly, and not answering, slouched lazily back to their waggons. When the hindmost waggon was level with the spot where the dead snake lay, the man with his face tied up standing over it turned to Panteley and asked in a tearful voice:

'Grandfather, what did he want to kill the grass snake for?'

His eyes, as Yegorushka saw now, were small and dingy-looking; his face was grey, sickly and looked somehow dingy too while his chin was red and seemed very much swollen.

'Grandfather, what did he kill it for?' he repeated, striding along beside Panteley.

'A stupid fellow. His hands itch to kill, and that is why he does it,' answered the old man; 'but he oughtn't to kill a grass snake, that's true ... Dymov is a ruffian, we all know, he kills everything he comes across, and Kiruha did not interfere. He ought to have taken its part, but instead of that, he goes off into "Ha-ha-ha!" and "Ho-ho-ho!" ... But don't be angry, Vassya ... Why be angry? They've killed it – well, never mind them. Dymov is a ruffian and Kiruha acted from foolishness – never mind ... They are foolish people without understanding – but there, don't mind them. Emelyan here never touches what he shouldn't; ... he never does; ... that is true ... because he is a man of education, while they are stupid ... Emelyan, he doesn't touch things.'

The waggoner in the reddish-brown coat and the spongy swelling on his face, who was conducting an unseen choir, stopped. Hearing his name, and waiting till Panteley and Vassya came up to him, he walked beside them.

'What are you talking about?' he asked in a husky muffled voice.

'Why, Vassya here is angry,' said Panteley. 'So I have been saying things to him to stop his being angry ... Oh, how my swollen feet hurt! Oh, oh! They are more inflamed than ever for Sunday, God's holy day!'

'It's from walking,' observed Vassya.

'No, lad, no. It's not from walking. When I walk it seems easier; when I lie down and get warm ... it's deadly. Walking is easier for me.'

Emelyan, in his reddish-brown coat, walked between Panteley and Vassya and waved his arms, as though they were going to sing. After waving them a little while he dropped them, and croaked out hopelessly:

'I have no voice. It's a real misfortune. All last night and this morning I have been haunted by the trio "Lord, have Mercy" that we sang at the wedding at Marionovsky's. It's in my head and in my throat. It seems as though I could sing it, but I can't; I have no voice.'

He paused for a minute, thinking, then went on:

'For fifteen years I was in the choir. In all the Lugansky works there was, maybe, no one with a voice like mine. But, confound it, I bathed two years ago in the Donets, and I can't get a single note true ever since. I took cold in my throat. And without a voice I am like a workman without hands.'

'That's true,' Panteley agreed.

'I think of myself as a ruined man and nothing more.'

At that moment Vassya chanced to catch sight of Yegorushka. His eyes grew moist and smaller than ever.

'There's a little gentleman driving with us,' and he covered his nose with his sleeve as though he were bashful. 'What a grand driver! Stay with us and you shall drive the waggons and sell wool.'

The incongruity of one person being at once a little

gentleman and a waggon driver seemed to strike him as very queer and funny, for he burst into a loud guffaw, and went on enlarging upon the idea. Emelyan glanced upwards at Yegorushka, too, but coldly and cursorily. He was absorbed in his own thoughts, and had it not been for Vassya, would not have noticed Yegorushka's presence. Before five minutes had passed he was waving his arms again, then describing to his companions the beauties of the wedding anthem, "Lord, have Mercy," which he had remembered in the night. He put the whip under his arm and waved both hands.

A mile from the village the waggons stopped by a well with a crane. Letting his pail down into the well, black-bearded Kiruha lay on his stomach on the framework and thrust his shaggy head, his shoulders, and part of his chest into the black hole, so that Yegorushka could see nothing but his short legs, which scarcely touched the ground. Seeing the reflection of his head far down at the bottom of the well, he was delighted and went off into his deep bass stupid laugh, and the echo from the well answered him. When he got up his neck and face were as red as beetroot. The first to run up and drink was Dymov. He drank laughing, often turning from the pail to tell Kiruha something funny, then he turned round, and uttered aloud, to be heard all over the steppe, five very bad words. Yegorushka did not understand the meaning of such words, but he knew very well they were bad words. He knew the repulsion his friends and relations silently felt for such words. He himself, without knowing why, shared that feeling and was accustomed to think that only drunk and disorderly people enjoy the privilege of uttering such words aloud. He remembered the murder of the grass snake, listened to Dymov's laughter, and felt something like hatred for the man. And as ill-luck would have it, Dymov at that moment caught sight of Yegorushka, who had climbed down from the waggon and gone up to the well. He laughed aloud and shouted:

'I say, lads, the old man has been brought to bed of a boy in the night.'

Kiruha laughed his bass laugh till he coughed. Someone else laughed too, while Yegorushka crimsoned and made up his mind finally that Dymov was a very wicked man.

With his curly flaxen head, with his shirt opened on his chest and no hat on, Dymov looked handsome and exceptionally strong; in every movement he made one could see the reckless daredevil and athlete, knowing his value. He shrugged his shoulders, put his arms akimbo, talked and laughed louder than any of the rest, and looked as though he were going to lift up something very heavy with one hand and astonish the whole world by doing so. His mischievous mocking eyes glided over the road, the waggons, and the sky without resting on anything, and seemed looking for someone to kill, just as a pastime, and something to laugh at. Evidently he was afraid of no one, would stick at nothing, and most likely was not in the least interested in Yegorushka's opinion of him ... Yegorushka meanwhile hated his flaxen head, his clear face, and his strength with his whole heart, listened with fear and loathing to his laughter, and kept thinking what word of abuse he could pay him out with.

Panteley, too, went up to the pail. He took out of

his pocket a little green glass of an ikon lamp, wiped it with a rag, filled it from the pail and drank from it, then filled it again, wrapped the little glass in the rag, and then put it back into his pocket.

'Grandfather, why do you drink out of a lamp?' Yegorushka asked him, surprised.

'One man drinks out of a pail and another out of a lamp,' the old man answered evasively. 'Every man to his own taste ... You drink out of the pail – well, drink, and may it do you good ...'

'You darling, you beauty!' Vassya said suddenly, in a caressing plaintive voice. 'You darling!'

His eyes were fixed on the distance; they were moist and smiling, and his face wore the same expression as when he had looked at Yegorushka.

'Who is it you are talking to?' asked Kiruha.

'A darling fox ... lying on her back, playing like a dog.'

Everyone began staring into the distance, looking for the fox, but no one could see it, only Vassya with his grey muddy-looking eyes, and he was enchanted by it. His sight was extraordinarily keen, as Yegorushka learnt afterwards. He was so long-sighted that the brown steppe was for him always full of life and interest. He had only to look into the distance to see a fox, a hare, a bustard, or some other animal keeping at a distance from men. There was nothing strange in seeing a hare running away or a flying bustard – everyone crossing the steppes could see them; but it was not vouchsafed to everyone to see wild animals in their own haunts when they were not running nor hiding, nor looking about them in alarm. Yet Vassya saw foxes playing, hares washing themselves with their paws, bustards preening their wings and hammering out their hollow nests. Thanks to this keenness of sight, Vassya had, besides the world seen by everyone, another world of his own, accessible to no one else, and probably a very beautiful one, for when he saw something and was in raptures over it it was impossible not to envy him.

When the waggons set off again, the church bells were ringing for service.

V

THE train of waggons drew up on the bank of a river on one side of a village. The sun was blazing, as it had been the day before; the air was stagnant and depressing. There were a few willows on the bank, but the shade from them did not fall on the earth, but on the water, where it was wasted; even in the shade under the waggon it was stifling and wearisome. The water, blue from the reflection of the sky in it, was alluring.

Styopka, a waggoner whom Yegorushka noticed now for the first time, a Little Russian lad of eighteen, in a long shirt without a belt, and full trousers that flapped like flags as he walked, undressed quickly, ran along the steep bank and plunged into the water. He dived three times, then swam on his back and shut his eyes in his delight. His face was smiling and wrinkled up as though he were being tickled, hurt and amused.

On a hot day when there is nowhere to escape from the sultry, stifling heat, the splash of water and the loud breathing of a man bathing sounds like good music to the ear. Dymov and Kiruha, looking at Styopka, undressed quickly and one after the other,

laughing loudly in eager anticipation of their enjoyment, dropped into the water, and the quiet modest
little river resounded with snorting and splashing and
shouting. Kiruha coughed, laughed and shouted as
though they were trying to drown him, while Dymov
chased him and tried to catch him by the leg.

'Ha-ha-ha!' he shouted. 'Catch him! Hold him!'

Kiruha laughed and enjoyed himself, but his expression was the same as it had been on dry land, stupid,
with a look of astonishment on it as though someone
had, unnoticed, stolen up behind him and hit him on
the head with the butt-end of an axe. Yegorushka
undressed, too, but did not let himself down by the
bank, but took a run and a flying leap from the height
of about ten feet. Describing an arc in the air, he fell
into the water, sank deep, but did not reach the bottom; some force, cold and pleasant to the touch,
seemed to hold him up and bring him back to the surface. He popped out and, snorting and blowing
bubbles, opened his eyes; but the sun was reflected in
the water quite close to his face. At first blinding spots
of light, then rainbow colours and dark patches, flitted
before his eyes. He made haste to dive again, opened
his eyes in the water and saw something cloudy-green
like a sky on a moonlight night. Again the same force
would not let him touch the bottom and stay in the
coolness, but lifted him to the surface. He popped out
and heaved a sigh so deep that he had a feeling of space
and freshness, not only in his chest, but in his stomach.
Then, to get from the water everything he possibly
could get, he allowed himself every luxury; he lay on
his back and basked, splashed, frolicked, swam on his
face, on his side, on his back and standing up – just as

he pleased till he was exhausted. The other bank was thickly overgrown with reeds; it was golden in the sun, and the flowers of the reeds hung drooping to the water in lovely tassels. In one place the reeds were shaking and nodding, with their flowers rustling – Styopka and Kiruha were hunting crayfish.

'A crayfish, look lads! A crayfish!' Kiruha cried triumphantly and actually showed a crayfish.

Yegorushka swam up to the reeds, dived, and began fumbling among their roots. Burrowing in the slimy, liquid mud, he felt something sharp and unpleasant – perhaps it really was a crayfish. But at that minute someone seized him by the leg and pulled him to the surface. Spluttering and coughing, Yegorushka opened his eyes and saw before him the wet grinning face of the daredevil Dymov. The impudent fellow was breathing hard, and from a look in his eyes he seemed inclined for further mischief. He held Yegorushka tight by the leg, and was lifting his hand to take hold of his neck. But Yegorushka tore himself away with repulsion and terror, as though disgusted at being touched and afraid that the bully would drown him, and said:

'Fool! I'll punch you in the face.'

Feeling that this was not sufficient to express his hatred, he thought a minute and added:

'You blackguard! You son of a bitch!'

But Dymov, as though nothing were the matter, took no further notice of Yegorushka, but swam off to Kiruha, shouting:

'Ha-ha-ha! Let us catch fish! Mates, let us catch fish.'

'To be sure,' Kiruha agreed; 'there must be a lot of fish here.'

'Styopka, run to the village and ask the peasants for a net!'

'They won't give it to me.'

'They will, you ask them. Tell them that they should give it to us for Christ's sake, because we are just the same as pilgrims.'

'That's true.'

Styopka clambered out of the water, dressed quickly, and without a cap on he ran, his full trousers flapping, to the village. The water lost all its charm for Yegorushka after his encounter with Dymov. He got out and began dressing. Panteley and Vassya were sitting on the steep bank, with their legs hanging down, looking at the bathers. Emelyan was standing naked, up to his knees in the water, holding on to the grass with one hand to prevent himself from falling while the other stroked his body. With his bony shoulder-blades, with the swelling under his eye, bending down and evidently afraid of the water, he made a ludicrous figure. His face was grave and severe. He looked angrily at the water, as though he were just going to upbraid it for having given him cold in the Donets and robbed him of his voice.

'And why don't you bathe?' Yegorushka asked Vassya.

'Oh, I don't care for it . . .' answered Vassya.

'How is it your chin is swollen?'

'It's bad . . . I used to work at the match factory, little sir . . . The doctor used to say that it would make my jaw rot. The air is not healthy there. There were three chaps beside me who had their jaws swollen, and with one of them it rotted away altogether.'

Styopka soon came back with the net. Dymov and

Kiruha were already turning blue and getting hoarse
by being so long in the water, but they set about fishing eagerly. First they went to a deep place beside the
reeds; there Dymov was up to his neck, while the
water went over squat Kiruha's head. The latter
spluttered and blew bubbles, while Dymov stumbling
on the prickly roots, fell over and got caught in the
net; both flopped about in the water, and made a
noise, and nothing but mischief came of their fishing.

'It's deep,' croaked Kiruha. 'You won't catch
anything.'

'Don't tug, you devil!' shouted Dymov trying to
put the net in the proper position. 'Hold it up.'

'You won't catch anything here,' Panteley shouted
from the bank. 'You are only frightening the fish, you
stupids! Go more to the left! It's shallower there!'

Once a big fish gleamed above the net; they all drew
a breath, and Dymov struck the place where it had
vanished with his fist, and his face expressed
vexation.

'Ugh!' cried Panteley, and he stamped his foot.
'You've let the perch slip! It's gone!'

Moving more to the left, Dymov and Kiruha picked
out a shallower place, and then fishing began in earn-
est. They had wandered off some hundred paces from
the waggons; they could be seen silently trying to go
as deep as they could and as near the reeds, moving
their legs a little at a time, drawing out the nets, beating the water with their fists to drive them towards
the nets. From the reeds they got to the further bank;
they drew the net out, then, with a disappointed air,
lifting their knees high as they walked, went back into
the reeds. They were talking about something, but

what it was no one could hear. The sun was scorching their backs, the flies were stinging them, and their bodies had turned from purple to crimson. Styopka was walking after them with a pail in his hands; he had tucked his shirt right up under his armpits, and was holding it up by the hem with his teeth. After every successful catch he lifted up some fish and letting it shine in the sun, shouted:

'Look at this perch! We've five like that!'

Every time Dymov, Kiruha, and Styopka pulled out the net they could be seen fumbling about in the mud in it, putting some things into the pail and throwing other things away; sometimes they passed something that was in the net from hand to hand, examined it inquisitively, then threw that, too, away.

'What is it?' they shouted to them from the bank.

Styopka made some answer, but it was hard to make out his words. Then he climbed out of the water and, holding the pail in both hands, forgetting to let his shirt drop, ran to the waggons.

'It's full!' he shouted, breathing hard. 'Give us another!'

Yegorushka looked into the pail: it was full. A young pike poked its ugly nose out of the water, and there were swarms of crayfish and little fish round about it. Yegorushka put his hand down to the bottom and stirred up the water; the pike vanished under the crayfish, and a perch and a tench swam to the surface instead of it. Vassya, too, looked into the pail. His eyes grew moist and his face looked as caressing as before when he saw the fox. He took something out of the pail, put it to his mouth and began chewing it.

'Mates,' said Styopka in amazement, 'Vassya is eating a live gudgeon! Phoo!'

'It's not a gudgeon, but a minnow,' Vassya answered calmly, still munching.

He took a fish's tail out of his mouth, looked at it caressingly, and put it back again. While he was chewing and crunching with his teeth it seemed to Yegorushka that he saw before him something not human. Vassya's swollen chin, his lustreless eyes, his extraordinary sharp sight, the fish's tail in his mouth, and the caressing friendliness with which he crunched the gudgeon made him like an animal.

Yegorushka felt dreary beside him. And the fishing was over, too. He walked about beside the waggons, thought a little, and, feeling bored, strolled off to the village.

Not long afterwards he was standing in the church, and with his forehead leaning on somebody's back, listened to the singing of the choir. The service was drawing to a close. Yegorushka did not understand church singing and did not care for it. He listened a little, yawned, and began looking at the backs and heads before him. In one head, red and wet from his recent bathe, he recognized Emelyan. The back of his head had been cropped in a straight line higher than is usual; the hair in front had been cut unbecomingly high, and Emelyan's ears stood out like two dock leaves, and seemed to feel themselves out of place. Looking at the back of his head and his ears, Yegorushka, for some reason, thought that Emelyan was probably very unhappy. He remembered the way he conducted with his hands, his husky voice, his timid air when he was bathing,

and felt intense pity for him. He longed to say something friendly to him.

'I am here, too,' he said, putting out his hand.

People who sing tenor or bass in the choir, especially
those who have at any time in their lives conducted,
are accustomed to look with a stern and unfriendly air
at boys. They do not give up this habit, even when
they leave off being in a choir. Turning to Yegorushka,
Emelyan looked at him from under his brows and said:

'Don't play in church!'

Then Yegorushka moved forwards nearer to the
ikon-stand. Here he saw interesting people. On the
right side, in front of everyone, a lady and a gentleman
were standing on a carpet. There were chairs behind
them. The gentleman was wearing newly ironed shan-
tung trousers; he stood as motionless as a soldier
saluting, and held high his bluish shaven chin. There
was a very great air of dignity in his stand-up collar,
in his blue chin, in his small bald patch and his cane.
His neck was so strained from excess of dignity, and
his chin was drawn up so tensely, that it looked as
though his head were ready to fly off and soar
upwards any minute. The lady, who was stout and
elderly and wore a white silk shawl, held her head on
one side and looked as though she had done someone
a favour, and wanted to say: 'Oh, don't trouble yourself to thank me; I don't like it ...'. A thick wall of
Little Russian heads stood all round the carpet.

Yegorushka went up to the ikon-stand and began
kissing the local ikons. Before each image he slowly
bowed down to the ground, without getting up,
looked round at the congregation, then got up and
kissed the ikon. The contact of his forehead with the

cold floor afforded him great satisfaction. When the
beadle came from the altar with a pair of long snuffers
to put out the candles, Yegorushka jumped up quickly
from the floor and ran up to him.

'Have they given out the holy bread?' he asked.

'There is none; there is none,' the beadle muttered
gruffly. 'It is no use your . . .'

The service was over; Yegorushka walked out of the
church in a leisurely way, and began strolling about
the market-place. He had seen a good many villages,
market-places, and peasants in his time, and everything that met his eyes was entirely without interest
for him. At a loss for something to do, he went into a
shop over the door of which hung a wide strip of red
cotton. The shop consisted of two roomy, badly
lighted parts; in one half they sold drapery and gro-
ceries, in the other there were tubs of tar, and there
were horse-collars hanging from the ceiling; from both
came the savoury smell of leather and tar. The floor of
the shop had been watered; the man who watered it
must have been a very whimsical and original person
for it was sprinkled in patterns and mysterious sym-
bols. The shopkeeper, an overfed-looking man with
a broad face and round beard, apparently a Great
Russian, was standing, leaning his person over the
counter. He was nibbling a piece of sugar as he drank
his tea, and heaved a deep sigh at every sip. His face
expressed complete indifference, but each sigh seemed
to be saying:

'Just wait a minute; I will give it you.'

'Give me a farthing's worth of sunflower seeds,'
Yegorushka said, addressing him.

The shopkeeper raised his eyebrows, came out from

behind the counter, and poured a farthing's worth of sunflower seeds into Yegorushka's pocket, using an empty pomatum pot as a measure. Yegorushka did not want to go away. He spent a long time in examining the box of cakes, thought a little and asked, pointing to some little cakes covered with the mildew of age:

'How much are these cakes?'

'Two for a farthing.'

Yegorushka took out of his pocket the cake given him the day before by the Jewess, and asked him:

'And how much do you charge for cakes like this?'

The shopman took the cake in his hands, looked at it from all sides, and raised one eyebrow.

'Like that?' he asked.

Then he raised the other eyebrow, thought a minute, and answered:

'Two for three farthings . . .'

A silence followed.

'Whose boy are you?' the shopman asked, pouring himself out some tea from a red copper teapot.

'The nephew of Ivan Ivanitch.'

'There are all sorts of Ivan Ivanitchs,' the shopkeeper sighed. He looked over Yegorushka's head towards the door, paused a minute and asked: 'Would you like some tea?'

'Please . . .' Yegorushka assented not very readily, though he felt an intense longing for his usual morning tea.

The shopkeeper poured him out a glass and gave him with it a bit of sugar that looked as though it had been nibbled. Yegorushka sat down on the folding chair and began drinking it. He wanted to ask the price of a pound of sugar almonds, and had just broached the subject when a customer walked in, and the shopkeeper, leaving his glass of tea, attended to his business. He led the customer into the other half, where there was a smell of tar, and was there a long time discussing something with him. The customer, a man apparently very obstinate and pig-headed, was continually shaking his head to signify his disapproval, and retreating towards the door. The shopkeeper tried to persuade him of something and began pouring some oats into a big sack for him.

'Do you call those oats?' the customer said gloomily. 'Those are not oats, but chaff. It's a mockery to give that to the hens; enough to make the hens laugh ... No, I will go to Bondarenko.'

When Yegorushka went back to the river a small camp-fire was smoking on the bank. The waggoners were cooking their dinner. Styopka was standing in the smoke, stirring the cauldron with a big notched spoon. A little on one side Kiruha and Vassya, with eyes reddened from the smoke, were sitting cleaning the fish. Before them lay the net covered with slime and water weeds, and on it lay gleaming fish and crawling crayfish.

Emelyan, who had not long been back from the church, was sitting beside Panteley, waving his arm and humming just audibly in a husky voice: 'To Thee we sing ...' Dymov was moving about by the horses.

When they had finished cleaning them, Kiruha and Vassya put the fish and the living crayfish together in the pail, rinsed them, and from the pail poured them all into the boiling water.

'Shall I put in some fat?' asked Styopka skimming off the froth.

'No need. The fish will make its own gravy,' answered Kiruha.

Before taking the cauldron off the fire Styopka scattered into the water three big handfuls of millet and a spoonful of salt; finally he tried it, smacked his lips, licked the spoon, and gave a self-satisfied grunt, which meant that the grain was done.

All except Panteley sat down near the cauldron and set to work with their spoons.

'You there! Give the little lad a spoon!' Panteley observed sternly. 'I dare say he is hungry too!'

'Ours is peasant fare,' sighed Kiruha.

'Peasant fare is welcome, too, when one is hungry.'

They gave Yegorushka a spoon. He began eating, not sitting but standing close to the cauldron and looking down into it as in a hole. The grain smelt of fish and fish-scales were mixed up with the millet. The crayfish could not be hooked out with a spoon, and the men simply picked them out of the cauldron with their hands; Vassya did so particularly freely, and wetted his sleeves as well as his hands in the mess. But yet the stew seemed to Yegorushka very nice, and reminded him of the crayfish soup which his mother used to make at home on fast-days. Panteley was sitting apart munching bread.

'Grandfather, why aren't you eating?' Emelyan asked him.

'I don't eat crayfish ... Nasty things,' the old man said, and turned away with disgust.

While they were eating they all talked. From this conversation Yegorushka gathered that all his new acquaintances, in spite of the differences of their ages and their characters, had one point in common which made them all alike: they were all people with a splendid past and a very poor present. Of their past they all – every one of them – spoke with enthusiasm; their attitude to the present was almost one of contempt. The Russian loves recalling life, but he does not love living. Yegorushka did not yet know that, and before the stew had been all eaten he firmly believed that the men sitting round the cauldron were the injured victims of fate. Panteley told them that in the past, before there were railways, he used to go with trains of waggons to Moscow and to Nizhni, and used to earn so much that he did not know what to do with his money; and what merchants there used to be in those days! what fish! how cheap everything was! Now the roads were shorter, the merchants were stingier, the peasants were poorer, the bread was dearer, everything had shrunk and was on a smaller scale. Emelyan told them that in the old days he had been in the choir in Lugansky works, and that he had a remarkable voice and read music splendidly, while now he had become a peasant and lived on the charity of his brother, who sent him out with his horses and took half his earnings. Vassya had once worked in a match factory; Kiruha had been a coachman in a good family, and had been reckoned the smartest driver of a three-in-hand in the whole district. Dymov, the son of a well-to-do peasant, lived at ease, enjoyed himself and had known no trouble till he was twenty, when his stern harsh father, anxious to train him to work, and afraid he would be spoiled at home, had sent him to a carrier's to work as a hired labourer. Styopka was the only one who said nothing, but from his beardless face it was evident that his life had been a much better one in the past.

Thinking of his father, Dymov frowned and left off eating. Sullenly from under his brows he looked round at his companions and his eye rested upon Yegorushka.

'You heathen, take off your cap,' he said rudely. 'You can't eat with your cap on, and you a gentleman too!'

Yegorushka took off his hat and did not say a word, but the stew lost all savour for him, and he did not hear Panteley and Vassya intervening on his behalf. A feeling of anger with the insulting fellow was rankling oppressively in his breast, and he made up his mind that he would do him some injury, whatever it cost him.

After dinner everyone sauntered to the waggons and lay down in the shade.

'Are we going to start soon, grandfather?' Yegorushka asked Panteley.

'In God's good time we shall set off . . . There's no starting yet; it is too hot . . . O Lord, Thy will be done. Holy Mother . . . Lie down, little lad.'

Soon there was a sound of snoring from under the waggons. Yegorushka meant to go back to the village, but on consideration, yawned and lay down by the old man.

VI

THE waggons remained by the river the whole day, and set off again when the sun was setting.

Yegorushka was lying on the bales again; the wag-gon creaked softly and swayed from side to side. Pan-teley walked below, stamping his feet, slapping himself on his thighs and muttering. The air was full of the churring music of the steppes, as it had been the day before.

Yegorushka lay on his back, and, putting his hands under his head, gazed upwards at the sky. He watched the glow of sunset kindle, then fade away; guardian angels covering the horizon with their gold wings dis-posed themselves to slumber. The day had passed peacefully; the quiet peaceful night had come, and they could stay tranquilly at home in heaven ... Yego-rushka saw the sky by degrees grow dark and the mist fall over the earth – saw the stars light up, one after the other ...

When you gaze a long while fixedly at the deep sky thoughts and feelings for some reason merge in a sense of loneliness. One begins to feel hopelessly solitary, and everything one used to look upon as near and akin becomes infinitely remote and valueless; the stars that have looked down from the sky thousands of years already, the mists and the incomprehensible sky itself, indifferent to the brief life of man, oppress the soul with their silence when one is left face to face with them and tries to grasp their significance. One is reminded of the solitude awaiting each one of us in the grave, and the reality of life seems awful ... full of despair ...

Yegorushka thought of his grandmother, who was sleeping now under the cherry trees in the cemetery. He remembered how she lay in her coffin with pennies on her eyes, how afterwards she was shut in and let down into the grave; he even recalled the hollow sound of the clods of earth on the coffin lid ... He pictured his granny in the dark and narrow coffin, helpless and deserted by everyone. His imagination pictured his granny suddenly awakening, not understanding where she was, knocking upon the lid and calling for help, and in the end swooning with horror and dying again. He imagined his mother dead, Father Christopher, Countess Dranitzky, Solomon. But however much he tried to imagine himself in the dark tomb, far from home, outcast, helpless and dead, he could not succeed; for himself personally he could not admit the possibility of death, and felt that he would never die ...

Panteley, for whom death could not be far away, walked below and went on reckoning up his thoughts.

'All right ... Nice gentlefolk ...' he muttered. 'Took his little lad to school – but how he is doing now I haven't heard say – in Slavyanoserbsk. I say there is no establishment for teaching them to be very clever ... No, that's true – a nice little lad, no harm in him ... He'll grow up and be a help to his father ... You, Yegory, are little now, but you'll grow big and will keep your father and mother ... So it is ordained of God, "Honour your father and your mother" ... I had children myself, but they were burnt ... My wife was burnt and my children ... that's true ... The hut caught fire on the night of Epiphany ... I was not at home, I was driving in Oryol. In Oryol ... Marya dashed out into the street, but remembering that the children were asleep in the hut, ran back and was burnt with her children ... Next day they found nothing but bones.'

About midnight Yegorushka and the waggoners were again sitting round a small camp fire. While the dry twigs and stems were burning up, Kiruha and Vassya went off somewhere to get water from a creek; they vanished into the darkness, but could be heard all the time talking and clinking their pails; so the creek was not far away. The light from the fire lay a great flickering patch on the earth; though the moon was bright, yet every thing seemed impenetrably black beyond that red patch. The light was in the waggoners' eyes, and they saw only part of the great road; almost unseen in the darkness the waggons with the bales and the horses looked like a mountain of undefined shape. Twenty paces from the camp fire at the edge of the road stood a wooden cross that had fallen aslant. Before the camp fire had been lighted, when he could still see things at a distance, Yegorushka had noticed that there was a similar old slanting cross on the other side of the great road.

Coming back with the water, Kiruha and Vassya filled the cauldron and fixed it over the fire. Styopka, with the notched spoon in his hand, took his place in the smoke by the cauldron, gazing dreamily into the water for the scum to rise. Panteley and Emelyan were sitting side by side in silence, brooding over something. Dymov was lying on his stomach, with his head propped on his fists, looking into the fire ... Styopka's shadow was dancing over him, so that his handsome face was at one minute covered with darkness, at the next lighted up ... Kiruha and Vassya were wandering about at a little distance gathering dry grass and bark for the fire. Yegorushka, with his hands in his pockets, was standing by Panteley, watching how the fire devoured the grass.

All were resting, musing on something, and they glanced cursorily at the cross over which patches of red light were dancing. There is something melancholy, pensive, and extremely poetical about a solitary tomb; one feels its silence, and the silence gives one the sense of the presence of the soul of the unknown man who lies under the cross. Is that soul at peace on the steppe? Does it grieve in the moonlight? Near the tomb the steppe seems melancholy, dreary and mournful; the grass seems more sorrowful, and one fancies the grasshoppers chirrup less freely, and there is no passer-by who would not remember that lonely soul and keep looking back at the tomb, till it was left far behind and hidden in the mists ...

'Grandfather, what is that cross for?' asked Yegorushka.

Panteley looked at the cross and then at Dymov and asked:

'Nikola, isn't this the place where the mowers killed the merchants?'

Dymov not very readily raised himself on his elbow, looked at the road and said:

'Yes, it is ...'

A silence followed. Kiruha broke up some dry stalks, crushed them up together and thrust them under the cauldron. The fire flared up brightly; Styopka was enveloped in black smoke, and the shadow cast by the cross danced along the road in the dusk beside the waggons.

'Yes, they were killed,' Dymov said reluctantly. 'Two merchants, father and son, were travelling, sel-

ling holy images. They put up in the inn not far from
here that is now kept by Ignat Fomin. The old man
had a drop too much, and began boasting that he had
a lot of money with him. We all know merchants are
a boastful set, God preserve us ... They can't resist
showing off before the likes of us. And at the time
some mowers were staying the night at the inn. So
they overheard what the merchants said and took
note of it.'

'Oh Lord! ... Holy Mother!' sighed Panteley.

'Next day, as soon as it was light,' Dymov went
on, 'the merchants were preparing to set off and the
mowers tried to join them. "Let us go together, your
worship. It will be more cheerful and there will be
less danger, for this is an out-of-the-way place ..."
The merchants had to travel at a walking pace to
avoid breaking the images, and that just suited the
mowers ...'

Dymov rose into a kneeling position and stretched.

'Yes,' he went on, yawning. 'Everything went all
right till they reached this spot, and then the mowers
let fly at them with their scythes. The son, he was a
fine young fellow, snatched the scythe from one of
them, and he used it too ... Well, of course, they got
the best of it because there were eight of them. They
hacked at the merchants so that there was not a
sound place left on their bodies; when they had finished they dragged both of them off the road, the
father to one side and the son to the other. Opposite
that cross there is another cross on this side ...
Whether it is still standing, I don't know ... I can't
see from here ...'

'It is,' said Kiruha.

'They say they did not find much money afterwards.'

'No,' Panteley confirmed; 'they only found a hundred roubles.'

'And three of them died afterwards, for the merchant had cut them badly with the scythe too. They died from loss of blood. One had his hand cut off, so that they say he ran three miles without his hand, and they found him on a mound close to Kurikovo. He was squatting on his heels, with his head on his knees, as though he were lost in thought, but when they looked at him there was no life in him and he was dead ...'

'They found him by the track of blood,' said Panteley.

Everyone looked at the cross, and again there was a hush. From somewhere, most likely from the creek, floated the mournful cry of the bird: 'Sleep! sleep! sleep!'

'There are a great many wicked people in the world,' said Emelyan.

'A great many,' assented Panteley, and he moved up closer to the fire as though he were frightened. 'A great many,' he went on in a low voice. 'I've seen lots and lots of them ... Wicked people! ... I have seen a great many holy and just, too ... Queen of Heaven, save us and have mercy on us. I remember once thirty years ago, or maybe more, I was driving a merchant from Morshansk. The merchant was a jolly handsome fellow, with money, too ... the merchant was ... a nice man, no harm in him ... So we put up for the night at an inn. And in Russia the inns are not what they are in these parts. There the yards are roofed in and look like the ground floor, or let us say like barns in good

farms. Only a barn would be a bit higher. So we put
up there and were all right. My merchant was in a
room, while I was with the horses, and everything was
as it should be. So, lads, I said my prayers before going
to sleep and began walking about the yard. And it was
a dark night, I couldn't see anything; it was no good
trying. So I walked about a bit up to the waggons, or
nearly, when I saw a light gleaming. What could it
mean? I thought the people of the inn had gone to bed
long ago, and besides the merchant and me there were
no other guests in the inn ... Where could the light
have come from? I felt suspicious ... I went closer ...
towards the light ... The Lord have mercy upon me!
and save me, Queen of Heaven! I looked and there was
a little window with a grating ... close to the ground,
in the house ... I lay down on the ground and looked
in; as soon as I looked in a cold chill ran all down
me ...'

Kiruha, trying not to make a noise, thrust a hand-
ful of twigs into the fire. After waiting for it to leave
off crackling and hissing, the old man went on:

'I looked in and there was a big cellar, black and dark
... There was a lighted lantern on a tub. In the middle
of the cellar were about a dozen men in red shirts with
their sleeves turned up, sharpening long knives ...
Ugh! So we had fallen into a nest of robbers ... What's
to be done? I ran to the merchant, woke him up
quietly, and said: "Don't be frightened, merchant,"
said I, "but we are in a bad way. We have fallen into a
nest of robbers," I said. He turned pale and asked:
"What are we to do now, Panteley? I have a lot of
money that belongs to orphans. As for my life," he said,
"that's in God's hands. I am not afraid to die, but it's

dreadful to lose the orphans' money," said he ... What were we to do? The gates were locked; there was no getting out. If there had been a fence one could have climbed over it, but with the yard shut up! ... "Come, don't be frightened, merchant," said I; "but pray to God. Maybe the Lord will not let the orphans suffer. Stay still," said I, "and make no sign, and meanwhile, maybe, I shall think of something ..." Right! ... I prayed to God and the Lord put the thought into my mind ... I clambered up on my chaise and softly ... softly so that no one should hear, began pulling out the straw in the thatch, made a hole and crept out, crept out ... Then I jumped off the roof and ran along the road as fast as I could. I ran and ran till I was nearly dead ... I ran maybe four miles without taking breath, if not more. Thank God I saw a village. I ran up to a hut and began tapping at a window. "Good Christian people," I said, and told them all about it, "do not let a Christian soul perish ..." I waked them all up ... The peasants gathered together and went with me ... one with a cord, one with an oakstick, others with pitchforks ... We broke in the gates of the innyard and went straight to the cellar ... And the robbers had just finished sharpening their knives and were going to kill the merchant. The peasants took them, every one of them, bound them and carried them to the police. The merchant gave them three hundred roubles in his joy, and gave me five gold pieces and put my name down. They said that they found human bones in the cellar afterwards, heaps and heaps of them ... Bones! ... So they robbed people and then buried them, so that there should be no traces ... Well, afterwards they were punished at Morshansk.'

Panteley had finished his story, and he looked round at his listeners. They were gazing at him in silence. The water was boiling by now and Styopka was skimming off the froth.

'Is the fat ready?' Kiruha asked him in a whisper.

'Wait a little . . . Directly.'

Styopka, his eyes fixed on Panteley as though he were afraid that the latter might begin some story before he was back, ran to the waggons; soon he came back with a little wooden bowl and began pounding some lard in it.

'I went another journey with a merchant, too . . .' Panteley went on again, speaking as before in a low voice and with fixed unblinking eyes. 'His name, as I remember now, was Pyotr Grigoritch. He was a nice man . . . the merchant was. We stopped in the same way at an inn . . . He indoors and me with the horses . . . The people of the house, the innkeeper and his wife, seemed friendly good sort of people; the labourers, too, seemed all right; but yet, lads, I couldn't sleep. I had a queer feeling in my heart . . . a queer feeling, that was just it. The gates were open and there were plenty of people about, and yet I felt afraid and not myself. Everyone had been asleep long ago. It was the middle of the night; it would soon be time to get up, and I was lying alone in my chaise and could not close my eyes, as though I were some owl. And then, lads, I heard this sound, "Toop! toop! toop!" Someone was creeping up to the chaise. I poke my head out, and there was a peasant woman in nothing but her shift and with her feet bare . . . "What do you want, good woman?" I asked. And she was all of a tremble; her face was terror-stricken . . . "Get up,

good man," said she; "the people are plotting evil ...
They mean to kill your merchant. With my own ears
I heard the master whispering with his wife ..." So it
was not for nothing, the foreboding of my heart! "And
who are you?" I asked. "I am their cook," she said ...
Right! ... So I got out of the chaise and went to the
merchant. I waked him up and said: "Things aren't
quite right, Pyotr Grigoritch ... Make haste and rouse
yourself from sleep, your worship, and dress now while
there is still time," I said; "and to save our skins, let
us get away from trouble." He had no sooner begun
dressing when the door opened and, mercy on us!
I saw, Holy Mother! the innkeeper and his wife come
into the room with three labourers ... So they had
persuaded the labourers to join them. "The merchant
has a lot of money, and we'll go shares," they told
them. Every one of the five had a long knife in their
hand ... each a knife. The innkeeper locked the door
and said: "Say your prayers, travellers ... and if you
begin screaming," they said, "we won't let you say
your prayers before you die ..." As though we could
scream! I had such a lump in my throat I could not
cry out ... The merchant wept and said: "Good Christian people! you have resolved to kill me because my
money tempts you. Well, so be it; I shall not be the
first nor shall I be the last. Many of us merchants
have been murdered at inns. But why, good Christian
brothers," says he, "murder my driver? Why should
he have to suffer for my money?" And he said that so
pitifully! And the innkeeper answered him: "If we
leave him alive," said he, "he will be the first to bear
witness against us. One may just as well kill two as
one. You can but answer once for seven misdeeds ...

Say your prayers, that's all you can do, and it is no good talking!" The merchant and I knelt down side by side and wept and said our prayers. He thought of his children. I was young in those days; I wanted to live ... We looked at the images and prayed, and so pitifully that it brings a tear even now ... And the innkeeper's wife looks at us and says: "Good people," said she, "don't bear a grudge against us in the other world and pray to God for our punishment, for it is want that drives us to it." We prayed and wept and prayed and wept, and God heard us. He had pity on us, I suppose ... At the very minute when the innkeeper had taken the merchant by the beard to rip open his throat with his knife suddenly someone seemed to tap at the window from the yard! We all started, and the innkeeper's hands dropped ... Someone was tapping at the window and shouting: "Pyotr Grigoritch," he shouted, "are you here? Get ready and let's go!" The people saw that someone had come for the merchant; they were terrified and took to their heels ... And we made haste into the yard, harnessed the horses, and were out of sight in a minute ...'

'Who was it knocked at the window?' asked Dymov.

'At the window? It must have been a holy saint or angel, for there was no one else ... When we drove out of the yard there wasn't a soul in the street ... It was the Lord's doing.'

Panteley told other stories, and in all of them 'long knives' figured and all alike sounded made up. Had he heard these stories from someone else, or had he made them up himself in the remote past, and afterwards, as his memory grew weaker, mixed up his experiences with his imaginations and become unable to distinguish one from the other? Anything is possible, but it is strange that on this occasion and for the rest of the journey, whenever he happened to tell a story, he gave unmistakable preference to fiction, and never told of what he really had experienced. At the time Yego-rushka took it all for the genuine thing, and believed every word; later on it seemed to him strange that a man who in his day had travelled all over Russia and seen and known so much, whose wife and children had been burnt to death, so failed to appreciate the wealth of his life that whenever he was sitting by the camp fire he was either silent or talked of what had never been.

Over their porridge they were all silent, thinking of what they had just heard. Life is terrible and marvel-lous, and so, however terrible a story you tell in Russia, however you embroider it with nests of rob-bers, long knives and such marvels, it always finds an echo of reality in the soul of the listener, and only a man who has been a good deal affected by education looks askance distrustfully, and even he will be silent. The cross by the roadside, the dark bales of wool, the wide expanse of the plain, and the lot of the men gathered together by the camp fire – all this was of itself so marvellous and terrible that the fantastic col-ours of legend and fairy-tale were pale and blended with life.

All the others ate out of the cauldron, but Panteley sat apart and ate his porridge out of a wooden bowl. His spoon was not like those the others had, but was made of cypress wood, with a little cross on it. Yego-rushka, looking at him, thought of the little ikon glass and asked Styopka softly:

'Why does Grandfather sit apart?'

'He is an Old Believer,' Styopka and Vassya answered in a whisper. And as they said it they looked as though they were speaking of some secret vice or weakness.

All sat silent, thinking. After the terrible stories there was no inclination to speak of ordinary things. All at once in the midst of the silence Vassya drew himself up and, fixing his lustreless eyes on one point, pricked up his ears.

'What is it?' Dymov asked him.

'Someone is coming,' answered Vassya.

'Where do you see him?'

'Yo-on-der! There's something white . . .'

There was nothing to be seen but darkness in the direction in which Vassya was looking; everyone listened, but they could hear no sound of steps.

'Is he coming by the highroad?' asked Dymov.

'No, over the open country . . . He is coming this way.'

A minute passed in silence.

'And maybe it's the merchant who was buried here walking over the steppe,' said Dymov.

All looked askance at the cross, exchanged glances and suddenly broke into a laugh. They felt ashamed of their terror.

'Why should he walk?' asked Panteley. 'It's only those walk at night whom the earth will not take to herself. And the merchants were all right . . . The merchants have received the crown of martyrs.'

But all at once they heard the sound of steps; someone was coming in haste.

'He's carrying something,' said Vassya.

They could hear the grass rustling and the dry twigs crackling under the feet of the approaching wayfarer. But from the glare of the camp fire nothing could be seen. At last the steps sounded close by, and someone coughed. The flickering light seemed to part; a veil dropped from the waggoners' eyes, and they saw a man facing them.

Whether it was due to the flickering light or because everyone wanted to make out the man's face first of all, it happened, strangely enough, that at the first glance at him they all saw, first of all, not his face nor his clothes, but his smile. It was an extraordinarily good-natured, broad, soft smile, like that of a baby on waking, one of those infectious smiles to which it is difficult not to respond by smiling too. The stranger, when they did get a good look at him, turned out to be a man of thirty, ugly and in no way remarkable. He was a tall Little Russian, with a long nose, long arms and long legs; everything about him seemed long except his neck, which was so short that it made him seem stooping. He was wearing a clean white shirt with an embroidered collar, white trousers, and new high boots, and in comparison with the waggoners he looked quite a dandy. In his arms he was carrying something big, white, and at the first glance strange-looking, and the stock of a gun also peeped out from behind his shoulder.

Coming from the darkness into the circle of light, he stopped short as though petrified, and for half a minute looked at the waggoners as though he would have said: 'Just look what a smile I have!'

Then he took a step towards the fire, smiled still more radiantly and said:

'Bread and salt, friends!'

'You are very welcome!' Panteley answered for them all.

The stranger put down by the fire what he was carrying in his arms – it was a dead bustard – and greeted them once more.

They all went up to the bustard and began examining it.

'A fine big bird; what did you kill it with?' asked Dymov.

'Grape-shot. You can't get him with small shot; he won't let you get near enough. Buy it, friends! I will let you have it for twenty kopecks.'

'What use would it be to us? It's good roast, but I bet it would be tough boiled; you could not get your teeth into it . . .'

'Oh, what a pity! I would take it to the gentry at the farm; they would give me half a rouble for it. But it's a long way to go – twelve miles!'

The stranger sat down, took off his gun and laid it beside him.

He seemed sleepy and languid; he sat smiling, and, screwing up his eyes at the firelight, apparently thinking of something very agreeable. They gave him a spoon; he began eating.

'Who are you?' Dymov asked him.

The stranger did not hear the question; he made no answer, and did not even glance at Dymov. Most likely this smiling man did not taste the flavour of the porridge either, for he seemed to eat it mechanically, lifting the spoon to his lips sometimes very full and sometimes quite empty. He was not drunk, but he seemed to have something nonsensical in his head.

'I ask you who you are?' repeated Dymov.

'I?' said the unknown, starting. 'Konstantin Zvonik from Rovno. It's three miles from here.'

And anxious to show straight off that he was not quite an ordinary peasant, but something better, Konstantin hastened to add:

'We keep bees and fatten pigs.'

'Do you live with your father or in a house of your own?'

'No; now I am living in a house of my own. I have parted. This month, just after St Peter's Day, I got married. I am a married man now! ... It's eighteen days since the wedding.'

'That's a good thing,' said Panteley. 'Marriage is a good thing ... God's blessing is on it.'

'His young wife sits at home while he rambles about the steppe,' laughed Kiruha. 'Queer chap!'

As though he had been pinched on the tenderest spot, Konstantin started, laughed and flushed crimson.

'But, Lord, she is not at home!' he said quickly, taking the spoon out of his mouth and looking round at everyone with an expression of delight and wonder. 'She is not; she has gone to her mother's for three days! Yes, indeed, she has gone away, and I feel as though I were not married ...'

Konstantin waved his hand and turned his head; he wanted to go on thinking, but the joy which beamed in his face prevented him. As though he were not comfortable, he changed his attitude, laughed, and again waved his hand. He was ashamed to share his happy thoughts with strangers, but at the same time he had an irresistible longing to communicate his joy.

'She has gone to Demidovo to see her mother,' he said, blushing and moving his gun. 'She'll be back to-morrow ... She said she would be back to dinner.'

'And do you miss her?' said Dymov.

'Oh, Lord, yes; I should think so. We have only been married such a little while, and she has gone away ... Eh! Oh, but she is a tricksy one, God strike me dead! She is such a fine, splendid girl, such a one for laughing and singing, full of life and fire! When she is there your brain is in a whirl, and now she is away I wander about the steppe like a fool, as though I had lost something. I have been walking since dinner.'

Konstantin rubbed his eyes, looked at the fire and laughed.

'You love her, then ...' said Panteley.

'She is so fine and splendid,' Konstantin repeated, not hearing him; 'such a housewife, clever and sensible. You wouldn't find another like her among simple folk in the whole province. She has gone away ... But she is missing me, I kno-ow! I know the little magpie. She said she would be back to-morrow by dinner-time ... And just think how queer!' Konstantin almost shouted, speaking a note higher and shifting his position. 'Now she loves me and is sad without me, and yet she would not marry me.'

'But eat,' said Kiruha.

'She would not marry me,' Konstantin went on, not heeding him. 'I have been struggling with her for three years! I saw her at the Kalatchik fair; I fell madly in love with her, was ready to hang myself ... I live at Rovno, she at Demidovo, more than twenty miles apart, and there was nothing I could do. I sent matchmakers to her, and all she said was: "I won't!"'

Ah, the magpie! I sent her one thing and another,
earrings and cakes, and twenty pounds of honey –
but still she said: "I won't!" And there it was. If you
come to think of it, I was not a match for her! She
was young and lovely, full of fire, while I am old:
I shall soon be thirty, and a regular beauty, too; a
fine beard like a goat's, a clear complexion all covered
with pimples – how could I be compared with her!
The only thing to be said is that we are well off, but
then the Vahramenkys are well off, too. They've six
oxen, and they keep a couple of labourers. I was in
love, friends, as though I were plague-stricken.
I couldn't sleep or eat; my brain was full of thoughts,
and in such a maze, Lord preserve us! I longed to see
her, and she was in Demidovo. What do you think?
God be my witness, I am not lying, three times a
week I walked over there on foot just to have a look
at her. I gave up my work! I was so frantic that
I even wanted to get taken on as a labourer in Demidovo, so as to be near her. I was in misery! My
mother called in a witch a dozen times; my father
tried thrashing me. For three years I was in this
torment, and then I made up my mind. "Damn my
soul!" I said, "I will go to the town and be a cab-
man ... It seems it is fated not to be." At Easter
I went to Demidovo to have a last look at her ...'

Konstantin threw back his head and went off into a
mirthful tinkling laugh, as though he had just taken
someone in very cleverly.

'I saw her by the river with the lads,' he went on.
'I was overcome with anger ... I called her aside and
maybe for a full hour I said all manner of things to
her. She fell in love with me! For three years she did

not like me! she fell in love with me for what I said to her . . .'

'What did you say to her?' asked Dymov.

'What did I say? I don't remember . . . How could one remember? My words flowed at the time like water from a tap, without stopping to take breath. Ta-ta-ta! And now I can't utter a word . . . Well, so she married me . . . She's gone now to her mother's, the magpie, and while she is away here I wander over the steppe. I can't stay at home. It's more than I can do!'

Konstantin awkwardly released his feet, on which he was sitting, stretched himself on the earth, and propped his head in his fists, then got up and sat down again. Everyone by now thoroughly understood that he was in love and happy, poignantly happy; his smile, his eyes, and every movement, expressed fervent happiness. He could not find a place for himself, and did not know what attitude to take to keep himself from being overwhelmed by the multitude of his delightful thoughts. Having poured out his soul before these strangers, he settled down quietly at last, and, looking at the fire, sank into thought.

At the sight of this happy man everyone felt depressed and longed to be happy, too. Everyone was dreamy. Dymov got up, walked about softly by the fire, and from his walk, from the movement of his shoulder-blades, it could be seen that he was weighed down by depression and yearning. He stood still for a moment, looked at Konstantin and sat down.

The camp fire had died down by now; there was no flicker, and the patch of red had grown small and dim . . . And as the fire went out the moonlight grew clearer and clearer. Now they could see the full width

of the road, the bales of wool, the shafts of the waggons, the munching horses; on the further side of the
road there was the dim outline of the second cross ...

Dymov leaned his cheek on his hand and softly
hummed some plaintive song. Konstantin smiled
drowsily and chimed in with a thin voice. They sang
for half a minute, then sank into silence. Emelyan
started, jerked his elbows and wriggled his fingers.

'Lads,' he said in an imploring voice, 'let's sing
something sacred!' Tears came into his eyes. 'Lads,' he
repeated, pressing his hands on his heart, 'let's sing
something sacred!'

'I don't know anything,' said Konstantin.

Everyone refused, then Emelyan sang alone. He
waved both arms, nodded his head, opened his mouth,
but nothing came from his throat but a discordant
gasp. He sang with his arms, with his head, with his
eyes, even with the swelling on his face; he sang passionately with anguish, and the more he strained his
chest to extract at least one note from it, the more
discordant were his gasps ...

Yegorushka, like the rest, was overcome with
depression. He went to his waggon, clambered up on
the bales and lay down. He looked at the sky, and
thought of happy Konstantin and his wife. Why did
people get married? What were women in the world
for? Yegorushka put the vague questions to himself,
and thought that a man would certainly be happy if
he had an affectionate, merry and beautiful woman
continually living at his side. For some reason he
remembered the Countess Dranitsky, and thought it
would probably be very pleasant to live with a woman
like that; he would perhaps have married her with

pleasure if that idea had not been so shameful. He recalled her eyebrows, the pupils of her eyes, her carriage, the clock with the horseman ... The soft warm night moved softly down upon him and whispered something in his ear, and it seemed to him that it was that lovely woman bending over him, looking at him with a smile and meaning to kiss him ...

Nothing was left of the fire but two little red eyes, which kept on growing smaller and smaller. Konstantin and the waggoners were sitting by it, dark motionless figures, and it seemed as though there were many more of them than before. The twin crosses were equally visible, and far, far away, somewhere by the highroad there gleamed a red light – other people cooking their porridge, most likely.

'Our Mother Russia is the he-ad of all the world!' Kiruha sang out suddenly in a harsh voice, choked and subsided. The steppe echo caught up his voice, carried it on, and it seemed as though stupidity itself were rolling on heavy wheels over the steppe.

'It's time to go,' said Panteley. 'Get up, lads.'

While they were putting the horses in, Konstantin walked by the waggons and talked rapturously of his wife.

'Good-bye, mates!' he cried when the waggons started. 'Thank you for your hospitality. I shall go on again towards that light. It's more than I can stand.'

And he quickly vanished in the mist, and for a long time they could hear him striding in the direction of the light to tell those other strangers of his happiness.

When Yegorushka woke up next day it was early morning; the sun had not yet risen. The waggons were at a standstill. A man in a white cap and a suit of cheap grey material, mounted on a little Cossack stallion, was talking to Dymov and Kiruha beside the foremost waggon. A mile and a half ahead there were long low white barns and little houses with tiled roofs; there were neither yards nor trees to be seen beside the little houses.

'What village is that, Grandfather?' asked Yegorushka.

'That's the Armenian Settlement, youngster,' answered Panteley. 'The Armenians live there. They are a good sort of people ... the Armenians are.'

The man in grey had finished talking to Dymov and Kiruha; he pulled up his little stallion and looked across towards the settlement.

'What a business, only think!' sighed Panteley, looking towards the settlement, too, and shuddering at the morning freshness. 'He has sent a man to the settlement for some papers, and he doesn't come ... He should have sent Styopka.'

'Who is that, Grandfather?' asked Yegorushka.

'Varlamov.'

My goodness! Yegorushka jumped up quickly, getting upon his knees, and looked at the white cap. It was hard to recognize the mysterious elusive Varlamov, who was sought by everyone, who was always 'on his rounds,' and who had far more money than Countess Dranitzky, in the short, grey little man in big boots, who was sitting on an ugly little nag and talking to peasants at an hour when all decent people were asleep.

'He is all right, a good man,' said Panteley, looking towards the settlement. 'God give him health – a

splendid gentleman, Semyon Alexandritch ... It's
people like that the earth rests upon. That's true ...
The cocks are not crowing yet, and he is already up
and about ... Another man would be asleep, or galli-
vanting with visitors at home, but he is on the steppe
all day ... on his rounds ... He does not let things
slip ... No-o! He's a fine fellow ...'

Varlamov was talking about something, while he
kept his eyes fixed. The little stallion shifted from one
leg to another impatiently.

'Semyon Alexandritch!' cried Panteley, taking off
his hat. 'Allow us to send Styopka! Emelyan, call out
that Styopka should be sent.'

But now at last a man on horseback could be seen
coming from the settlement. Bending very much to
one side and brandishing his whip above his head like
a gallant young Caucasian, and wanting to astonish
everyone by his horsemanship, he flew towards the
waggons with the swiftness of a bird.

'That must be one of his circuit men,' said Panteley.
'He must have a hundred such horsemen or maybe
more.'

Reaching the first waggon, he pulled up his horse,
and taking off his hat, handed Varlamov a little book.
Varlamov took several papers out of the book, read
them and cried:

'And where is Ivantchuk's letter?'

The horseman took the book back, looked at the
papers and shrugged his shoulders. He began saying
something, probably justifying himself and asking to
be allowed to ride back to the settlement again. The
little stallion suddenly stirred as though Varlamov
had grown heavier. Varlamov stirred too.

'Go along!' he cried angrily, and he waved his whip at the man.

Then he turned his horse round and, looking through the papers in the book, moved at a walking pace alongside the waggons. When he reached the hindmost, Yegorushka strained his eyes to get a better look at him. Varlamov was an elderly man. His face, a simple Russian sunburnt face with a small grey beard, was red, wet with dew and covered with little blue veins; it had the same expression of businesslike coldness as Ivan Ivanitch's face, the same look of fanatical zeal for business. But yet what a difference could be felt between him and Kuzmitchov! Uncle Ivan Ivanitch always had on his face, together with his businesslike reserve, a look of anxiety and apprehension that he would not find Varlamov, that he would be late, that he would miss a good price; nothing of that sort, so characteristic of small and dependent persons, could be seen in the face or figure of Varlamov. This man made the price himself, was not looking for anyone, and did not depend on anyone; however ordinary his exterior, yet in everything, even in the manner of holding his whip, there was a sense of power and habitual authority over the steppe.

As he rode by Yegorushka he did not glance at him. Only the little stallion deigned to notice Yegorushka; he looked at him with his large foolish eyes, and even he showed no interest. Panteley bowed to Varlamov; the latter noticed it, and without taking his eyes off the sheets of paper, said lisping:

'How are you, old man?'

Varlamov's conversation with the horseman and the way he had brandished his whip had evidently made an overwhelming impression on the whole party. Everyone looked grave. The man on horseback, cast down at the anger of the great man, remained stationary, with his hat off, and the rein loose by the foremost waggon; he was silent, and seemed unable to grasp that the day had begun so badly for him.

'He is a harsh old man ...' muttered Panteley. 'It's a pity he is so harsh! But he is all right, a good man ... He doesn't abuse men for nothing ... It's no matter ...'

After examining the papers, Varlamov thrust the book into his pocket; the little stallion, as though he knew what was in his mind, without waiting for orders, started and dashed along the highroad.

VII

ON the following night the waggoners had halted and were cooking their porridge. On this occasion there was a sense of overwhelming oppression over everyone. It was sultry; they all drank a great deal, but could not quench their thirst. The moon was intensely crimson and sullen, as though it were sick. The stars, too, were sullen, the mist was thicker, the distance more clouded. Nature seemed as though languid and weighed down by some foreboding.

There was not the same liveliness and talk round the camp fire as there had been the day before. All were dreary and spoke listlessly and without interest. Panteley did nothing but sigh and complain of his feet, and continually alluded to impenitent deathbeds.

Dymov was lying on his stomach, chewing a straw in silence; there was an expression of disgust on his

face as though the straw smelt unpleasant, a spiteful
and exhausted look ... Vassya complained that his
jaw ached, and prophesied bad weather; Emelyan was
not waving his arms, but sitting still and looking
gloomily at the fire. Yegorushka, too, was weary. This
slow travelling exhausted him, and the sultriness of
the day had given him a headache.

While they were cooking the porridge, Dymov, to
relieve his boredom, began quarrelling with his
companions.

'Here he lolls, the lumpy face, and is the first to put
his spoon in,' he said, looking spitefully at Emelyan.
'Greedy! always contrives to sit next the cauldron.
He's been a church-singer, so he thinks he is a gentleman! There are a lot of singers like you begging along
the highroad!'

'What are you pestering me for?' asked Emelyan,
looking at him angrily.

'To teach you not to be the first to dip into the
cauldron. Don't think too much of yourself!'

'You are a fool, and that is all about it!' wheezed
out Emelyan.

Knowing by experience how such conversations
usually ended, Panteley and Vassya intervened and
tried to persuade Dymov not to quarrel about
nothing.

'A church-singer!' The bully would not desist, but
laughed contemptuously. 'Anyone can sing like that –
sit in the church porch and sing "Give me alms, for
Christ's sake!" Ugh! you are a nice fellow!'

Emelyan did not speak. His silence had an irritating effect on Dymov. He looked with still greater hatred at the ex-singer and said:

'I don't care to have anything to do with you, or I would show you what to think of yourself.'

'But why are you pushing me, you Mazeppa?' Emelyan cried, flaring up. 'Am I interfering with you?'

'What did you call me?' asked Dymov, drawing himself up, and his eyes were suffused with blood. 'Eh! I am a Mazeppa? Yes? Take that, then; go and look for it.'

Dymov snatched the spoon out of Emelyan's hand and flung it far away. Kiruha, Vassya, and Styopka ran to look for it, while Emelyan fixed an imploring and questioning look on Panteley. His face suddenly became small and wrinkled; it began twitching, and the ex-singer began to cry like a child.

Yegorushka, who had long hated Dymov, felt as though the air all at once were unbearably stifling, as though the fire were scorching his face; he longed to run quickly to the waggons in the darkness, but the bully's angry, bored eyes drew the boy to him. With a passionate desire to say something extremely offensive, he took a step towards Dymov, and brought out, gasping for breath:

'You are the worst of the lot; I can't bear you!'

After this he ought to have run to the waggons, but he could not stir from the spot, and went on:

'In the next world you will burn in hell! I'll complain to Ivan Ivanitch. Don't you dare insult Emelyan!'

'Say this too, please,' laughed Dymov: ' "every little sucking-pig wants to lay down the law." Shall I pull your ear?'

Yegorushka felt that he could not breathe; and

something which had never happened to him before –
he suddenly began shaking all over, stamping his feet
and crying shrilly:

'Beat him, beat him!'

Tears gushed from his eyes; he felt ashamed, and
ran staggering back to the waggon. The effect produced by his outburst he did not see. Lying on the
bales and twitching his arms and legs, he whispered:

'Mother, mother!'

And these men and the shadows round the camp
fire, and the dark bales and the far-away lightning,
which was flashing every minute in the distance – all
struck him now as terrible and unfriendly. He was
overcome with terror, and asked himself in despair
why and how he had come into this unknown land in
the company of terrible peasants? Where was his
uncle now, where was Father Christopher, where was
Deniska? Why were they so long in coming? Hadn't
they forgotten him? At the thought that he was forgotten and cast out to the mercy of fate, he felt such
a cold chill of dread that he had several times an
impulse to jump off the bales of wool, and run back
full speed along the road; but the thought of the huge
dark crosses, which would certainly meet him on the
way, and the lightning flashing in the distance,
stopped him ... And only when he whispered,
'Mother, mother!' he felt as it were a little better.

The waggoners must have been full of dread, too.
After Yegorushka had run away from the camp fire
they sat at first for a long time in silence, then they
began speaking in hollow undertones about something, saying that it was coming and that they must
make haste and get away from it ... They quickly

finished supper, put out the fire and began harnessing the horses in silence. From their fluster and the broken phrases they uttered it was apparent they foresaw some trouble. Before they set off on their way, Dymov went up to Panteley and asked softly:

'What's his name?'

'Yegory,' answered Panteley.

Dymov put one foot on the wheel, caught hold of the cord which was tied round the bales, and pulled himself up. Yegorushka saw his face and curly head. The face was pale and looked grave and exhausted, but there was no expression of spite in it.

'Yera!' he said softly, 'here, hit me!'

Yegorushka looked at him in surprise. At that instant there was a flash of lightning.

'It's all right, hit me,' repeated Dymov. And without waiting for Yegorushka to hit him or to speak to him, he jumped down and said: 'How dreary I am!'

Then, swaying from one leg to the other and moving his shoulder-blades, he sauntered lazily alongside the string of waggons and repeated in a voice half weeping, half angry:

'How dreary I am! Oh Lord! Don't you take offence, Emelyan,' he said as he passed Emelyan. 'Ours is a wretched cruel life!'

There was a flash of lightning on the right, and, like a reflection in the looking-glass, at once a second flash in the distance.

'Yegory, take this,' cried Panteley, throwing up something big and dark.

'What is it?' asked Yegorushka.

'A mat. There will be rain, so cover yourself up.'

Yegorushka sat up and looked about him. The distance had grown perceptibly blacker, and now oftener than every minute winked with a pale light. The blackness was being bent towards the right as though by its own weight.

'Will there be a storm, Grandfather?' asked Yegorushka.

'Ah, my poor feet, how they ache!' Panteley said in a high-pitched voice, stamping his feet and not hearing the boy.

On the left someone seemed to strike a match in the sky; a pale phosphorescent streak gleamed and went out. There was a sound as though someone very far away were walking over an iron roof, probably barefoot, for the iron gave a hollow rumble.

'It's set in!' cried Kiruha.

Between the distance and the horizon on the right there was a flash of lightning so vivid that it lighted up part of the steppe and the spot where the clear sky met the blackness. A terrible cloud was swooping down, without haste, a compact mass; big black shreds hung from its edge; similar shreds pressing one upon another were piling up on the right and left horizon. The tattered, ragged look of the storm-cloud gave it a drunken disorderly air. There was a distinct, not smothered, growl of thunder. Yegorushka crossed himself and began quickly putting on his great-coat.

'I am dreary!' Dymov's shout floated from the foremost waggon, and it could be told from his voice that he was beginning to be ill-humoured again. 'I am so dreary!'

All at once there was a squall of wind, so violent that it almost snatched away Yegorushka's bundle and mat; the mat fluttered in all directions and flapped on the bale and on Yegorushka's face. The wind dashed whistling over the steppe, whirled round in disorder and raised such an uproar from the grass that neither the thunder nor the creaking of the wheels could be heard; it blew from the black storm-cloud, carrying with it clouds of dust and the scent of rain and wet earth. The moonlight grew mistier, as it were dirtier; the stars were even more overcast; and clouds of dust could be seen hurrying along the edge of the road, followed by their shadows. By now, most likely, the whirlwind eddying round and lifting from the earth dust, dry grass and feathers, was mounting to the very sky; uprooted plants must have been flying by that very black storm-cloud, and how frightened they must have been! But through the dust that clogged the eyes nothing could be seen but the flash of lightning.

Yegorushka, thinking it would pour with rain in a minute, knelt up and covered himself with the mat.

'Panteley-ey!' someone shouted in the front. 'A ... a ... va!'

'I can't!' Panteley answered in a loud high voice. 'A ... a ... va! Arya ... a!'

There was an angry clap of thunder, which rolled across the sky from right to left, then back again, and died away near the foremost waggon.

'Holy, holy, holy, Lord of Sabaoth,' whispered Yegorushka, crossing himself. 'Fill Heaven and earth with Thy glory.'

The blackness in the sky yawned wide and breathed white fire. At once there was another clap of thunder. It had scarcely ceased when there was a flash of light-

ning so broad that Yegorushka suddenly saw through
a slit in the mat the whole highroad to the very horizon, all the waggoners and even Kiruha's waistcoat.
The black shreds had by now moved upwards from
the left, and one of them, a coarse, clumsy monster
like a claw with fingers, stretched to the moon. Yegorushka made up his mind to shut his eyes tight, to pay
no attention to it, and to wait till it was all over.

The rain was for some reason long in coming. Yegorushka peeped out from the mat in the hope that perhaps the storm-cloud was passing over. It was
fearfully dark. Yegorushka could see neither Panteley,
nor the bale of wool, nor himself; he looked sideways
towards the place where the moon had lately been,
but there was the same black darkness there as over
the waggons. And in the darkness the flashes of lightning seemed more violent and blinding, so that they
hurt his eyes.

'Panteley!' called Yegorushka.

No answer followed. But now a gust of wind for the
last time flung up the mat and hurried away. A quiet
regular sound was heard. A big cold drop fell on Yegorushka's knee, another trickled over his hand. He
noticed that his knees were not covered, and tried to
rearrange the mat, but at that moment something
began pattering on the road, then on the shafts and
the bales. It was the rain. As though they understood
one another, the rain and the mat began prattling of
something rapidly, gaily and most annoyingly like two
magpies.

Yegorushka knelt up or rather squatted on his
boots. While the rain was pattering on the mat, he
leaned forward to screen his knees, which were sud-

denly wet. He succeeded in covering his knees; but in less than a minute was aware of a penetrating, unpleasant dampness behind on his back and the calves of his legs. He returned to his former position, exposing his knees to the rain, and wondered what to do to rearrange the mat, which he could not see in the darkness. But his arms were already wet, the water was trickling up his sleeves and down his collar, and his shoulder-blades felt chilly. And he made up his mind to do nothing but sit motionless and wait till it was all over.

'Holy, holy, holy!' he whispered.

Suddenly, exactly over his head, the sky cracked with a fearful deafening din; he huddled up and held his breath, waiting for the fragments to fall upon his head and back. He inadvertently opened his eyes and saw a blinding intense light flare out and flash five times on his fingers, his wet sleeves, and on the trickles of water running from the mat upon the bales and down to the ground. There was a fresh peal of thunder as violent and awful; the sky was not growling and rumbling now, but uttering short crashing sounds like the crackling of dry wood.

'Trrah! tah! tah! tah!' the thunder rang out distinctly, rolled over the sky, seemed to stumble, and somewhere by the foremost waggons or far behind to fall with an abrupt angry 'Trrra!'

The flashes of lightning had at first been only terrible, but with such thunder they seemed sinister and menacing. Their magic light pierced through closed eyelids and sent a chill all over the body. What could he do not to see them? Yegorushka made up his mind to turn over on his face. Cautiously, as though afraid of being watched, he got on all fours, and his hands slipping on the wet bale, he turned back again.

'Trrah! tah! tah!' floated over his head, rolled under the waggons and exploded 'Kraa!'

Again he inadvertently opened his eyes and saw a new danger: three huge giants with long pikes were following the waggon! A flash of lightning gleamed on the points of their pikes and lighted up their figures very distinctly. They were men of huge proportions, with covered faces, bowed heads, and heavy footsteps. They seemed gloomy and dispirited and lost in thought. Perhaps they were not following the waggons with any harmful intent, and yet there was something awful in their proximity.

Yegorushka turned quickly forward, and trembling all over, cried: 'Panteley! Grandfather!'

'Trrah! tah! tah!' the sky answered him.

He opened his eyes to see if the waggoners were there. There were flashes of lightning in two places, which lighted up the road to the far distance, the whole string of waggons and all the waggoners. Streams of water were flowing along the road and bubbles were dancing. Panteley was walking beside the waggon; his tall hat and his shoulder were covered with a small mat; his figure expressed neither terror nor uneasiness, as though he were deafened by the thunder and blinded by the lightning.

'Grandfather, the giants!' Yegorushka shouted to him in tears.

But the old man did not hear. Further away walked Emelyan. He was covered from head to foot with a big mat and was triangular in shape. Vassya, without anything over him, was walking with the same wooden step as usual, lifting his feet high and not bending his knees. In the flash of lightning it seemed as though the waggons were not moving and the men were motionless, that Vassya's lifted foot was rigid in the same position . . .

Yegorushka called the old man once more. Getting no answer, he sat motionless, and no longer waited for it all to end. He was convinced that the thunder would kill him in another minute, that he would accidentally open his eyes and see the terrible giants, and he left off crossing himself, calling the old man and thinking of his mother, and was simply numb with cold and the conviction that the storm would never end.

But at last there was the sound of voices.

'Yegory, are you asleep?' Panteley cried below. 'Get down! Is he deaf, the silly little thing? . . .'

'Something like a storm!' said an unfamiliar bass voice, and the stranger cleared his throat as though he had just tossed off a good glass of vodka.

Yegorushka opened his eyes. Close to the waggon stood Panteley, Emelyan, looking like a triangle, and the giants. The latter were by now much shorter, and when Yegorushka looked more closely at them they turned out to be ordinary peasants, carrying on their shoulders not pikes but pitchforks. In the space between Panteley and the triangular figure, gleamed the window of a low-pitched hut. So the waggons were halting in the village. Yegorushka flung off the mat, took his bundle and made haste to get off the waggon. Now when close to him there were people talking and a lighted window he no longer felt afraid, though the thunder was crashing as before and the whole sky was streaked with lightning.

'It was a good storm, all right ...' Panteley was muttering. 'Thank God ... my feet are a little softened by the rain. It was all right ... Have you got down, Yegory? Well, go into the hut; it is all right ...'

'Holy, holy, holy!' wheezed Emelyan, 'it must have struck something ... Are you of these parts?' he asked the giants.

'No, from Glinovo. We belong to Glinovo. We are working at the Platers'.'

'Threshing?'

'All sorts. Just now we are getting in the wheat. The lightning, the lightning! It is long since we have had such a storm ...'

Yegorushka went into the hut. He was met by a lean hunchbacked old woman with a sharp chin. She stood holding a tallow candle in her hands, screwing up her eyes and heaving prolonged sighs.

'What a storm God has sent us!' she said. 'And our lads are out for the night on the steppe; they'll have a bad time, poor dears! Take off your things, little sir, take off your things.'

Shivering with cold and shrugging squeamishly, Yegorushka pulled off his drenched overcoat, then stretched out his arms and straddled his legs, and stood a long time without moving. The slightest movement caused an unpleasant sensation of cold and wetness. His sleeves and the back of his shirt were sopped, his trousers stuck to his legs, his head was dripping.

'What's the use of standing there, with your legs apart, little lad?' said the old woman. 'Come, sit down.'

Holding his legs wide apart, Yegorushka went up to

the table and sat down on a bench near somebody's head. The head moved, puffed a stream of air through its nose, made a chewing sound and subsided. A mound covered with a sheepskin stretched from the head along the bench; it was a peasant woman asleep.

The old woman went out sighing, and came back with a big water melon and a little sweet melon.

'Have something to eat, my dear! I have nothing else to offer you ...' she said, yawning. She rummaged in the table and took out a long sharp knife, very much like the one with which the brigands killed the merchants in the inn. 'Have some, my dear!'

Yegorushka, shivering as though he were in a fever, ate a slice of sweet melon with black bread and then a slice of water melon, and that made him feel colder still.

'Our lads are out on the steppe for the night ...' sighed the old woman while he was eating. 'The terror of the Lord! I'd light the candle under the ikon, but I don't know where Stepanida has put it. Have some more, little sir, have some more ...' The old woman gave a yawn and, putting her right hand behind her, scratched her left shoulder.

'It must be two o'clock now,' she said; 'it will soon be time to get up. Our lads are out on the steppe for the night; they are all wet through for sure ...'

'Granny,' said Yegorushka, 'I am sleepy.'

'Lie down, my dear, lie down,' the old woman sighed, yawning. 'Lord Jesus Christ! I was asleep, when I heard a noise as though someone were knocking. I woke up and looked, and it was the storm God had sent us ... I'd have lighted the candle, but I couldn't find it.'

Talking to herself, she pulled some rags, probably her own bed, off the bench, took two sheepskins off a nail by the stove, and began laying them out for a bed for Yegorushka. 'The storm doesn't grow less,' she muttered. 'If only nothing's struck in an unlucky hour. Our lads are out on the steppe for the night. Lie down and sleep, my dear ... Christ be with you, my child ... I won't take away the melon; maybe you'll have a bit when you get up.'

The sighs and yawns of the old woman, the even breathing of the sleeping woman, the half-darkness of the hut, and the sound of the rain outside, made one sleepy. Yegorushka was shy of undressing before the old woman. He only took off his boots, lay down and covered himself with the sheepskin.

'Is the little lad lying down?' he heard Panteley whisper a little later.

'Yes,' answered the old woman in a whisper. 'The terror of the Lord! It thunders and thunders, and there is no end to it.'

'It will soon be over,' wheezed Panteley, sitting down; 'it's getting quieter ... The lads have gone into the huts, and two have stayed with the horses. The lads have ... They can't ... the horses would be taken away ... I'll sit here a bit and then go and take my turn ... We can't leave them; they would be taken ...'

Panteley and the old woman sat side by side at Yegorushka's feet, talking in hissing whispers and interspersing their speech with sighs and yawns. And Yegorushka could not get warm. The warm heavy sheepskin lay on him, but he was trembling all over; his arms and legs were twitching, and his whole inside was shivering ... He undressed under the sheepskin, but that was no good. His shivering grew more and more acute.

Panteley went out to take his turn with the horses, and afterwards came back again, and still Yegorushka was shivering all over and could not get to sleep. Something weighed upon his head and chest and oppressed him, and he did not know what it was, whether it was the old people whispering, or the heavy smell of the sheepskin. The melon he had eaten had left an unpleasant metallic taste in his mouth. Moreover he was being bitten by fleas.

'Grandfather, I am cold,' he said, and did not know his own voice.

'Go to sleep, my child, go to sleep,' sighed the old woman.

Tit came up to the bedside on his thin little legs and waved his arms, then grew up to the ceiling and turned into a windmill ... Father Christopher, not as he was in the chaise, but in his full vestments with the sprinkler in his hand, walked round the mill, sprinkling it with holy water, and it left off waving. Yegorushka, knowing this was delirium, opened his eyes.

'Grandfather,' he called, 'give me some water.'

No one answered. Yegorushka felt it insufferably stifling and uncomfortable lying down. He got up, dressed, and went out of the hut. Morning was beginning. The sky was overcast, but it was no longer raining. Shivering and wrapping himself in his wet overcoat, Yegorushka walked about the muddy yard and listened to the silence; he caught sight of a little shed with a half-open door made of reeds. He looked into this shed, went into it, and sat down in a dark corner on a heap of dry dung.

There was a tangle of thoughts in his heavy head; his mouth was dry and unpleasant from the metallic taste. He looked at his hat, straightened the peacock's feather on it, and thought how he had gone with his mother to buy the hat. He put his hand into his pocket and took out a lump of brownish sticky paste. How had that paste come into his pocket? He thought a minute, smelt it; it smelt of honey. Aha! it was the Jewish cake! How sopped it was, poor thing!

Yegorushka examined his coat. It was a little grey overcoat with big bone buttons, cut in the shape of a frock-coat. At home, being a new and expensive article, it had not been hung in the hall, but with his mother's dresses in her bedroom; he was only allowed to wear it on holidays. Looking at it, Yegorushka felt sorry for it. He thought that he and the great-coat were both abandoned to the mercy of destiny; he thought that he would never get back home, and began sobbing so violently that he almost fell off the heap of dung.

A big white dog with woolly tufts like curl-papers about its face, sopping from the rain, came into the shed and stared with curiosity at Yegorushka. It seemed to be hesitating whether to bark or not. Deciding that there was no need to bark, it went cautiously up to Yegorushka, ate the sticky plaster and went out again.

'There are Varlamov's men!' someone shouted in the street.

After having his cry out, Yegorushka went out of the shed and, walking round a big puddle, made his way towards the street. The waggons were standing exactly opposite the gateway. The drenched waggoners, with their muddy feet, were sauntering beside them or sitting on the shafts, as listless and drowsy as flies in autumn. Yegorushka looked at them and thought: 'How dreary and comfortless to be a peasant!' He went up to Panteley and sat down beside him on the shaft.

'Grandfather, I'm cold,' he said, shivering and thrusting his hands up his sleeves.

'Never mind, we shall soon be there,' yawned Panteley. 'Never mind, you will get warm.'

It must have been early when the waggons set off, for it was not hot. Yegorushka lay on the bales of wool and shivered with cold, though the sun soon came out and dried his clothes, the bales, and the earth. As soon as he closed his eyes he saw Tit and the windmill again. Feeling a sickness and heaviness all over, he did his utmost to drive away these images, but as soon as they vanished the daredevil Dymov, with red eyes and lifted fists, rushed at Yegorushka with a roar, or there was the sound of his complaint: 'I am so dreary!' Varlamov rode by on his little Cossack stallion; happy Konstantin passed, with a smile and the bustard in his arms. And how tedious these people were, how sickening and unbearable!

Once – it was towards evening – he raised his head to ask for water. The waggons were standing on a big bridge across a broad river. There was black smoke below over the river, and through it could be seen a steamer with a barge in tow. Ahead of them, beyond the river, was a huge mountain dotted with houses and churches; at the foot of the mountain an engine was being shunted along beside some goods trucks ...

Yegorushka had never before seen steamers, nor engines, nor broad rivers. Glancing at them now, he was not alarmed or surprised; there was not even a look of anything like curiosity in his face. He merely felt sick, and made haste to turn over to the edge of the bale. He was sick. Panteley, seeing this, cleared his throat and shook his head.

'Our little lad's taken ill,' he said. 'He must have got a chill to the stomach. The little lad must ... away from home; it's a bad lookout!'

VIII

THE waggons stopped at a big inn for merchants, not far from the quay. As Yegorushka climbed down from the waggon he heard a very familiar voice. Someone was helping him to get down, and saying:

'We arrived yesterday evening ... We have been expecting you all day. We meant to overtake you yesterday, but it was out of our way; we came by the other road. I say, how you have crumpled your coat! You'll catch it from your uncle!'

Yegorushka looked into the speaker's mottled face and remembered that this was Deniska.

'Your uncle and Father Christopher are in the inn now, drinking tea; come along!'

And he led Yegorushka to a big two-storied building, dark and gloomy like the almshouse at N. After going across the entry, up a dark staircase and through a narrow corridor, Yegorushka and Deniska reached a little room in which Ivan Ivanitch and Father Christopher were sitting at the tea-table. Seeing the boy, both the old men showed surprise and pleasure.

'Aha! Yegor Ni-ko-la-aitch!' chanted Father Christopher. 'Mr Lomonosov!'

'Ah, our gentleman that is to be,' said Kuzmitchov, 'pleased to see you!'

Yegorushka took off his great-coat, kissed his uncle's hand and Father Christopher's, and sat down to the table.

'Well, how did you like the journey, *puer bone?*' Father Christopher pelted him with questions as he poured him out some tea, with his radiant smile. 'Sick of it, I've no doubt? God save us all from having to travel by waggon or with oxen. You go on and on, God forgive us; you look ahead and the steppe is always lying stretched out the same as it was – you can't see the end of it! It's not travelling but regular torture. Why don't you drink your tea? Drink it up; and in your absence, while you have been trailing along with the waggons, we have settled all our business capitally. Thank God we have sold our wool to Tcherepahin, and no one could wish to have done better ... We have made a good bargain.'

At the first sight of his own people Yegorushka felt an overwhelming desire to complain. He did not listen to Father Christopher, but thought how to begin and what exactly to complain of. But Father Christopher's voice, which seemed to him harsh and unpleasant, prevented him from concentrating his attention and confused his thoughts. He had not sat at the table five minutes before he got up, went to the sofa and lay down.

'Well, well,' said Father Christopher in surprise. 'What about your tea?'

Still thinking what to complain of, Yegorushka leaned his head against the wall and broke into sobs.

'Well, well!' repeated Father Christopher, getting

up and going to the sofa. 'Yegory, what is the matter with you? Why are you crying?'

'I'm ... I'm ill,' Yegorushka brought out.

'Ill?' said Father Christopher in amazement. 'That's not the right thing, my boy ... One mustn't be ill on a journey. Aie, aie, what are you thinking about, boy ... eh?'

He put his hand to Yegorushka's head, touched his cheek and said:

'Yes, your head's feverish ... You must have caught cold or else have eaten something ... Pray to God.'

'Should we give him quinine? ...' said Ivan Ivanitch, troubled.

'No; he ought to have something hot ... Yegory, have a little drop of soup? Eh?'

'I ... don't want any,' said Yegorushka.

'Are you feeling chilly?'

'I was chilly before, but now ... now I am hot. And I ache all over ...'

Ivan Ivanitch went up to the sofa, touched Yegorushka on the head, cleared his throat with a perplexed air, and went back to the table.

'I tell you what, you undress and go to bed,' said Father Christopher. 'What you want is sleep now.'

He helped Yegorushka to undress, gave him a pillow and covered him with a quilt, and over that Ivan Ivanitch's great-coat. Then he walked away on tiptoe and sat down to the table. Yegorushka shut his eyes, and at once it seemed to him that he was not in the hotel room, but on the highroad beside the camp fire. Emelyan waved his hands, and Dymov with red eyes lay on his stomach and looked mockingly at Yegorushka.

'Beat him, beat him!' shouted Yegorushka.

'He is delirious,' said Father Christopher in an undertone.

'It's a nuisance!' sighed Ivan Ivanitch.

'He must be rubbed with oil and vinegar. Please God, he will be better to-morrow.'

To be rid of bad dreams, Yegorushka opened his eyes and began looking towards the fire. Father Christopher and Ivan Ivanitch had now finished their tea and were talking in a whisper. The first was smiling with delight, and evidently could not forget that he had made a good bargain over his wool; what delighted him was not so much the actual profit he had made, as the thought that on getting home he would gather round him his big family, wink slyly and go off into a chuckle; at first he would deceive them all, and say that he had sold the wool at a price below its value, then he would give his son-in-law, Mihail, a fat pocket-book and say: 'Well, take it! that's the way to do business!' Kuzmitchov did not seem pleased; his face expressed, as before, a businesslike reserve and anxiety.

'If I could have known that Tcherepahin would give such a price,' he said in a low voice, 'I wouldn't have sold Makarov those five tons at home. It is vexatious! But who could have told that the price had gone up here?'

A man in a white shirt cleared away the samovar and lighted the little lamp before the ikon in the corner. Father Christopher whispered something in his ear; the man looked, made a serious face like a conspirator, as though to say, 'I understand,' went out, and returned a little while afterwards and put something under the sofa. Ivan Ivanitch made himself a bed on the floor, yawned several times, said his prayers lazily, and lay down.

'I think of going to the cathedral to-morrow,' said Father Christopher. 'I know the sacristan there. I ought to go and see the bishop after mass, but they say he is ill.'

He yawned and put out the lamp. Now there was no light in the room but the little lamp before the ikon.

'They say he can't receive visitors,' Father Christopher went on, undressing. 'So I shall go away without seeing him.'

He took off his full coat, and Yegorushka saw Robinson Crusoe reappear. Robinson stirred something in a saucer, went up to Yegorushka and whispered:

'Lomonosov, are you asleep? Sit up; I'm going to rub you with oil and vinegar. It's a good thing, only you must say a prayer.'

Yegorushka roused himself quickly and sat up. Father Christopher pulled down the boy's shirt, and shrinking and breathing jerkily, as though he were being tickled himself, began rubbing Yegorushka's chest.

'In the name of the Father, the Son, and the Holy Ghost,' he whispered, 'lie with your back upwards – that's it ... You'll be all right to-morrow, but don't do it again ... You are as hot as fire. I suppose you were on the road in the storm.'

'Yes.'

'You might well fall ill! In the name of the Father, the Son, and the Holy Ghost ... you might well fall ill!'

After rubbing Yegorushka, Father Christopher put
on his shirt again, covered him, made the sign of the
cross over him, and walked away. Then Yegorushka
saw him saying his prayers. Probably the old man
knew a great many prayers by heart, for he stood a
long time before the ikon murmuring. After saying his
prayers he made the sign of the cross over the window,
the door, Yegorushka, and Ivan Ivanitch, lay down on
the little sofa without a pillow, and covered himself
with his full coat. A clock in the corridor struck ten.
Yegorushka thought how long a time it would be
before morning; feeling miserable, he pressed his forehead against the back of the sofa and left off trying to
get rid of the oppressive misty dreams. But morning
came much sooner than he expected.

It seemed to him that he had not been lying long
with his head pressed to the back of the sofa, but
when he opened his eyes slanting rays of sunlight were
already shining on the floor through the two windows
of the little hotel room. Father Christopher and Ivan
Ivanitch were not in the room. The room had been
tidied; it was bright, snug, and smelt of Father Christopher, who always smelt of cypress and dried cornflowers (at home he used to make the holy-water
sprinklers and decorations for the ikon stands out of
cornflowers, and so he was saturated with the smell of
them). Yegorushka looked at the pillow, at the slanting sunbeams, at his boots, which had been cleaned
and were standing side by side near the sofa, and
laughed. It seemed strange to him that he was not on
the bales of wool, that everything was dry around
him, and that there was no thunder and lightning on
the ceiling.

He jumped off the sofa and began dressing. He felt splendid; nothing was left of his yesterday's illness but a slight weakness in his legs and neck. So the vinegar and oil had done good. He remembered the steamer, the railway engine, and the broad river, which he had dimly seen the day before, and now he made haste to dress, to run to the quay and have a look at them. When he had washed and was putting on his red shirt, the latch of the door clicked, and Father Christopher appeared in the doorway, wearing his top-hat and a brown silk cassock over his canvas coat and carrying his staff in his hand. Smiling and radiant (old men are always radiant when they come back from church), he put a roll of holy bread and a parcel of some sort on the table, prayed before the ikon, and said:

'God has sent us blessings – well, how are you?'

'Quite well now,' answered Yegorushka, kissing his hand.

'Thank God . . . I have come from mass . . . I've been to see a sacristan I know. He invited me to breakfast with him, but I didn't go. I don't like visiting people too early, God bless them!'

He took off his cassock, stroked himself on the chest, and without haste undid the parcel. Yegorushka saw a little tin of caviare, a piece of dry sturgeon, and a French loaf.

'See; I passed a fish-shop and brought this,' said Father Christopher. 'There is no need to indulge in luxuries on an ordinary weekday; but I thought, I've an invalid at home, so it is excusable. And the caviare is good, real sturgeon . . .'

The man in the white shirt brought in the samovar and a tray with tea-things.

'Eat some,' said Father Christopher, spreading the caviare on a slice of bread and handing it to Yego-rushka. 'Eat now and enjoy yourself, but the time will soon come for you to be studying. Mind you study with attention and application, so that good may come of it. What you have to learn by heart, learn by heart, but when you have to tell the inner sense in your own words, without regard to the outer form, then say it in your own words. And try to master all subjects. One man knows mathematics excellently, but has never heard of Pyotr Mogila; another knows about Pyotr Mogila, but cannot explain about the moon. But you study so as to understand everything. Study Latin, French, German ... geography, of course, history, theology, philo-sophy, mathematics ... and when you have mastered everything, not with haste but with prayer and with zeal, then go into the service. When you know every-thing it will be easy for you in any line of life ... You study and strive for the divine blessing, and God will show you what to be. Whether a doctor, a judge or an engineer ...'

Father Christopher spread a little caviare on a piece of bread, put it in his mouth and said:

'The Apostle Paul says: "Do not apply yourself to strange and diverse studies." Of course, if it is black magic, unlawful arts, or calling up spirits from the other world, like Saul, or studying subjects that can be of no use to yourself or others, better not learn them. You must undertake only what God has blessed. Take example ... the Holy Apostles spoke in all languages, so you study languages. Basil the Great studied mathematics and philosophy – so you study them; St Nestor wrote history – so you study and write history. Take example from the saints.'

Father Christopher sipped the tea from his saucer, wiped his moustaches, and shook his head.

'Good!' he said. 'I was educated in the old-fashioned way; I have forgotten a great deal by now, but still I live differently from other people. Indeed, there is no comparison. For instance, in company at a dinner, or at an assembly, one says something in Latin, or makes some allusion from history or philosophy, and it pleases people, and it pleases me myself ... Or when the circuit court comes and one has to take the oath, all the other priests are shy, but I am quite at home with the judges, the prosecutors, and the lawyers. I talk intellectually, drink a cup of tea with them, laugh, ask them what I don't know ... and they like it. So that's how it is, my boy. Learning is light and ignorance is darkness. Study! It's hard, of course; nowadays study is expensive ... Your mother is a widow; she lives on her pension, but there, of course ...'

Father Christopher glanced apprehensively towards the door, and went on in a whisper:

'Ivan Ivanitch will assist. He won't desert you. He has no children of his own, and he will help you. Don't be uneasy.'

He looked grave, and whispered still more softly:

'Only mind, Yegory, don't forget your mother and Ivan Ivanitch, God preserve you from it. The commandment bids you honour your mother, and Ivan Ivanitch is your benefactor and takes the place of a father to you. If you become learned, God forbid you should be impatient and scornful with people

because they are not so clever as you, then woe, woe
to you!'

Father Christopher raised his hand and repeated in
a thin voice:

'Woe to you! Woe to you!'

Father Christopher's tongue was loosened, and he
was, as they say, warming to his subject; he would not
have finished till dinner-time but the door opened and
Ivan Ivanitch walked in. He said good-morning hurriedly, sat down to the table, and began rapidly swal-
lowing his tea.

'Well, I have settled all our business,' he said. 'We
might have gone home to-day, but we have still to
think about Yegor. We must arrange for him. My sister told me that Nastasya Petrovna, a friend of hers,
lives somewhere here, so perhaps she will take him in
as a boarder.'

He rummaged in his pocket-book, found a
crumpled note and read:

' "Little Lower Street: Nastasya Petrovna Toskunov, living in a house of her own." We must go at once
and try to find her. It's a nuisance!'

Soon after breakfast Ivan Ivanitch and Yegorushka
left the inn.

'It's a nuisance!' muttered his uncle. 'You are
sticking to me like a burr. You and your mother want
education and gentlemanly breeding and I have nothing but worry with you both . . .'

When they crossed the yard, the waggons and the
drivers were not there. They had all gone off to the
quay early in the morning. In a far-off dark corner of
the yard stood the chaise.

'Good-bye, chaise!' thought Yegorushka.

At first they had to go a long way uphill by a broad street, then they had to cross a big market-place; here Ivan Ivanitch asked a policeman for Little Lower Street.

'I say,' said the policeman, with a grin, 'it's a long way off, out that way towards the town grazing ground.'

They met several cabs but Ivan Ivanitch only permitted himself such a weakness as taking a cab in exceptional cases and on great holidays. Yegorushka and he walked for a long while through paved streets, then along streets where there were only wooden planks at the sides and no pavements, and in the end got to streets where there were neither planks nor pavements. When their legs and their tongues had brought them to Little Lower Street they were both red in the face, and taking off their hats, wiped away the perspiration.

'Tell me, please,' said Ivan Ivanitch, addressing an old man sitting on a little bench by a gate, 'where is Nastasya Petrovna Toskunov's house?'

'There is no one called Toskunov here,' said the old man, after pondering a moment. 'Perhaps it's Timoshenko you want.'

'No, Toskunov ...'

'Excuse me, there's no one called Toskunov ...'

Ivan Ivanitch shrugged his shoulders and trudged on farther.

'You needn't look,' the old man called after them. 'I tell you there isn't, and there isn't.'

'Listen, auntie,' said Ivan Ivanitch, addressing an old woman who was sitting at a corner with a tray of pears and sunflower seeds, 'where is Nastasya Petrovna Toskunov's house?'

The old woman looked at him with surprise and laughed.

'Why, Nastasya Petrovna lives in her own house now!' she cried. 'Lord! it is eight years since she married her daughter and gave up the house to her son-in-law! It's her son-in-law lives there now.'

And her eyes expressed: 'How is it you didn't know a simple thing like that, you fools?'

'And where does she live now?' Ivan Ivanitch asked.

'Oh, Lord!' cried the old woman, flinging up her hands in surprise. 'She moved ever so long ago! It's eight years since she gave up her house to her son-in-law! Upon my word!'

She probably expected Ivan Ivanitch to be surprised, too, and to exclaim: 'You don't say so,' but Ivan Ivanitch asked very calmly:

'Where does she live now?'

The old woman tucked up her sleeves and, stretching out her bare arm to point, shouted in a shrill piercing voice:

'Go straight on, straight on, straight on. You will pass a little red house, then you will see a little alley on your left. Turn down that little alley, and it will be the third gate on the right ...'

Ivan Ivanitch and Yegorushka reached the little red house, turned to the left down the little alley, and made for the third gate on the right. On both sides of this very old grey gate there was a grey fence with big gaps in it. The first part of the fence was tilting forwards and threatened to fall, while on the left of the gate it sloped backwards towards the yard. The gate itself stood upright and seemed to be still undecided which would suit it best – to fall forwards or backwards. Ivan

Ivanitch opened the little gate at the side, and he and Yegorushka saw a big yard overgrown with weeds and burdocks. A hundred paces from the gate stood a little house with a red roof and green shutters. A stout woman with her sleeves tucked up and her apron held out was standing in the middle of the yard, scattering something on the ground and shouting in a voice as shrill as that of the woman selling fruit:

'Chick! ... Chick! ... Chick!'

Behind her sat a red dog with pointed ears. Seeing the strangers, he ran to the little gate and broke into a tenor bark (all red dogs have a tenor bark).

'Whom do you want?' asked the woman, putting up her hand to shade her eyes from the sun.

'Good-morning!' Ivan Ivanitch shouted, too, waving off the red dog with his stick. 'Tell me, please, does Nastasya Petrovna Toskunov live here?'

'Yes! But what do you want with her?'

'Perhaps you are Nastasya Petrovna?'

'Well, yes, I am!'

'Very pleased to see you ... You see, your old friend Olga Ivanovna Knyasev sends her love to you. This is her little son. And I, perhaps you remember, am her brother Ivan Ivanitch ... You are one of us from N.... You were born among us and married there ...'

A silence followed. The stout woman stared blankly at Ivan Ivanitch, as though not believing or not understanding him, then she flushed all over, and flung up her hands; the oats were scattered out of her apron and tears spurted from her eyes.

'Olga Ivanovna!' she screamed, breathless with excitement. 'My own darling! Ah, holy saints, why am I standing here like a fool? My pretty little angel ...'

She embraced Yegorushka, wetted his face with her tears, and broke down completely.

'Heavens!' she said, wringing her hands. 'Olga's little boy! How delightful! He is his mother all over! The image of his mother! But why are you standing in the yard? Come indoors.'

Crying, gasping for breath and talking as she went, she hurried towards the house. Her visitors trudged after her.

'The room has not been done yet,' she said, ushering the visitors into a stuffy little drawing-room adorned with many ikons and pots of flowers. 'Oh, Mother of God! Vassilisa, go and open the shutters anyway! My little angel! My little beauty! I did not know that Olitchka had a boy like that!'

When she had calmed down and got over her first surprise Ivan Ivanitch asked to speak to her alone. Yegorushka went into another room; there was a sewing-machine; in the window was a cage with a starling in it, and there were as many ikons and flowers as in the drawing-room. Near the machine stood a little girl with a sunburnt face and chubby cheeks like Tit's, and a clean cotton dress. She stared at Yegorushka without blinking, and apparently felt very awkward. Yegorushka looked at her and after a pause asked:

'What's your name?'

The little girl moved her lips, looked as if she were going to cry, and answered softly:

'Atka . . .'

This meant Katka.

'He will live with you,' Ivan Ivanitch was whispering in the drawing-room, 'if you will be so kind,

and we will pay ten roubles a month for his keep. He
is not a spoilt boy; he is quiet ...'

'I really don't know what to say, Ivan Ivanitch!'
Nastasya Petrovna sighed tearfully. 'Ten roubles
a month is very good, but it is a dreadful thing to
take another person's child! He may fall ill or something ...'

When Yegorushka was summoned back to the
drawing-room Ivan Ivanitch was standing with his
hat in his hands, saying good-bye.

'Well, let him stay with you now, then,' he said.
'Good-bye! You stay, Yegor!' he said, addressing his
nephew. 'Don't be troublesome; mind you obey Nastasya Petrovna ... Good-bye; I am coming again to-
morrow.'

And he went away. Nastasya once more embraced
Yegorushka, called him a little angel, and with a tear-
stained face began preparing for dinner. Three
minutes later Yegorushka was sitting beside her,
answering her endless questions and eating hot
savoury cabbage soup.

In the evening he sat again at the same table and,
resting his head on his hand, listened to Nastasya
Petrovna. Alternately laughing and crying, she talked
of his mother's young days, her own marriage, her
children ... A cricket chirruped in the stove, and there
was a faint humming from the burner of the lamp.
Nastasya Petrovna talked in a low voice, and was continually dropping her thimble in her excitement; and
Katya, her granddaughter, crawled under the table
after it and each time sat a long while under the table,
probably examining Yegorushka's feet; and Yegorushka listened, half dozing and looking at the old

woman's face, her wart with hairs on it, and the stains of tears ... and he felt sad, very sad. He was put to sleep on a chest and told that if he were hungry in the night he must go out into the little passage and take some chicken, put there under a plate in the window.

Next morning Ivan Ivanitch and Father Christopher came to say good-bye. Nastasya Petrovna was delighted to see them, and was about to set the samovar; but Ivan Ivanitch, who was in a great hurry, waved his hands and said:

'We have no time for tea! We are just setting off.'

Before parting they all sat down and were silent for a minute. Nastasya Petrovna heaved a deep sigh and looked towards the ikon with tear-stained eyes.

'Well,' began Ivan Ivanitch, getting up, 'so you will stay ...'

All at once the look of business-like reserve vanished from his face; he flushed a little and said with a mournful smile:

'Mind you work hard ... Don't forget your mother, and obey Nastasya Petrovna ... If you are diligent at school, Yegor, I'll stand by you.'

He took his purse out of his pocket, turned his back to Yegorushka, fumbled for a long time among the smaller coins, and, finding a ten-kopeck piece, gave it to Yegorushka.

Father Christopher, without haste, blessed Yegorushka.

'In the name of the Father, the Son, and the Holy Ghost ... Study,' he said. 'Work hard, my lad. If I die, remember me in your prayers. Here is a ten-kopeck piece from me, too ...'

Yegorushka kissed his hand, and shed tears; something whispered in his heart that he would never see the old man again.

'I have applied at the high school already,' said Ivan Ivanitch in a voice as though there were a corpse in the room. 'You will take him for the entrance examination on the seventh of August ... Well, good-bye; God bless you, good-bye, Yegor!'

'You might at least have had a cup of tea,' wailed Nastasya Petrovna.

Through the tears that filled his eyes Yegorushka could not see his uncle and Father Christopher go out. He rushed to the window, but they were not in the yard, and the red dog, who had just been barking, was running back from the gate with the air of having done his duty. Yegorushka, he could not have said why, leapt up and flew out of the room. When he ran out of the gate Ivan Ivanitch and Father Christopher, the former waving his stick with the crook, the latter his staff, were just turning the corner. Yegorushka felt that with these people all that he had known till then had vanished from him for ever. He sank helplessly on to the little bench, and with bitter tears greeted the new unknown life that was beginning for him now ...

What would that life be like?

ABOUT THE TRANSLATOR

CONSTANCE GARNETT (1862–1946) was a distinguished translator responsible for introducing many of the great Russian classics to English readers. As well as Chekhov she translated Tolstoy, Dostoevsky, Turgenev, Gogol and Herzen. She was married to the author Edward Garnett and mother of the novelist and critic David Garnett.

ABOUT THE INTRODUCER

RICHARD FREEBORN is Professor of Russian Literature at the University of London. He has translated a number of the works of Turgenev and is the author of *The Rise of the Russian Novel*, *The Russian Revolutionary Novel* and *Turgenev, the Novelist's Novelist*. He has also written several novels himself.

CHINUA ACHEBE
Things Fall Apart

THE ARABIAN NIGHTS
(2 vols, tr. Husain Haddawy)

MARCUS AURELIUS
Meditations

JANE AUSTEN
Emma
Mansfield Park
Northanger Abbey
Persuasion
Pride and Prejudice
Sanditon and Other Stories
Sense and Sensibility

HONORÉ DE BALZAC
Cousin Bette
Eugénie Grandet
Old Goriot

SIMONE DE BEAUVOIR
The Second Sex

SAUL BELLOW
The Adventures of Augie March

WILLIAM BLAKE
Poems and Prophecies

JORGE LUIS BORGES
Ficciones

JAMES BOSWELL
The Life of Samuel Johnson

CHARLOTTE BRONTË
Jane Eyre
Villette

EMILY BRONTË
Wuthering Heights

MIKHAIL BULGAKOV
The Master and Margarita

SAMUEL BUTLER
The Way of all Flesh

ITALO CALVINO
If on a winter's night a traveler

ALBERT CAMUS
The Outsider

MIGUEL DE CERVANTES
Don Quixote

GEOFFREY CHAUCER
Canterbury Tales

ANTON CHEKHOV
My Life and Other Stories
The Steppe and Other Stories

KATE CHOPIN
The Awakening

CARL VON CLAUSEWITZ
On War

S. T. COLERIDGE
Poems

WILKIE COLLINS
The Moonstone
The Woman in White

JOSEPH CONRAD
Heart of Darkness
Lord Jim
Nostromo
The Secret Agent
Typhoon and Other Stories
Under Western Eyes
Victory

THOMAS CRANMER
The Book of Common Prayer

DANTE ALIGHIERI
The Divine Comedy

DANIEL DEFOE
Moll Flanders
Robinson Crusoe

CHARLES DICKENS
Bleak House
David Copperfield
Dombey and Son
Great Expectations
Hard Times
Little Dorrit
Martin Chuzzlewit
Nicholas Nickleby
The Old Curiosity Shop
Oliver Twist
Our Mutual Friend
The Pickwick Papers
A Tale of Two Cities

DENIS DIDEROT
Memoirs of a Nun

JOHN DONNE
The Complete English Poems

FYODOR DOSTOEVSKY
The Brothers Karamazov
Crime and Punishment

GEORGE ELIOT
Adam Bede
Middlemarch
The Mill on the Floss
Silas Marner

WILLIAM FAULKNER
The Sound and the Fury

HENRY FIELDING
Joseph Andrews and Shamela
Tom Jones

F. SCOTT FITZGERALD
The Great Gatsby
This Side of Paradise

GUSTAVE FLAUBERT
Madame Bovary

FORD MADOX FORD
The Good Soldier
Parade's End

E. M. FORSTER
Howards End
A Passage to India

ELIZABETH GASKELL
Mary Barton

EDWARD GIBBON
The Decline and Fall of the
Roman Empire
Vols 1 to 3: The Western Empire
Vols 4 to 6: The Eastern Empire

J. W. VON GOETHE
Selected Works

IVAN GONCHAROV
Oblomov

GÜNTER GRASS
The Tin Drum

GRAHAM GREENE
Brighton Rock
The Human Factor

THOMAS HARDY
Far From the Madding Crowd
Jude the Obscure
The Mayor of Casterbridge
The Return of the Native
Tess of the d'Urbervilles
The Woodlanders

JAROSLAV HAŠEK
The Good Soldier Švejk

NATHANIEL HAWTHORNE
The Scarlet Letter

JOSEPH HELLER
Catch-22

ERNEST HEMINGWAY
A Farewell to Arms
The Collected Stories

GEORGE HERBERT
The Complete English Works

HERODOTUS
The Histories

HINDU SCRIPTURES
(tr. R. C. Zaehner)

JAMES HOGG
Confessions of a Justified Sinner

HOMER
The Iliad
The Odyssey

VICTOR HUGO
Les Misérables

HENRY JAMES
The Awkward Age
The Bostonians
The Golden Bowl
The Portrait of a Lady
The Princess Casamassima
The Wings of the Dove
Collected Stories (2 vols)

JAMES JOYCE
Dubliners
A Portrait of the Artist as
a Young Man
Ulysses

FRANZ KAFKA
Collected Stories
The Castle
The Trial

JOHN KEATS
The Poems

SØREN KIERKEGAARD
Fear and Trembling and
The Book on Adler

RUDYARD KIPLING
Collected Stories
Kim

THE KORAN
(tr. Marmaduke Pickthall)

CHODERLOS DE LACLOS
Les Liaisons dangereuses

GIUSEPPE TOMASI DI
LAMPEDUSA
The Leopard

D. H. LAWRENCE
Collected Stories
The Rainbow
Sons and Lovers
Women in Love

MIKHAIL LERMONTOV
A Hero of Our Time

PRIMO LEVI
If This is a Man and The Truce
The Periodic Table

NICCOLÒ MACHIAVELLI
The Prince

THOMAS MANN
Buddenbrooks
Death in Venice and Other Stories
Doctor Faustus

KATHERINE MANSFIELD
The Garden Party and Other
Stories

GABRIEL GARCÍA MÁRQUEZ
Love in the Time of Cholera
One Hundred Years of Solitude

ANDREW MARVELL
The Complete Poems

HERMAN MELVILLE
The Complete Shorter Fiction
Moby-Dick

JOHN STUART MILL
On Liberty and Utilitarianism

JOHN MILTON
The Complete English Poems

YUKIO MISHIMA
The Temple of the
Golden Pavilion

MARY WORTLEY MONTAGU
Letters

THOMAS MORE
Utopia

TONI MORRISON
Song of Solomon

MURASAKI SHIKIBU
The Tale of Genji

VLADIMIR NABOKOV
Lolita
Pale Fire
Speak, Memory

V. S. NAIPAUL
A House for Mr Biswas

THE NEW TESTAMENT
(King James Version)

THE OLD TESTAMENT
(King James Version)

GEORGE ORWELL
Animal Farm
Nineteen Eighty-Four

THOMAS PAINE
Rights of Man
and Common Sense

BORIS PASTERNAK
Doctor Zhivago

PLATO
The Republic

EDGAR ALLAN POE
The Complete Stories

ALEXANDER PUSHKIN
The Collected Stories

FRANÇOIS RABELAIS
Gargantua and Pantagruel

JOSEPH ROTH
The Radetzky March

JEAN-JACQUES ROUSSEAU
Confessions
The Social Contract and
the Discourses

SALMAN RUSHDIE
Midnight's Children

WALTER SCOTT
Rob Roy

WILLIAM SHAKESPEARE
Comedies Vols 1 and 2
Histories Vols 1 and 2
Romances
Sonnets and Narrative Poems
Tragedies Vols 1 and 2

MARY SHELLEY
Frankenstein

ADAM SMITH
The Wealth of Nations

ALEXANDER SOLZHENITSYN
One Day in the Life of
Ivan Denisovich

SOPHOCLES
The Theban Plays

CHRISTINA STEAD
The Man Who Loved Children

JOHN STEINBECK
The Grapes of Wrath

STENDHAL
The Charterhouse of Parma
Scarlet and Black

LAURENCE STERNE
Tristram Shandy

ROBERT LOUIS STEVENSON
The Master of Ballantrae and
Weir of Hermiston
Dr Jekyll and Mr Hyde
and Other Stories

HARRIET BEECHER STOWE
Uncle Tom's Cabin

JONATHAN SWIFT
Gulliver's Travels

JUNICHIRŌ TANIZAKI
The Makioka Sisters

W. M. THACKERAY
Vanity Fair

HENRY DAVID THOREAU
Walden

ALEXIS DE TOCQUEVILLE
Democracy in America

LEO TOLSTOY
Anna Karenina
Childhood, Boyhood and Youth
The Cossacks
War and Peace

ANTHONY TROLLOPE
Barchester Towers
Can You Forgive Her?
Doctor Thorne
The Eustace Diamonds

ANTHONY TROLLOPE *cont.*
Framley Parsonage
The Last Chronicle of Barset
The Small House at Allington
The Warden

IVAN TURGENEV
Fathers and Children
First Love and Other Stories
A Sportsman's Notebook

MARK TWAIN
Tom Sawyer
and Huckleberry Finn

JOHN UPDIKE
Rabbit Angstrom

GIORGIO VASARI
Lives of the Painters, Sculptors
and Architects

VIRGIL
The Aeneid

VOLTAIRE
Candide and Other Stories

EVELYN WAUGH
The Complete Short Stories
Brideshead Revisited
Decline and Fall
The Sword of Honour Trilogy

EDITH WHARTON
The Age of Innocence
The Custom of the Country
The House of Mirth
The Reef

OSCAR WILDE
Plays, Prose Writings and Poems

MARY WOLLSTONECRAFT
A Vindication of the Rights of
Woman

VIRGINIA WOOLF
To the Lighthouse
Mrs Dalloway

W. B. YEATS
The Poems

ÉMILE ZOLA
Germinal

This book is set in Old Style. Throughout the first half of
the nineteenth century, modern typefaces were predominant in all areas of publishing. In 1852, however, Miller and Richard, who had been in the
forefront of modern face production, set a
new trend when they issued specimens
of a regularized old face which was
named Old Style. Types of this
kind became popular in
the second half of
the nineteenth
century.